# PARNO'S COMPANY

## THE BLACK SHEEP OF SOULAN

### BOOK ONE

Creative Texts Publishers products are available at special discounts for bulk purchase for sale promotions, premiums, fund-raising, and educational needs. For details, write Creative Texts Publishers, PO Box 50, Barto, PA 19504, or visit www.creativetexts.com

PARNO'S COMPANY
The Black Sheep of Soulan: Book One by N.C. REED
Published by Creative Texts Publishers
PO Box 50
Barto, PA 19504
www.creativetexts.com



The following is a work of fiction. Any resemblance to actual names, persons, businesses, and incidents is strictly coincidental. Locations are used only in the general sense and do not represent the real place in actuality.

ISBN: 978-0-692-47563-8

# PARNO'S COMPANY

## N.C. Reed

**CREATIVE TEXTS PUBLISHERS**
Barto, Pennsylvania

It's not what we planned Jabo, but it's a start.
Love and miss you.

# TABLE OF CONTENTS

# CHAPTER ONE

-

"Well? Have you anything to say for yourself?"

Parno McLeod met his father's gaze levelly, almost defiantly. He was more than accustomed to the older man's berating and had long since lost his fear of such encounters.

Parno was the youngest of four children in the House McLeod, the ruling dynasty of the Kingdom of Soulan. His mother having died shortly after giving birth to him, Parno had for all his life been blamed for the death of Queen Margolynn McLeod. The fact that Parno had no say in the matter seemed to have escaped his remaining family's collective memory over the years. Parno had grown up to the daily hatred of both his father and siblings. His oldest brother, Memmnon, was the Heir. He was followed by the twins, Therron and Sherron. A mild contempt was the best Parno had ever managed to gain from any of them.

As a result, Parno had grown up virtually alone in a palace surrounded by people who despised him. He had grown callous to their hatred over the years and to any import that his actions might have on his 'loving' family.

Parno McLeod was infamous among the soldiers of Nasil as one of the hardest drinking, hardest fighting men in the city. It had been said on more than on occasion that Parno would fight at the drop of a hat...or knock the hat from your head, if you were too slow in dropping it. All agreed that there was little animosity toward him, however. Parno always paid for any damages his brawls might cause and he always bought a round of drinks for all involved, win or lose.

It was such an encounter that had caused the meeting here today.

"Nothing I say will appease you, Father, and you and I both know it. Were it not this it would merely be something else that attracted your ire." The retainers in the room stirred uncomfortably. Few had the courage to speak to Tammon in such a manner. Whatever faults Parno McLeod might be cursed with, cowardice was not among them.

"You impertinent whelp!" Tammon snarled. "Would that you had died in birth rather than your blessed mother, then I would not be saddled with your insolence! A drunken brawl with common soldiers in the Royal City! Could you possibly have acted any worse? Could you have somehow brought even more shame to the McLeod name?"

"Since I have been old enough to know anything, Father, I have known your desire that I had died rather than my Mother," Parno replied evenly. "Indeed, you and my noble brothers and sister have made that abundantly clear to me over the span of my life. I assure you it is the one thing we have in common. Had the choice been mine to make, I would gladly have perished that the one person who loved me had lived."

"Damn you!" Tammon screeched, his face red with rage. "How dare you speak to me in such a manner! It is you that has forced this meeting today, not I. With your drunken revelry and common brawling! Such behavior is far beneath a Prince of Soulan. I expect better of my sons. Even you."

"It is a blow to my heart, Father, that my behavior has caused you such difficulty." Parno's tone was heavy with sarcasm. In truth, he didn't care even a tithe about his father's difficulties. He had decided long ago that his days of playing the beaten pup were at an end. He had learned to live without fear of his father or older siblings soon after he entered his teen years.

"Get out!" Tammon ordered. "Leave my sight while I retain the memory of your blessed mother and her love for you! Lest I forget it and deal with you as you deserve!"

Parno bowed stiffly and far less deeply than protocol required before he turned and departed the room. Tammon sat upon his throne seething with anger.

"Father," Memmnon McLeod said from his father's side, "you must not let him provoke you to anger. Physician Smith has warned you that such anger is ..."

"Oh, be silent!" Tammon snarled, waving aside his oldest son's complaints. "I have recovered my senses. I cannot help it if the very sight of him irks my blood."

"I understand, Father," Memmnon, who felt the same way, nodded. "Yet there is little more we can do, save banish him from the city and such an action would not be looked upon with favor."

"I know, curse the luck! Is there not something he can do well enough that he can be given duties? Duties which, regrettably, would require him to travel? Travel as far from here as possible, mind you."

"What duties would you risk in the hands of Parno, Father?" the Crown Prince asked quietly.

"I'm open to almost anything that removes him from underfoot," the King retorted. "At least then his brawling and drinking and womanizing won't be here right in front of us."

"Well," Memmnon said after a brief pause, "there is one project which I have been considering. One which would, indeed, require not only a great deal of travel, but would leave him permanently posted outside the city."

"What?" Tammon asked, voice rising with hope.

"It has been considered for some time," Memmnon said, "that we form a military unit from elements of the King's Prisons. Men would serve their time in service to the King rather than in the cells of the territorial prisons. Such a unit would be ideal for breaking the Norland charges when war comes again and the men would be considered expendable at any rate."

"A prison company?" Tammon asked skeptically.

"Essentially, yes," Memmnon nodded. "It would require a leavening of real soldiers to provide security, of course, and it would take time to ready them for combat but it would be a job which took years. In fact, it would never truly be finished. Even as some of the soldiers left the service with their time served, others would be entering the service at the same time. Of course, such a company could never be posted in Nasil."

"No," Tammon agreed thoughtfully. "No that would never do, having a company of prison soldiers in the Royal City."

"It is but a thought, Father," Memmnon said. "I have been interested in the idea for some months but with everything else that's been happening I simply haven't taken the time to get it started."

"Assign it to Parno," Tammon said at once. "Give him the job. Tell him that you want him to have the chance to prove he can behave in the manner of a Prince and prove to me that he is of value to the realm. Anything like that. Just make sure that he leaves."

"I will see to it, Father," Memmnon promised with a smile. "Today."

Later Memmnon summoned Parno to his office and greeted the youngest prince with a smile. "Thank you for coming, Brother," Memmnon said, "Please, take a seat. May I get you anything?"

"Let's get to the chase, Memmnon," Parno said, though not unpleasantly. "I know you didn't ask me here to exchange pleasantries. I also know that you dislike my company as much as our father. I'm sure my being here is keeping you from important matters of state." Memmnon, as Heir to the Throne, was the defacto Foreign Minister for the Kingdom of Soulan. Therron, the Heir Secondary, commanded the Soulan Army.

"Very well," Memmnon's smile faded. "I asked you here because I have an assignment for you. One that's long ended, I'm afraid, and will require no small amount of travel. I wanted to stress to you that it would be good if you reel in your desire for questionable company and drinking to excess while your job carries you about the kingdom."

"An assignment?" Parno's brow creased in frown. "What possible assignment could there be that you would entrust to me?"

"That's not fair, Parno," Memmnon replied, his face showing hurt. "I admit I have never been over fond of you. I cannot help blame you for the death of our mother. I know it's wrong of me, and I have tried to overcome it, but every time I see you I am reminded of her…or rather of her absence."

"I would that she had lived as well," Parno said quietly. "Would have been better all-around had I been the one to perish."

"I've never said that," Memmnon pointed out.

"You've never had to," Parno replied calmly, and Memmnon flushed slightly in anger.

"What is this job you would have me do?" Parno asked, changing the subject.

"It's not a pleasant one, I'll warn you now. But it is of some importance, especially in the long run. A new military unit is being formed from elements of prisoners from the Provincial King's Prisons. It will be your job to select the men, and oversee their training and organization." Memmnon handed Parno a sheaf of papers.

"You'll find the information on the soldiers under your command in here, along with information concerning the most likely individuals to be acceptable to the program. The details of the program itself are in the folder. Familiarize yourself with them before you begin."

"Prisoners?" Parno asked skeptically. "You want to make King's Soldiers out of King's Prisoners?"

"If possible, yes," Memmnon affirmed. "We hope to ease crowding in the prisons, for one thing. To be honest, there are many men now in prison who have attributes useful to the crown. This is a way to get service from them while they serve their sentences. The Norland Army has far more resources than do we to draw upon, Parno,"

Memmnon added quietly. "We must try and use everything at our disposal."

"And you just naturally thought of me, I guess, to lead this effort?" Parno's voice betrayed his sarcasm.

"No," Memmnon answered, surprising Parno. "I didn't. It was only this morning that I thought of using you in this position. I suggested it to Father not long after you left, in fact." Memmnon knew he was skating around the truth but didn't want to tell Parno why the job was being given to him. There was no point in throwing oil onto an already burning fire.

"Get me from underfoot?" Parno asked, and smiled at the surprise on

Memmnon's face. Though the diplomat recovered quickly, the damage was done.

"That was the idea," he sighed. "To get you and Father as far apart as possible."

"Don't pretend you won't be happy to see me go as well, Brother," Parno said.

Memmnon's face clouded. "Not because I hate you, Parno," Memmnon said quietly. "It is just that I have never been able to look at you, not once, without thinking of the death of my mother. It is painful, even now. I cannot help that."

"How do you know, Memmnon?" Parno asked, his voice not quite hard. "I've never seen you, any of you, make the effort. I was offered no choice as whether to come into the world or not. You might bear that in mind once in a while. You all hate me," the words grated passed tightly clenched teeth, "for something I had no say in. Now, as Heir to the King's Justice, does that strike you as fair?"

"Life isn't always fair, Parno," Memmnon said quietly. "If it were, Mother would still be here, where she belongs."

"And I would be dead," Parno finished. Memmnon did not meet his eyes.

"Yes, you would."

"Well, at least you're honest," Parno said with a sigh. "I suppose I should be grateful for that." He reviewed the papers in his hands.

"Cove?" he asked, seeing the home of his new 'unit'. "My headquarters will be in Cove? That's not too close to Nasil, you think? I can ride that in two days, or three."

"It was the site of the unit before you entered into it," Memmnon said. "I saw no reason to change it."

"Right," Parno snorted. "Okay, Memmnon, I'll take the 'job', but I have a few conditions."

"Conditions?" Memmnon said, his features betraying a hint of anger. "Your King gives you instructions and you set conditions?"

"You can put away that dung," Parno shot back. "This isn't the act of a King and a Subject. It's the act of a father who hates his son. So yes, the son will set some conditions."

"Name them," Memmnon said, his voice noncommittal.

"I want the original order extended to cover those hunted by King's Warrant," Parno said. Memmnon thought for a moment, then nodded.

"I will agree to that. The basic idea is the same. What else?"

"I want my 'unit' fully funded. Soldiers paid, descent quarters, good food. I want a King's Writ to make sure I can get what I need." A King's Writ was basically a command from the King to offer any and all assistance requested by the bearer, with expenses paid by the Crown. King's Writs were not that common. Memmnon studied his brother closely.

"I will see to it myself," Memmnon said finally, "provided that you provide receipts for your expenditures. I will not pay for your boozing and brawling from the Royal Treasury."

"No," Parno agreed, "you won't. I'll pay for that, from the General's pay you'll be giving me and the allowances that go along with it."

"Forget it," Memmnon said at once. "I haven't the authority to make you a General, and Therron would see you in Hell first."

"I didn't say anything about making me a General," Parno smiled. "I said I'd be paid like one, including all allowances."

Memmnon considered that. Generals in the Soulan army were well paid by anyone's standards. Their allowances were almost as good. A building that served as quarters and office, a valet, a cook, a secretary, a personal physician and an escort. All on the King's crown.

Parno had never been interested in the trappings of power. Even as a child he had been fiercely independent, relying on no one other than himself unless there was no possible alternative. His request for such things now surprised the Crown Prince.

"I will agree, except to the escort," Memmnon said at last. "You already have a company of veteran soldiers at your command. That should be sufficient to get you out of any fights you find yourself in."

"I do my own fighting, Memmnon," Parno replied with a smile. "You remember that, don't you?" The older brother flushed at that, remembering.

Memmnon had set his retainer, a veteran soldier, upon his brother one day in a fit of rage. Parno, fourteen at the time, had nearly killed the soldier and then administered a severe beating to Memmnon as well. Only the intervention of Parno's own retainer had saved Memmnon from being crippled, or perhaps killed, at the hands of his enraged younger brother. Memmnon still bore scars from the encounter.

"Your other conditions?" Memmnon snapped.

"Darvo Nidiad is to be made Colonel and placed in command," Parno said. Nidiad was Parno's faithful retainer and the young Prince's one true friend.

"That I can do," Memmnon agreed. "Nidiad should have been Colonel long before now, anyway. Would have been, had he not chosen. . . ."

"Not chosen to remain at my side," Parno finished the unspoken part of his brother's sentence. "I'm aware of the reason he has been passed over. I am loyal to those who deserve my loyalty." Memmnon chose not to respond to that barb. It had hit too close to home for comfort.

"Anything else?"

"No, I think that will cover it," Parno said amiably. "Please make sure that the King's Writ includes orders to the Prison Wardens. I assume that I'll be able to hire or appropriate some suitable instructors for my new soldiers?"

"Yes, the Writ will cover that," Memmnon assured him. "Submit your payroll each month. Nidiad can decide appropriate ranks for the instructors, but no one over the rank of Captain, mind you. Higher rank will require Therron's approval."

"Which I will never receive," Parno nodded in agreement as he stood. "Very well, Prince Memmnon. I will endeavor to fulfill my duty to the best of my ability. Tell me true, though, Brother. It will not affect my decision. Is this a true and actual duty, or did you invent it to get rid of me?"

"The idea was presented to me over four months ago," Memmnon told him. "I had not acted upon it yet.  In truth, I haven't had the time but I was convinced the idea was worth exploring. Had you not received the project, someone else would have."

"Fair enough," Parno nodded. "Where do I find my soldiers?"

"King's Barracks," Memmnon answered. "Right here in the grounds. Captain Willard is in command."

"Enri Willard?" Parno asked. "The sword champion?" Enri Willard was the holder of the coveted King's Sword, acknowledged as the finest swordsman in Soulan. He was also Captain of the Palace Guard.

"No. His younger brother, Karls." Memmnon corrected. "Not quite as good as Enri, but very good nonetheless and his men are fine soldiers."

"I will leave tomorrow or the day after then. Does that meet with the Crown's approval?" There was only a slight tinge of sarcasm in Parno's voice.

"Parno, you needn't voice your disdain of the King to me. I assure you, I know all too well your feelings for Father."

"I doubt that very much, Memmnon," Parno said quietly. "I doubt it very much indeed." With that Parno turned and departed, leaving his brother to look at his departing back.

-

"You're daft, lad!"

Darvo Nidiad had never minced words, even with the Prince he had served so faithfully for nineteen years. He saw no reason to start now.

"Darvo, it's not as bad as all that," Parno objected. "And it makes your Colonelcy, something you wouldn't have gotten any other way, so long as you remained with me."

"I care not for that," Nidiad replied. "I am near to retiring at any rate, lad. I'm too old to start trying to make soldiers out of thieves and killers."

"Then consider this retirement with pay and benefits," Parno offered. "Look at it! A King's Writ, our own garrison, and little in the way of expectations! Select a few trainers, oversee the organization of the unit, and sit back and watch the fun. You know as well as I do that no one will ever interfere with us. They'll likely never think of us so long as I am out of Nasil, which is the true objective after all. We'll live out our lives in relative comfort on the King's Crown, far from the cares of the great city of Nasil and the scrutiny of King Tammon the Terrible."

"Don't be treasonous," Nidiad chided. Parno scoffed.

"Don't be a hypocrite," he shot back. "Come on Darvo! I can't do this without you."

"You can't do it period," Nidiad replied. "Make soldiers from the dregs of the King's Prison? They couldn't stay out of prison, lad. They aren't likely to be paragons of virtue, you know. Thieves, killers, brawlers and the like. Men who would cheat their own mothers out of their life savings, then kill the poor woman to keep her from calling the constable. Forget it lad," the old soldier said kindly. "'Tis folly to even consider such a notion workable."

"Fine," Parno said, disgusted. "Stay here, then, and enjoy your retirement. But I don't have much of a choice. I will never be allowed another opportunity to get away from here and keep at least some dignity. My family hates me, wishes me dead. There's nothing here for me, Darvo. Nothing to keep me here. This is a chance for me to get away from here and do it without living from a saddlebag the rest of my life. I can't afford to turn it down."

"But that's exactly what you should have done," Nidiad told his young charge. "Turned it down. It's a fool's errand they've sent you on. Your 'company' will be the laughing stock of the army!"

"Not if you're in command," Parno persisted, sensing the old man weakening despite his objections. "And we have a full company of veteran soldiers assigned to us as well."

"Led by who?" Nidiad asked scornfully. "A wet-behind-the-ears ass kisser? Looking to get ahead by doing a Royal 'favor'?"

"Karls Willard," Parno said smugly. "Enri's younger brother.

"Indeed?" Darvo's interest seemed to perk up a bit at that.

"Indeed," Parno nodded emphatically. "So there's at least one indication that the idea, despite my involvement, is being taken seriously. For all his faults, and his dislike of me, Memmnon isn't a liar. He told me plainly that he had intended to pursue the idea even before he suggested my involvement."

Nidiad did not respond right away. His eyes gave away the fact that he was calculating. Parno decided to sweeten the pot.

"You can move, lock stock and barrel, Darvo. Dahlia can be placed on the books as the cook, and ..."

"My daughter will not play servant to a bunch o' crooks and killers, Parno McLeod!" Darvo roared.

"My cook, you irritable old fart," Parno sighed in exasperation. "The only people she'll be cooking for is yourself, and perhaps the physician and secretary. Not the soldiery."

"Leaving out yourself, o' course," Nidiad pointed out.

"I'll be eating with the troops," Parno said quietly. Darvo's eyes rose at that.

"A Prince of Soulan? Scion of the House McLeod? Messing with common soldiers? A scandal for sure."

"So be it," Parno shrugged. "Look, Darvo. This is the only opportunity I'm ever likely to have to make a name for myself as something besides the son Tammon McLeod loves to hate. The men we choose will have to be loyal to me if this is going to work. Who are they likely to respect more? A Prince who lives in a big house and eats privately? Or a man who shares the same food and discomforts they themselves endure?"

Nidiad looked fondly at the young man he had served as surrogate father for so long. Parno had always applied himself wholeheartedly to everything he'd set his mind to. The boy had been a sponge, soaking up knowledge like a rag-soaked water. In truth, Parno was something of a military tactician himself, though neither his father nor especially his brother Therron would never give him credit for it even if they knew.

Nidiad knew for a fact they didn't know. Just as they were unaware of the younger McLeod's horsemanship or swordsmanship. Had the law not forbid his competing Nidiad had no doubt that Parno could have defeated even Enri Willard in the annual King's Sword competition.

For the first time since the conversation began, Darvo Nidiad gave serious thought to the idea of making soldiers out of prisoners. True, there were likely to be some stalwart lads found in the King's Prisons. Men with savvy and spirit. Many of them would be skilled in at least some of the attributes needed by a good soldier.

"Just what kind of unit were you planning on forming, anyway?" Darvo asked.

"Cavalry," Parno replied at once. "A mixed bag of mounted men. Lancers, swordsmen, and archers. Every man trained expert on one weapon and proficient with at least one other." Nidiad smiled to himself as he recognized his own influence on Parno's thinking.

"And where, pray, do you intend to get the horses and saddlery for such a unit? For that matter, the swords, lances and bows?"

"King's Writ," Parno replied smugly. "I can get anything I want, remember? As to the swords and the lances, I hope to find an able blacksmith and sword-maker who can provide us with quality weapons without depending on the King's Armory. As to the bows, I thought to venture into the Apples and seek out a bow-master. It might be that we can find a man who can teach us to make our own."

"If not, then we'll find the best we can and purchase them with King's Crown."

"Thought of everything, have you?" Nidiad smiled.

"No," Parno replied. "But I've tried to. I've been turning the problem over in my head trying to see what problems I might encounter and then working on a solution. Of course," he smiled, "no plan survives contact with the enemy."

"Indeed, lad," Nidiad laughed, slapping his leg as Parno used another of his own teachings against the old soldier. "Very well, Parno, me lad, I'm in. But," he said, a thick and calloused finger raised in point, "my daughter will not accompany us. She can make the trip after we have set the place to order and I'm satisfied it's safe."

"Fine," Parno agreed. Darvo's own wife had died in childbirth just as Parno's mother had. Parno had always wondered if that had influenced the older man's decision to remain in his post as retainer, despite the fact that he could not rise above the rank of Major in doing so. His daughter, Dahlia, was his pride and joy.

"Very well, then," Darvo rose. "Let's be over to the Barracks and meet Captain Willard. I'm sure he's as thrilled as I am to be on this mission."

"Have to get your uniform fixed first," Darvo said. "You're a Colonel, now."

# CHAPTER TWO

-

Parno and his 'troop' had departed Nasil on the third day after Memmnon's summons. Their first stop would be the city of Jax far to the south. Jax was the Capital of the Misi province and also home to a King's Prison. One of the smallest but a King's Prison no less.

The trip was uneventful. Parno, Darvo, and Karls Willard had spent most evenings around the fire, discussing the job before them. Willard, it turned out, did not share Nidiad's misgivings.

"There are some likely lads behind the gates," Willard said on one such evening. "Men who will be strong in body, mind, and spirit. Have to strain rather fine, I admit, but still, there's bound to be some potential there."

"It's finding the potential that gives me cause for concern," Nidiad countered. "The same men you will find those attributes in will also have no desire for military life. Many of them will see this as simply a way out of prison. We'll be lucky to pass the winter before finding half of them gone and the other waiting for their chance."

"Not likely," Parno said quietly. "Penalty for desertion in this unit is hanging."

"You can't do that, lad," Nidiad objected. "King's Law specifies imprisonment for desertion, equal to the remaining term of service at the time of desertion."

"This isn't a normal unit," Parno pointed out. "Besides, it isn't my idea. It was written into the overall plan and Memmnon signed off to it. So desertion, in this outfit, will be on penalty of death."

"Well, that will take the starch right out of any snowbirds," Willard observed in a near whisper.

"I hope it will cut down on any frivolous enlistments as well," Parno agreed. "We've a big enough task without throwing any more problems into the mix."

-

Their arrival in Jax was unheralded. Parno disliked the pomp and preening associated with his rank anyway but there had been no warning of his impending visit regardless. The first word the Governor had of the Royal Presence was when his secretary entered the office stating that Prince Parno desired an audience.

Parno was ushered into the Governor's office at once, while the governor, a kindly appearing man named Jerl Harkin, made abundant apologies for not having received the young Prince 'properly'.

"I'm quite satisfied that I am properly received, Governor," Parno said, silencing Harkin's apologies. "I am not the King, nor even the Heir. No such dignitary welcome is needed or even desired."

"Still your Majesty should have been received properly," Harkin insisted.

"I will state for the record that I have been so received, Governor."

"Thank you, milord," Harkin bowed. "How may I be of use to you? My office and I stand at your disposal."

"Quartering for my men and care for our horses would be much appreciated, Governor," Parno replied. "Other than that, I am here on business that should not affect your office. I merely wanted to make a courtesy call to inform you of my presence and that of my men for a few days. It seemed only proper that you be notified of my presence in your province and your city."

"I thank you, Highness, for that courtesy," Harkin bowed, "and of course, your men and horses will be placed in the House Barracks here, if that's agreeable to you."

"More than agreeable, Governor," Parno bowed slightly. "I thank you for that kindness."

"Is it Royal business that brings you here, milord? Or is that too forward of me? I ask only to see if there is any way in which I might render assistance."

"Not forward at all, and I thank you," Parno replied. "I am, in fact, here on King's business. I am looking to form a military unit of inmates from the various King's Prisons. I am touring the facilities in person looking for likely candidates. Any recommendations you have on that issue would be welcome."

"Prisoners? Make soldiers of King's Prisoners?"

"If possible, yes." Parno explained the basis of the unit, including attributes that he was likely to find useful.

"I must say, milord, such is an extremely . . . interesting idea," Harkin said when Parno had finished. "In all candor, however, I must say odds are long against you in succeeding."

"To be sure," Parno nodded. "Still, the idea has attracted attention at the highest level, so there's aught to be done but try." 'Highest Level' in Soulan meant Royal involvement. Coming as it did from a member of the Royal Family itself, the term likely meant the King himself.

"My wife's cousin, Felden Bates, is the warden at the Jax prison, Your Highness," Harkin volunteered. "He would probably be able to point out any suitable candidates among his inmates. Though I must remind the Prince that the King's Prison here is quite small compared to most of the others."

"May I mention you to Warden Bates, Governor? By way of introduction?" Parno asked. The Governor looked appalled.

"Certainly not, Your Highness!" he exclaimed. "I will accompany you there, and make the introduction myself!"

"Very kind of you, Governor, but hardly necessary," Parno replied.

"It's the least I can do, milord," Harkin insisted. "Besides, it will give me a reason to leave this office, even if it's only for a few hours." Parno laughed.

"Then I accept, and gladly, Governor," he said. "Far be it from me to deprive you of a few hours peace."

-

The Jax prison was small with no more than three hundred inmates. Compared to the one in Lana, the Capital of the Gera province, it was almost non-existent.

But among those three hundred or so prisoners might be one or two that Parno could make use of.

"Welcome to Jax Territorial Prison, Your Highness," Warden Bates bowed after the introduction by the Governor. "Myself and staff are at your disposal."

"Thank you, Warden," Parno replied graciously. "I have no desire to impact your duties. However, I am, as the Governor explained, here on a Crown matter. Right now, I'd like to begin by reviewing the records of all prisoners in your custody. Afterward, should I find any suitable candidates, I will require only a minimal guard to escort the prisoners to me and then back to their cells. Will that be a problem?"

"Of course not, Highness," Bates replied. "I must add my opinion to Governor Harkin's though that this enterprise is unlikely to be successful. The sort of men you are likely to find suitable in other ways will likely prove uncooperative."

"I doubt it not," Parno smiled. "Yet it is a Royal Order, thus I have to try."

"Of course, Your Majesty," Bates replied with a small bow. "I will set you up in the meeting hall and provide you with the records you seek. I will assign a clerk to you as well, to help with the records."

"That's more than helpful, Warden. Are there any of your inmates that you think might bear special scrutiny?"

"Well, milord, there are a few poachers among the prisoners who are excellent woodsmen and skilled archers. They are here for hunting on King's Land. Whether they would participate or not, I cannot say."

"Send me their records first then," Parno ordered.

"As you will, milord."

-

"What a sorry lot," Nidiad offered an hour later. He and Karls Willard had been helping Parno peruse the records of inmates confined in the prison and so far had found only two dozen or so likely candidates.

"What did you expect, Darvo?" Parno asked with a chuckle. "As you yourself pointed out, these are criminals."

"Aye, that I did," Nidiad nodded. "Still.."

"Here's an interesting one," Willard offered. "Blacksmith. Killed a man in a drunken brawl. Felled him with one blow. Only the circumstances kept him from the noose."

"What circumstances?"

"Never in trouble before, and the man he killed started the fight," Willard said, still reading. "Had this case been sent before the Bench in Nasil he'd never have gone to prison. Ah," Willard added suddenly, "now I see. The man he killed was a minor official. Off duty constable, also drunk. Apparently, he was nephew to the Judge who pronounced sentence."

Parno took the file, reading for himself. Willard was correct it seemed. In a proper court, such a case would have been dismissed. Clearly the judge in question had allowed his own sentiment to interfere with his duty.

"I'll bring this to Memmnon's attention when we return to Nasil," Parno murmured.

"Meantime, we'll add him to the list."

"That brings us to a grand total of twenty-nine likely candidates, plus the poachers Warden Bates mentioned," Nidiad informed the Prince.

"Let's start talking to them."

-

"You are Brenack Wysin? Currently serving a life sentence for the slaying of a Provincial Constable?" Parno asked.

"I am milord" the giant in the chair opposite the Prince rumbled. Corded muscle bulged beneath the thin prison shirt and Wysin's giant neck threatened to burst the collar. Rough hands carried the callouses associated with long hours and hard work. Parno wasn't sure he'd ever seen such a large man before. Wysin was easily a head and a half taller than Parno himself and Parno was six feet three inches tall.

"So, tell me, Brenack, what led you to slay a Constable?"

"Strong drink, milord," Wysin replied at once. "I am unused to such and it fogged my mind. When the constable accosted me in the tavern, I struck back much harder than I should have."

"Should you have struck a Constable at all?" Willard asked.

"I didn't know he was a Constable, sir," Wysin answered. "He was drunk as well, and wore no uniform of office. He decided that he could beat me. He was mistaken."

Parno nodded thoughtfully. According to the record the Constable in question had been a man of small stature. Many such men, when under the influence of strong drink, seemed to feel that brawling with larger men was a way of proving themselves. The Constable's choice of 'victim' had cost him his life in this case.

"Tell me, Brenack," Parno said, "are you a good blacksmith?"

"I was a good smith, milord," Wysin corrected. "Now I'm merely a prisoner."

"Are you skilled at weapon making?" Parno asked. "Sword making perhaps?"

"I have made swords, milord," Wysin nodded. "Their quality I must leave to those who own them. I myself have no skill with a blade."

"Brenack," Parno said, leaning back in his chair, "I am here recruiting men for the army. For a new type of unit. I have need of a blacksmith, more than one actually. I also have need of skilled sword smiths if any are to be found. Does that sound like something that might interest you?"

"Would I be out of here, milord?"

"Yes, but on conditions," Parno replied. "Your term of service will be equal to your prison sentence. You will be paid and eventually be able to earn freedom of movement if you prove trustworthy. But desertion carries the penalty of death, Brenack Wysin. I ask you to consider that before giving me your answer."

"I accept, milord," Wysin said at once. "Any chance of freedom is better than this."

"Very well, Brenack," Parno said after a pause. "Your name shall be entered upon the roles. You will remain here for a bit longer, perhaps two months or so. You will then be transferred to our post in the Tinsee Province. Once there, you will begin your service to the Crown as a regimental smith and armorer."

"Thank you, milord," Wysin said, his deep voice threatening to crack. "I will work very hard to reward your confidence in me."

"I have no doubt," Parno nodded. "I will see you again, in Tinsee." The guards entered, escorting Wysin back to his cell. Willard watched him go, then turned to Parno.

"Milord, you may not find another useful soul in all the prisons of Soulan, but there is one you'll not have cause to regret."

"I agree," Nidiad said at once. "That one will be loyal to the death. Well done lad. Well done indeed."

"Let's see if there's another among our choices, then."

Much later, Parno's spirits had deflated quite far when the guards escorted a small oriental prisoner into the room. Twenty-four men had been seen since Brenack Wysin. Some had declined the offer, others had been deemed unsuitable by the panel. Outside Warden Bates' poachers, only three men remained. Three men and this foreign monk.

Cho Feng entered the room slowly, dragging a large quantity of heavy chain with him. Fettered hand and foot, the monk could barely walk.

"I take it you deem this man a danger?" Parno asked the guards.

"Orders, milord," the senior guard replied with a small bow. "The prisoner is well behaved, but dangerous. He has fighting abilities the likes of which none of us have ever seen. Nor can we compete with."

"How interesting," Willard murmured.

Feng took his seat, where he sat stoically, not speaking, not moving. Parno studied him closely. The man was small, compared to most, but a wiry strength was evident, strength that would prove surprising to those who looked merely at the man's size.

Cho Feng had been arrested as a pirate by the Navy on the Southern Sea. Claiming to be a paying passenger on his way to the continent, Feng had pleaded ignorance of any pirating activity. He had paid for passage north from the southern countries, he said, and was not a member of the crew.

Unfortunately, his deal had been made with the Captain of the pirate vessel and he had not survived the encounter. Unable to prove his story, Feng had been convicted of piracy. A charge which carried at the least a life sentence.

"Tell me, Cho Feng," Parno said at last, "why were you coming here to 'the continent' as you put it?"

"I wished to see the Face Mountain," Feng said finally. "Such a thing is not seen in my lands. I wished to see it for myself."

"And you just happened to book passage on a pirate vessel?" Willard asked.

"It was the only vessel in the Brazees coming this way," Feng replied. "One must use the means one is given. It was taking passage aboard the ship, or walk. One does not walk through many of the southern kingdoms alone. Not if he wishes to live. I did not know the vessel was that of a pirate. It was clean and appeared well kept. I thought it a merchant vessel and inquired of the Captain if I might pay or earn passage north."

"You did not fight the Navy when they took the ship, I see," Nidiad spoke.

"I did not," Feng agreed. "One does not fight authority in my land. I had broken no laws and did not expect to be sent to prison. As it turns out, no law breaking is required in your lands for one to be sent to prison."

"Thus, you claim to be innocent," Willard said.

"I do not claim anything," said Feng, his voice tinged with bitterness. "Your own record tells you that I did not resist your navy. No proof that I am or ever have been a pirate was presented to your court. I was labeled a pirate because I was aboard the ship. Having paid the equivalent of three years wages for passage here to see the Mountain of Faces. Which I will now never see."

Parno said nothing, studying the man closely. If his tale was true, and Parno suspected it was, then he didn't blame the man for being bitter. Cho Feng fairly radiated a quiet dignity, a formal bearing which spoke of good raising and education. This man would be a boon to his work, of that Parno was certain. He wasn't sure how, at the moment, but knew it for the truth. But could Feng be trusted? How could Parno decided if the man was trustworthy? A sudden inspiration seized him. He looked at the guard.

"Free him," Parno ordered.

"Milord," the guard began hesitantly.

"Mind yourself," Nidiad warned, and the guard acquiesced, quickly removing the chains.

"Leave us," Parno ordered. The guards didn't argue this time, but withdrew hesitantly. Parno nodded to Nidiad and Willard.

"You as well," he added. Now it was Darvo's turn to protest.

"Go," Parno ordered. He looked at Feng.

"Cho Feng, are you an honorable man?" The oriental was caught by surprise at the question, but nodded.

"I have always sought to be."

"May I have your word of honor that you will not seek to harm me, or to escape?"

"I will not seek to harm you, on my honor," Feng answered. "I cannot give you my word not to try and escape, for I do not belong here. Any chance I have to flee this horrid place, I will take."

"Fair enough," Parno nodded, convinced now that he was right. "Go," he ordered again, and this time Nidiad went, Willard having already gone through the door.

Once they were alone, Parno sat quietly for a moment. Suddenly he picked up an apple left from lunch and drew his knife.

"Would you share my apple, Cho Feng?" he asked, cutting the apple with a deft slice. He handed one half to Feng, made a small cut on his left hand, and re-sheathed his blade.

"You have cut yourself," Feng pointed.

"The blade must taste blood once drawn," Parno shrugged. "I have no other knife, and the apple must be cut." Feng's eyes registered surprise, but he said nothing as he ate the apple.

"Cho Feng, I am Prince Parno McLeod, third son of Tammon McLeod, King of Soulan. I must warn you, however, that you will gain no bargain by taking me as hostage. Indeed, my father would be more likely to reward you for killing me, than for setting me free. Though he wouldn't. He'd hang you and play the bereaved father."

"I know who you are, Prince of Soulan," Feng said. "And I have given you my word, regardless of your father's reaction."

"Yes, you have," Parno nodded. "Tell me, Cho Feng, do you believe in fate? Believe that all things, regardless of time, happen for a reason?"

"I do," Feng nodded, surprise again evident in his eyes.

"So do I," Parno said between bites of apple. "I have heard of a bare-handed fighting ability among sailors who sail the orient. Is it this type of skill that inspires such fear among the guards?"

"I am skilled at many disciplines of combat," Feng replied with a smile. "I worked for many years as trainer to the Imperial Army in my homeland."

"I thought as much," Parno nodded. "Here is my problem, Cho Feng. I have been given a task. To take men from prisons such as these and make them soldiers. You may know that the kingdom to the north, Norland, is much larger than our own and has a much larger army."

"Three times in recent memory, including once in my father's reign, Norland has attacked us. Each time we have been victorious, but the cost in lives was ruinous. Our land is much smaller, much less populous, than the Nor. We cannot continue to face them on the battlefield on equal terms."

"I plan to create a unit that can fight many times its own numbers, and emerge the victor. Skill such as yours could well make the difference in that battle."

"You wish me to teach your soldiers? A pirate?" Feng's voice didn't drip sarcasm so much as ooze with it. Parno nodded.

"I understand your anger. I have read the account of your arrest. I am inclined to believe that you are truthful and so, I make you this offer. Serve me as instructor of hand-to-hand combat and any other form you know of that might help. In return, you will be paid, given room and board, and a measure of freedom that depends upon you."

"And," Parno added, "if you do so, I will petition the King's Bench to review your conviction. Failing that, I will appeal directly to the King for pardon. I won't lie, the fact that I'm doing the asking will work against you. But I will try, nonetheless."

"If I succeed, you may return to your country and have the pay in your pockets when you do. It is little to offer, I know. But I believe you to be a man of your word and I am of mine. All I require is your word that you will not flee, not attempt to escape during your service, and I will take you from here when I leave today."

"You place great faith in a man you do not know," Feng said finally.

"I place faith in fate," Parno corrected. "I need someone of your skills. Fate has placed you here that we should meet. Am I a fool to trust you, and fate? Or a fool to ignore what fate has placed before me?"

Feng sat silently for so long that Parno was about to decide the monk would refuse. That was when he spoke.

"You have patience, young Prince," Feng smiled. "Such is not always the case with Royalty. Nobles tend to want what they want, now. Regardless of any other considerations. You are also wise beyond your years, Scion of Soulan. Yes, I do believe in fate. For long years I was driven to venture here and see the Mountain of Faces, though I could not tell you why. I do not, even now, know why."

"It seems," the monk said, "that fate has indeed placed me here for you to meet. If that is so, then who am I to question such things? I give you my word, Parno McLeod, that I will neither harm you, nor your people. I will not seek to escape and I will teach you and your soldiers all that I can."

"I can ask no more than that," Parno bowed. "I will be your first student, Cho Feng. I promise I will be an apt pupil."

"I have no doubt, My Prince," Feng smiled yet again.

Parno had signed his second man.

-

"Milord, this is most unusual," Warden Bates said, "but of course your wishes will be met." Parno had given instruction for the Brenack Wysin and twelve others to be delivered to Cove by the time Parno had returned there, but Cho Feng would accompany him when he left today.

"I want to thank you, Warden, for your hospitality, and your assistance," Parno said graciously. "I will inform His Majesty's Chief Constable of your service personally." Bates fairly beamed at that.

"Most kind of you, Your Highness," he bowed deeply.

"We take our leave, Warden," Parno said offering his hand. "Please inform the families of the prisoners I have selected to be ready to move when the train departs. I will ask Governor Harkin to provide wagons, drivers, and a suitable escort."

"I will see to it myself, Milord," Bates promised.

Parno, with Willard, Nidiad, and Cho Feng in tow, walked outside where their horses were waiting. Bates had provided a horse for Feng, until the group returned to Jax, where one would be acquired.

"Where now, Milord?" Nidiad inquired, eyeing Feng from the corner of his eye.

"We shall return to Jax for the night and depart upon the morrow," Parno said, stepping into the saddle. "We must see to clothing and accessories for Feng, and the men will likely need a night in barracks to recuperate from a night upon the town."

"Likely so," Willard chuckled. "They're a good lot, mind you, Your Highness, but high spirited."

"I'd have it no other way, Karls."

-

Parno swung at Cho Feng, his right hand driving straight at the monks smiling face. Suddenly the Prince was flying through the air. He landed on his back with a loud 'oomph'. He lay still for a moment; the impact having jarred every bone in his body.

"Well done!" Darvo Nidiad howled with laughter. Willard and his soldiers joined in, having learned that Parno was not one to lord his position over those who served with him.

"You must learn to strike without warning," Feng was speaking to the assembled soldiers. It was the first night on the road after leaving Jax, and Parno had decided that no time would be wasted. The soldiers and himself would learn what they could from Feng as they traveled.

Feng was much more impressive after a hot scrubbing bath and once adorned in new, proper fitting clothes. He now wore a dirk, and a sword adorned his saddle. Parno had kept his word. Feng was as free as possible in his new role.

"With no time to prepare, your enemy is less likely to parry your attack and even less likely to counter-attack."

"Aye," Nidiad laughed. "I think that the Prince would agree he's not in any position to counter-attack. 'Least not at the moment," he added with an evil snicker.

"Very funny, old man," Parno half groaned, half growled, rising stiffly to his feet.

"I'm not the one picking myself up from the ground, Your Highness," Darvo pointed out.

"I can arrange that, if you'd like," Parno smiled nastily.

"Not a chance," Nidiad shook his great head. "I'm far too old for that sort of thing. But I can see real possibilities in this, I can. Master Feng will make good soldiers better ones, that's for sure."

Feng bowed, pleased with the compliment from the old soldier.

"Please take note of the stiffness Prince Parno is experiencing. Such is the result of improper conditioning. There are exercises which will free you from that state, and allow you to roll with such impacts, lessening their severity."

"We will begin those exercises on the morrow," Feng concluded. "They will also make long travel by horseback easier on the body."

"Well, we need another volunteer for the next move," Parno announced, limping back to his seat. "I don't think I'm up to another 'lesson' at the moment."

"None of us are," Nidiad ordered, rising. "Captain, set the guard and let's to bed. We've hard riding to do yet and Master Feng's 'exercise' will take some time in the morning. Best we be rested."

Willard saluted and called for his sergeant. Parno sank carefully into his camp chair, sighing in relief as he did so.

"You have great potential, My Prince," Feng said. "And you desire knowledge. Such is the true mark of the wise. I have known many great leaders in my lifetime. All were such men."

"I'm not a great leader, Cho," Parno smiled, "just a black sheep. A black mark upon the name McLeod."

"Wool from the black sheep is many times more valuable than that of the others, My Prince," Feng said quietly. "Do not underestimate yourself." With that Feng went to his tent. Darvo and Parno sat alone in the failing light of the fire.

"He's quite the man, Parno me lad," Darvo observed quietly. "And a teacher of rare value. You have made a good choice there."

"You seem to have changed your opinion rather quickly," Parno observed quietly. "Wasn't because he threw me around so easily was it?"

"Well," Nidiad smiled at the memory, "I admit that might have played a small part in my decision. But it's the bearing of the man strikes me hardest. There's a man knows what he can do and make no mistake, I doubt there's a more dangerous man in all of Soulan."

"I'm of the same mind," Parno nodded. "If he can teach our men even a third of what he knows, our soldiers will be near unstoppable on the battlefield."

"An arrow will stop anyone, lad, regardless of rank, knowledge, or skill," Darvo reminded him. "But I agree in spirit. Soldiers with Feng's abilities will be a force to be reckoned with, no doubt."

-

The morning saw the entire company, even Darvo Nidiad, engaged in Cho Feng's exercises. The soldiers were skeptical, to say the least, when the first command was to sit upon the ground, one leg thrust forward, the other pulled behind.

"Now, lean toward the extended leg with the opposite hand, attempting to touch the toe of the foot. You will feel the leg stretch to accommodate this action. Likewise, you will feel the extended arm and its shoulder stretch slightly. Go no further should you encounter real pain. Such must begin slowly, progressing as the body adjusts."

The soldiers obeyed, stretching first one leg, then the other. Then came what Feng referred to as 'calisthenics'. More stretching intermingled with jumping, bending and pushing up from the ground. Finally, after nearly an hour, Feng called the class over.

Groaning troopers pulled themselves erect, heading for the meal the cook had prepared. Soon they were in the saddle, riding east. Their next destination was the city of Bingham, in the Alba province.

Parno had a feeling that they would all be in remarkably better condition when they arrived. If they survived.

# CHAPTER THREE

-

The small command made good time venturing across the southern half of the kingdom, following one of the ancient trade routes left from before the fall. No one knew who had built the great roads, but the McLeod family had invested a great deal of Crown Treasury over the centuries to keep the roads serviceable. Travelers who had ventured to Norland had reported similar roads crisscrossing the northern land as well.

The trip to Bingham had taken most of three weeks. As promised, Cho Feng's 'exercises' had indeed proven to ease the pains of travel on horseback. The soldiers were no longer grumbling about the instructor's conditioning program. Instead their ire had a new target.

Running.

Two weeks after the basic exercise programs had started, Feng announced that the command would begin running each morning after their stretches and workouts. The soldiers, all cavalrymen, objected instantly.

"We've no need of running, Master Feng. We ride into battle."

"We're not in the habit of running away from a fight, Master Feng."

Despite their protests, the men obeyed. And found, to their amazement, that the running was at least as beneficial as the exercises had been. Already they were leaner, harder and breathed easier than before. They also found that working with the high-spirited mounts favored by all cavalry men was no longer a great and exhausting chore.

"I'd not of believed it," Nidiad shook his head as he, Parno, Karls Willard, and Cho Feng sat beneath the fly of Parno's tent. "I feel at least ten years younger. A month ago, I was set upon retirement, now I feel like I'm back in the Nasil Lancers."

"Good exercise can keep one young far longer than without, Colonel," Feng said. "In my homeland, active soldiers serve in the ranks well into their sixties."

"Sixties?" Willard exclaimed. "Why, that's incredible!"

"Not at all, Captain," Feng replied. "When one's body and spirit are in harmony, one can do much more in his advanced years than those who have not made the necessary training and conditioning a part of their lives."

-

The column was approaching an outlying village of Bingham when they heard the shouting.

"What the devil is that?" Willard asked, reigning his horse to a stop and motioning for the following cavalry to do the same.

"Sounds like a riot, almost," Nidiad said, ears straining to hear more.

"Or a raid," Parno said grimly. "Let's see."

"Forward!" Willard shouted, and the column, Parno, Nidiad, and Karls Willard in the lead, moved at a gallop into the village.

-

The village was nearly in a riot, it turned out. Most of the town's people seemed to be hovering around the town square. A massive bonfire had been erected, but not yet lit. In the middle of that structure, tied to a pole, was a somewhat grizzled man, howling like a banshee.

"What goes on here?" Parno demanded from the nearest man.

"Burning a witch," the man replied without looking at his questioner. "Warlock or wizard I guess, seeing as he's a man."

"Witch? Wizard?" Willard was fighting the urge to laugh, while Nidiad was already laughing.

"A witch!" the old soldier roared in laughter. "Oh, deliver me from the ignorant of the world, even amongst my own!" Parno wasn't so amused.

"Who's in charge?" Parno demanded.

"Priest yonder," the man pointed toward the bonfire. "Him and the constable."

Parno kicked his horse, pushing him through the crowd. Willard motioned for the soldiers to spread out around the crowd, then he, Feng and Nidiad, along with five cavalrymen, followed Parno into the crowd.

Parno arrived at the fire just as the priest was finishing his rant, working the crowd into a fevered pitch. The arrival of the horsemen took some of the steam from him, but he looked up defiantly.

"Who are you, and what business do you have interrupting this proceeding?"

"Who are you, sir," Parno snapped, "that you take it upon yourself to burn another at the stake as if we were ignorant savages?"

"I am the Priest of the local church, young man, fully empowered by the King himself to tend to matters such as this and have the backing of the constable as well!" The priest shot back, his voice carrying across the crowd. At his words, the crowd once again began shouting.

"You sir, are a liar," Parno said savagely. "Never has the King authorized any but the King's Bench and their subordinates to dispense justice in the Kingdom of Soulan." He glanced at the constable. "And you give weight of your office to this travesty, then, constable?"

"You're overstepping your bounds, young visitor," the constable grated. "Let's have no more talk from you, less you want to spend the night in the cells."

"And who is it that will put me there, constable," Parno asked with a smile. "Yourself?"

"This is none of your affair, you interloper. Be gone or we'll . . ." the priest began, but Nidiad moved his horse forward in an instant, cutting him off.

"Mind your tongue, or I'll have it out right here and now!" Nidiad snarled. "This is Prince Parno McLeod you're speaking to!"

That put a whole new light on things. The constable went deathly white, knowing that he was in trouble. The priest too, went pale, realizing that he was trapped in a pit of his own making. He had assured the people that he had the full authority to prosecute and then persecute anyone accused of witchcraft. Now his lies had caught up with him.

"I want the priest and the constable taken into custody," Parno ordered. "We'll take them to Bingham for trial before the bench." Soldiers began to move into the area, still astride their mounts. Parno turned to face the crowd.

"Go home, all of you!" he ordered. "They'll be no burning here today, nor any other. This is unlawful, and any who remain will face the King's Justice!"

The crowd melted away in record time. No one doubted that the speaker was, indeed, Prince Parno, though none had ever seen him. It was enough that he acted like a prince and that's what mattered.

Satisfied that the crowd was breaking up, Parno dismounted. Easing up to the still howling man, he drew his knife.

"Be still!" Parno snarled, and cut the ropes. The man fell against Parno, nearly in tears.

"Thank you, milord, thank you! Had you not happened along when you did, they'd have burned me alive!"

"I'm afraid that's likely," Parno nodded, anger still fresh from the abuse of power he had seen. "Who are you, man? And what have you done to arouse such ire among these people?"

"It was the holy man who did the ire rousing, milord," the man snarled. "Any he falls afoul of, or threatens his hold over the village, come to no good. I am Roda Finn, milord, late of the King's University in Bingham."

"Almost very late," Nidiad observed. "How come you to be in this fix, Finn?"

"I am smarter than the priest, good sir, that's how," Finn said with a sniff. "I retired here to work on my projects, you see. The priest enjoys, or did enjoy, perhaps I should say, a large degree of power. Some of my projects here have aided more than one poor farmer, which in turn led to some small degree of popularity for me. The priest cannot stand for any challenge to his power, so he accused me of sorcery, and convinced the townsfolk, and that witless oaf of a constable, that I should be burned alive for my 'crimes'."

"And just what have you done that has aided the poor folk of this community that was so quickly forgotten?" Parno asked with a grin.

"I've not aided everyone, milord, only those few who asked. Nor have I charged any monies or goods for my services, before you ask. One small thing I did was erect a windmill on a small ranch not far from here. A simple device that harnesses the power of the wind to pump water from a deep well. The stock man there now has an ample supply of water year around."

"Sounds reasonable enough," Nidiad nodded. "We use them in the Tinsee province as well."

"Of course you do, sir," Finn snorted. "You are not ignorant savages who, spurred by a power mad priest, see evil in anything that is beyond your simple knowledge. Unfortunately, some areas of the Kingdom are not so enlightened."

"Was this all you did, then, Roda Finn?" Parno asked.

"No. I also developed a supply of ancient powder to help another man clear stumps from a new field. Used with a length of fuse, one can pour the powder under the stump, light the fuse, and the stump is blown from the ground by the force of the powder exploding. I'm afraid that's probably what gave the priest the leverage he needed."

"Exploding?" Parno asked.

"Yes milord," Finn replied. "The ancient formula was used for many things, including warfare. Mixed in large quantities it has great power. It can also be used to propel objects for great distance. Objects that can also be made to explode when they strike their target."

"Indeed," Nidiad muttered softly, glancing at Parno. "Such a thing might well be . . . useful, milord."

"Indeed it might," Parno smiled. He turned to the scientist, now trying vainly to straighten his clothing. "Tell me, Roda Finn. Are you interested in pursuing your, 'work', elsewhere? North to the Tinsee, perhaps? As a member of my staff?"

"Staff?" Finn said, halting his brushing. "You wish me to work for you?"

"I do," Parno nodded. "In exchange, I will fund your work." The scientist's eyes glowed at that. "But you will need to help me in developing these ideas of yours to military uses. A fair trade?"

Finn said nothing for a moment, clearly considering. After a long moment, he nodded.

"A fair trade, milord," he said. "I will help you, and you will keep me safe from ignorant savages. One brush with a bonfire is quite enough."

"Indeed, I will," Parno said with a laugh. "Come then, Master Finn. Let us gather your things."

-

Finn, it turned out, had a good bit to gather. The fussy scientist insisted on carrying everything he owned with him, as he planned to 'never return to this backwards place'. Parno laughed as the former professor supervised the soldiers loading his belongings. His fussing and muttering turned to outright jabbering when it came time to load his 'laboratory'.

"Mister Finn," Parno said finally, "might I get a word in private?" Parno could tell that Finn's constant attention was wearing thin on the soldiers.

"Certainly, milord," Finn said, coming to Parno's side.

"Roda, I know you are concerned about your things, and I understand that you must still be shaken by the events of this morning. But my soldiers are not accustomed to dealing with someone of your background and while they are not, perhaps, the scholars you are accustomed to dealing with, they are intelligent men. Tell them once what to do and then be silent. If an object needs special care, then point that out, but do not hover over them as a hawk would a chicken. Understand?"

Finn's face flushed red at the reprimand, but then he looked at the soldiers. In his absence, they were still working. He noted they took great care with his equipment, books and parchments, and they packed his goods as carefully as they might were they their own. He looked back to Parno rather shame faced.

"I am sorry, milord," he said contritely. "I am not . . . I am unused to having skilled help. Many of my things are rare and likely would prove difficult, and expensive, to replace. I'm afraid it is an old habit. One I see I will need to break myself of."

Parno smiled at that, pleased with Finn's reaction. He had half expected the professor to respond poorly to criticism and was pleased to be wrong. He wanted Finn on good terms with the soldiers. If even half of what the man claimed were possible, it would be extremely helpful to the young prince. He reached into his pocket and pulled a handful of coins from his purse.

"Take this," Parno instructed Finn, placing the coin into Finn's hand, "and when we reach Bingham, buy a round, or two, for the men who are loading for you. Tell them what a good job they did and how much you appreciate it."

"Why?" Finn asked, confused. "They are following your orders are they not? Why is it necessary to buy . . . ." Finn trailed off as Parno raised a hand.

"They are soldiers, Master Finn," the prince replied, his voice taking on a slightly sharper edge. "In the world you are accustomed to, I know that hirelings do their work because you pay them. But these are fighting men, Roda, not menial servants. They are following my orders, but I will also buy them a drink tonight for doing what they, and I, consider extra duty. If you are to become part of our outfit, you would do well to learn how we do things."

"And they did help me save your life, after all, if you recall."

Again, Roda Finn blushed red, now from shame. He did recall.

"I'm sorry, milord. You are right, I have much to learn."

"Not as much as you think, Roda," Parno smiled. "And not nearly as much as we have to learn from you."

-

As the column entered Bingham, several heads turned to follow the soldiers and their captives. Parno inquired of a passing constable of the location of the Justice Hall, and directed the column in that direction. The priest was protesting his treatment, sounding off loud and long for the people on the streets.

The captive constable, however, was quiet. He had allowed himself to be used by the priest and knew he was about to pay a stiff price. Clan McLeod was founded on law, justice, and equality of all its subjects in that law. As a constable, he enjoyed a position of trust, which he had violated. His punishment would be correspondingly more severe.

Willard signaled a halt before the Justice Hall. Parno, Willard, Feng, and Nidiad all dismounted, as did four troopers. These four took possession of the prisoners, guiding them none too gently into the doorway.

Inside, Parno was less than impressed with what he saw. The hall wasn't unkept, exactly, but it was untidy. The desk constable looked up at the new arrivals, frowning at the sight of a constable being held prisoner.

"What the blazes? Who are you, to be holding a constable captive?" The stout constable was on his feet, projecting his voice. Several constables sitting in the hall roused themselves to see what was happening.

"Are you in charge here?" Parno inquired politely. "I'm afraid I have some unpleasant business to attend to. This constable has misused his authority."

"And who are you to make that determination?" the desk constable snarled. "I've a good mind to teach you -" The sergeant's tirade cut off abruptly as both Willard and Nidiad stepped in front of their Prince. Both were in the uniform of the Royal Military, and while neither spoke, their anger was evident.

"My name," Parno answered agreeably, "is Parno McLeod, constable, and I asked if you were in charge."

The constable's face paled. His fellow constables were suddenly studiously seeing to their own affairs. Licking his dry lips, the desk constable nodded.

"Y-yes, Milord," he finally croaked. "Constable Sergeant Nevers, sire."

"Very well, Sergeant Nevers," Parno smiled. "I wish these men held here for trial. The charges are attempted murder, inciting a riot, and for the constable here you may add dereliction of duty and abuse of office. I will return in the morning to speak with the Chief Constable of the District and take care of any formalities. Please ensure that the Chief knows that I will call upon him and ask that he make himself available."

"Of course, Milord," the Sergeant replied at once. "Turner, Miller! See to the prisoners. At once!" The last command was bellowed as the two constables detailed to take charge of the prisoners didn't move fast enough to suit the Sergeant.

"Should the Chief Constable desire to speak to me before morning, Sergeant, he may call for me at the Royal Barracks. Understood?"

"Aye, Milord. I shall so inform the Chief of Constabulary."

"Thank you, Sergeant."

"Let's go," he added in a quieter tone to his men. As the soldiers filed back outside, the priest could still be heard, yammering constantly.

"What a mess," Nidiad snorted as the men stepped outside. "I could understand it if we were in a smaller settlement, but this is the Provincial Capital, for Crown's sake!"

"Judge not," Parno smiled. "And let us waste no more time with such matters. There's baths, women, and strong drink awaiting us!"

"Hear, hear!"

The column moved along the street, eager for the promised recreation after over two weeks in the saddle.

-

"Milord! We were not expecting you! Had we known, proper accommodations would have already been prepared. I assure you, however, that we will -" Parno's raised hand silenced the young officer in mid-apology.

"Proper accommodation for me is with my men, Captain," Parno said quietly. "If it's good enough for them, then it's good enough for me. I would appreciate it if suitable barracks were made available for my Company to bunk together, however. And if you could have the stables care for our horses? We really are in need of a hot bath and cold beer, preferably with as little delay as possible."

"Of course, Milord," the Captain replied with a grin. "I'll see to it myself. If you and your men will follow me, I'll get you to your barracks, and then have the stable hands retrieve and care for your animals and wagons."

"Thank you, Captain."

-

"Well, these ain't bad," Willard said, as he followed Parno and Nidiad into the transient barracks assigned to the men in Parno's command.

The barracks were austere, of course, as all such buildings were. As transient barracks the interior lacked the touches of soldiers who called barracks home. There were no soldiers permanently billeted in these quarters and the walls and desks were empty. The barracks themselves were spotless.

"Whoever runs this place has things right on rail, seems to me," Nidiad agreed. "This place could stand inspection right now."

"Well, all I want to inspect is the tub," Parno said with a grin. "And after that, the nearest good beer."

"Sounds like a plan," Willard replied, his own face split by a grin. He turned to address his troops.

"All right, lads! Pick your bunks, by rank, then seniority. I expect every man back here in time for morning assembly. Leave until then." Cheers erupted from the soldiers at that news. After so many days on the road, they were more than ready for a few days in barracks, along with a few nights in town.

"First round is on me, boys!" Parno called, and the cheering increased. Parno laughed. "Course that means I get first crack at the bath!" General laughter followed that remark, as the men all piled in to shake down into bunk assignments.

Over the last month, Parno McLeod had proven to be most un-prince like, the soldiers had decided. Instead, they regarded the scion of their ruling family as one of them, high praise indeed from combat soldiers. While Parno's brother, Therron, commanded all the Soulan Armies, he was not considered a true soldier by the men he commanded. The Lord Marshal, as Therron insisted on being called, traveled in comfort wherever he went and would never dream of sharing a barracks, let alone a campfire, with 'common' soldiers.

Parno, on the other hand, held himself no higher, no more deserving of comfort, than the man next to him in the saddle, regardless of what rank that man might hold. Moreover, Prince Parno was by no means trying to convince the soldiers of his own toughness. Indeed, he complained just like the troopers did, of saddle sores, cramped muscles and long rides. But he endured all these things right alongside the soldiers he now commanded.

And that was the difference. While Parno McLeod would never be like them, he was one of them. That, after all, was all that mattered.

-

The next morning found the Chief Constable waiting upon the Prince's pleasure in the office of the barrack's Captain. He was in a somewhat foul mood, having been kept waiting by a mere captain and to see a non-entity like Parno McLeod at that.

Tumar Barone had been Chief Constable of Bingham for many years and was a fairly powerful man in his own right. He knew that Parno was the least favored of the ruling family and that the King couldn't stand the sight of him. Still, he was a member of the Royal Family and despite his knowledge of the relationship between Royal Father and Royal Son, Barone knew it was dangerous to rock the boat.

"Chief Constable?" Barone's thoughts were interrupted. He turned to see a young man in soldier's garb entering the door.

A damned aide, Barone thought sourly. Come, no doubt, to explain that his Highness is delayed. Probably due to illness, though no doubt the truth is that the whelp is hung over.

"Yes?"

"Parno McLeod," the young man said, offering his hand. Barone, taken aback by the off-handed way the young prince introduced himself, Barone took the hand without a thought.

"Milord," Barone nodded.

"I'm sorry to have brought you such a wad of trouble, Chief," Parno said. "I found the constable and priest I turned over to your men about to burn a man at the stake, alive, for witchcraft, of all things."

"I read the report, sire," Barone nodded. "I must confess, I was surprised. Both by the constable's actions and the priest's. The priest apparently convinced the constable and most of the townsfolk that he had some sort of official authority to practice such devilry."

"Well, he doesn't," Parno assured the Chief Constable. "I've made sure, as far as possible, that the people in town know that too. But this cannot be allowed to go unpunished."

"It won't, Milord," Barone replied. "I assure you. Both men will stand trial as charged. It will be necessary for you and your men to be here for that trial, however."

"Not a problem," Parno assured him. "I'll be here for a week, perhaps ten days. That should be enough time for the trial, shouldn't you think?"

"More than sufficient, Milord," Barone agreed. "I wasn't aware you were going to be staying with us so long."

"Let me know when you need me. If I'm not around, a message left with the barracks Officer will reach me quickly enough," Parno ordered, ignoring the Constable's deftly asked non-question. Normally Parno wouldn't have hesitated to let the Chief Constable of a town he visited know what he was doing, but there was something about Barone that didn't set well with him.

"As you will, Milord," Barone responded with a curt bow. He knew a dismissal when he heard it. "By your leave?"

"Good day to you, Chief," Parno nodded and the chief left the office, still surly.

"Quite a fellow, aye, Captain?" Parno noted to the Officer of Barracks. The young Captain hesitated for a few seconds, then nodded. "Aye, milord. Quite a fellow indeed."

Parno was about to ask the Captain about his hesitation when Nidiad opened the door and stepped in.

"Ready when you are, Milord," the old soldier informed him.

"Very well. Captain, should anyone be looking for me I shall return here this evening. You might make note that my men and I will occupy the barracks for at least ten days. Also note that we will require the training field at dawn each morning for roughly an hour and again before dark. If that interferes with anyone else, let me know. We'll work something out."

"Aye, Milord."

"Well then," Parno told Nidiad, "let's be off, shall we?"

-

The ride to the King's Prison outside Bingham was uneventful. The warden, a fat, red-faced and effusive man named Brickle made every effort to please the young prince.

Parno, Nidiad, and Willard spent most of the day interviewing prisoners. A number of the men they spoke to seemed ideal for their unit, while others seemed to try a bit too hard to seem ideal.

By the end of the day, another three dozen men had been added to the rolls of what everyone, save the prince, referred to as 'Parno's Company'. The warden assured the prince that the men and their families would be in Cove at the appointed time.

As the three men rode back onto town, Parno broached the subject of a name for the proposed regiment.

"Parno's Company? Who in blazes came up with that?"

"I did, actually," Willard replied, not the least put off. "The men will need a proper name for the unit in which they serve and you are the commander."

"Darvo is the commander, Karls," Parno pointed out. "I'm just along to give the project a royal boost and to keep me as far from my Father as possible, of course," he added with a wry smile. Parno had never made an effort to hide the problems he had with his family. He had no intention of starting now, least of all with Karls Willard.

"That may be how it came about, milord," Willard replied, "but my own men have already accepted as fact that you command. There is no grumbling, no murmuring, either. They are proud to serve with you. Whatever they may think of you elsewhere, you have earned the respect of these men and that's not something that's easily done."

"I agree," Nidiad spoke for the first time. "The regular soldiers of the King's Army are not, by and large, easy to impress. Nor is their respect something that is freely given."

"Look, it's well and good in such a small setting, for you and them to feel that way," Parno said. "And I'm honored, to be sure. Even more, if I'm honest, I'm pleased that I've been able to earn that respect. But the fact remains that I'm a figurehead. The only reason I was given this position was to get me out of Nasil."

"Mission accomplished, then," Karls grinned. "You are out of Nasil."

"So I am," Parno grinned back. "And up a creek."

The three men shared a laugh at that, and the conversation turned to other matters as they continued back into town. The subject of Parno's Company was raised no more.

-

The trial lasted only a half day, a busy morning of testimony and sputtering. The former from Parno and his men, the latter from the priest. The Constable spoke only twice, once to point out that the priest had presented official looking documents supporting his claim of royal authority and again to apologize for his ineptitude.

In the end, the priest was sent to prison for ten years, the charge of attempted murder guaranteeing him a cell for that long. The constable was dismissed and given a much lighter sentence, two years. All in all, Parno was quite pleased with the outcome of the trial itself. Yet his concern about the root cause of the incident refused to go away.

Was the royal family that out of touch with what was going on in its Kingdom? He knew that he hadn't made much effort to stay on top of events in the kingdom. There hadn't seemed much point to it. He knew, now, that was an error in judgment.

The problem was one of communication as much as anything else, he knew. Situated in the second most northern province, it took a long time for a message to reach Nasil from the southern part of the kingdom. Even Royal courier relays required ten to twelve days to make the journey from the Sunshine Peninsula, and that was in good weather. If a faster, more reliable method of communication was possible, then such problems as the one he had encountered might be reported long before conditions grew so serious.

Then there was the matter of the Provincial Capital's own Constabulary. Darvo had been right that the office was a mess. Parno had never had a reason to doubt the validity of Soulan's Justice system. Now, he had two reasons. First there were the cases of Cho Feng and Brenack Wysin. There had been no justice there, Parno was certain. Now, the apparent lack of concern over a constable who was party to what amounted to a lynching, albeit with fire rather than rope, and the pitiful state of Bingham's Constabulary. These two events had rocked Parno's faith in his Kingdom's justice system and he didn't like that feeling.

In the end, there wasn't much he could do about it, Parno knew. He was able to circumvent things in both cases, but the fact that the incidents occurred at all was troubling in the extreme and he was powerless to do anything about it.

Parno decided he would lay the problem before Memmnon upon his return to Nasil. He was better placed to investigate such an upheaval, anyway. His words would also carry far greater weight than that of a black sheep prince who would never ascend to the throne.

-

"So, tell me, Roda, how it is that you invented this 'blasting' powder of yours."

Finn looked at Parno. The two had not had much chance to speak since the prince had saved him from being burned alive. Between his work, which somehow involved prisons and the trial Parno had been quite busy. Now, as the group headed out of Alma, Parno had eased his horse into position alongside Finn's wagon.

"I didn't invent it, milord," Finn replied, appearing to weigh his words with care. "I simply rediscovered something that the ancients used. Before the Dying."

"Indeed?" Parno looked a tad surprised, though not shocked. "I didn't think there was much left of their knowledge." The world they lived in now was the by-product of a great dying time. Through the generations after that great dying much of the ancient's knowledge had been lost. There were simply too few people left in the world at that time who were capable of understanding and preserving it.

True, some things had survived, such as the technology for windmills and the ability to harness certain element found in nature. But compared to what legend said of the ancient's once proud world, it wasn't much.

"There isn't much in general use, that's true," Finn nodded. "The knowledge, at least some of it, remains, however. In books scattered throughout the kingdom and doubtless throughout the world for that matter. It's a matter of finding those bits and pieces that we can still make use of today."

"And that's something you do as what? A hobby?" Parno asked. "I remember you saying that you had been a teacher at some point."

"I was, milord," Finn nodded again. "I have served on the faculty at three of the King's Universities, teaching chemistry, mainly. It was only recently that I retired to pursue my studies of the ancient's knowledge full time."

"Fascinating," Parno shook his head. "I had no idea. I would imagine that you have read some very wonderful things, Roda Finn."

"Very, milord," Finn smiled.

"How did you come to study these things?" Parno asked, curious. "If so many believe that the knowledge is lost for all time, what made you look there at all?"

Finn looked at Parno for a long moment, weighing his reply. Parno returned his gaze steadily, wondering at the man's reluctance to speak. Until now, Finn had shown no hint of such reluctance. Interesting.

"Milord," Finn finally replied. "I will share with you something if you promise to keep it to yourself. May I be so bold as to ask your word on that?" Parno frowned at that. What could be so secretive as all that? Seeing the frown and misreading it, Finn hastened to explain.

"It isn't about. . .it's not a trust issue, milord, so much as my concern for safety. Some of the things we. . .I, have uncovered. . .well, would you like to see just anyone able to make the gunpowder? The 'blasting powder' as you call it?" Parno considered that and shook his head.

"No, I would not," he agreed. "But in any case, yes, you have my word. But if you'd prefer not to speak of it, then don't, Roda. I was asking from simple curiosity."

"No, I certainly don't mind speaking to you, milord," Finn assured him. "It's just not something I would want to be made common knowledge." He paused, lips pursed, as he considered how to explain.

"There exists within Soulan a society, a fraternal order, if you will. That society is dedicated to seeking out ancient knowledge, reconstructing the marvels of the time before the Dying and rebuilding those that would be of benefit to our fellow man. It is a painstaking process, milord, to say the least. Information found in a book in Nasil, for instance, might be useless without information from another book that might be in Jax, or Tallsee, for example. The ancient texts are not always easy to find. Far too often they are in such poor shape that it takes months, even years, to carefully reconstruct what is in them."

"But the work is worth it, milord. There exists in those ancient texts many wonderful, useful things. Information and knowledge that properly employed can make many facets of life easier. Safer."

"Knowledge of medicines and health for instance. Certain diseases, medical afflictions, and whatnot. Treatments that the ancient doctors knew of. Ways to make the same medicines they used themselves."

"And engineering," Finn continued, clearing warming to the subject so dear to his heart. "Bridge building, for instance. Building construction. Information about the earth itself. Earthquakes, weather patterns, ways of protecting ourselves against these disasters."

"And warfare," Parno said grimly. Finn nodded in agreement.

"Aye, milord," he said quietly. "The ancients were well versed at warfare. My 'gunpowder' is but a trivial thing when stacked against the weapons of the time before the Dying."

Parno considered that for a moment.

"I admit that I know little of the past," Parno admitted, almost shame faced. "I never took much time to study it. But, if this knowledge still exists, how is it that we don't use it today? How did it become lost? If lost is the term," he added with a frown. "What happened?"

"There are a number of reasons, milord," Finn shrugged. "First and foremost it seems, is that many of the people who knew how to make use of knowledge in certain areas were lost in the Dying. Some certainly survived, of course," he acknowledged, "but many did not. Too many, perhaps, for the necessary schools to continue."

"Another problem was the separation of peoples caused by the Dying. Histories from the time immediately after the Dying indicate that fierce battles were fought among the survivors over scraps of technology and dwindling resources. Leaders of many great cities, including Nasil, knew that once those scraps were gone or depleted, replacement of them would be difficult or completely impossible. The machines needed to make parts for much of their equipment had no one to operate them. Materials needed for some parts were made in faraway places, and there was no longer a way to get them."

"True, for a while there continued to be some sharing among the various places in the world of what the Ancients called 'hi-tech', but gradually their ways were lost to them as the few remaining skilled people in many areas died. In the time they had they tried to teach their skills to others but each generation naturally knew less and had less to work with than the generation before."

"So the lack of skilled workers resulted in the loss of the marvels of the Ancients," Parno said.

"To a degree," Finn nodded. "But in some places, superstition played a role it seems. The Dying was caused by a system a warfare known as Biological War. That means that weapons were derived that attacked our bodily systems, making us ill," Finn added at Parno's frown. "To them, the great technology of the their time had led to the near ruin of the entire world. As such, knowledge of those things became taboo among some races, in many parts of the world."

"Libraries were destroyed, machines disassembled. Skilled technicians killed. Laws passed that forbade the study of the 'old ways'. As a result, much was lost needlessly. We try to reconstruct what we can, when we can find it. We here in Soulan are fortunate. The Dynasty of Tyree mandated that all libraries were to be protected and they were. Your own father continues that even today, milord."

"The Guild works to restore those histories and technical 'manuals' in order to rebuild at least some of that glory."

"Who funds all this, Roda?" he asked finally.

"Those of us who search, milord," Finn shrugged. "We work at one job to support the other. It is often difficult," he admitted.

"How many of you are there, Roda?" the young prince inquired. "And are you. . .I assume that you are spread all over the kingdom?"

"Yes, we are," Finn nodded. "As to how many, I have no idea, to be honest. As we find students of rare skill and intelligence, we. . .encourage, I suppose, or foster, their interest in the pursuit. I know many of them but no one, I daresay, can know them all."

Parno pondered all this in silence. Finn noted the look on his face.

"What are you thinking, milord?" he asked, not without some concern. He had taken a large chance in sharing what he had with Parno.

"I'm thinking that I can help you and your fellows," Parno said simply. "I'm thinking that with proper funding there is much you could accomplish. Would such a sponsorship interest any of your fellows, Roda?" he asked plainly. "And would some of them be willing to apply what they know and what they learn in helping me?"

"I'm sure several of them would jump at the chance, milord," Finn answered thoughtfully. "In the past, some of our predecessors have sought Royal backing for certain projects. Not always with success, mind you," he added.

"As to helping you, I cannot say," he admitted. "None would deny you specific information as you are a Prince of the Realm, but," he shrugged again, "I cannot say that any would agree to work for you as I have. What areas would interest you the most? I may know of some who would be willing to help."

"I'm interested in all of it," Parno chuckled. "Anything that would help our people is always of interest to me, Roda. As to assisting me directly, I would be most interested in the medicinal aspect and the engineering."

"I see," Roda mused. "I know a few that might be open to working for you in those aspects."

"I would also be interested in the study of the weather," Parno mused. "If someone could predict weather patterns, even a few days in advance, then that would be most helpful. Especially in combat."

"Yes, I can see that," Roda nodded. "If I may have a few men to serve as couriers, then I can dispatch messages to a few of my colleagues who have great skill and knowledge in those areas."

"I would be willing to build a hospital on our post if one or more of the physicians would be willing to relocate," Parno added, hoping to sweeten the pot. "I'll provide anything they need, for any of them, as far as that goes."

"That would certainly appeal to many of them," Roda agreed. "I will draft the messages starting tonight. I cannot promise anything, mind you," he warned. "All I can do is present your proposal with my endorsement."

"That is all I can ask," Parno smiled. "And I thank you."

"It's the least I can do, considering that you kept me from being the guest of honor at a local stake burning," Roda replied.

# CHAPTER FOUR

-

"I give you a simple project and what happens? You stir up trouble all over the southern provinces," Tammon McLeod scowled at his youngest son, who stood before him unapologetic.

Parno and his men had returned to Nasil only the day before. Almost at once a courier had appeared, informing the youngest Prince of Soulan that the Kind demanded an audience first thing on the morrow.

The trip had been exhausting on both men and animals. They had, in fact, pushed into the night in order to reach Nasil rather than make camp again in the open. After three months in the saddle nearly every day, even the hardiest of the troopers were showing signs of fatigue.

Their travels had not been in vain, however. Over the course of their prison visitations, Parno, Darvo and Karls had found eight hundred and seventy-nine men they considered as 'possible' for the new regiment. True, some would undoubtedly have to be sent back. But considering the long odds they had faced at the outset, Parno was rather happy with the way things stood.

Or he had been, until now.

"I did not stir up trouble, My King," Parno said evenly, on his best behavior. "I have, in fact, stopped a crime from being committed. Committed in your name, in fact. The priest in question had forged official looking documents that granted him 'royal authority' to burn people at the stake."

"What?" Tammon's attitude changed abruptly.

"And had co-opted the local constable into helping him as well," Parno added with a nod, hoping to capitalize on the shift in Tammon's attention.

"In my name?" the King almost yelled.

"Yes, Milord," Parno answered. "I stopped the act before it could be finished and took both men into custody. Took them to the provincial capital where I handed them immediately over to the authorities. Our only involvement after that was to testify as to what we observed upon our arrival."

"I also," Parno continued, "took the liberty to speak for you in refuting the priest's claim of any such Royal authority. I pointed out your unswerving dedication to equal justice for all under the law and the fact that you would never authorize something like a man being burned alive.

"So, all this rumbling about your interference in affairs of justice?" Tammon inquired, his voice, for once, minus its normal sneer. Normal when dealing with Parno, at any rate.

"Just that, Milord," Parno nodded again. "Rumbling. I took no hand in the trial other than my testimony as to what I had witnessed. Something any good citizen should do and certainly something any member of the Royal Family is required to do."

"Just so," Memmnon nodded in agreement. Memmnon, in addition to his work as defacto foreign secretary, was also responsible for the King's Justice including appointments to the King's Bench. The appointment of the King's constables, a more powerful organization than the provincial constables, also fell to him. As such, all officers of the King's Justice, regardless of rank or position, were under his authority. Which meant under royal authority.

"It is the responsibility of all those of noble rank to ensure fair treatment and adherence to the law," Memmnon added firmly. "I deem you to have acted properly."

Parno nodded his thanks to his oldest sibling. While it irked him to need Memmnon's approval on his actions, the support from his brother was welcome in any setting.

"Very well," Tammon said abruptly. "Then you have indeed, for once, acted like a member of this family and fulfilled your duty. I trust you will return to your old self shortly, however, providing embarrassment and aggravation to the Crown."

Parno grimaced openly at that. For once, he had believed, he had won his father's approval. Leave it to Tammon McLeod, however, to crush those hopes while still new born.

"I'll do my best, Father," he replied, voice tinged with bitterness.

"How is your project coming, Parno?" Memmnon asked suddenly. He, too, was disappointed in Tammon's attitude.

"We have a good group," Parno replied. "I've no doubt that some will prove unsuitable, but I am fairly confident in the lot as a whole, as are Colonel Nidiad and Captain Willard," he added.

"Their training?" Memmnon pressed.

"Will begin soon," Parno nodded. "Probably within a fortnight, but no longer than a month. The prisoners are already under escort to Cove. I had planned to stay here only long enough to make my report to you."

"What is their reaction to being allowed into this trial?" Tammon asked, genuinely curious.

"They seem genuinely happy for the opportunity to prove themselves and to have a chance at making a contribution to society. The idea that they can earn even a limited freedom, especially with their families nearby, has convinced more than one to try his hand at soldiering."

"See to it they are not allowed too much freedom," Tammon growled. "They are still criminals."

"The rules are quite strict, Sire," Parno assured his father. "With Captain Willard's company there are sufficient soldiers on hand to ensure security."

"Well, so long as they don't cause any trouble," Tammon waved his hand in dismissal. "That will be all, Parno. I'm sure you will want to return to your men as soon as possible."

Parno knew a dismissal when he heard it. He bowed stiffly, and deeper than usual, then turned to go.

"I will walk out with you, brother," Memmnon said suddenly, surprising both Parno and Tammon.

"We meet with the Norland Ambassador in minutes, Memmnon," the King reminded his eldest son.

"I will be there," Memmnon assured his father.

-

Once outside, Memmnon looked at his youngest brother apologetically.

"I'm sorry, Parno," he said sincerely. "There was no call for those final remarks."

"It is a small thing anymore, brother," Parno lied easily. "I have long since learned to ignore him." *Just like I do the rest of you*, he had no need to add. Memmnon's face flushed just the same.

"Your actions were just and proper and I, for one, thank you for them," Memmnon said. His voice was not grudging, nor condescending. It rang with honesty, and sincerity.

"You need to take a closer look at what's going on in that region, Memmnon," Parno advised. "There is an ugly feel to the whole area. The Constable's office was a joke. I have to agree with Darvo. It would have been bad enough had it been in some backwards township, far removed from society as a whole. But the Provincial Capital?"

"I was only there a short time, of course," Parno continued. "But in that time I have to admit that things felt, well, off somehow. I can't tell you anything specific, just a general feeling of unease among the entire area. Especially around Bingham."

"I have already dispatched one of my best investigators, backed by a dozen King's Constables. If there is anything out of sorts, it will be dealt with, I promise."

"Good," Parno nodded. "There is something else. Two something's actually. Two cases I'd like you to look at, when time allows. I believe they were handled badly and I'd like your opinion of them. I know too little to trust my own judgment in these matters." He handed Memmnon a small leather valise. Inside were the records of Cho Feng and Brenack Wysin. Memmnon's eyebrows raised slightly.

"Interfering in the matters of Justice, Parno?" he asked lightly.

"There is no justice in these, if I am right," Parno said darkly. "It grieves me to say it, but it seems so. I will let you be the judge, since it is your position. I ask only that you do that which is right. You will see what I mean." Memmnon considered his brother carefully for a moment, then nodded.

"I will review this tonight, if possible," he said. "I make no promises. . . ."

"I ask you for no promises, Memmnon," Parno said evenly. "I ask only that you look for yourself. If it makes you feel better, it was Karls Willard who brought them to my attention." Memmnon's eyebrows rose to new height at that.

"As to Karls," Parno added, "I have a request to make, one that I cannot broach. Willard is, in fact if not law, Darvo's second. He should be promoted to Major, if not Lieutenant Colonel, something I am not allowed to do. Any suggestion I make to Therron will have negative consequences for his career, as you well know. Please mention to him that Karls is deserving of promotion."

"I will do that," Memmnon agreed immediately. "Today, in fact. Now, I must go. The Norland ambassador will be here presently and I am required to be there."

"The Norland Ambassador," Parno repeated. "Doesn't sound right, does it?"

"No," his brother snorted. "No, it doesn't. Nor does it feel right, I admit. The man is a weasel and his words are far too silky. But Father desires peace if at all possible and," Memmnon added, reluctantly, "the Norland Emperor has been very forthcoming in the last year, two years really."

"Too forthcoming, perhaps?" Parno asked.

"I. . .I would dislike to say that, in all honesty," Memmnon said, his voice absent its usual confidence. "But, I cannot shake this feeling that the man is simply going through the motions. There have been many things discussed between us, especially in the last year. He has not. . .fought, if you will, hard enough. There have been several concessions made by the Norland government. All very favorable to us. And the ambassador has offered only token resistance in our negotiations."

"It. . .bothers me, somehow," Memmnon concluded. Suddenly aware of what he had said and to whom he resumed his Crown Prince persona.

"Anyway, I will do as you request, brother," he said, voice now once again that of Ruler To Be. "I must go. Take care and safe journey." With that Memmnon turned abruptly and strode away. Parno watched him go, concern upon his face.

What was Norland up too, anyway? Among the Soulan people, it was an accepted fact that once every generation, two at most, the hordes of Norland would come sweeping down upon the Southern Kingdom. It was a fact of life that Soulan had long ago gotten used to, just as they had the sun's rising in the east and setting in the west. Now all of a sudden Norland wanted to play nice?

It made no sense, not from a ruling family that had sworn to see Soulan subdued, brought under the Norland heel. Peace would be nice, Parno agreed, and did not blame his father for pursuing any chance there might be to have it, but after centuries of ill will, two or three years of diplomatic niceties were not enough to erase the natural distrust that Soulan had for the Northern Kingdom. The Empire, as they liked to call it.

What Parno needed was someone who ventured North regularly, a merchant perhaps, taking advantage of the North's new trade allowances. Someone who would be able to simply look around. Not so much spy as simply observe.

As he returned to his rooms, Parno determined to find such a person. Someone who traveled to more than one area, if possible, and had an eye for detail. Maybe more than one person, even. He smiled as he thought of the possibilities. Parno McLeod, spymaster.

His father would have a stroke for sure.

# CHAPTER FIVE

-

Darvo Nidiad looked at the assembly of men before him, sighing heavily. Still dressed in their prison rags, they were a motley looking bunch, no doubt. The guards that had accompanied the trains were still on the grounds and Parno had impressed them into service for the time being to assist with getting the grounds organized.

Cove Canton, their small garrison, wasn't really a bad place, Darvo admitted. In the months that Parno had led them across Soulan gathering the men now standing on the parade ground, workmen had been erecting the fort itself, along with barracks, housing for senior officers, a mess hall, dispensary, everything the post needed to serve a garrison of soldiers.

Only the men before him weren't soldiers. Not yet at least. Maybe never. He stepped up on a raised podium placed there for the purpose. Soldiers of Karls Willard's command began circulating among the men, ordering them to be silent and pay attention. Darvo, ever impatient, decided to help.

"ATTENTION!" Darvo's loud voice cut across the grounds. The talking and movement dropped to nil at that bellow and Nidiad nodded.

Good start, anyway.

"You all know me," he began, voice carrying easily across the heads of the assembled prisoners. "You all know why you're here. You chose to be here. Never forget that. In the days and weeks ahead you will come to hate it here. You will come to hate me and every other person in the military. You will especially hate the people whose job it is to teach you how to be soldiers. You will want to hit them. You will want to disobey them. You may well want to kill them." He paused for effect.

"Before you take that or any other action that you have not been ordered to take, I suggest you remember this. You are no longer in prison. You are no longer a civilian. You are soldiers and as such you are subject to Army discipline. It is not in the nature of the Army of Soulan to be forgiving. Such actions as I have just described may well end with you taking a trip to the gallows." A small stir rippled through the ranks. Darvo almost nodded.

I think I've got their attention, now.

"This is not to say that the Army is unfair," he told them next. "In fact, just the opposite is true. If you become soldiers, good soldiers, you will find the Army a fine home. Good food, medical care when you need it, uniforms and equipment provided, and a dry place to sleep. All at no cost to you," he added with a grin. There were actually a few laughs among the men at this.

"Many of you were in prison because you made a mistake. Others were there because you felt forced by circumstances to take certain actions. A few of you were there because you're just plain ornery." Several more laughs came from the men at that statement, as several realized he'd just spoken to them on a personal level.

"I understand how it is that a man makes mistakes," Darvo told them. "Made a few myself in my younger years. It will only be natural that you wonder what kind of man it is who stands next to you. All of you know what you did, personally, to be sent to prison. You may know what some of the others were there for. I will tell you now, none of that matters anymore."

"There are no murders among you," he informed them. "There are no rapists among you. There are no traitors among you. The rest is meaningless. In the weeks, and months ahead, the men around you will become your brothers. Your fellow soldiers. They will work beside you, sleep beside you in the field, eat beside you at mess. Nothing that happened to you before you marched through those gates and into this fort means anything, anymore." The ripple was bigger, this time.

"During your training all of you have a blank slate. I don't care who you are, why you're here, or where you're from. That does not mean that I trust you. I don't. It does mean that I'm giving you a chance to earn my trust and the trust of the instructors, the officers, and perhaps most importantly, the men who will serve in your unit beside you. One chance, to prove yourselves. I will accept no excuses. There will be no second chances. This is your second chance, gentlemen."

"All of you lads were chosen for this because you seemed able and willing to serve your land in this manner, rather than rotting in prison. Don't make me regret having chosen you. If you cause trouble, you're on your way back to prison. If you disobey, you're on your way back to prison. If you at any point don't convince me and the others here that you're giving your dead level best effort, you're on your way back to prison. There's no room for slackers. Here, or anywhere else in the

Army."

"Your families, for those of you that have them, are outside these grounds right now. They will be provided shelter and food. Work will be made available to them. If you wind up going back, then so do they. Remember that." Darvo paused again, longer this time, allowing what he had said to sink in for a moment.

Enough stick, he decided, looking at the faces in front of him. Time for some carrot. "If you work hard, you will be rewarded," he told them. "You will become a part of something much bigger than you, yourself are. You will earn certain freedoms as well. Time to spend with your families outside these walls, for one." Cheers erupted at that and Willard's men worked to shush the noise.

"There are other privileges as well that can and must be earned. You will be paid, just like the other soldiers. How you get to spend that money depends on you." He paused again here, allowing the men to digest the fact that they weren't slave labor.

"If you're wondering when we'll get started, it's now. Today. You'll be separated into training companies as soon as I've finished. Some of you will be fitted for uniforms today. The rest will be working to help finish the buildings here. The groups will switch tomorrow." He leaned forward.

"Once that's finished, your real training starts."

-

It took a week, all totaled, to get the men into uniforms and for the remainder of the cabins and fortifications finished. Finally, with the work finished, Parno released the guards and escorts who had brought the men to Cove from the prisons. They were glad to go, having already been delayed a week longer than expected. Parno compensated them with a night in town, which eased the grumbling and complaining.

During that week Parno had not been idle. The first part of his recruiting mission was completed and he was pleased with it. Now, he went to work on the second.

Actually, he continued it was more accurate. Before leaving Nasil, Parno had ordered posters printed at the Royal Printers. Posters that announced his formation of a new Army regiment and the terms of enlistment. It also stated that men who were wanted by the law could apply and seek asylum. During his trek across the Kingdom to the various Provincial Prisons, Parno had distributed those fliers at every inn, roadhouse, saloon, brothel, and any other likely place he had passed.

He knew that some would be torn down, but felt that the news would spread. Since Darvo had things well in hand at the garrison, Parno had decided to circulate a bit more, spreading the word. The visits were short, never more than a day or so ride. He rode with a minimal escort, which he left behind when entering any place that might prove a good recruiting point.

He spoke to the men who ran those establishments, always in private and always with a small bag of coins left on the table when he departed. Patriotic fervor was all well and good, Parno knew, but money talked to even the most suspicious individual. All that Parno promised was that any wanted man who came to him to apply would not be taken into custody while in Cove Canton. The rest would depend upon the men who sought him out.

He hadn't expected his efforts to yield any immediate results, of course, and said as much to Cho Feng one night as the two of them sat around a campfire. Feng had chosen to accompany the Prince on his excursions as his particular skills weren't needed as yet and would not be for some time, in fact.

"It may well be some time before this work bears fruit," Feng agreed. "And yet, who can say? Some men who are wanted will undoubtedly desire a chance to escape that noose, so to speak."

"We'll see, I guess," was all Parno had said.

-

After one such foray Parno was on his way back to Cove Canton with his escort, Cho Feng by his side, when they rounded a bend in the road and came face to face with a group of over thirty horsemen. Parno raised his hand to halt his small column, and the soldiers, seeing the threat, moved into a line with Parno. Their orders were to protect the Prince at all costs.

"Steady, gentlemen," Parno ordered. "We don't know who they are, or what they want."

"I'd say who they are is apparent, milord," Sergeant Montrose Berry, the commander of his escort snorted. "They're brigands, no question."

"Perhaps," Parno nodded. "We'll let them open things, however."

The two men sat looking at each other for a good five minutes, during which some of Parno's men began to itch.

"I don't like this, milord," Berry said finally. "They could have men coming up behind us right now."

"True," Parno nodded. "Very well, Sergeant. Let's see. . . ." Parno broke off as one man left the opposing group, walking his horse toward Parno. No one spoke as the man made his way across the ground that separated the two parties. As he came nearer, Parno was able to see a man in his late thirties to early forties. He was dark complected and weathered looking, the man's skin bronzed by a life lived out of doors. His eyes were hard, taking in every detail of the men before him, though none so much as the Prince. He glanced at Cho Feng, his eyes betraying surprise at the sight of a foreigner, but then returned his gaze to Parno.

When he was five yards or so away, the man reined in his steed and sat, still looking at the Prince.

Parno returned the gaze calmly. Despite the potential danger involved, the Prince was calm. After the brief stare down, the man suddenly threw back his head, laughing.

"So it is true," he said. "A Prince of Soulan, riding the trails, practically alone." His voice had a slight gravel sound to it. The voice of a man who drank rough whiskey and was loud and boisterous.

"Practically," Parno nodded. "But not quite alone. You have the advantage of me, I'm afraid. You clearly know who I am, but I do not know you."

"So you don't," the man nodded. "And I've more than just that in advantage over you, Prince." He made the word sound like a slur.

"Do you?" Parno smiled at him. "Perhaps. We may see about that, shortly. In the meantime, who are you? And, more to the point, what is it that you want?" The man's eyes narrowed at that.

"You're a might lippy for a man that's in a pickle, your lordship," his voice was matter of fact.

"A pickle, you say?" Parno smiled again. "Again, perhaps," he nodded. "Then again, perhaps not. You haven't stated your business yet, by the way. And I still don't know who you are."

The man eyed him closely for a moment.

"Your bein' a Prince won't help you none here, boy."

"My being a Prince has never helped me," Parno shot back, no longer smiling. "Which you would know, if you really knew anything about me. Obviously you don't so I'll ask once more. Who are you, and what…do…you…want?" Parno bit the words off shortly. He was growing tired of this game.

"You've got courage, I give ya that," the man said finally. "My name is Doak Parsons." Berry's sharp intake of breath let Parno know that the man was, indeed, a brigand.

"And I should know you, I take it?" Parno asked, his voice disinterested. "Or at least know of you?" Parsons scowled at that.

"I'm a wanted man, Prince," he replied, his voice tinged with a warning that Parno cheerfully ignored.

"Well, thanks for clearing that up," he said derisively. Berry's men chuckled at that. Parno's calm detachment had bled over into them. They were now looking across the way at the rest of the bandits. No longer wondering how they could protect Parno, but instead how many of them they could kill before the ruffians ran off.

For his part Parsons was somewhat perturbed. Things weren't going as he had expected. The laughter of Berry's soldiers wasn't lost on him, either. Finally, with an exasperated sigh, he slapped his thigh.

"I wanted to talk to you 'bout that Army thing you're doin'."

-

Parsons' men had withdrawn a bit, giving the Prince room. Parno had ordered his men off the road onto a small clearing. Parno then turned his attention to Parsons.

"I'm listening," he said simply. Parsons eyed the Prince for a moment, then took a seat on a nearby log.

"You don't scare much, do ya?" Parsons asked. Parno grinned slightly.

"I grew up with far worse than you, Mister Parsons."

"Mister," Parsons threw his back at that. "That's a hoot. A Prince callin' me 'Mister'." His laughter soon trailed away, however.

"I heard you lookin' fer such as us, Prince," he said seriously. "Men as are wanted. Can ride, fight as needs be. Men who ain't done certain things, nor stand accused of 'em. Men as might want to leave a hard life behind 'em."

"I am," Parno nodded. "Are you such men?" Parsons guffawed at that.

"Yessir, I reckon we are at that," he replied. "We're thieves, milord. Good ones at that. Been slippin' about this country and the Norlands too, fer years." Parno's interest was piqued at once, hearing that.

"I see," was all he said. "What do you steal?"

"Horses, payrolls, things o' that nature," Parsons shrugged. "We ain't never stole from a poor man, mind you. Man's gotta have some standards. Stealin' from them as ain't got much to start with is a mite lower'n we aim to be thought of."

"Robbing from the rich and giving to the poor?" Parno asked, a hint of a grin on his face.

"I ain't big on 'givin', poor or otherwise, less'n there's som'at in it for me," Parsons shrugged, grinning slightly himself. "Ain't claimin' to be no saint, nor want to be one. Just makin' sure you know how it is."

"Very well," Parno nodded. He walked over to the log, and settled himself onto it beside Parsons. "What do you want from me?" he asked. Parsons looked at him.

"Thought that'd be evident, Prince," he replied. "I. . .we," his hand swept across the open grass to include those who followed him, "want a safe place to lay our heads. Somewhere no one'll turn us over for the price on our heads. Somewhere we can start over, so to speak."

"You do realize that you'll be joining the Army, right?" Parno asked, eyebrows raising. Parsons nodded.

"Yeah," he nodded, voice reluctant. "But way I figure it, man like you, might have need o' men like us, was we at war or whatnot. Be able to use us where you couldn't use reg'lar soldiers."

"But we're not at war," Parno pointed out. Parsons look spoke volumes.

"We ain't now," Parsons corrected. "But you know, well as I do, how quick that can change. Them Nor-heatherns, they'll be across the border one day in the future, sure as God makes little green apples. Just a matter o' when, milord, not if." Parno found himself reassessing Parsons. While his speech and mannerisms were those of someone from a rustic background, he was intelligent.

"Likely true," Parno nodded. "Still, were I to need someone such as yourself, they would still have to be part of the regiment. That's the only way I can guarantee that any wants and warrants will be suppressed. Otherwise. . . ." Parno shrugged helplessly.

"I figured that," Parsons nodded. "What's all involved in bein' in the Army?"

"Well, as to that, it's probably best if you meet the Regimental Commander."

-

"Doak Parsons," Darvo breathed it more than spoke it. Parno nodded.

"Yes. Just rode right up and wanted to join," he admitted.

"How 'bout that," Darvo scratched his head. "He's something else, lad, that he is. Wasn't always a brigand, either."

"I suspected as much," Parno replied. "He's very intelligent, though he makes an effort to hide it."

"I 'spect so, considerin' the company he keeps," Darvo agreed. "And he wants to join up, does he?" Parno nodded.

"Well, we can use him," Darvo nodded. "That bunch of his will be better than fair horsemen, lad. They can likely train the others that aren't so adept to the saddle."

"Parsons suggested I could use him for. . .other things," Parno mused idly. "If you can use them to train the others in horsemanship, then by all means do so. But I think maybe I might make use of Parsons, and perhaps a few of his men, for something else, later on."

"And what might that be?" Darvo asked, an all too familiar feeling settling in his stomach.

"We'll see."

-

There were thirty-seven men in Parsons' band, counting Parsons himself. All of them were standing before Darvo Nidiad now. Some looked calm, but others looked nervous. One of two looked outright afraid.

"Do you men realize that you're joining the Army of Soulan?" Darvo asked. He looked from each man to the next, making eye contact. Slowly, and not always surely, each man nodded.

"You also realize that you're subject to Army regulations and discipline, then?" Again, all nodded in understanding.

"I want you to think before you sign these papers," Parno said. "Once you do, there's no turning back. You will have sworn fealty to the Crown as Royal Troopers. Violating that oath will mean much harsher penalties than the crimes which you now stand accused. Much harsher."

"We understand, milord," Parsons spoke for them all. "Truth is, we all had our say when the idea came about. Them as wasn't willin' is gone their way. One's as are left, they want to be here. They may be scared, but they's willin'. Come's to that, I'm a bit scared myself."

"I don't believe it," Parno scoffed, and was rewarded with chuckles from Parsons' own men. Parsons himself grinned, but said nothing.

"Very well, then," Darvo nodded. "Form a line and we'll get started."

Parno watched as the official part of the deed was accomplished. He had decided that he would play as small a part as possible in the actual training of the men. Instead, he would train with them. Suffer the same hardships as they did. A small thing, perhaps, to some. But he hoped, among men such as these, that the little things would add up.

Eventually.

# CHAPTER SIX

-

As autumn consumed the Plateau, Parno and Company continued to train their new soldiers. The small town of Cove, nestled among the highlands east of the Royal City, had proved a fertile training ground. The rugged terrain, mixed with a few rolling hills and even the occasional plain, provided an ideal mixture of geographical challenges needed to properly train soldiers to move and fight in almost any conditions.

There were difficulties, of course. Among the initial recruits, thirty-eight had been returned to the prisons, most of them in the first two weeks of training. The training itself had also suffered more than one setback, due in part to the fact that the men selected were, as a rule, individualists that were unaccustomed to working with or depending upon others.

"Just takes time, lad," Darvo assured him. "Man has to re-learn things, that's all. It takes time."

And it had. But now three months into training the regiment was beginning to shape up nicely, he thought. The men knew their duties now, and performed them adequately, if not with the military precision one might have expected from a front line unit. Soon individual training would start as the men shook down into permanent companies, depending on where their greatest skill lay.

Doak Parsons and his men had, indeed, proved to be expert horsemen. With their basic training out of the way they would serve as instructors in horsemanship to those men who had little or no experience in the riding and care of horses.

In swordsmanship, there was no lack of competent men among the original company of Regulars. But in Cho Feng they had an expert swordsman as well, thus in that area there were also no worries.

Archery was another matter.

There were very few truly competent archers among the regiment and exactly one who knew how to build a serviceable long bow. As a result archer training was lagging but Parno was still confident that he would find the right man for that job, sooner or later.

And then there was the artillery. Two months into their station, Captain Danson Lars had arrived at the post, leading a small detail and hauling worn out machines. Six trebuchets, seven catapults, and an even dozen old ballistae, all with cracked and broken wood, frayed rope, and rusted mechanisms. Lars himself had a record as a troublemaker and his detail wasn't a great deal better. Parno had expected trouble from them but after talking to Lars he had felt better.

"This is our last post, Milord," Lars had said simply. "'We either do well here or we're cashiered. I'm sorry we're all you get, but we'll do our best if you'll give us the chance.'" Parno had considered that for a moment, then nodded.

"'First order of business is to get your equipment in working order, Captain,'" he had ordered. "'If you can accomplish that then you've got your chance. Everyone else here is working on a second chance. I see no reason you and your men should be any different.'"

It hadn't been done over-night but Lars and his men, working largely with Brenack Wysin and a carpenter named Plank, had managed to salvage the antiquated artillery and restore them to battery. Parno couldn't have asked for anything better.

Parno was more than pleased with the entire operation at that point. In fact, things had been going so well that Parno began wondering what was going to happen to offset their accomplishments.

-

"Milord!"

Parno turned to see Lieutenant Sprigs hurrying towards him, face flushed.

"What is it, Lieutenant?"

"Sir," the young man said breathlessly. "There's trouble in town, sir. Two of our men have been arrested by the constable and they're threatening to hang them!"

"Which two men?" Parno wanted to know. Had someone among the prison ranks violated their parole?

"Sergeant Fitch and Lance Corporal Diggs, sir," Sprigs informed him. "They're not. . . ."

"Have my horse saddled at once," Parno ordered, heading for his office at a trot. "And tell Major Willard I want a troop of his best men saddled and ready to ride in ten minutes!"

"Yes, milord!" Sprigs called to Parno's back, then ran to carry out his orders.

Parno's mind was racing. What in the Kingdom was going on? Fitch and Diggs were two of Karls' best men. Steady, reliable, and able soldiers. They had been assigned to escort the supply wagon to town and back and supervise the men responsible for the loading. He met Darvo Nidiad coming out of the house, obviously looking for him,

"Lad. . . ." he began.

"I know," Parno assured him, never slowing. "I've already ordered a troop mounted. We're going into town." Parno ducked into the main hallway, retrieved his sword, and walked right back out again. His horse was being led over by a trooper, along with Darvo's.

"Lad, let's not be hasty, here," Darvo cautioned.

"We've time for little else, it seems," Parno replied, walking to his horse. In the background he was aware of the hurried movement and organized confusion of twenty men saddling their horses as fast as possible.

"We should be cautious, is all I'm saying," Darvo told him, mounting his own horse. "We don't know the exact situation in the town at the moment."

"What do we know?" Parno demanded.

"The Quartermaster returned saying that Fitch and Diggs had been involved in an altercation with several of the townsmen," Darvo informed him. "As I have it, from the Quartermaster, five men approached the wagons, attempting to rile the men into a fight. Our men ignored them, as ordered."

"When insults didn't provoke the men, the good citizens accused our men of disrespecting them and tried to get physical. Fitch intervened, and when the men attacked him, Diggs went to his aid."

"The result?" Parno asked, as Willard led the now mounted cavalry troop towards his waiting liege.

"The civilians weren't up to the challenge," Darvo told him. "Unfortunately, two of them are dead and the rest in rather bad shape."

"Perfect," Parno growled. "Our men were behaving?"

"Absolutely," Darvo confirmed. "And the prisoners who were assigned to the labor detail refrained from joining the brawl. They aren't happy about that but they did follow your orders."

"Good," Parno nodded absently. "Let's head into town, gentlemen," Parno ordered as Willard rode up. "And make haste."

-

Parno galloped into town at the head of the short column, dust swirling around him as he drew reign in front of the constable's office in the town of Cove. Townspeople scattered as the group thundered into town, then closed in around the horsemen as they came to a halt.

Parno dismounted, throwing his reigns to a trooper who had dismounted to hold his horse. Darvo dismounted as well as Parno turned to Willard.

"Wait here, and keep things calm," he ordered. Willard nodded in return, remaining on his mount. Parno strode across the side walk with Darvo following closely and threw open the constable's door.

Inside, Parno saw his two men, hands and feet bound by iron fetters, being assaulted by at least five men. Without a thought, Parno grabbed the nearest man, turning him, and hit him squarely in the face.

"HOLD!" Darvo shouted as the others turned to face the Prince. "You're in the presence of Prince Parno McLeod! Any man who touches him will answer to the King!"

The men reacted as if they had been burned, backing away. Parno's eyes fell on the Constable.

"If you have any notion of remaining a freeman beyond this day, there had better be an excellent excuse for this." Parno's words were clipped as he waved to the two beaten soldiers. "And if they aren't out of those irons in the next ten seconds, you'll be in them inside the minute."

"These men. . . ." the constable began, only to be cut off.

"I'm not asking," Parno said coldly. Colonel Willard!" Parno called loudly over his shoulder.

"Aye, Milord?" Willard answered from outside.

"I need five of your men in here, please!" Parno called.

"On the way, Milord!" Willard replied. In seconds a squad of large, very angry Soulan troopers, led by a sergeant, filled the small office.

"I want these men in fetters," Parno ordered, looking at the sergeant. "They'll be returning to the fort with us to face charges of assaulting men of the King's Army."

Grim faced troopers took charge of the five men who'd been administering the beating and escorted them outside. Parno looked again at the Constable.

"Your time is almost up," he said coldly. Ashen faced the Constable nodded to his deputy, who quickly freed the two beaten soldiers.

"Are you men hurt?" Parno asked, his voice softening slightly.

"We can walk, I think, Milord," Fitch said, his voice heavy with pain.

"Wait outside," Parno ordered. The two men saluted and limped to the doorway.

"They're under law!" the Constable exclaimed. "You've no right, milord, to interfe. . . ." His protests died unfinished as cold grey eyes fell on his own.

"I'm still waiting for that explanation," Parno informed him coldly.

"Those criminals came in here disrespecting honest folk and started a brawl!" the Constable spat out. "I enforce the law here, under the provisions of the King's Bench!"

"Criminals?" Parno asked, his voice deceptively mild.

"We know about those heathen out there at your fort!" The Constable hissed. He knew that Parno wasn't well thought of by the rest of the Royal Family and risked being surly because of it. "And I won't have them in this town, disrupting the piece. They killed two men of this town and I aim to see them hang for it! Was they still in prison, where they belonged, this wouldn't have happened. You've no one to blame but yourself. Milord." The last word was spoken almost as a slur. Darvo stiffened, but Parno held out his hand, stilling the older man.

"Colonel Willard!" Parno called again. "Join us at the door, if you please!" Within seconds a furious looking Willard was at the office door.

"Milord?" Karls' face was distorted with rage over the treatment of his two troopers.

"Would you identify the two criminals, please, Constable, to Major Willard?"

"Those two right there!" the Constable pointed out Fitch and Diggs, both being ministered to by a pair of their fellow troopers.

"Who are those men, Major?" Parno asked.

"Sergeant Fitch, milord, and Lance Corporal Diggs. Both good men, milord," Willard added, almost defensively.

"How long have they been under your command?" Parno asked.

"Both men have served under my command for the past two years, milord," Willard's voice betrayed his confusion. The Prince knew all this.

"Has either man ever been a prisoner of the King's Justice?" Parno asked mildly.

"No, sir!" Willard seethed. "Both men are career soldiers in the Soulan Army!" Parno nodded, turning to the Constable, who suddenly seemed less sure of himself.

"That will be all, Colonel, thank you," Parno said, never taking his eyes from the lawman. "Constable, you are guilty of aiding and abetting the attack on two men in the King's service, while in the normal performance of their duties. The penalty for that crime is quite severe, as I'm sure you're aware. What say you?"

"Before you answer," Parno smiled, though it wasn't a pretty smile, "I suggest that the word 'criminal' be scrubbed from your vocabulary for the time being. As I think you just learned, both of those men are not only soldiers, but decorated soldiers."

"Milord, I. . . ." the Constable licked suddenly dry lips, unsure of what to do or say. "I. . .that is we. . .it was understood that the men of your command were criminals, sire," the Constable's voice was respectful now, as the import of what he'd done, or at least allowed to happen, hit him.

"It might interest you to know that the men who stood by and took no actions were the 'criminals' you so detest, Constable," Parno told the sweating man coldly. "Your actions, or perhaps merely inaction, have shown you unfit for your post."

"The death of those two men is directly attributable to their assaulting two of the King's men, again, while fulfilling their service to the crown. I assume you saw the attack?" The Constable's face paled at that.

"I. . .that is, I was across the street and down a ways, Milord, when the ruckus broke out," he replied carefully. "I hurried right along when the commotion came about."

"And did you make any move to prevent the attack on my men once you arrived?" Parno demanded. "Or did you, perhaps, participate in the attack?"

"Sir, milord, that is," the Constable stammered. "I took it that the soldiers had started to ruckus and moved to secure them, seeing as they had already felled two men dead."

"What weapons were used by the soldiers?" Parno asked.

"We. . .weapons, milord?"

"If they had killed two men, apparently in cold blood to hear you tell it, I assume weapons were involved."

"Milord, I saw no weapons," the Constable answered truthfully. "But two men are dead and your men did it!"

"In defense of themselves and the King's property," Parno stated. "Is that not correct? A defense that you, as the town's appointed lawman, did nothing to bolster, is that correct? Were the local men, by any remote chance, intoxicated?" Trapped by his own words, the Constable remained silent.

"I will be forwarding a report of this incident to Prince Memmnon, for his consideration, Constable," Parno informed him. "Those five men I arrested will be tried by military tribunal for their attack on my soldiers. I'm sorely tempted to add you to that complaint, considering that had you done your job, those two men would likely still be alive. Have you anything to say in your defense before I go?"

"Milord. . .sire, I made. . .there was a mistake, here, milord," the Constable forced himself to speak. "It. . .I should have stopped the ruckus before it started. I. . .those two men were known to me and I allowed that to cloud my judgment"

Parno considered that for a moment, eying the Constable coldly. After a long consideration that saw the Constable trying not to squirm under the eyes of the furious Prince, Parno spoke.

"Constable, this type of behavior, as you know, is unacceptable. Do I have your assurance that such as this won't occur again?"

"On my word of honor, milord!" the Constable squeaked out, flinching at Darvo Nidiad's derisive snort, his opinion of the Constable's 'word of honor' rather clear.

"My men were assailed by drunken townspeople while carrying out their duties," Parno continued. "I assume that your desire to hold them for any trial has been satisfied?"

"Yes, milord," the Constable nodded.

"I will require a signed statement, written in your hand, that your investigation has yielded that the townsmen were in the wrong and that their deaths, while regrettable, was entirely due to their attack on troopers of the King's Army, while said troopers were performing their sworn duty. But only," Parno smiled, "if you're satisfied that's what happened. Otherwise, I'll have to refer the entire matter to the district Bench in Nasil, making it a matter of the King's Justice. As you have said, I cannot interfere in the matters of justice."

The Constable stared for a moment while examining the Prince's statement. After considering what might await him in the outcome of such an investigation and trial, the Constable nodded.

"Aye, milord, I'd have to say that's accurate, right enough."

"Excellent," Parno nodded. "I will also require you to inform the townsfolk that it was your inaction that led to this tragedy, thus leaving my troopers blameless. I assume that won't be a problem?"

"No, milord," the Constable winced as the trap closed about him. He had hoped to get away with this, then claim that the Prince, backed by his soldiers, had forced him to accede. If he made a public announcement, then those hopes would be dashed.

"Milord," Darvo said quietly, "I'd rather see this entire event laid before the Royal Bench. This kind of thing can be made to look like somewhat other than it is." Parno seemed to contemplate his mentor's words momentarily. Finally, he nodded.

"I agree," Parno sighed wearily, as if accepting Darvo's recommendation over his own. Panic flashed across the Constable's face.

"Milord, I've agreed to all that you've asked for!" he protested.

"So you have," Parno acknowledged. "However, the Colonel makes a good point. This is the kind of thing that can be turned into something ugly by someone who knows how to manipulate the facts. Perhaps it would be better, in the interest of justice and fairness, to have it laid properly to rest in the courts, rather than allow it to fester like an open wound in summer."

"Sire, I can make sure that this incident stops where it is!" the Constable exclaimed, now fearful. "I'll tell the townsfolk what happened, the truth of it, right now, should you like." Parno seemed to consider that.

"If the townsfolk accept your explanation and are happy with it to my satisfaction, then I will consider that. I don't know how you can make that so, however," he added, with a note of caution in his voice.

"Let me show you!" the Constable exclaimed, heading for the door. Parno and Darvo followed him outside. Many of the town's residents had gathered near the office, curious as to what was happening. Some, no doubt having witnessed, or been part of the attack, looked angry, but also fearful in the presence of the soldiers. Their attention had been on the two injured soldiers, but now drifted up to the constable.

"Good people!" the Constable called, attracting the attention of everyone around. Those farthest came closer, wanting to hear what was said.

"This whole affair," the Constable's voice boomed with authority, "has been regrettable. Men of our town, apparently in their cups, took it upon themselves to attack two troopers of the King's Army in our town! Those two soldiers are blameless in this attack and acted only in their own defense and in the defense of the King's property."

"Further, I have compounded the error by not conducting a proper investigation before taking action! Two men are dead and several others injured due to an altercation that was entirely the fault of those men who attacked these soldiers," he motioned to Fitch and Diggs. "After consultation with Prince Parno McLeod, I have decided that it would be improper, as well as illegal, to charge the troopers in any way, as they were not responsible for the brawl. Nor was it their fault that two men involved in the attack upon their persons are now dead. The fault for that lies entirely with the men who instigated the attack and with me, for not executing my duties as I should have."

"They killed two o' my friends!" a yelled a man from the front of the crowd. His face showed signs of a recent fight, indicating that he had likely been involved in the brawl.

"And you're as much to blame as any!" the Constable shot back. "You was, I'd say from your face, in the brawl as well. Do you know what the penalty is for assaulting a man in King's service, whilst in the performance of his duties?" The man paled slightly, wisely deciding to stay quiet.

"When I arrived," Parno announced, "I found these five. . .men," he made the word a slur, "beating two of my troopers who were bound hand and foot. By King's Law, I have taken them into custody, to be tried for that crime." Parno paused, allowing that to sink in.

"In light of my discussion with the Constable he has prevailed upon me and I have decided that these men will not be tried, after all." Karls Willard stiffened at that, but said nothing. His soldiers stirred uneasily, though they held their tongues.

"Enough have suffered today," Parno continued in a gentler tone. "The Constable would like to conclude this matter and he has my support for the plan he has devised and lain before me. My only proviso was that the final decision be up to you, the townspeople."

Many of the gathered citizens looked shocked at that. The Constable winced as Parno's words laid full responsibility for everything squarely upon him.

"What say you, citizens?" Parno called. "Can we let this be laid to rest, with no further unpleasantness between us?" All but a stubborn handful of people nodded in agreement. Some of their discussion reached Parno's ears, and they were satisfied that the affair had been settled fairly.

"Very well, then," Parno nodded. He looked to the Constable.

"I'll need that statement."

-

"That was deftly handled, milord," Darvo spoke quietly as the troop filed out of town, returning to the fort. Parno drew reign, seeing they were safely out of town.

"Gather around, men," Parno told them gently. The angry troopers formed a loose circle around the Prince.

"I know you're unhappy with this," he told them frankly. "And I'm not overjoyed about it myself in all honesty. However," he added, "I think that two men dead, all in all, evens the balance. Sergeant Fitch and Corporal Diggs gave a good accounting of themselves it would seem." Parno smiled at the two injured men, who managed to chuckle softly.

"Were it not for the beatin' afterward, milord, I'd be inclined to agree," Fitch replied for both men. "We weren't at fault here, sire."

"I know that," Parno smiled kindly. "And now, so does the entire town. I want you men to understand something."

"This unit is a test, of sorts, to see if something along these lines is workable. We've done well up until today. An incident like this," he pointed back toward the distant town, "could have destroyed everything we've accomplished to this point."

"We were able," he continued, "to secure our men without further bloodshed. I dislike the notion of using the King's Army against the civil authorities, even when they're somewhat less than civil." This brought a round of chuckles from the troopers. Good.

"In allowing this matter to be settled in this way, further bloodshed wasn't necessary. We avoided it and perhaps started to heal the rift between ourselves and the townspeople. That pathetic excuse of a Constable has, without even realizing it, taken full responsibility for everything that happened. I want peace between us and the townspeople wherever possible."

"I also want every man of you to know something else," he added, his voice grim. "Had it been necessary to force the release of Sergeant Fitch and Lance Corporal Diggs, I would have done so. I would not have relished it," he added, seeing the shocked looks on the faces surrounding him, "but I would have done so, and hang the consequences."

"You men, all of you troopers and criminal troopers in waiting," he smiled, and the men laughed outright at that, "are my men. My responsibility. I will never allow anything like this to happen to you, any of you, so long as I can prevent it. And that includes the use of force."

"Yes, we could have taken those men and had them tried in open court. Not doing so let's the people in town, those not responsible for what happened, to see that we do not consider ourselves above the law. I want, always, for us to have mercy for our own people, wherever possible. Use all of your mercy, men, on the people of Soulan."

"That way, when we meet the Nor in battle, or perhaps find banditry running in our area, we will have used up all our mercy where it's deserved and have none left for those who aren't so deserving. Do you understand, now, why I acted as I did?"

A chorus of assenting growls and nodded heads answered that question. Parno nodded. "Very well, then. Thank you for your understanding. Let's reform and head back." As the troop reformed their column, Parno managed to separate Karls Willard from the rest.

"Are you satisfied, Karls, with the arrangement I've made? Note that I don't ask if you're happy, because I'm not happy myself, but is it satisfactory?"

"Of course, milord," Karls replied at once. Under Parno's pointed look, Willard frowned slightly.

"I admit, I wasn't happy at the time," Willard nodded. "but, without my anger up over what happened, I can see that this if for the best. There's more to be considered here than my feelings or those of the men," he added.

"Good," Parno nodded, pleased. "I'm glad you see that. This won't happen again. Not like this," he added at Karls' look of doubt. "I'm going to see to opening a store of our own and have supplies brought into there. From Nasil, if needed."

"That won't make the store owners very happy," Karls smiled.

"That's a problem they'll have to take up with the good constable and his drunks. I'll also build a canteen for the men. I don't want them back in that town, for any reason."

"I notice that you didn't say anything about this in town," Willard smiled.

"They'll figure it out," Parno snorted. "Eventually."

-

When Parno and his men returned to the fort, he had a messenger waiting to see him.

"Will this day never end?" he groused. Leaving his horse with an idle trooper to be cared for, Parno stomped his way up to the headquarters building where his office was. Standing beside his office door was an older man dressed in the simple utilitarian uniform of a personal footman.

"Milord," the man bowed deeply. Parno resisted the urge to snap at him.

"What can I do for you, Mister. . . .?"

"My name is Benson, milord," the older man smiled. "I am the Lady Edema Willows, Duchess of Cumberland's, personal footman. I bear an invitation for you written in my lady's own hand." He offered Parno an envelope, bearing the wax seal of the Duke of Cumberland. He walked into his office, motioning for Benson to follow.

He knew the Duke and Duchess, ever so slightly. Basically just well enough to say hello to. He couldn't imagine what the invitation was for.

"You are invited to attend the Cumberland House Harvest Ball," Parno read aloud, then looked up at Benson. "A cotillion, I suppose?"

"Mostly, milord," Benson nodded respectfully. "Though there will be a dinner beforehand."

"I see," Parno mused, looking back to the invitation. "This is tomorrow night!" he exclaimed suddenly, looking back up at Benson. The older man looked a bit distraught at that.

"Milady instructed me to tell you, Milord, that she has been away until day before yesterday. She was unaware of you presence here until this very day. She sends her apologies concerning the lateness of the invitation and points out that you are under no obligation to attend." Parno considered that.

Probably be best if he didn't, he admitted. He wasn't well liked and today would add to that dislike in the community.

Probably be better for them and myself if I don't go, he thought.

"If I may, sir," Benson broke into his train of thought. "Milady was especially delighted to find that you were here. It would mean a great deal to her if you can attend. Forgive my forwardness," he asked, bowing.

"Oh, stop that," Parno ordered. Benson looked up in surprise.

"I can't stand to have all that bowing and scraping," Parno told him bluntly. "I'm a man, just like any other, save for an accident of birth that left me in a Royal Household. You may tell the Lady Willows. . . ." Parno paused, taking a deep breath, then plunged ahead.

"Tell her that myself and my retainers will be delighted to attend." Benson smiled widely.

"I will relay your message, milord. Thank you." With that the man was gone.

Oh, why did I do that?

-

"Exactly what kin are you to this man, Milord?" Willard asked as they moved through the gate leading to a very large house high upon a hill. The place was nearly as large as a castle, or a country manor.

"I have no idea, to be honest," Parno admitted. "In all truth, the blood will have been so watered down by now that there exists no true kinship, I suppose, as most people reckon things. As you know, those siblings not in line for the throne, at least not directly, are given titles commiserate with their status as Royals. The Duke of Cumberland, the original that is, was my great-great-great-great, I think, grandfather's brother. I think."

Nidiad chuckled at Parno's hesitant identification. In truth he was off by only two 'greats', and Darvo saw no need to correct his young charge.

"Well, it's close enough," Parno said in response to that chuckle.

"Aye, lad. That it is," Darvo nodded.

"We'll be on our best behavior tonight, while I'm thinking about it," Parno said suddenly, changing the subject. "I almost impressed my father after what happened in Bingham with that wacky priest and doofus constable," he informed them. "While I'm not overly concerned by the need to impress him further, it would be nice if nothing happened to erase that stain of good service, if you catch my meaning. So if either of you see me making, or about to make, an ass of myself, feel free to intervene."

"I'll just do that," Darvo muttered. Willard laughed, but nodded his agreement.

"I'm serious," Parno smiled. "There's no need to rattle his cage and it might hurt the outfit. I'll have a, as in one, drink before dinner; no more than two glasses of wine during, and no more than one drink after. Neither will either of you since you need to be sober, ensuring that I stay sober."

"We understand, Milord," Willard nodded, seriously this time.

-

"Parno, how nice to see you!" The Prince turned at the voice to see Edema Willows the Duchess of Cumberland approaching.

"Duchess" Parno bowed formally, taking the extended hand and kissing it lightly. "I am honored by your invitation, and don't you look lovely," he added.

Edema Willows was lovely. Blonde hair cascading down her back, radiant blue eyes, and a figure that would set any man's mouth to watering. Parno didn't know her exact age but it was more than her looks would reveal.

"Aren't you sweet," Edema slapped his shoulder lightly with her fan. "And so gallant. And how could we have a dinner and not invite a member of the Royal Family not more than five miles distant? Why, half these people are here just to say they rubbed elbows with you!"

"I seriously doubt that, My Lady," Parno smiled crookedly. "No one wants it known they have 'rubbed elbows' with the Black Sheep."

"Oh, stuff," Edema said lightly, her fan striking him again. "What nonsense! Yes, yes," she waved off Parno's next comment, "I know that you and your father seldom see eye to eye. That changes nothing. You are still Prince Parno. Devilishly handsome, slyly charming, and quite a catch. There are numerous young ladies here tonight who have chosen to attend without escort. Young ladies who do not normally attend these gatherings alone, you understand? There's no doubt why that is so."

"I am flattered, My Lady," Parno smiled. "Yet I doubt that any good father would want me within arm's reach of his daughter, given my reputation. Still, I yield to your greater knowledge of such things." The Duchess laughed lightly and took Parno by the arm. The Prince did not object. Edema was one of the few nobles who treated him as something other than a blot.

"Come, dear boy," she said quietly. "We must make the rounds, of course. I would not be a good hostess otherwise."

-

Dinner, it turned out, was excellent. Beef, pork, and poultry, all having been slow cooked over roasting smoke wood, along with piles of vegetables fresh from the harvest and bread made from freshly gathered wheat. Parno had eaten well, as had Karls and Darvo. Both had been seated a fair ways away, though Parno's obvious friendship with the pair had forced their inclusion in the main dining hall, otherwise they would have eaten with the other retainers.

Willard, a handsome young man and now a Lieutenant Colonel in the King's Army, struck quite a figure in his uniform. It was obvious that he was enjoying himself and also the attention he received from at least three young women. The attention of their fathers, which was lost on the young soldier, had amused Parno. The men would say nothing in all likelihood since Willard was, in fact, a Royal retainer, but they brooded none the less.

Darvo, less interested in the female attractions, had set into the meal with gusto and was now leaning back, nursing a goblet of wine. He caught Parno looking his way and raised his glass in salute, a smile on his face. Parno nodded, returning the smile.

"Parno, dear," Edema said suddenly, "let us walk out to the veranda, shall we? There are refreshments there, and music. The party should be moving there and no one will go until you do."

"Of course, My Lady," Parno rose at once. "At your service."

"Such a dear boy," Edema smiled, taking his arm. Sure enough, as Parno and the Duchess started for the veranda, others rose to follow. Parno hid a small smile at the thought of his being the center of attention.

"Such a smile," the Duchess said at his side. "Much like that of your mother."

Parno halted so suddenly that someone crashed into his back. A muffled curse was bit off as the source realized who it was he was mouthing about. Parno ignored it in any case, his attention focused on the Duchess.

"My mother?" he said, voice threatening, but not quite breaking.

"Yes," Edema Willows sighed softly. "I knew your mother, Parno. Knew her quite well, in fact. We attended King's college together. The main university, in fact, in Nasil. We were friends till the day. . ." her voice trailed off.

"Till the day I was born," Parno nodded, walking again, albeit more stiffly now.

"Don't go pouty on me, young man," Edema's voice hardened. "I was going to say 'she died', just for your information. I know how the Family has regarded you these many years as being responsible for Margolynn's death. Such rubbish!"

"You -"

"I do not think you are responsible for your mother's death, Parno. No, nor do I blame you in any way. Your family is foolish to do so as well, though it's not unexpected I suppose. Your father can be one of the most obstinate, pig-headed, foolish men I believe it has ever been my pleasure to spend the day with."

"So you have met my father," Parno grinned, and Edema laughed suddenly.

"Oh, yes, Parno McLeod, I have, indeed, met Tammon, King of Soulan. Edward and I met about the same time as he and your mother. We often took rides together, serving as each other's chaperones. Hardly necessary, of course. Never went anywhere without a detachment of cavalry in those days."

"Tell, me, My Lady, of my mother," Parno said suddenly. His voice was one of wonder, of a child. Very few people had ever spoken to him of his mother, save to lay the blame for her death at his feet.

"Poor, dear boy," Edema said quietly, her hand coming to rest on Parno's cheek. "It has been very rough for you, has it not? These many years in the shadow of your father and the rest of your family?" She paused for a moment, then turned to look out over the lighted courtyard.

"Your mother was, without exception, the kindest, most gentle hearted person I have ever met. I have often wondered, even now, how she ever came to be married to Tammon McLeod. She loved him, I know. Loved him without reason, in fact.

She was completely devoted to him in all ways, but never were two people so very different."

"Your mother was my best friend, Parno," she continued, looking him in the eye. "A wonderful woman, wonderful person. Someone who loved fiercely and without reservation, or hesitation. Oh, and she loved you." Edema's eyes watered slightly.

"The twins' birth was hard on your mother," the Duchess said. "She was so small, and both of them were large infants, built more like your father. When she had recovered, she told me that Smithe, the Royal Physician, had informed her that she could no longer bear children. Indeed, that she could no longer conceive. Tammon, of course, was upset, but with two healthy sons and a daughter, his line was secure."

"And he loved your mother, Parno," she said firmly. "Never doubt that. If there is an ounce of gentleness in the man, it was reserved for her. Only for her. There was no one in the world who owned his affections, save your mother. He simply told her, 'we'll raise the children we have and be thankful for them'. End of story."

"But it wasn't the end," Parno said darkly.

"No," Edema's voice was almost a whisper. "No, it wasn't. They were young, of course, and there was much love between them. Nature takes its course in such things. One day when I was visiting, Margolynn confided in me that she was, once again, with child. I was shocked at first, knowing that Smithe had told her this was impossible."

"Your mother was convinced that you were her gift from God," she smiled at the memory. "That you were a sign that He had not forgotten her. Smithe was insistent that the rigor of another child birth would be her death and suggested. . ." she stopped and looked at Parno.

"I know," he nodded slowly. "Many is the time that point has been made to me. I am aware of the discussion." Edema's eyes watered at that admission, but Parno was not looking at her and did not see.

"Dear boy," she voiced softly. "There was never any danger of that, I assure you. Your life was more precious to her than her own and she proved that. Your mother refused to even entertain the idea, saying that she would trust in God to take care of her. That whatever He decided, she would accept without question."

"Tammon was furious, of course," she laughed. "Stomped about the palace, making decrees, giving orders. He went to your mother and insisted that she end the pregnancy. She refused, of course. It was a terrible argument, she told me later, but it was lost before Tammon started. There was steel in your mother, Parno, despite her frail looks. Steel far stronger than the furnaces of Tammon McLeod could ever harm."

"The rest, you know, sweet child. Your mother died a few minutes after your birth. But," Edema said, her voice suddenly stronger, "she held you in her arms before she died, Parno. Laid you to her breast and sang to you. Sang so softly that no one could hear. She told me that it was all she could give you, her time was so short. Then she smiled and told me that you were destined to do great things. That you would be a great man, a man of your people. That one day the name Parno would be yelled in every village of Soulan."

"It was the last thing she ever said, Parno," the Duchess concluded. "The last thought of her beautiful, peaceful soul, the last thing in her heart, was you."

No one had ever had the kindness to tell him these things. Never. Not once. The household followed the lead of the older McLeods and had treated him only as well as his Royal birth had required. Even the women charged with his care as a child had never spoken to him about his mother, other than to remind him that her death was his fault.

"Thank you for that," he said quietly. Edema hugged him tightly and after a few seconds, Parno felt himself returning the embrace.

*This must be what it feels like to have a mother.*

-

Darvo Nidiad watched the scene between the Duchess of Cumberland and the Prince of Tinsee play out with concern. As the Duchess enfolded the young prince in her arms, Darvo glanced around.

Sure enough, the Duke was watching. He regarded the scene with interest, but with no apparent anger. Finally, as the two broke apart, the Duke returned his attention to other visitors. Darvo relaxed slightly, but vowed he would talk to Parno about his. . . actions. He did not need the ire of one of the wealthiest Dukes in all Soulan upon his head.

-

"Forgive me, My Lady," Parno said quietly, turning away from her and wiping away threatening tears. "I am too forward by half, but I thank you for taking the time to tell me of these things."

"There is nothing to forgive, dear boy," Edema replied, her own eyes misty. "If your father had the compassion of even a snake he would have told you these things long ago or had them told you, and he would have loved you as she would have. Sadly, he lacks in compassion as much as he does in true wisdom." Her voice was hard.

"What do you mean?" Parno asked, turning to face her once again.

"Parno, do you know that Edward and I travel to Norland at least three times a year?"

"No, My Lady, I did not," Parno admitted, his interest aroused.

"I thought not," Edema nodded firmly. "Edward is a merchant, you know. He has taken great advantage of the new trade policies between the two kingdoms. You know of what I speak?"

"Vaguely," the Prince allowed. "Memmnon and I were discussing that very thing, among others, the last time I was in Nasil, some months past."

"Well," the Duchess continued, "the policy of open trade has been very good to us, Parno. Edward was in a very good position to take immediate advantage of them and we have profited handsomely. But I have seen things. . ." her voice trailed off.

"What sort of things, My Lady?" Parno pressed, interest fully awakened now.

"The Nor have horses, now, Parno," she said quietly. "Many, many, horses, in fact and they have trained cavalry to ride them. Not the helpless oafs they normally send, but real horsemen. And," she added darkly, "I have seen several of the Wild Folk among them. Not in charge, exactly, but. . ." the Duchess paused, frustrated by her lack of military vocabulary.

"Training them, perhaps?" Parno offered, and Edema nodded at once.

"Yes! That's it exactly. I was going to say instructing. And it's not simply one or two, or even a dozen. There seem to be Wild Folk everywhere I look."

"You believe that the Nor have made some type of treaty with the Wilds?" Parno asked. The lands across the Great River were all known as the Wild Lands, the inhabitants as the Wild Folk, or Wildmen. Fierce warriors who rode horseback just as most of the Soulan army did and fought from horseback even better, if anything, than most Southron Cavalry. An alliance between the two, Nor and Wild, could be trouble for Soulan. Bad trouble.

"That is my. . .opinion," Edema said carefully. "I mentioned the number of Wildmen present in the Nor provinces that we visit to Edward once in passing. He brushed it off as no more than the Heathen taking advantage of the new trading policies of the North. Which would make sense, except..."

"Except they aren't trading?" Parno finished for her.

"Exactly," she nodded firmly. "And the men I have seen, they are not 'traders' of any sort. They are fighting men, and fair ones at that, I'd wager."

Parno considered this. The Wildmen were fierce fighters. The Nor were playing nice, and there appeared to be a connection of some importance between Nor and the Wild Lands.

Were the Nor training their men to ride, and fight, from horseback? And buying horses from the Wildmen? The Nor had never enjoyed the large herds that Soulan possessed. Their mounted units were limited in number, and their training was laughable next to that of similar Soulan regiments. But if that were to change?

Large numbers of Norland troopers, mounted on the tough and powerful horses of the Wild Lands, might be more than a match for the Soulan Army.

"We should rejoin the gala," he said suddenly, smiling. "I have monopolized your good company for too long. But what say I call upon you again, soon. A week, perhaps? A bit longer? I would be very interested in hearing anything you can tell me of what you have observed."

He extended his arm and the two walked back into the light, to the sound of music.

-

"Lad, you've a mind of your own, I'm knowing. But it's a bad business to play patty-cake in the dark with another man's wife. Especially when the other man can see you."

"What?" Parno turned in the saddle to face his adviser. They were on their way home, at last, and Darvo had waited until the others were out of earshot before speaking. Parno, thinking on what Edema had told him concerning Norland, had not been paying attention.

"I said it's a bad business -"

"I heard what you said," Parno retorted. "I'm wondering what the hell you're talking about."

"You and the Duchess," Darvo said quietly. "He was watching the two of you, in the shadows."

"There was nothing in the shadows for him to see," Parno shrugged. "Lady Cumberland was kind enough to tell me of my mother. More than simply that her death was my fault. She and mother were close, before my mother passed."

"Ah," Darvo muttered. "So that's it, then."

"It is," Parno said, not quite testily. "Do you think me so foolish as that Darvo? Have I been such an ass during my life that you think I'd seek to seduce a man's wife, in his own home? With a crowd looking on?"

Darvo didn't know how to respond to that, so he wisely said nothing. He had angered his young charge, and was now sorry he had broached the subject.

"Ah, hell," Parno said suddenly, anger gone in a rush of breath. "I did tell you to keep an eye on me, so I shouldn't complain. But I assure you, what you saw was the Lady Edema telling me of my mother. Nothing more."

"I know, lad," Darvo nodded.

"So, there is to be no more talk, even hint, of anything improper, where the Lady Edema is concerned."

"It will be so."

# CHAPTER SEVEN

-

It was one day over two weeks before Parno had a chance to return to Cumberland House. He traveled early, accompanied as always by Sergeant Berry and his men. Parno had long since stopped trying to be rid of them. Berry had orders from both Darvo and Karls to protect Parno. And he wasn't going to go away.

"I'll likely be there for a good bit of the day," Parno warned. Berry nodded.

"We'll stay from underfoot, milord," was all he had said. He had a basket prepared for Edema and Edward Willows, which one of Berry's men had promptly relieved him of. Parno sighed in defeat, and set off.

When he arrived, Edema was actually on the porch of the great house, watching as some of the staff cared for the yard. She didn't interfere, he noted, simply scowling when something wasn't quite as she wanted it.

I suppose I could learn something from that, Parno thought idly as he dismounted, and reclaimed his gift basket. Berry and his men, careful not to intrude upon the work being done, carried his horse with them as they headed for the holding corral outside the barn. Parno heard Edema giving orders that his men be fed as he walked up the steps to where she stood. By the time he got to the porch, she was facing him, all smiles.

"Hello, Parno!" she exclaimed, kissing him lightly on the cheek. "I'm delighted to see you back so soon!"

"Thank you, my lady," Parno bowed slightly. "I have brought this for your home," he told her, handing over the basket. Inside was a bottle of very good wine, a smaller bottle of excellent brandy for the Duke, and various delicacies he had acquired from a sutler from Nasil. Edema took the basket with a gracious bow.

"You honor us, and our home, with your presence, Prince Parno." Handing the basket to a maid, she took Parno's arm.

"Edward is away, I'm afraid," she told him as they entered the house. "Perhaps I can impose upon you to take lunch with me on the veranda?"

"No imposition, Lady Edema," Parno assured her. "I'd be delighted."

-

"So," Parno said as they sat at the small table on the veranda, "I'd like to hear more about your travels in the Nor lands, my Lady." Edema looked at him closely for a moment.

"Very well," she nodded. "I suspected as much, since you were so interested in what I said at the ball. It's odd, you know," she added. "When I spoke to Edward about my suspicions, he simply ignored them. Politely, of course."

"I'm not ignoring them," Parno told her plainly. "I am not satisfied that all is well between us and the Nor, despite their aggressive outreach to the King. I have suspicions, but no proof. I need evidence of what is happening in the North, Edema. Something I can show to Memmnon, if it's warranted." Edema nodded again.

"As I said earlier, Parno, all I have is suspicions as well."

"But you have seen, Edema," Parno insisted. "Whereas I have not. Tell me, if you will, what you have seen."

For the next hour, Edema rattled off the things she had noticed during the Willow's last trip to Norland. Somewhere small, especially taken alone. Others, however, stood out at once to someone who knew what they were looking at.

"And you say they now have much greater numbers of mounted soldiers?" Parno asked, as he clarified what he'd been told.

"I honestly lost count of the groups, companies I suppose, of mounted men that we encountered along the trade routes, Parno. It became so common place, I came to ignore them, I'm afraid."

"I'm more interested in their skill, at this point, than in their numbers," Parno admitted. "If those you encountered are an example of how well they're training their cavalry these days, then that, alone, should be cause for concern."

"I thought that as well, considering that it has always been our own advantage in horsemanship that has helped us prevail in the past," Edema replied. "Granted, I'm not a military historian, but I can read." Parno laughed at that.

"You've no need to be a historian to see good horsemanship, and count flags, Lady Edema," he assured her.

"I'm used to being ignored, I'm afraid, when it comes to such discussions," Edema sighed. "I've come to expect it from everyone, I fear."

"Well, I'm not ignoring you," Parno replied. "In fact, I have a favor to ask. When do you think you will go north again?" Edema looked surprised at that.

"I usually don't go this time of year," she admitted. "But Edward will always try to make one last trip before the winter sets in. In fact, that is why he's not here, today. He has another expedition scheduled to leave in a fortnight."

"Could I prevail upon you to take that trip?" Parno asked bluntly. "More importantly, would you make notations of what you see?" Edema looked stunned.

"Parno, dear boy!" she exclaimed. "I wouldn't know what information would be useful to you!"

"You needn't know," Parno told her calmly. "In fact, it's better that you don't know, to be honest." He was skating on thin ice here, and knew it. He was all but asking Edema Willows to be a spy.

"What I'd like you to do, My Lady, is simply keep a diary. Something airy, and light. What most men would call 'typical female drivel'," he laughed. "For instance, 'we passed a splendid looking cavalry unit today. All one hundred of them turned out in uniform, looking and stepping smartly. What a wonderful sight to see!' That sort of thing." Edema looked at him for a moment, then burst out laughing.

"Oh, my boy!" she was nearly whispering. "How sly and clever you truly are. Is your brother, Memmnon, aware of how smart you are?"

"I doubt it," Parno replied honestly. "None of them care much for me, in truth."

"Tut, tut," she shook a small finger at him. "None of that in my house!" She leaned back for a moment, studying her visitor.

"Very well, Parno," she agreed. "I will do this. I don't know how much good it will do you, mind. But I will do it."

"Thank you, Lady," Parno sighed. Taking her hand, he kissed it lightly. "I appreciate this. My suspicions may be nothing, of course, but. . . ."

"But if they are something, it's best that we know it now," she concluded. Parno nodded. He was about to speak again when Benson appeared.

"Beg pardon, milady," he spoke quietly, "but the Tinker is here. You wished him to look at the mantle clock, I recall." Edema stood suddenly.

"Yes, I did," she nodded. "I'll see him at once." Benson bowed, and departed. Edema looked at Parno.

"Come with me," she ordered. "This is a man you should meet."

Parno wordlessly followed Edema back to the front portico of Cumberland house. He wondered who or what a Tinker was.

As the two of them followed Benson out onto the porch, Parno saw a man standing at the foot of the large steps. He noted that one of Berry's troopers was nearby. He wasn't doing anything obvious. Just watching. Parno sighed, and turned his attention to the man before him.

Tall, slender without being skinny, prominent nose and cheekbones. Skin dark, though not just from the sun. The man was dressed in blacks and browns, including a flat brimmed black hat. Several gold rings dangled from his ears, and a smaller chain hung around his neck.

He's a gypsy! Parno realized with a start. Well, probably not an actual gypsy, as I learned about in history. But a descendent of them, I'd wager.

"Tinker!" Edema enthused. She allowed the man to take her hand, which he kissed lightly. He smiled in return, showing a mouthful of white teeth.

"Hello, Lady Edema," his voice was firm, yet soft. Cultured even, Parno decided.

"I'm very glad to see you, Tinker," Edema said, turning to Parno. "Prince Parno McLeod, may I present the Tinker. Tinker, this is Prince Parno, of the House McLeod." Parno stepped forward, offering his hand, which the Tinker accepted. Firm handshake, but not overtly powerful.

A very confident man, Parno decided. He liked the man at once.

"Pleased to meet you, Master Tinker," Parno smiled.

"The pleasure is mine, Milord," Tinker bowed deeply. "I apologize, Lady Cumberland. I did not know that you were entertaining."

"Oh, stuff!" Edema slapped the Tinker lightly on the shoulder. "Come inside, you swindler. I really am glad you're here. I wanted the Prince to meet you. Come, and regale us with tales of your travels. You will stay the night. No, no, I insist," she pressed when the man began to object. Her eyes were twinkling.

"I think you and Parno will have much to discuss."

-

The Tinker was as much an entertainer as he was a repairman, Parno decided. Edema had allowed most of the staff to gather on the Veranda as the Tinker spoke, all the while working on her mantle clock.

As his fingers deftly searched for, and then repaired the problem, the Tinker told them of his last several stops, news that he had gathered, and a few tidbits of non-malicious gossip. Parno could tell from the way everyone had gathered so quickly that this must be a normal routine.

"How often do you pass this way, Master Tinker?" Parno asked, later on. The clock was repaired, and Edema had ordered food brought for him. It was still early enough in the day that the sun warmed them.

"Depends on which way the wind blows me, Milord," the Tinker shrugged. "I was here last time, in May I believe." He shrugged again. "Dates mean little to me, Milord, traveling as I do. When I am here, I am here. When I am there, then I am there."

Parno smiled at that, suddenly very envious of the Tinker. To have such freedom! To go, and do, and see, and be, without anyone telling you that you shouldn't, couldn't or won't be allowed to! How marvelous that must be.

"I envy you, Master Tinker," Parno told him honestly. "I would, I think, likely enjoy work such as yours." The Tinker looked at Parno for a moment, head cocked to the side. Finally, he leaned back in his chair.

"You want to ask me something, Prince," he remarked. It was a statement, not a question. Parno regarded him carefully for a moment, then nodded.

"Yes, I do," Parno agreed. "But I would not wish to offend you, and I worry that my question might do so."

"Ask your question, Parno McLeod," the Tinker told him firmly. "There will be no offense taken, if none is meant." Parno chuckled at how carefully that had been phrased.

"I was wondering if you ever traveled among the Nor lands," Parno admitted. The Tinker smiled.

"Indeed I do, Prince McLeod. But it is Soulan that I call home." Again, Parno noted how that was spoken. The choice of words.

"I wonder if you might tell me of what you've seen there," Parno leaned forward. "Certain things, anyway."

"Things like whether or not the Nor have learned to ride a horse, perhaps?" he smiled. "About whether or not they are buying large numbers of horses from the Wild Tribes from across the Great River? Or perhaps that they are buying large numbers of cattle from our own Kingdom in order to feed their people, yet their people remain hungry? Things like that, perhaps?" Parno felt a chill at the words, spoken so calmly, yet so full of information.

"Just like that, Master Tinker," Parno agreed. "If you're willing. I'd be glad to compensate you, of course. In whatever way you may desire," he added, trying to make sure he didn't offend the man.

"A Royal Favor, eh?" the Tinker smiled. "That might be. . .interesting, milord. Perhaps you and I should take a walk."

-

"I have no love for the Nor, Prince McLeod," the Tinker told him. "They persecute people like me all the time, when they can find reason. I give them no reason. I work for them, repairing their machinery, their gadgets, and still, they look at me as if I am something to be removed from their shoe before entering the home." He looked out across the field. The hay had recently been cut, and the smell was almost intoxicating. The two men had walked a short distance from the house, with one of Berry's men trailing at a respectful distance.

"I know what it is you want, Prince," he said finally. "And I will do it. It will require money," he warned. "I have not the resources I would need to travel in the Nor lands during winter. And I would need gold to provide those who gave me information. It is the way of things," he shrugged.

"I'm aware," Parno grinned. "And I can give you anything you need, including the gold. But, will it be safe for you?" The Tinker laughed at that.

"I'm safe nowhere, Milord," he replied. "My kind have been hunted almost to extinction. I, myself, am a half-breed. But it will be as safe as anything else I would do across the border." Parno considered that.

"What do you need, and when?" Parno asked. As the two walked back toward the house, the Tinker explained what he needed, and why. Parno listened raptly, but his ears perked up even further when the Tinker began to tell him of the things he's already encountered.

"Their discipline in the ranks is a savage as anything I've ever seen, milord," Tinker told him. "And I've been traveling their lands for a good while. Their horsemanship has improved, but it's more than just individual horsemanship. The troopers, and their horses, move as a unit. Well drilled, well instructed, and well equipped. They are rebuilding their army from the ground up it seems, and doing a magnificent job of it."

"And I keep wondering why, considering their overtures to the South, of late. Some of which allow me to travel openly now, whereas before I was forced to slink about."

"Yes, surely that is a coincidence," Parno remarked drily, and the Tinker laughed.

"I cannot promise you the results you seek, you know," the Tinker told him as they neared the house. "I can go, and I can look. That is all."

"That's all I'm asking," Parno nodded. "That, and when you return, you visit me at my home, and place all that you've seen on a map for me." The Tinker considered that briefly.

"Yes, I will do that," he nodded finally. "I have your word that a favor is owed?"

"If I am able to grant it, yes," Parno agreed. "Bear in mind, however, that I am limited in what I can do, Master Tinker. I'm not exactly well liked in Nasil."

"It will be within your power, milord," the Tinker assured him. "But if you renege, then I will be forced to curse you," he warned, eyes twinkling.

"That might actually improve things for me," Parno told him ruefully. "I've been cursed since about an hour after I was brought into this world."

The Tinker's laughter rolled across the hills.

-

At Edema's insistence, Parno had also spent the night at Cumberland House. Berry had dispatched a man back to the Canton to inform Colonel Nidiad, informing him of the change in plans. Edema had placed Parno's escort in an empty bunkhouse, not far from the main house. Two men stood guard through the night, despite Parno's insistence that it was unnecessary. Berry was almost as immovable as Darvo himself.

Parno and the Tinker had talked quietly into the wee hours before the fire in Parno's room. The dark man had told the King of everything he had seen, or heard, and Parno made notes of it. If Edema was disappointed in that the two of them had left her early in the evening, she showed no sign of it.

Finally, with the lamp oil beginning to grow low, the two men had retired.

The next morning Edema had a good breakfast prepared, for Parno and the Tinker, and had sent a similar repast to Sergeant Berry's men as well. Parno offered his good-byes to her perhaps an hour later.

"It was good to see you, Parno," Edema smiled from the porch. "Please, do visit again when you have time. Hopefully Edward will be here next time."

"I will come back whenever I can," Parno replied truthfully. "I do enjoy spending time here. It's peaceful. Homey." Edema beamed at that praise, and then Parno was off, heading for Cove Canton.

-

Once he had returned, Parno set off again, ditching his escort deftly by simply telling them to report to the stables. He would ride the training fields, and then go to his office. He hated to lie to Berry, but would make sure the man didn't get into any trouble.

He rode a short distance away, to the east. There, near an abandoned line cabin, the Tinker waited. Parno smiled, and returned the man's greeting.

"I made sure no one would know that we had met here," Parno told him. "I'm sure that my men are trustworthy, but the fewer who know of our connection, the better for you it is, I think." The Tinker nodded.

"Very good, milord," he replied. "I don't know when I will be able to return, exactly. I cannot simply ride through, you understand? To variate from my usual patterns will draw attention. I'm already changing enough, just going North when I usually go south."

"How will you explain that?" Parno asked, curious.

"Ah, there is a woman, you see," the Tinker shook his head theatrically. "I must see her again, though it be the death of me." Parno laughed. The Tinker, for all his seriousness, had a sense of humor.

"You know," the Tinker said, pocketing the bag of gold the Prince had just handed over, "I could just take your gold and run with it." Parno nodded.

"You can," he agreed. "And you might, I suppose, if you take a notion. But I think you won't."

"Why?" the Tinker asked, his own curiosity pricked.

"I don't really know," Parno admitted. "I just have the feeling I can trust you. You're trusting me," he shrugged. "It has to go both ways."

"That is true," the Tinker agreed. "I will do as best I can for you, Prince. I have no love for the Nor. Well, at least not their Emperor, and their ruling class. Their common people are not so unlike Soulan's, to be honest."

"I've heard that more than once," Parno shrugged again. "Perhaps, one day, we'll be able to live in peace. But I don't think that day has come, just yet."

"Nor do I," the Tinker nodded. "Nor do I. Farewell, Prince Parno McLeod. We will see each other again when we do. As my father once said, 'look for me only when you see me coming'."

"I like it," Parno grinned, shaking hands with the man. "Ride careful."

Parno watched the man out of sight, then turned his horse for home.

-

"Where in blazes have you been?" Darvo demanded as soon as Parno entered the Headquarters building.

"Nowhere, really," Parno lied just a little. "Just out around the grounds. Seeing what I could. Why?"

"You shouldn't be out, alone, lad," Darvo frowned. "It isn't safe."

"I'm quite capable of taking care of myself, you know," Parno replied sardonically. "It's not like I couldn't get help if I needed it, anyway." Darvo nodded, reluctantly.

"True enough, far as it goes," he admitted. "Well, I have work to do," he declared to no one in particular, and stomped out of the office building. Parno grinned at his mentor's gruff exterior. Shaking his head, he went to his office. After two days of idleness, he was sure something needed his attention.

-

In the weeks that followed, Parno watched the regiment take shape. Good shape, in fact. True, there were rough spots, still. But not so many, and not so rough, as before.

Parno walked among the tents and cabins of the camp almost everyday, speaking to different men, asking after their families if they had them, inquiring to their well being.

At first the men were, if not surly, then only as friendly as they deemed necessary to stay out of trouble. The young Prince was patient, however, and never called attention to their attitudes. Nor did he allow others to do so.

Gradually, the men began to lose their innate distrust of Parno as man of privilege and power. It wasn't that they lost respect for Parno, the Prince, but rather they that they gained respect for Parno, the man.

The young Royal often rode with them on training missions, though never in a command capacity. When he did, he rode alone, without retainers, other than a runner, who did not, the men took note, wait on the prince.

Parno took care of his own horse, and saw to his own needs. He used a fire just as they did, and slept on the ground when the ride was an extended one. He demanded no special considerations, and accepted none, when they were offered.

Parno trained with them, when on rides, running and stretching and doing Cho Feng's 'calisthenics', often cursing right alongside them at the need. He ate the same meals they ate, and complained just as loudly as they did when the food wasn't good.

Grudgingly the men around him began to see Parno not as a Prince, but as one of them. A man.

Then there was the fact that all of them who had families now had those families with them. Wives, sons, daughters, even siblings in some cases, had been moved lock, stock, and barrel to the camp. Small but well made cabins had been constructed outside the camp walls, and the families were all settled before winter.

Those with families, as they gained the trust of their commanders, were allowed to move into those cabins as well, reporting for duty each morning just as other freemen would have done. The small selection of cabins grew, as men were added to the roster. After Parno ordered a store built, following the events in Cove, and stocked with goods, attitudes improved again. No longer did anyone have to go into town in order to buy the things they needed and wanted. And the prices in the camp store were far more reasonable than in the nearby town of Cove.

Merchants had grumbled at the presence of the unit so near town, and had often been surly with those families who ventured into town to shop. Now they grumbled again, complaining that Parno's 'store' had cost them business. The attitude in town meant that few if any of the dependents around the fort were welcome in town. They were treated with a surly disrespect at best, and outright hostility more often than not.

As a result, Parno had an even larger building erected, near the center of the small village of homes. When it was finished, the residents were stunned to discover that this building was for their use, as a place to hold dinners, dances, and other gatherings. The women were delighted, which, in turn, made the men happy. Now with practically their own 'town', no one had any need to venture into town at all. And no one wanted to, either.

Thus, within the five months that all that had taken, Parno had not only gained their respect, but also their loyalty. Many of them considered themselves so far in Parno's debt that no amount of service could erase it.

This feeling of debt, however, was not so unsettling as it would have normally been to such men, who considered their independence something worth more than any amount of money. In fact, they learned that depending on each other, and Parno, wasn't a bad thing. Men who had long been accustomed to going at the world alone, learned that making one's way was much easier when there were men who could be trusted, counted on to help when the need arose.

And they learned that being beholden to offer that same help in return wasn't the millstone around their neck they'd always considered it to be. In fact, the men of the regiment learned that the feeling was comforting.

All of these things served to assist in gelling the men into the beginning of a unit, not just a collection of men who might or might not be someone they could trust.

-

Winter was looming. Colder air was blowing across the Cumberland Plateau each day it seemed. Winter uniforms were issued, along with 'union suits', of long sleeved and legged underwear. Parno wondered, more than once, where that term had come from. No one seemed to know.

Still, Parno continued his habit of making his way through the post at least once each day. In this way, he felt, he stayed in touch with the soldiery. He often knew about problems before they were actual problems. And he dealt with them as quickly as possible. And the men, they noticed that too.

"Good mornin', Milord," Parno heard over and over as he walked through the camp in the early morning hours. Parno returned each greeting, by name if he could remember, by the term 'Trooper' if not. Inwardly, Parno smiled as he thought back on how things had changed in so short a time.

"Good morning, Brenack," Parno smiled, as he walked over to where the huge blacksmith was laboring at his forge. "Getting an early start, I see." Brenack Wysin looked up at Parno, and smiled.

"Mornin' milord," he replied. "Always best to get going early, sir. Never know what the day'll bring."

"So true," Parno gave a sigh of long suffering. "So true." Brenack laughed at that.

"You're far too young to know that kind of misery, milord," he told his young liege.

"I've suffered greatly in the time I've been here, my friend," Parno laughed in reply. "So horrible. It hurts merely to contemplate."

"You've done well for yourself, here, milord," Brenack said seriously. "This lot," he waved to the camp around him, "aren't the kind to give respect to any man, let alone one of noble birth. But you," he added, smiling slightly, "you've earned their respect, milord. No small accomplishment, to my way o' thinking."

"I'm glad I've managed that," Parno admitted, "but all I've done is try to treat them fairly."

"And that's the secret, sire," Brenack nodded firmly. "All men such as these want, the good ones, mind," he added with a pointed finger, "is to be treated like a man. With respect. And you've done that."

"Them as had to be sent back?" a huge shoulder shrugged. "That's as it is, milord. Not all men are good ones, sir. And careful as you was, a few was bound to get through the sifting. Like bugs in the flour."

"And don't think that these men don't know that," he added. "They're wise enough to see a truly bad man, and know 'im for what he is. They ain't a man in this camp, as I know of, is sad about seein' them as has gone back depart."

"I'm glad of that," Parno admitted. "I confess, I did wonder at the effect it would have on those who remained."

"Well, they note that they ain't been sent back," Brenack chuckled in his deep baritone. "And they note that only them as was unwillin' was sent back. They know that so long as they stay straight, they're good with you. And bein' good with you has become somethin' important to most of us." Brenack eyed Parno closely.

"Not cause you're a prince, mind," he told his liege. "But account o' you giving us all a second chance at life. And a not bad life, at that," he added, smiling. "Those I know, or come to know in the time I been here, they don't aim to throw that away."

"Good," Parno nodded, pleased.

"Well," Brenack said suddenly, mindful of how casually he'd been talking to a Prince of the Royal Family. "I best get back workin', milord. Don't wanna get sent back, myself," he added with a final grin.

"I don't think that will happen, Brenack," Parno assured him, starting on his way again. "Take care."

"And yourself, milord. And yourself."

Parno continued on through the camp, taking note how the men were working. He was very pleased with what he saw. Maybe they weren't a 'crack' fighting outfit as yet, but they were coming along nicely.

Very nicely indeed.

Which was good, since they would likely be needed sooner, rather than later. Thinking on that made Parno think on the Willows, and the Tinker. Even now, this minute, either one might well be seeing something worth knowing. Something that Parno could point to, one way or another, and allay his fears. His suspicions.

He wanted to believe that peace was possible. He wanted to think that there was nothing suspicious about the Norland overtures to Soulan.

Try as he might, however, he couldn't.

We'll know soon enough, I imagine, he thought to himself. Still worrying over what might well be nothing, Parno started for his office. He too, had work to do.

-

For once, Parno had been undisturbed. As a result, he had worked most of the day, clearing his desk of reports, receipts, requisitions, and all the other paperwork that made the regiment work. He was surprised that no complaint had been made of his expenditures, but Memmnon had, so far, been true to his word.

Parno had been careful with his money. Work done on the post was done by the soldiers, especially any labor-intensive projects. Several of the men had carpentry experience, and worked for the quartermaster one or two days a week, making repairs to buildings, seeing to it that all was in order. The helped to keep costs down as well.

But there was no real way to hide the money he was spending on Roda Finn. The fussy inventor wasn't a real drain on the treasury, of course, but the materials that he needed rightfully had no place on an army base. Parno had partially solved that problem by giving Roda Finn his own bunker, house, barracks, and range roughly one mile from the fort itself. Roda had assured him that any disaster that befell him in his work would leave the fort undamaged.

"Probably," he had murmured, qualifying himself, as he almost always did. Parno winced at that thought. Fussy though he might be, however, Roda Finn was making war materials that Parno was sure he could make use of. Powerful tools that might mean the difference between victory and defeat, someday.

Realizing that it was near dark, Parno finished up his current project, a list of promotional candidates, and rose. Donning his jacket and cap, he walked out into the near dark, just past sunset. Looking across the grounds, he saw a solitary figure standing on the platform above the East Gate. Recognizing the figure, Parno headed that way. As he topped the steps, he found Cho Feng.

"Good evening, Master Feng," Parno spoke quietly, walking up to where the oriental weapons master was looking at the stars.

"Good evening, young Prince," Feng replied, without turning. "How was your day?"

"Not bad, considering," Parno admitted, looking to the stars himself. He often wondered what Feng saw in the heavens at times like these.

"Indeed," Feng replied. "You are, perhaps, wondering what I see in the stars?"

"How do you do that?" Parno asked, exasperated. It seemed that Feng always knew what was on his mind.

"Do what, Prince Parno?" Feng asked, stifling a grin.

"Know what I'm thinking?"

"I do not know what you're thinking," Feng replied laconically. "I do know your habits, however," he added, turning to face the younger man.

"You have an innate curiosity, Parno," Feng told him. "This is not a bad thing," he added. "It is, in fact, a good thing, especially in a man who would lead other men. Perhaps many men, before your life reaches its fulfillment."

"I assure you, Master Cho, that these are all the men I'll ever lead," Parno scoffed in good humor. "But they are enough."

"Things will not always be as they are now, young Prince," Feng told him cryptically, returning his gaze to the heavens.

"My people," he continued, after a moment, "have believed for many generations that the future is often written among the stars. That one can gaze into their lights, and see the path that his life will follow." He turned to grin at Parno slightly.

"His fate, if you will."

"You share this belief?" Parno asked, curious.

"I do," Feng nodded. "I cannot explain how. I think that no one can. I cannot even explain how I can see, at least not easily. I often wonder if it is not simply my inner being, seeing what comes my way."

"A handy gift," Parno replied ruefully. "One I wish I shared."

"Perhaps you do, in a way," Feng told him. "I know that you are troubled by the actions of your Northern adversaries. That you seek a reason behind their actions."

"They aren't our adversaries anymore, apparently," Parno sighed. "But yes, I am suspicious. And I don't think I'm alone in that. My brother, Memmnon, deals with many affairs of State for my father. As Crown Prince, he is, in effect, the Minister of State for Soulan. He, too, is suspicious." *Just not enough, I fear,* he didn't add.

"And that merely fuels your own feelings," Feng nodded. "Fanning the flames, so to speak."

"It does," Parno admitted. "I don't know why, in all honesty. Except. . . ." Parno trailed off, looking out over the camp for a moment. Feng waited patiently as Parno worked to gather his thoughts.

"Except it feels wrong," he admitted finally. "I don't know any other way to put it. There's just something wrong with this whole. . .thing."

"The leopard does not change his spots," Feng nodded. "They have been your enemy for as long as memory and history can tell. They have invaded your lands repeatedly, killed your countrymen, your family members. It is impossible to trust such a people. Such an enemy."

"I suppose that's part of it, anyway," Parno agreed after a minute of thought. "But it's. . .it's more than that. It's as if I can feel the storm coming in my bones, Cho. Feel it coming, and there's nothing I can do to stop it."

"No, there is not," Feng told him sadly, looking back to the stars once more. "You cannot stop what comes, young Prince. Therefore, you must free your mind of that worry. There is no profit in worrying over things you cannot change."

"Instead," he continued, "you must turn your efforts toward seeing through the veil your enemy is weaving. Seek the truth of their intentions, and prepare yourself for their coming." He looked once more at Parno.

"You must be ready, when the time comes."

"Ready for what?" Parno asked, confused.

"To meet your destiny, Parno McLeod. For Destiny rides a swift horse, and she gallops headlong for you." With that, Feng turned and left the dais before Parno could question him further. Parno watched him go, then turned to look into the stars himself.

Finally, he shook his head.

"What the hell is he seeing up there?"

# CHAPTER EIGHT

-

Parno watched as the column rode out of the small fort. A full company, mounted and in full armor. Provisions for three days. One hundred miles to go. It was a circle that never ended.

Between the prisoners, those on the 'wanted' list who had come in seeking a fresh start, and a few hardy volunteers who had simply walked in, the regiment was becoming a true regiment, with just over twelve hundred troops. Since the basic training had pretty much ended, the men had been shaken down into companies. Each company had a 'specialty' of sorts, be it archery, infantry, artillery, and one company of cross bowmen. In keeping with his plans, however, everyone was required to master that one weapon, and be at least moderately skilled with another.

And everyone had to be able to ride, and fight, as cavalry.

Each month, each company was required to make one long patrol, one hundred miles give or take. Everything they might need had to be in their packs or saddlebags, though in winter, forage for the horses was taken out by wagon.

Each week, every company was required to march twenty five miles on patrol. While he didn't envision that the need would arise, Cho had convinced him that the marches were good exercise, conditioning the men to hardship in the field. Parno agreed.

He wasn't excused from the patrols, himself, nor was anyone else who might find themselves in combat. He took his patrols with different companies each time, always as just another soldier. He had no desire to disrupt the chains of command that each company had developed. The soldiers he accompanied treated him with no deference to his position, per his own orders. The fact that he shared their hardships was not lost on them, and slowly he won their respect as a fellow soldier, rather than just as their liege lord.

Glad it wasn't his turn, this time, to go out, Parno walked on into the headquarters building, and then into the small office he maintained there. Most of his work he did from the house, so he kept an office little larger than a closet in the main building. His argument, when others protested, was that there was little enough room as it was, and he didn't need a large work area, as he had a spacious study in the main house.

"Good morning, milord," Harrel Sprigs nodded as his Commander walked into the building.

"Morning, Harrel," Parno replied. "Anything needing my attention this morning?"

"We have a delegation from the town here, sir," Sprigs told him, sighing. "Complaining that we are no longer allowing the men into town. Or buying supplies from their merchants."

"After the fiasco with the constable?" Parno was shocked. "I'd not have thought they wanted us there again, were we to come bearing gifts from afar."

Sprigs shrugged helplessly. There was no accounting for people.

"Send them into my office in five minutes."

"There are several of them, sir," Sprigs warned. "Eight, to be exact."

"Fine," Parno nodded in satisfaction. "They can crowd in, and stand."

-

Parno looked up casually as Sprigs knocked lightly, then opened the door.

"The delegation from Cove, milord," he said firmly.

"Very well, show them in," Parno smiled. He watched as the sullen, even angry looking men trooped into his small office. One of them, well dressed and well fed, looked around him in disdain.

"I'd think someone of your station would keep better quarters, Prince," he remarked, just a hint of sarcasm entering his voice.

"I do keep better quarters," Parno said flatly. "This is my office. How may I be of service to you, gentlemen." The slight inflection on the word gentlemen wasn't lost on the fat man, as he flushed slightly.

"We'd like to know why you have declared our town off limits to your soldiers," he said bluntly. "I'm Mayor Hagerly, Prince. Your men used to spend their money in town, and now, thanks to you, that's no longer the case. Likewise, you no longer give our merchants your patronage when buying supplies. We'd like an explanation."

"I see," Parno nodded, ignoring, for now, the barely disguised 'demand'. "I'd think that, after the incident two or so months back, there would be no need for explanations, Mayor. My men were attacked in your town, and your constable took two of my troopers, Royal troopers, mind you, into custody for defending themselves. He made it quite clear that my men weren't welcome in Cove. As did any number of townspeople. I believe you were there, in fact," he added.

"That was a misunderstanding," Hagerly said. "Your men. . . ."

"Did nothing other than defend themselves," Parno cut him off. "Something that shouldn't have even been needed, or necessary, in a town of this kingdom. Men who are sworn to protect the people and land of Soulan should not be targets for those they protect."

"That was just drunken brawling," Hagerly's face reddened further, "and your men were just as drunk. . . ."

"You, sir, are a liar," Parno said it flatly, his voice void of emotion. "I have entertained your desire for an audience today out of courtesy. Yet no courtesy has been returned. You come here, insulting me, my men, my office of all things, and expect to make demands of me." Parno stood suddenly, and Hagerly and his followers almost jumped back away from his desk.

"Need I remind you who you're talking to?" he said softly.

Hagerly licked his lips, nervously. Knowing as he did Parno's status among the Royals, he had expected the young Prince to be intimidated.

"Perhaps we should speak to the Crown, then," he threatened, trying to regain his composure.

"Perhaps you should," Parno nodded. "I'd welcome that, in fact," he smiled. "Since, once you do, the report of the incident in question will have to be made available to the Crown. Merely as supporting evidence, of course," he added. Hagerly's face paled.

"I. . .I was not aware that no report had been made," he said quietly. He had assumed that the report had indeed been made, and ignored, due to the fact that it was Parno McLeod who filed it.

"Not at all," Parno smiled. "As part of the arrangement with your Constable, and with the consent of the townspeople present at the time I might add, there was a report prepared, but not filed. Had it been, I've no doubt that a Royal Constable would have been dispatched to investigate. Attacks upon the Crown's troopers are not taken lightly."

"So I urge you, Mayor, by all means, appeal to the Crown. Lay this matter before the King."

Hagerly looked like a trapped rat now. He had intended, indeed, he had promised, to force the Prince to allow his men into town once more, and to resume purchasing his supplies from the local merchants. At a substantial profit, of course. Now, he had walked into a bear trap, and there was no available escape route.

"I think this matter is concluded, gentlemen," Parno said finally. "Mister Sprigs will show you out." As if he'd been listening all the time, which, of course, he had, Sprigs opened the door.

"This way if you please, gents. I'll show you to your carriages." Two large, stone faced Royal Troopers were now in the hall. Placed there by Sprigs.

"I'm sorry we disturbed you, milord," Hagerly managed to say without venom. "And thank you for your time."

"No problem at all, Mayor," Parno smiled. "I always have time for my people." Hagerly flinched at that but made no other comment as he and his 'delegation' were shown the door.

Parno sighed, sitting back in his chair. He'd thought that whole mess was behind them for good.

Maybe it was, this time.

-

The day wasn't over for Parno. Just after lunch, there was a soft knock at his office door. Parno looked up from the stack of company progress reports.

"Milord, there's a visitor here to see you," Lt. Sprigs said quietly.

"Who is it?"

"He says his name is Hubbel. Whip Hubbel."

"Hubbel? The archer?" Parno asked, eyebrows raised. Sprigs nodded.

"I think so, sir. He's carrying a magnificent long bow."

"Show him in!" Parno exclaimed, rising. Springs bowed slightly and retreated. Seconds later he ushered the man in question into the room. Hubbel was a large man, wide of shoulder, and tall. He was weathered looking and heavily muscled. He wore buckskins, Parno noted, not unusual for men who lived in the mountains.

"Prince Parno, Whip Hubbel," Sprigs announced calmly, and then closed the door.

"Welcome, Mister Hubbel," Parno smiled, extending his hand. Hubbel took the proffered hand with a firm grip. Not crushing, not limp, simply a strong, firm grip. Parno returned the pressure equally.

"Thank you for seein' me, milord," the older man said gruffly.

"Certainly," Parno nodded. "How may I be of service?" Hubbel grinned at that, and Parno noted that the man's weathered face crinkled in amusement.

"Was thinkin' it was me, might be o' service to you, milord," he replied. Parno chuckled softly.

"I'm thinking the same thing, sir. May I offer you anything to drink?"

"Beer, if'n ya got it'd go mighty fine," Hubbel said. Parno's grin returned.

"This is an army post, Mister Hubbel. If we didn't have beer, we'd have a mutiny on our hands." The older man chuckled this time. Parno walked to a small barrel, where a large chunk of ice was floating in clear water, and removed two bottles.

"You don't mind if I join you, I hope?" Parno asked, uncorking the bottles, and handing one to Hubbel. "Please, take a chair." The two men took seats, and each raised their bottle.

"Your health, milord," Hubbel smiled, and took a large drought.

"And yours, sir," Parno replied, taking a healthy drink himself. With the formalities out of the way, Parno turned to business.

"What's on your mind, Mister Hubbel?"

"'Spect it's wrong, man o' yer station callin' me 'sir', or 'mister'," Hubbel noted. Parno shrugged.

"I'm not much on 'stations' Mister Hubbel. But if you prefer I call you something else, I will oblige."

"Whip'll do, I reckon," the older man rumbled after a pause. "I must say, you ain't what I expected."

"I hope that's a good thing," Parno managed to smile. Whip nodded.

"It is," he assured the young prince. "I expected a fop, or fancy pants, playin' at bein' somethin' he ain't. You don't 'pear to be neither."

"Well, I'm not much on pretense either, Whip," Parno shrugged again. "This is what I am." Whip nodded.

"Hear tell you need bowmen," the older man changed the subject. Parno regarded the man carefully.

"I need bowyers," Parno corrected. "And bow masters. Bowmen I have in plenty, provided I can find someone to teach them."

"I see," the older man mused. "I'm a fair hand at bow makin'," he said after a few seconds.

"You're said to be the finest bow-maker in the Apple Mountains, Whip," Parno smiled slightly. The old man looked at Parno intently, then laughed out loud.

"I see you've done yer schoolin', Milord."

"I do what I can," Parno nodded. "But I'm curious. Where you interested in enlisting? You do realize that this regiment is made up of former prisoners and men who have found themselves on the wrong side of the law, so to speak."

"So I'd heard," the old man nodded. "Might be I was thinkin' on it," he added carefully. "Bein' as I might be wanted, a bit."

"A bit?" Parno's eyes rose. "How much of a bit?"

"Mighta killed a deer or two I hadn't oughta," the old man shrugged. "Mighta had need, at the time."

"I see," Parno nodded. "Well, Whip, I'm sorry to say that I don't think I can use you in the regiment. Despite your notable abilities you're a bit old to enter military service. Not that I doubt your stamina," he added when Whip frowned. "But this truly is a young man's game and the training is rigorous enough that even the younger men are finding the going difficult."

"What I can use you for, however, is to teach my men how to use their bows better, and to teach the actual archers how to make their own bows. All of my men are required to be able to use a bow, but several of them are already fairly adept and the long bow is their primary weapon."

"If you're interested in that, then I can offer you a position."

"What about my wants?" Whip asked, sounding unconvinced.

"I can take care of that," Parno smiled. "And, as you aren't a convicted criminal," Parno added slyly, "I can pay you for your services and provide you a place to live." Whip looked at Parno for a long minute. Parno sat quietly, returning the older man's gaze levelly. He needed this man's help and they both knew it. There was no point in pretending otherwise and, as he'd said, Parno didn't much care for pretense.

"I got a daughter, milord," Whip said finally. "Just turned seventeen. Need a place for her. A safe place, was somethin' to happen to me. Ain't no one but me and her, anymore. I'm all she has."

"All the men's families are welcome here, Whip," Parno replied. "Your daughter is no different. Should something, untoward, shall we say, happen to you, then she'll be welcome to remain here. Many of the men's family members work here as well. In the kitchens…doing laundry…sewing…any number of things. All paid work, by the way. No one's required to work, but the work is available."

"Girl's a fair hand with the bow, herself," Whip commented. "And knows how to fashion a bow herself."

"Does she now?" Parno leaned forward, eyes alight with interest. "That. . .that might change things a bit, then," he smiled. "Perhaps she'd like to actually work for me. By which I mean, the regiment. We've need of skilled bowyers, and arrow makers as well. Is she up to that, you think?"

"She is," Whip nodded without thought.

"Well, then, Whip," Parno smiled. "Let's discuss terms, shall we?"

-

Winifred Hubbel, 'Winnie' to her father and few friends, eyed the assembled company in front of her with no little trepidation. She refused to let it show on her face but she was sure that the Captain standing in front of her could see it in her eyes.

Winnie was a comely lass, tall, willowy, and rather full of figure. Pretty, with green eyes and flame colored hair she looked far older than her seventeen years. Life in the mountains could be hard, and very unforgiving.

But her bow, made by her own hands, was obviously a fine one.

"We'll be here with you, miss," Captain Roland, commander of Archery Company 'B' assured her. "And they're not a bad lot, ma'am."

"I ain't scared of'em," she assured the Captain, with more bravado than she actually felt. She could hear some of the troopers, who had yet to be called to attention, had to say.

"A skirt?"

"What's next? Kiddies to teach us how to fight?"

"Whose blunderin' idea was this, I wonder?"

Suddenly tired of the muttering, she drew and knocked an arrow. The target line was over fifty yards down range, about the best the men before her could be hoped to attain. She turned, raising her bow in a fluid motion, and let fly.

The talk behind her trickled, and then halted, as the arrow lodged firmly into the target's center. Her hair trailing out in the light breeze, Winnie turned back to the assembled men.

"Any more questions 'bout why I'm here?" she demanded, her voice carrying easily across the company assembly.

"Bleedin' hell," someone gasped. The archers were all open mouthed. Roland, having already been informed of who his young charge was, smirked slightly. She was all that the Prince had promised, and a good bit more, besides.

"Sergeant Price," Roland said softly.

"ATTEN-SHUN!" the non-com boomed, and the soldiers almost clicked as they assumed the rigid posture. Roland nodded slightly, then stepped to the front of the ranks.

"That, gentlemen, is the proper way to use a long bow," he said, his voice almost, but not quite, taunting. "Something none of you, I might point out, have so far been able to demonstrate. This young woman," he indicated Winnie, "is our new instructor. Her name is Hubbel. Winifred Hubbel. You will refer to her as ma'am, or Miss Hubbel. And you will listen raptly to her instructions."

"You will give her your undivided attention at all times when she is speaking. And you will exhibit exemplary behavior in her presence at all times. Is that understood?"

"YES SIR"! Company 'B' shouted. Roland nodded.

"She can make you better archers," he continued, his voice not quite so frosty. "And she can teach you to make your own bows, so that you no longer have to depend upon bows made by someone else." He turned to Winnie.

"Miss Hubble. They're yours." She nodded, stepping forward without hesitation.

"Today we will focus on proper form, and execution," she announced. "I'm informed that this range will accommodate one entire platoon at the time. While that platoon is on the line, I ask that you pay particular attention to the instructions given. It will speed your training and get us to the point where we can begin your own bowyer training.  Perhaps then we can move into arrow making as well. Sergeant Price?" she called and the large non-com snapped to.

"Ma'am!"

"Please designate one platoon for the first shooting and post the others where they can pay rapt attention."

"Ma'am!" Price grinned. She might not be that old, but she knew what she knew.

Roland nodded as well.

Yes, I think this will do nicely. Very nicely indeed.

-

About the same time that Winnie Hubbel was creating such a stir among Roland's company of archers, Parno had decided to pay Roda Finn a visit.

"Master Finn, how goes it today?" Parno walked into the fussy scientist's workshop carefully. One never knew what might come flying by.

"Hello, Prince Parno," Finn smiled happily. "How is my favorite benefactor today, ah?" Finn had been working on something inside a small glass tube. He now set the tube aside and looked to his prince.

"I'm your only benefactor, Roda," Parno smiled easily.

"That's true, that's true," Finn chuckled. "But no matter how many more I have between now and my final destination, you shall always be my favorite. Thanks to you, I am not ashes, spread over some fanatic's flower bed and sprinkled with Holy Water."

"Well, I thank you for that special place in your. . .heart," Parno grinned. "What are you working on today, by the way?"

"Well, let me show you," Finn said, waving the Prince closer to his workbench. When Parno hesitated, Finn chuckled. "Come on, come on. I promise, no fire, no explosions."

"Very well, if you promise." Parno eased forward carefully. Though he tried to appear at ease, he was also ready to bolt for the door at a seconds notice. Finn's experiments sometimes got away from him.

"See this?" Finn said triumphantly. 'This' was a small, round ball. Iron, Parno realized as he took it. The ball weighed perhaps two pounds. As he turned it in his hands, he was surprised to see that a hole had been bored into the iron.

"I see it," Parno nodded. "What is it?"

"It's a small ball of iron, but that's not really important," Finn replied with a smirk. Parno shot the inventor a murderous glance, which Finn chose to ignore. He picked up the test tube, waving it toward a basin along the wall.

"Bring it along, and I'll show you what it's for," he promised. "No one around here has a sense of humor," he grumped.

"It doesn't pay to bring one's sense of humor into your place of business, Roda," Parno pointed out politely. "It's far too easy to get something blown off that way."

"Ah," Finn made a pushing motion with his hand, as if waving off the comment. Finn really had made some spectacular . . . 'miscalculations', as he preferred to call them.

"Let me have the ball," he ordered, and Parno gladly passed it over. He watched as Finn carefully poured the substance from the beaker into the hole. Stopping before it was filled, Finn handed the glass back to Parno.

"Set that back on the bench, if you would," Finn asked. Parno had taken it and started for the bench when Finn added, "And do be careful. You don't want to drop that." Parno cursed under his breath, his feet softly treading across the roughhewn floor as if walking on eggs. He was very careful to set the glass down softly, and level, then backed away. When he returned, Finn had sealed the ball with wax and was slowly tossing it a few inches into the air over his hand, then catching it again.

Parno stopped suddenly, trying to gauge where it was safer, near the table, or the basin. Finn laughed.

"Don't worry, Prince. We're fine, long as I don't drop it."

"Then might I suggest you stop doing that?" Parno said tersely. Finn only laughed again as he headed for the door.

"Come along, Prince Parno. I have something to show you. Something I think you will like. Like very much, in fact." Parno gingerly followed Finn outside, the inventor still juggling the ball.

"Roda, please," Parno said urgently.

"Oh, it's fine, so long as I don't -"

"Drop it, yes I know. And if you aren't juggling it like that, the odds of your dropping it are so much lower, that's all."

"Well, I'm about to throw it, so it's a moot point anyway," the scientist cackled harshly. With that he grabbed what looked like a miniature catapult and began pulling the cocking arm into place. This caused him to further juggle the small iron 'bomb', (Parno had decided it had to be some kind of bomb, that being the name that Finn gave to so many of his exploding toys), which in turn caused Parno much grief. Finally he stepped forward and grabbed the lever himself.

"Allow me, if you will keep that thing firmly in your hand." Finn growled under his breath, but allowed the younger man to ready the small catapult. Once the weapon was ready, Finn placed the small iron ball into the cradle. Attaching a string to the releasing mechanism, he began to walk away. When he saw Parno wasn't following, he turned back to the Prince.

"You might want to follow me, Milord," he said, almost without sarcasm. "You were so worried about my dropping it. This thing might not launch correctly, you know." Parno, his face showing his shock at the thought, hastily followed Finn.

The scientist retreated thirty feet or so, Parno figured, to a small wooden barricade, made with close fitted oak logs. The logs were staggered so that no part of the barrier was less than two feet thick. A sturdy and formidable shield, Parno thought thankfully. He huddled behind the barricade with Finn. The little inventor looked at him, grinned evilly, and then pulled the cord.

As soon as the catapult fired, Finn was on his feet. Parno followed a tad slower, but was still in time to see fire blossom down range, roughly one hundred yards away, followed immediately by the 'boom' now so familiar to those who worked with, or around, Roda Finn.

"YES!" Finn shouted, and jumped for joy. The sight of the little professor behaving so was comical, and Parno laughed despite himself. Finn turned to him, abashed at his outburst.

"Well, I wasn't sure that would work, to tell the truth," he admitted.

"What did it do?" Parno asked. "More to the point, what's it for?"

"Come on, I'll show you," Finn said, excitement back in his voice. Parno followed Roda Finn down the 'range', as he called it, again laughing at the sight of the fussy and stuffy inventor running. It was like following a duck with arthritis.

Parno's grin faded, however, as he neared what Roda called the 'impact area'. Several scarecrows had been set up on the range, all wearing various types of armor, ranging from leather jerkins and buff coats, to mail and even plate armor. As he examined the figures, most of them now on the ground, Parno felt a chill in his bones.

Every one of them was shredded, as if a giant knife had been plunged into each target over and over again. Gaping holes filled the leather and mail clad figures, and smaller, but no less wicked wounds afflicted even the plate armor. A small whistle escaped Parno's lips as he looked over the carnage in front of him.

"Now. You see?" Finn asked smugly.

"How is this possible, Roda?" Parno breathed. "I've never seen anything like this."

"No one has, Milord. Not in several centuries, anyway, unless I miss my guess. This is from an ancient form of warfare called 'artillery'."

"We have artillery," Parno objected. "You used one of our artillery pieces to launch this. . .thing!"

"True," Finn allowed grudgingly. "You have a form of artillery, in your catapults, trebuchets, and what not. Even ballistae are a form of such, though they are what the ancients referred to as 'direct fire' weapons. But the secret of artillery fire, my Prince, lies where?"

"In range, and in damage done," Parno answered immediately.

"Correct," Finn nodded. "The weapons themselves do not cause the damage. They are merely delivery systems. In ancient times, Milord, such delivery systems could hit targets miles from where they sat and cause significantly more damage than this."

"Miles," Parno said softly, shaking his head. "With weapons like that-"

"Unfortunately," Finn squelched that thought, "we do not have the technology to make that work. Such weapons as I have described are beyond us, certainly for the present. Too much of the knowledge needed to create those weapons was lost in the Great Dying, but," Roda waved to the ground about him, "we can do this!"

"It's not much range," Parno objected mildly. "Good as a last ditch defensive weapon, of course, and deadly too, but. . . ."

"But, but, no buts," Finn interjected. "What you just saw was simply a scale model demonstration, with a one-quarter scale catapult. Imagine, Milord, a ball weighing ten pounds, rather than two, and fired from a full size catapult, rather than my toy, there. Imagine that! And what do you see?"

Parno opened his mouth, but found no words. A ten pound. . .bomb, causing five times the damage this one had! At far greater ranges, to boot! With such a weapon, and in good defenses, a force could hold its ground against an attacker many times its own strength.

"Roda, how big can you make these things and have them still function?" he asked finally.

"I have no idea," Finn admitted with a shrug. "I suppose that the bomb can be made as large as needed, or wanted. Transporting them would be, difficult in the extreme, I fear, if they were too large. Not to mention. . . ."

"Not to mention the danger involved in grinding over bumpy roads, tree roots, or a wheel coming off," Parno finished for him. He frowned, considering the problem.

"What if," he said suddenly, "we transport the balls, bombs," he corrected at Finn's grimace, "unloaded? Fill them with. . .whatever it is you fill them with after we arrive? Could that work?"

"It could," Finn replied, hand rubbing his chin in thought. "Still leaves the trouble of transporting the concoction, of course, but maybe I can work something out for that as well. We might, for instance, use many small beakers, sized for only one shot. That way, anyone, well, not anyone, of course, but someone very careful, could simply load and seal the bombs on the battlefield."

"And," he continued excitedly, mind racing, "we can rig some kind of framing that will allow the beakers to move with the motion of the wagon. Swaying gently to the rocking, like in a boat upon the water, instead of rattling around inside a wagon box. That would make moving the compound safer, though it won't eliminate the risk altogether, mind you."

"Some risk is acceptable if it means having a weapon like this at our backs," Parno assured him. "I want it to be the least risk possible, mind you. And, I'd say you're going to need some assistants, too. Men will have to be trained to transport the...concoction, as you called it, and to assemble the bombs once we reach we ever it is we're going."

"They'll have to be steady men, Milord," Finn warned, with no trace of humor or his usual smugness. "Steady, and have some intelligence. This isn't a sword or shield."

"I'll talk to the Colonel tonight, and with his Second," Parno assured him. "We'll find the right men for the job. You just make sure we can move this stuff without killing them, or the rest of us if it comes to that."

# CHAPTER NINE

-

Tilden Carmichael Jefferson Bane, the Emperor of Norland, stood alone in his study. Quietly, he studied the map before him.

The paper was old, so old that Bane feared it would one day simply turn to dust in his hands. The map itself was replaceable, since many copies had been made, but this map was a part of his birthright. For that reason, he seldom opened it and never in the presence of others.

The map before him resembled the maps of his kingdom, at least in part. The northern part of the map. The southern part, as the eastern and western parts for that matter, were not represented as themselves. Instead, on this map, all of the kingdoms were part of one, United Kingdom.

For long ago, Norland, Soulan, the United Coastal Provinces, and the wild western lands across the great river had been one. One. A single, undivided kingdom that had ruled most of the world. Bane considered this kingdom, this nation, his as well. His to rule.

For Bane was the direct descendent of the last ruler of the great land that had once been. The last descendent, if he failed to sire an heir.

His family, for generations innumerable, had fought to reunite the old kingdom. Despite initial successes, the war always seem to turn once the fighting fell into the south. There the Soulanies refused to budge, choosing instead to fight to the death for every square inch of soil.

Bane's own father, Jefferson Johnston Bane, had led one such foray, one of the most successful in history, in point of fact. Yet that war, too, had ended in defeat. Despite all the then Emperor Jefferson could do, the Norland armies floundered once they penetrated too far into the Soulan territory.

The simple fact was that despite their numbers, Norland lacked the strength to occupy Soulan. It galled Bane to admit that, but it was true, nonetheless. He saw no reason to deny it. If he were to seize that which was meant to be his, then he had no time for half-truths or frivolity. Lying to himself was as bad, if not worse, than someone else lying to him…and it accomplished nothing.

But now, things were different.

Always the Soulan cavalry had made the difference. Raiding, burning, destroying baggage trains and supply trains, disrupting communications, attacking headquarters units, and generally wreaking havoc. The Norland Army had never been able to develop an effective counter to the Soulan horsemen.

Until now. Maybe.

Bane grimaced at the qualifier, but the truth was still the truth. He had laid his plans carefully over the years of his reign. Full diplomatic relations with the Southrons had been established- embassies, ambassadors, everything. The border had been opened to trade with Soulan, with free traffic back and forth. There were no excise taxes and no charge for crossing into Norland territory with trade goods. Many of his people had grumbled at that, albeit quietly, but he had held firm. It was only for a time.

With diplomatic relations restored, Bane had worked through the Soulan ambassador to establish trade and other treaties, all designed to show how reasonable he was. Only Bane's closest advisers knew his true ambitions.

While the one hand was stroking the southern kingdom, the other was making deals under the table with the wild tribes of the west. Horses, tens of thousands of them, had been imported from the west. Advisers from the western lands had been hired to train Norland soldiers how to fight from horseback.

It had been slow going, to be sure. The only experience most of the men in Norland had with horses was staring at the ass-end of one while steering a plow behind the beast and not everyone could master the near wild mustangs from the west. Those who couldn't returned to the infantry.

But those who could had mastered the art of horsemanship. The ranks of the Norland cavalry had grown to forty thousand. Forty thousand well trained, well mounted and highly disciplined troopers, plus another sixty thousand mounted infantry, men who could ride well enough, but would fight on foot once they reached the battlefield. They would join the two hundred thousand infantry, one hundred thousand archers, and hundreds of catapults, siege engines, and ballistae that made up the Norland Army.

Soon, very soon, it would be time to unleash those forces upon the south. Along with a few surprises. Surprises that would ensure, once and for all, control of the eastern half of the ancient kingdom. With Soulan defeated, the Atlantic Provinces would fall into line with little or no trouble. The coasters had little in the way of military forces, dependent for generations on the South for protection from Northern aggression.

Without them, those of the smaller republic would surrender without a fight, he was sure.

With the coming of the spring, war would come once again, as it had countless times in the past. But this time, the outcome would be different.

Very different.

-

Bane walked briskly into the ornate hall that served as his Council chamber. Already assembled were the generals and diplomats who were privy to his plans. They numbered fewer than twenty.

All stood as he entered and Bane graciously waved them back down to their seats, taking his own at the head of the long table.

"Please, gentlemen, sit," he smiled. "We have much to discuss today. General Meade, how are your preparations going?" The aged man who commanded all of Norland's military looked down from his seat next to Bane.

"Our army is as near ready as it can be, without having stood the test of battle," he said firmly. "The training regimens we have in place have worked wonders among the troops. I am confident that the army can carry out its mission."

"Our navy," he went on, glancing back to his Emperor, "is also prepared. Though their part is more limited, it is no less important to our overall plans. They are ready, and able, to carry out their mission."

"We have stockpiled sufficient supplies and equipment for a protracted campaign against Soulan, though we do not expect the campaign to last so long, we have preferred to err on the side of caution. Our planners have worked for weeks, some for many months, to try and anticipate every problem we might encounter and devise a solution for that problem."

"In addition, we have excellent intelligence from the south. We know where their army units are stationed, their make-up, and their combat readiness. Their readiness," he grinned, "I am happy to report is at an all-time low."

"As it should be," the Emperor smiled. "Minister Steadon, what have you to report?" Chance Steadon was the Foreign Minister of the Norland Empire. The tall, graying statesman was the primary architect for the 'outreach' program currently in place in Soulan.

"The Soulan King has been most receptive of our 'negotiations'," he reported with a reptilian smile. "We have convinced him and his heir that we no longer desire armed confrontation between our peoples. That what we desire instead is trade and good relations." He leaned forward, still smiling, "Their desire for peace has made them blind to anything else."

"Good," Bane nodded. "Have we any problems that need to be discussed?" This was a standard part of his meetings. His father had rarely consulted his advisers during his near ruinous rule. Bane had no intention of repeating that mistake.

"I am not convinced that we will be ready so soon after the spring rains," Lieutenant General Gerald Wilson spoke carefully. "Our timetable is very difficult to coordinate, Emperor. If we face an Ohi River still in flood, then our frontal attack may have to be delayed. If that is the case, other attacks will take place before ours and the element of surprise will be lost. Without that element of surprise, our casualties crossing the Ohi are sure to be heavy. So heavy," he added grimly, "that we could be unable to fulfill the rest of our mission."

Bane considered that. Wilson commanded the Norland 1st Field Army. His task was to force a crossing over the Ohi River bridges at Loville, securing those bridges to maintain a line of communications and supply during the war. With the bridges in hand, his Army was then to spearhead the campaign, striking deep into the heartland of Soulan, his ultimate goal to engage and destroy the Soulan Army.

Wilson was not a timid man. He was not afraid to fight, else he would not be here. Bane had made certain of the men who commanded his armies himself. He would not allow bumbling idiots to sabotage his efforts to regain his rightful place.

"Do you have a solution for that issue, General?" Bane asked. Wilson shook his head.

"No, sir, I do not. There are only two options, and neither is workable. One, delay the campaign by two weeks' time, ensuring that the floods from the rains have subsided. This is unacceptable because it takes two weeks off our campaign time."

"The other is improved communications with the Western Army. I know of no way to do that. We already have courier outposts and the best riders, with the best horses, along the route. As I said, neither is workable." He leaned back slightly.

"All that I can do is my best to make sure that we don't have any difficulties and keep my force from being so depleted that it cannot complete its objectives. This I will do, to the best of my abilities. I simply wanted you to know my concerns. And," he admitted, "I hoped that you might see something I have overlooked." This last wasn't a sop to his pride, Bane knew. Wilson meant what he'd said.

Again, Bane paused to consider the problems. Down the table, he heard a throat being cleared. He gazed down to see Admiral Frederic Porter looking at him.

"You have a suggestion, Admiral?" he asked.

"I do, Your Lordship," Porter nodded, then looked at Wilson.

"I can supply you with boats and skilled sailors that will allow you to place a goodly portion of your men on the south bank of the Ohi, both above and below the Soulan fortifications." He said it quietly, simply. Wilson's eyebrows rose at that.

"In what number?" he inquired, leaning forward again, hopeful.

"I would have to consult with my subordinates for exact figures," Porter admitted, "but I think, in the time we have, I could have at least three thousand boats, and the ten thousand or so sailors needed to operate them, in place before you are due to attack."

That announcement caused a small stir around the table, but Bane squelched it with an upraised hand.

"Would that help, General?" Bane asked. Wilson nodded eagerly.

"It would, My Lord," he said at once. "We had considered boats before, but too few of my men are able enough to do the work. We risked losing more men to drowning than to enemy action. With the Admiral's experienced sailors manning the boats, the idea is almost sure to succeed."

"Your men may have to row them," Porter warned. "Three or four of my men per boat is enough to return it to the north bank, but not to carry twenty men across, against the current."

"That is not a problem," Wilson assured him. "If you can provide the skilled assistance, I can supply the manual labor." Porter nodded in reply, then looked to the Emperor. Bane was pleased. Two of his hand-picked men had discussed, and solved, a problem without his help or intervention. Something his father had never learned could happen. All that remained was for him to approve.

"Very well, then," Bane smiled. "That problem is solved. I will leave it to the two of you to work out the details. Do not disappoint me," he warned. The two nodded their agreement. Disappointing the Emperor was more than just a bad career move. It was usually fatal, both for the disappointing officer, and for his family.

"General Brasher, do you foresee any difficulty in your mission?" Bane asked. Brasher commanded the smaller 3rd Field Army, consisting mainly of cavalry and mounted infantry, a fast-moving force.

"No, My Lord, I do not," the cocky general replied. "My men are ready. We will be triumphant."

Bane looked at Brasher for a full minute, searching for any sign of doubt, or weakness. He saw none. True, the man had an ego the size of the palace. But he was capable and he was ruthless. To him had fallen the most important strike in Bane's plan to win a fast and furious war. If he failed, then the war would become one of attrition. One the Nor should still win, Bane granted, but one that was sure to be longer and more costly.

This was something he could ill afford. His people were hungry, and disgruntled. While that, in and of itself, didn't concern him, the persistent rumors of possible rebellion did. Once his army was committed to battle, Bane would have few resources to call on in the event of an actual uprising. He needed to win the war as quickly as possible.

With a victory to brag about, and the resources of the South to shower his people with, such talk would die down and the suspected plotting would wither, and die. With his people united, he could easily turn the war machine that had conquered the South against the Coastal Provinces. Once the eastern half of the ancient Empire were under his rule, then would come the drive to subdue the west.

I'm getting ahead of myself, he thought angrily. Something that my father often did. He looked again at his assembled advisers.

"Is there anything else?" he asked. No one had anything else.

"Then let's get back to work," he ordered, rising. Everyone rose as he did and remained standing until he left the room.

It's going to work, Bane told himself as he strode down the hall to his private offices.

We are going to succeed!

# CHAPTER TEN

-

Parno arrived at Cumberland House just before lunch. He had received word from Edema that she and Edward were due to depart in two days' time, and could they expect to see him before they departed.

Accustomed by now to traveling with the Prince, Berry and his men headed toward the corral with little pause, leading Parno's own steed along with them. They would remain 'from underfoot', as Berry called it, taking mess in the bunkhouse that was now, for all intents and purposes, theirs.

Parno strode calmly up to the porch where Edema stood waiting. She hugged him tightly, placing a slight kiss upon his cheek.

"Welcome, dear boy," she told him, smiling. "I didn't know if you would make it or not."

"I could hardly allow you two to depart without saying farewell," Parno smiled in return. "Where is the Duke?"

"He's down with the train," Edema frowned. "I asked him to be back here for lunch, so hopefully we'll see him then. He cannot trust preparations to others, of course," she grumped. Parno laughed.

"I well understand that feeling," he assured her. They entered the house, walking to the study, where Edema had hot cocoa waiting for him. Parno smiled at the smell. He had always loved the stuff.

"So, you plan to leave day after tomorrow, is that right?" Parno asked after first taking a wonderful, warming sip of the delicious drink.

"That is the plan," she nodded. "I have never before gone with him, in this type of weather, nor even at this time of year. He was surprised when I asked to go," she added.

"Pleasantly, I hope?" Parno asked, as neutrally as possible.

"Oh, yes," Edema nodded. "Seemed very pleased with the arrangement for some reason." Parno nodded.

"It could be that he is glad of your company," he ventured.

"It could," she smiled beautifully and Parno wondered, idly, if Edward Willows had any idea how lucky he was.

"Regardless, I am going," she continued. "I've already prepared. My bags are already packed into our carriage for the most part."

"I really do appreciate this, you know," Parno said softly. She smiled at him again.

"I know," she nodded. "And, in truth, I'm happy to do it. The more I think on it, the less I like how things are going. If I can help in some way, then I want to."

Just then, Edward Willows came bounding into the study.

"My Lord!" he exclaimed, taking Parno's offered hand. "So glad you could come and see us off! How was the ride over?"

"Very enjoyable," Parno assured him. "Beautiful country here, Duke. I can see why you love it so."

"It is a great place," Edward agreed. "Edema, my dear, I am here, as ordered, for lunch." Edema laughed lightly at that.

"Ordered, is it?" she scowled playfully. "As if you would take orders from me. Very well, then," she rose gracefully. "Lunch should already be prepared. Shall we?"

-

"I tell you, milord," Edward Willows struggled to say around a piece of fried chicken, "the trade agreements between us and the Nor are one of the smartest moves your Father, the King, has ever made. Merchants such as I are making good money on trade good at the moment and the taxes will go a long way toward filling the King's coffers as well," he added with a conspiratorial wink. Parno smiled.

"He and Memmnon have been working very hard with the Norland ambassador," he agreed. "I'm glad that these arrangements are good for you, and others. I know that many of our ranchers are selling great numbers of cattle to the Nor as well, and at good prices."

"I've seen some of them on the trail," Edward agreed. "Huge herds of the lumbering beasts. Terrible smell, though, if you happen to get caught behind one for any length of time."

"So I'm told," he laughed, looking to Edema, whose nose crinkled.

"Well, it is," she agreed. "Not that I mind someone making a good living, mind you," she smiled at Edward. "But I do wish there were trails set aside specifically for the cattle drives. It would make our own travels so much. . .sweeter, shall we say." Both men laughed at that.

"Well, that's one problem we shan't face on this trip," Edward assured her. "The drives are pretty much done with winter coming. And our own trip will be a quick one, of course. Five weeks, perhaps six, but no more, and much of that spent simply getting to the border crossings in Loville." He looked at Parno.

"That is one drawback of being so far into the countryside, milord," he informed the younger man. "True, we could follow the trade route, but that would take us days to the west, before turning north. Despite the difficulty of following the smaller routes to Loville, we actually make a faster trip this way."

"How are the roads in Norland, Duke?" Parno asked, suddenly curious.

"Oh, they aren't bad, really," Edward waved a hand. "Not up to the trade routes that your Father maintains for us, here, to be sure. Nor even, in all honesty, equal to most of our secondary routes. But the winters there can be harsher than ours and I'm told that takes its own toll on roadways."

"The roads are at least well designed," he went on, "and their intersections are well planned with alternate routes around most towns for use by large parties such as ours. If we don't intend to stop in a town, we can use their by-pass roads to go around and avoid the inevitable snarls of carrying large numbers of wagons and men into a small area. That, I admit, is good engineering."

"Perhaps you should mention this to my Father," Parno suggested. "It sounds like something that would be a long ended project, but ultimately worthwhile." Edward looked at him for a moment, then nodded.

"Why, I hadn't thought of that, Milord, but it's an excellent suggestion! I will do just that when we return! Edema, dear, remind me to have some sketches made of the routes we take, as well." Parno suppressed a smile, having just given Edema an excellent cover for doing his bidding on the trip.

"I shall do that, Edward," she nodded, winking at Parno. The Prince raised his glass to her and then his host before hiding his smile behind it.

Well, that went well.

-

"Please be careful, Lord and Lady," Parno said formally as he prepared to leave. "I have grown very fond of visiting here. Return quickly."

"Oh, it's a short trip," Edward assured him. "And safe, as well. We have guards, and the Nor patrol the trade routes heavily. Very little banditry along them."

"Then enjoy the trip," Parno smiled. "I will see you again when you return." With that he headed down the steps. Edward watched him go, then turned to Edema.

"Quite a charmer, isn't he?" he said, his voice conversational.

"He can be," she smiled, not looking at Edward at the moment. "I have to find him a wife, Edward," she turned to look at him then, only to find him looking at her.

"Oh?" he asked. "And why is that?"

"Why, because he needs one!" Edema replied at once. "He's a man grown, and no one to care for him. He needs a wife to look after him."

"It seems to me that you're looking after him quite well, dear."

"What do you mean by that?" she spluttered.

"Just that you seem to have taken a great interest in our wayward Prince," Edward shrugged. "You dote upon him as would his mother. Which, considering how hard it's been for him without her, is a good thing, and now you want him married. He can take care of himself, I imagine."

"Well," Edema almost huffed, looking back at the departing Parno. "He has had it terribly hard in many ways, and I admit, it's good for me, as close as I was to his mother, to care for him any way I can. It's like I'm doing one last thing for Margolynn and I like it."

"Then by all means, find him a wife," Edward smiled, leaning in to kiss her cheek. "I must get back. Still a lot to do before we can leave and I am glad you decided to come along. The trip is always better when you're present." With that, Edward headed down to the walk to his waiting horse.

Edema watched him go, then returned to the house. She had preparations of her own to make.

-

Unaware that his matrimonial status was deemed 'ready to change', Parno rode back toward Cove Canton in silence, his mind working over various things. Chief among them the Nor.

He was sure, after speaking to Edema and the Tinker, that the Nor were using their diplomatic exchanges to hide a military build-up. That in and of itself was a cause for concern, but it wasn't proof that they were contemplating an attack upon Soulan.

On the other hand, why else would they build up their army? It could be that they were thinking of invading the Coastal provinces. More of a coalition that a true nation or kingdom, the United Coastal Provinces banded together for military aid, and little else. Outside defensive matters, each Province ruled itself, had its own leadership.

Soulan had always had a good relationship with the 'Coasties'. For over five hundred years Soulan had also been a member of their mutual aid treaties as well. Should the Nor, or anyone else, attack the UCP, then Soulan would march to their aid.

Was that the reason for Norland's diplomatic maneuvers with the south? Would the King risk the new trade and travel agreements made with the Nor to help the Coastal Provinces against a Nor invasion? Parno didn't know the answer to that. He doubted that Tammon did either. He doubted if his father had considered that.

But, Parno allowed, he might have. Despite the fact that he and his father did not get along very well, Parno knew that his father wasn't a fool by any stretch of the imagination. And Memmnon was, if anything, even more canny, more savvy, than their father was. So it was at least possible that one or both of them had considered the possibility. If they had, Parno wondered what decision they had come to in the event of such a scenario.

Still, Parno couldn't help but feel that the Nor were aiming more at Soulan. First, anyway. If they could defeat Soulan, then the UCP would have little chance, alone, of opposing the Nor when they attacked. They would fight, Parno was certain. But ultimately they would lose.

No, if Norland was contemplating war it would be against Soulan. Nothing else made sense. If he, Parno, were leading the Nor and wanted to bring the rest of the continent under his control, he would certainly start with his strongest enemy. With the largest, most powerful opponent defeated, or at least subdued, the smaller ones would be much easier to overcome.

All of which made the information that Edema and the Tinker could gather that much more vital. Yet, whatever those two happened to see would only be a part of the overall picture. He needed more information. Confirmation of Norland's buildup from other sources if nothing else. Underlying all of his efforts Parno had to be mindful of the fact that he would have to be able to convince his father, and his brother, that the Nor were intending to attack. Two sources of information would not be enough.

He needed someone who could circulate among others who were traveling to the north. Trading, sightseeing, whatever their purpose, they would have seen things. Things that might mean nothing to them and might mean nothing at all if taken alone, but what about once they were added to what Parno already knew?

He knew someone who would be able to do what he needed.

-

Doak Parsons stepped into Parno's office quietly, clearing his throat to get the Prince's attention. Parno looked up at him, smiling.

"You wanted to see me, Prince?" Parsons asked.

"I did," Parno nodded, rising. "Come in, please. Close the door if you would, and take a seat. Beer?"

"Beer would go mighty fine, sir," Parsons smiled, closing the door as ordered. He took the bottle Parno retrieved from the barrel and sat down across from the Prince. Parno looked at him for a moment.

"Your health, Mister Parsons," Parno raised his bottle.

"And yours, milord," Parsons returned the salute, careful not to drink until the Prince did.

"How are you and your men doing, Doak?" Parno asked.

"We're fine, milord," Parsons didn't try to hide his surprise. "Doin' right well, in fact. My boys are mostly teaching horse skills to others, nowadays."

"Yes, I was glad to have you men for that," Parno smiled easily. "You've done well, too," he added.

"Thank you, milord," Parsons nodded.

"I need you to do something for me," Parno said finally. Parsons leaned forward, waiting.

"I want you and a few of your men to take a trip," Parno continued. "Visit odd and end places in Kenty, here in Tinsee. I want. . ." Parno paused, thinking of how he wanted to word things.

"I want you to speak to people that have recently traveled in the Nor lands. See what they noticed while they were there. Where their troops were, what they were doing, how they acted. That sort of thing. Also," he added, "if they observed any of the Wild Tribes while they were there and what they might have been doing. I'd like you to leave as soon as possible." Parno reached into his desk, and withdrew a leather pouch, which he tossed across the desk to the former thief.

"This should cover your expenses," he smiled. "You'll need to buy a few drinks, I'd imagine. And you can stay inside rather than make camp. I want you back here in six weeks, give or take. Think you can handle that?"

Parsons looked at Parno for a moment, weighing the bag in his hand.

"Good bit o' money here, milord," he commented quietly. "Might just take it and run, ya know." Parno smiled.

"You might," he nodded, "but I don't think you will. You gave your word to be loyal. You might have been a thief, but I think you're a man of your word. And you did say I'd have need of men like you. Remember?" Parsons looked at him for a moment, then chuckled.

"That I did, milord," he nodded. "That I did. Mind if I ask why you're interested in all this?"

"I can't tell you," Parno shrugged. "I can't tell you because I don't know myself," he admitted. "I just have a feeling...a hunch, if you will. I need information. Until I know something, all I have is a hunch."

"All right," Parsons nodded. "I'll take a few boys and see what I can find. We'll leave first thing in the mornin', that's all right."

"Sooner the better," Parno agreed. "Don't press too hard," Parno cautioned, "and under no circumstances are you to cross the border. Just see what you can see. Don't discount anything you're told or that you see," Parno warned, "no matter how trivial it seems, I want to know."

Parsons finished his beer, rising.

"We'll see what we can see." With that the former horse thief was gone and Parno was once more alone in his office. He looked out his window for a time, thinking on what he'd done.

If his father ever found out what he was doing there would be hell to pay to say the least. His father would not be so understanding of his son's suspicions. In fact, even if Parno managed to acquire evidence that the Nor were planning something untoward the King would likely be inclined to ignore it, simply because of where it came from. Parno sighed.

It wasn't fair. He seldom allowed himself to engage in pity games. There was no point and it had never helped him before. He would have to find some way to convince his father to listen to him if his fears proved real.

If they didn't, then it wouldn't matter. Parno could relax and go back to living the life of comfort and leisure he had imagined when he'd taken this post. He didn't owe his father, nor any of his family, anything.

But he did owe Soulan and it was for that reason that he was willing to risk the anger of his father in order to safeguard the people of his kingdom. Because he owed his people.

And Parno McLeod paid his debts.

# CHAPTER ELEVEN

-

Doctor Stephanie Freeman-Corsin gazed out the window of the carriage, watching as the small fort grew steadily closer. For perhaps the tenth time she almost regretted her decision to answer Roda Finn's summons.

Freeman-Corsin was a physician of some renown in the world of medicine, despite the fact that she was a woman in what had become a man's world. She, however, was the latest in a very long line of physicians. Her family's medical legacy predated the Kingdom. In fact, the Freeman-Corsin's were able to trace their lineage back to before the Dying. As a result of that, the family's medical practice was generally regarded as the best in the Kingdom. Her own uncle, Clifford Flaherety Smithe was the Royal Physician.

She admitted that the offer presented by Finn had been. . .interesting. It also presented a challenge of no small size. A military hospital. Funding to pursue the study of medicine, including delving into the history of medicine from before the Dying, and, above all, the opportunity to serve her Realm. To support the work of the men who kept the Kingdom safe from threats. Her family's founding Patriarch and Matriarch had done so, as had any number of ancestors since then. Loyalty and patriotism ran deep in her family and none of them could have turned down this particular offer. House McLeod was descended from the House of Tyree, after all.

Still, the wonder of such a chance had worn thin after four bump-filled days on the road from Nasil to Cove and seeing the dirty collection of buildings ahead did nothing to brighten her mood.

The stockade was the dominant feature, of course, housing the fort itself. There were numerous houses outside the fortress, all in neat rows, with graveled streets laid out in neat squares and lines. She was slightly surprised to see lampposts along those streets, something she'd never have expected in such a far out-of-the-way place.

Of course, a member of the ruling family did make his home here, she reminded herself, even if it was Parno McLeod. She smiled thinly at that. The infamous Black Sheep of the McLeod Dynasty. Boy Prince playing soldier.

Everyone in Nasil society knew of Parno, of course. Hard drinking, hard fighting, womanizing, the list of 'crimes' went on and on. Her own mother, however, clucked at such gossip.

"Just a high-spirited boy, caught in a world that has no place for him," she'd said more than once. Stephanie could sympathize with that. Even with her family name and background, let alone her skill, she constantly met with opposition from the 'learned' men of her profession. She'd been told more than once that she was too 'delicate' for such work. Too beautiful and lady-like to lay hands on the sick and injured. She snorted at the idea.

While her pale complexion and dark hair did give her fresh-faced good looks a certain zest, she disdained the term 'beauty'. She was smart, and skilled. A highly intelligent woman, better at her chosen profession than at least ninety-eight percent of those 'learned men'. Her mother had often cackled with unrestrained glee at her daughter's often searing reply to such comments. No woman in her family would ever be denied a station as a physician, despite what anyone thought or said.

Even that irked the young woman. She shouldn't have to depend upon her name. No woman should. If she was capable of performing her job that should be all that mattered. That was one of the main reasons she's decided to come here to Cove Canton, to pursue an even more unorthodox career than simple physician. Here, she would be a military doctor. More than that, she would be the head of a military hospital that served a member of the ruling family.

That should put a crick in their stiff old necks, she thought with amusement. Which made coming here all the more worthwhile.

"We're arriving ma'am."

Startled from her reverie by the voice, she turned to the young lieutenant in charge of her escort detail.

"I see that, Lieutenant Caufield, thank you," she smiled. The young man nodded and rode on ahead. Stephanie sighed as the red-faced young officer rode stiffly away.

You have got to get a hold of that tongue, woman, she chided herself. She hadn't meant to sound disdainful, but, after all, she could see the bloody fort. Shaking her head, she gathered her things as the carriage pulled into the cantonment. Stopping in front of a building that a wooden sign proclaimed as 'Headquarters', the driver stepped down from the seat and opened her door.

Lieutenant Caufield offered her his hand in assistance, and she took it gracefully, trying to make up for her earlier retort.

"Thank you, Lieutenant."

"Service, ma'am," Caufield nodded curtly. He turned as an older man stepped out onto the portico of the Headquarters Office and saluted sharply.

"Freeman-Corsin detail returning, sir," he reported. "Party of one."

"Very good Lieutenant," the older man nodded, returning the salute. "See to your men and your horses. Your detail is excused for the rest of the day."

"Thank you, sir. Ma'am," He nodded again to Freeman-Corsin, then departed. The older man stepped down from the portico and offered his hand in greeting.

"Welcome to Cove Canton, Doctor. I'm Colonel Nidiad, commanding officer."

"You are?" Stephanie frowned, accepting the hand. "I thought that Prince Parno was in command."

"Aye, he commands the post," Nidiad smiled. "I command the Regiment in his name.

"I see," the confused doctor rallied. "At any rate, thank you, Colonel. It's been a long trip."

"I trust everything went well?" Nidiad inquired.

"Very well, thank you, just long. And bumpy," she added ruefully.

"That it is, miss, that it is," the colonel surprised her by chuckling. "If you wish, I'll escort you to your residence so that you can get settled in. After that, I'll summon the Prince, and Master Finn. I suspect they'll want to see you."

"That would be fine, Colonel," Stephanie smiled.

"Come this way, then," Nidiad ordered. "Greene, see to the lady's baggage."

"Yes, sir," the sergeant at the doorway acknowledge. "Right away."

-

One of Stephanie's worst apprehensions had been concerning her living quarters. Cove Canton was, to be blunt, in the middle of nowhere. She had worried, more than once, that she would be living in a tent.

Thus she was pleasantly surprised to find herself standing before a very neat looking house, complete with a small fence and flowers. She could see curtains in the windows and there were chairs on the small but comfortable front porch. Even a swing.

"Not quite what you were expecting?" Nidiad asked, amusement clear in his voice. She turned to face him, aware that her face had betrayed her surprise.

"I admit, I had wondered what living conditions would be like," she admitted, not quite shame faced. "I suppose. . .well, I don't know what I expected, Colonel."

"I understand," Nidiad nodded. "The Prince is extremely grateful to you for accepting his invitation. To you and to the others. His orders were that all of you were to be made a comfortable as was possible. He would be here himself to welcome you, save that he is currently meeting with some of the others who arrived before yourself."

"Others?"

"Aye, others," Nidiad smiled. "Several of Master Finn's contemporaries have likewise accepted the Prince's invitation. None are physicians such as yourself, mind you. Engineers, and the like. The Prince was intrigued by the notion that people were trying to reclaim technical information from the past. So much so that he has devoted a good deal of his own money to fund that work."

"We don't really study things that are useful to the military, by-and-large, Colonel," Freeman-Corsin said, a bit more primly than she had intended.

"He isn't interested in purely military applications, Miss," Nidiad's tone turned slightly frosty. "You'll find that Parno McLeod cares about nothing so much as his homeland and its people. If your work makes life easier for his people, then you will have his support. Your work will be militarily significant in that it will save the lives of his men, should they be injured, or wounded in combat. He takes his position as commander here very seriously."

"I'm sure he does," the young woman managed to stammer, red faced from the dressing down. "If you don't mind I'd like to freshen up a bit before meeting him."

"As you will. Here comes your luggage now. Your assistant should be inside."

"Assistant?"

"The wife of one of the soldiers," Nidiad explained. "Cook and maid, laundress and the like. The Prince wanted to make sure you were comfortable, and could apply yourself fully to your work, especially during the construction of the hospital."

"He's building a hospital?" the doctor blurted. "I assumed he would just use an existing structure."

"Not at all," the colonel assured her. "He has already selected the site for the building and acquired the materials. He waits only for your input before setting to work."

"I see," she replied, trying to recover from one surprise too many. "Well, then, I best see to my needs. I don't want to be the reason for any hold up."

"Good day, then, Miss." She watched the older man walk back toward the Headquarters offices, then turned again to look at 'her' house. Just as she started for the door, it opened. Standing inside it was a middle aged, pleasantly plump woman, smiling broadly.

"You'd be the lady doctor, I'd suspect," she said, her voice warm, and friendly. "I'm Maureen Downs, your cook and maid. I've the house ready for you, miss."

"I am the lady doctor," Stephanie smiled back, instantly liking the woman. "Please, call me Stephanie. I'm pleased to meet you."

-

"We of the Guild are not lackeys, milord, here to do your bidding on a royal whim!"

Professor Jason Pearl's normally jovial face was somewhat red at the moment. Having made the trip to Cove Canton all the way from Lana, he was both disappointed, and angry, to find that his skill and knowledge of engineering was being sought as a military weapon of sorts.

Facing Prince Parno, he had decided to make that known.

"Jason," Roda Finn interjected, "that's not the case at all. As I explained to you in my message, the Prince is interested in helping us to . . ."

"And you had no business revealing Guild business to the Prince without at least consulting one of us!"

"That will be quite enough," Parno McLeod's calm voice cut off Roda's rebuttal. "I'll remind you, sir, once, that I will tolerate only a certain amount of disdain and attitude in my own quarters, and you are near that limit."

As if suddenly remembering he was addressing a member of the ruling family, Pearl fell into silence. A sullen silence to be sure, but silence none-the-less.

"Now," Parno stood, walking around to lean upon his desk. "I did not request you, per se, Professor. I asked for someone skilled in engineering. Someone who could help me and to whom I could offer assistance to in return. Master Roda deemed you to be that someone, above any and all others he may know of with your background and experience. That should speak somewhat to the regard in which he holds you." Pearl's face reddened a bit more at that, this time in a bit of embarrassment.

"As to the 'lackey' business, I have no need of them. I do my own work, Professor. I didn't ask you here to 'do my bidding' as you so blithely put it. I asked you here because I'm interested in what you know and in what you can do. Further, I'm interested in assisting you, and others of your kind, in studying the past and reclaiming as much as possible from the workings of our ancestors."

"Roda has informed me that your. . . 'guild', as you call it, has sought Royal funding in the past for your research and been turned away. I cannot answer as to why that was so, and won't try. Nor can I, as a tertiary heir to the throne, grant you an all- encompassing grant to simply study what you wish. I don't have those resources or that authority at my disposal. I'm skating on thin ice as it is and funding most of this from my own pockets, which are not nearly so deep as my father's."

"What I want," Parno continued, "is someone who can train my Pioneers to do real engineering work. Build bridges, lay roads and trails, make maps, and so forth. I don't expect a man of your standing to go galloping around the country at my 'whim'. I have soldiers to do that, should the need arise. Understand?"

"Yes, milord," Pearl muttered, beginning to realize the depths of his mistake.

"Good," Parno nodded. "Now, what I can do, in return, is provide you with what authority I have to continue your research and provide the funds and means for you to do so. I can grant you access to any Royal or Provincial Library in the Kingdom, including the Royal Archives in Nasil. I've no idea, to be honest, what you're looking for, but I do know that the Royal Library, which the Archives are a part of, contains the most complete listing of pre-Dying books anywhere. Not all of them are located in Nasil, but they will be somewhere you can access in most cases."

"Those in private hands might prove harder to get to, and there's likely no way to secure them, but a letter of introduction from me, as my personal engineer and archivist, could possibly gain you access to some of them as well. Correct?"

"That is. . .very likely, milord. Yes," Pearl nodded, his enthusiasm growing, while his anger diminished. "That would be most helpful."

"Then consider this," Parno smiled for the first time since being introduced to the man. "The Royal Family maintains quarters in every Provincial Capital. I rarely make use of them myself, but I have the authority to grant you privileges in those quarters as my guest. I can provide you with an escort to ensure your safety, and with funds to purchase needed materials. You may then pursue your quest for knowledge wherever it leads you. All I ask in return are two things."

"First, I need my Pioneers trained as highly as possible, by you. I need them to be able to do the things I mentioned earlier. Not necessarily up to the skill of a true engineer, at least not at first, but well enough that if I need a bridge erected ahead of my column, they can get it done. Safely," he added. Pearl nodded.

"Secondly, I want whatever you discover that can ease the life of our people put to good use. I'm not interested in just the military aspect of your Guild's activities. I want the lives of our people to be better, longer, and more productive. Medicine and medical practices will certainly play a great role in that, but so do other things. Better bridges, better roads, stronger and better buildings are just a few of those areas which interest me, Professor."

Parno went still for a moment, studying the other man. Finn squirmed slightly, but remained silent, allowing Pearl to contemplate what he had been told. To his credit, the engineer smiled.

"Firstly, I must offer an apology, milord," he spoke firmly. "I'm afraid your reputation preceded you, and I jumped to a conclusion. A wrong one."

"You aren't the first, I assure you," Parno laughed in genuine humor. "And, I'm honest enough to admit that most of that reputation is richly deserved. That does not, however, mean that I can't have a serious side, so to speak. I love my land, Professor, and my people. I will never be King and don't want to be. I'm not interested in a 'legacy'. All I'm trying to accomplish is to leave this world, or at least our part of it, better off than I found it. I believe that people like you, with my help, can accomplish that far better than someone like me."

"I see your point, milord," Pearl nodded. "I see it, and agree. At first I thought. . .well, never mind what I thought. I was wrong. That's all that matters. So yes, milord, I will train your engineers, or Pioneers, or whatever you wish to call them, and will be honored to do so."

"Excellent!" Parno beamed. "I'll set to work at once gathering the best men I can find. What sort of men would make the best candidates? My original plan was to merely have a company of my own trained, but as I think of it, I'd also like to train a core of officers, educated men, who can go back on to other units and share what they learn with still more men."

"A good plan," Pearl nodded. "Well, the ideal candidate. . .hmm. . . ." Pearl fell silent for a moment, clearly thinking about the question.

"I'd say that the men you plan to train for your 'core' group should have strong math skills, certainly. That's one of the most important things, of course," Pearl began after a moment. "Certainly, a degree of experience in the engineering needs of a military unit on the move would be likewise helpful. Some skill in geology, the study of the earth itself," Pearl explained, "would also be a great help. One needs to know the best foundations for buildings and bridges. I assume the military has its own map makers?"

"Yes," Parno nodded. "Men who are skilled surveyors."

"Another handy skill," Pearl nodded. "A few of them should be included to form your training group. . .may I make a suggestion?"

"Of course," Parno replied eagerly. "You're the authority here, Professor."

"Firstly, a question. The men you have doing these jobs now, in the military I mean, how are they trained?"

"Well," Parno mused, "mostly within the Army itself. The War Academy trains officers in certain areas of expertise, of course. Men who have the qualities you just mentioned, especially the math. But by-and-large, training is accomplished by those who are already doing the work in the field. As new men come into the units, they simply learn to do what the men before them have done. There's nothing inherently wrong with the system," Parno added. "It's just not as complete as it should be, in my opinion. For large tasks, the Royal Engineers are used, of course. But there aren't many of them and they can only do so much at a time and not to mention that we can hardly expect to use them in a pinch."

The Royal Engineers were highly skilled men, many of them tradesmen, who both maintained the existing infrastructure of the Kingdom and performed new construction needs. Their schedule was laid out years in advance, with major projects sometimes being planned a full decade ahead of time. They did excellent work, but their projects were more along civilian lines than military.

"True," Pearl nodded. "Then my suggestion would be to create a school where your military engineers, or Pioneers as you call them, can be trained by the best minds in your military. Men already uniquely suited to the needs of a military unit, especially one in the field, on the move, so to speak. I will take those men and raise their standard of training even higher so that they can pass along that knowledge to others in both a classroom setting and in field work. You can use projects here in this area as work and test beds, allowing them to get hands on experience, while serving the greater good as well."

"Outstanding," Parno beamed. "I hadn't thought that far along. Now, professor, do you see why I wanted someone like you? In just a few minutes you've taken a simple idea that I had, and turned it into something not only far better, but longer ended. Such a facility could well train new generations of Pioneers for decades to come."

"Well, it wasn't that far a leap, really," Pearl murmured in a self-depreciating tone.

"But I wouldn't have thought of it," Parno pointed out. "Thank you, Professor. May I assume by your suggestion that you will undertake this project?" Pearl looked at Parno for a moment, then stood, drawing himself up to his full five feet and six inches.

"Yes, milord," he said formally. "I will."

-

"It's not like I'm a bloody gypsy, Roda!"

Roda Finn snorted at that. Hiram Wiggins was one of his oldest friends, the two of them having studied together years before as idealistic young men. Wiggins had studied chemistry at first, then turned his attention to geology. Geology had led him to the study of what the ancients had termed 'meteorology', or the study of weather and weather patterns.

"I never said you were, Hiram," the fussy chemist sighed. "And I didn't tell the Prince you were, either. He asked if anyone I knew was a weather expert, and if so, would I invite them to meet with him. Nothing more."

"What would the Prince want with me?" Wiggins asked, perplexed. Finn sighed again. For all his brilliance in books, Hiram had a true knack for overlooking the obvious.

"You predict weather patterns, Hiram," he explained patiently. "Don't you think that if the Prince were taking the field with his regiment, it might be well for him to have some idea what the weather would be like for him? Whether he could expect rain, or snow, or clear weather? Whether there was a chance it might turn cold or unexpectedly warm so that his men might be better prepared, and not carry things they don't need, or not carry things they do?"

"Oh," Wiggins said softly, scratching his head. "I hadn't thought of that."

"I know," Roda nodded. "Nor had I, really. Prince Parno is rather intelligent, despite what you may have heard to the contrary."

"I really hadn't heard anything," Wiggins shrugged. "I know who he is, of course. Everyone does, I imagine."

"He's a good man," Finn told him, "and as smart a young man as I have ever met. A long thinker, too." Wiggins stared at Finn. So long as he had known Roda Finn, the man's compliments were spare, as if he only had so many for a lifetime and he was parceling them out with great care. If Finn thought the Prince was a 'long thinker', or someone who thought in terms of years rather than months or weeks, then there was more to him than his title, that was certain.

"Well, I'm here, anyway," Wiggins finally shrugged again. "What is it you wish of me?"

"It's actually more a question of what you wish of him," Finn smiled. "What do you need to determine your weather patterns?"

"Well," Wiggins mused, "the most important thing is information, of course. Data from the field in a timely manner. Only there's no real way to get it, at least not quick enough to matter. If, for instance, I knew what the temperature and barometer was in Loville, right now, then I could predict what the weather might be here within a day or so, but you see the problem with that, I suspect? I can't get the information soon enough to matter. By the time a rider could get here, the information would be hopelessly out of date."

"Hm," Finn nodded. "Yes, I can see that. Very well. For short term weather we need a constant source of data. What about long term?"

"Well, we have the historical record, of course," Wiggins was warming to his subject now. "Basing what has happened before on what conditions are like today. For instance, I can tell you that there's no rain in the offing at this location for at least three days. Probably longer, but at least three days."

"How can you know that?" Parno McLeod asked, walking into the room as Wiggins made his prediction. Wiggins turned sharply, while Finn merely rose to his feet.

"Milord, this is Hiram Wiggins. He is an expert in weather prognostication. Hiram, allow me to introduce Prince Parno McLeod, of the House McLeod."

"Milord," Hiram bowed. "Pleasure," he murmured, unsure of himself.

"Pleasure is mine, Mister Wiggins," Parno smiled, offering his hand. The small weatherman looked nonplussed for a second, then awkwardly grasped the young Royal's hand.

"Now," Parno took a seat, "please tell me how you can know we won't have rain for at least three days. I'm not challenging you," Parno raised a hand in assurance. "I'm just curious."

"Well," Wiggins scratched his head absently. "Well, milord, there are several things. Firstly, there's the barometer. The amount of pressure in the air. It's rather high here at the moment, which you can thank for the slight wind, and the clear sky. High pressure dominating the area will keep weather patterns at a standstill for a few days."

"Secondly, is the hydrometer, or the measure of humidity, water vapor, present in the atmosphere. It's low at the moment, below twenty percent. Very dry. Thirdly, the wind, for the moment, is from the north to northwest. Very little moisture will come from that direction. Most of our rainfall is dictated by the flow of moist air from the Gulf of Storms, milord. Without that moisture in the air, there's no rain."

"Fascinating," Parno shook his head. "Roda, it seems you were quite correct about Mister Wiggins."

"Of course I was," Finn almost huffed, then added, "milord." Parno laughed.

"So, what can I do to help you advance your study of weather patterns, Mister Wiggins?"

"As I was explaining to Roda, milord, the most important thing is data from the field. If I know what the conditions are in Loville, the example I used earlier, then I can predict, with fair accuracy, what we might expect in the next thirty-six to forty-eight hours. The problem. . . ."

"The problem being that there's no way to know what it's like in Loville in time to matter," Parno nodded, finishing for him.

"That's the rub, milord," Wiggins agreed, surprised. Parno McLeod was, indeed, smarter than the average person. "It's just not possible to gather that information."

"True," Parno mused. "I'll work on it." Parno stood.

"What can you do, milord?" Wiggins asked, puzzled.

"No idea," Parno admitted, heading for the door, "but we'll come up with something. Welcome to Cove Canton, Mister Wiggins."

"Well," Roda sighed, standing, "you've met the benefactor, Hiram. Are you interested?"

"I guess," Wiggins shrugged, scratching his head. "Be interesting to see what he does."

"Well, let's see to getting you settled, then," Roda motioned to the door. "You'll like the accommodations, I should think. Very nice, with room for your wife and child."

"Huh," was Wiggins' only comment. Roda rolled his eyes.

"Come along, Hiram."

-

Parno made his way toward the guest quarters, cursing the blind luck that had all three of his visitors arriving on the same day. Not that he wasn't grateful they had responded to Roda's request, for he was. He just wished they had arrived a day apart, so that he hadn't needed to use an entire afternoon welcoming them, not to mention seeing what their needs were and how he could meet them.

As he approached the small collection of houses he'd had erected for the newest additions to Cove Canton, a young woman emerged onto the porch of one of the houses. The Doctor's house, he remembered, and hadn't Roda mentioned that. . . .

"You there!" the woman called to him. Surprised, Parno looked around him.

"Yes, you," the woman informed him. "Come here, please." Parno stood for just a second, then, with a half-smile playing on his lips, walked directly to the house.

"Can you tell me where I can find Prince McLeod?" the woman demanded. "He was supposed to meet me, but I've yet to see him."

"You have now," Parno told her, smiling. The woman looked nonplussed for a moment, then blushed.

"You're Parno McLeod, then? Prince McLeod?" she asked, her speech more subdued now.

"I am, indeed," Parno bowed graciously, "and I apologize, milady. I assume you are Doctor Freeman-Corsin?"

"Please, milord, call me Stephanie," the woman blushed again. "I apologize as well. I. . .”

“Quite all right, Stephanie, I assure you,” Parno smiled, walking up onto the porch, “and please, call me Parno. We are far from Nasil and I care little for formal address, save in a formal setting. I’m sorry I wasn’t here sooner, but several people decided to arrive here today and I’m having to make rounds to see all of you.”

“I remember,” she nodded. “Colonel Nidiad told me I wasn’t the only one who had been invited here. Please, take a seat,” she waved. She and Parno settled easily onto the comfortable porch chairs. Before they were settled, Mrs. Downs appeared on the porch.

“Can I get you some tea, milord? St. . .Doctor Corsin?”

“Hello, Maureen,” Parno smiled. “Water for me, thanks.”

“Milord?” Downs dimpled in a smile.

“Same for me, please, Maureen,” Stephanie nodded, watching how at ease Parno made the woman. The two exchanged pleasantries until Mrs. Downs returned with their glasses and a pitcher, before disappearing into the house once more.

“You know her well?” Stephanie asked.

“Barely at all, I fear,” Parno shook his head. “Her husband is one of my troopers. She’s a very nice woman, however. A good person.”

“I believe so as well,” Stephanie nodded. “Do you make a habit of using the spouses of your soldiers as menial labor?” Parno blinked at that.

“When we can,” he replied carefully, knowing that this woman was somehow upset over Mrs. Downs being here, but with no idea why.

“How very noble of you,” Stephanie didn’t quite sneer. Parno blinked again.

“I’m sorry? I thought you liked her. If there’s a problem, we can find someone else. I thought she’d be perfect for the job, but. . . .”

“I can’t believe that you would force a soldier’s wife into serving one of your staff!” Stephanie exclaimed.

“Force her?” Parno was still reeling. “I didn’t force her! The job was posted on the board in town and she was the best qualified applicant!”

“What?” It was Stephanie’s turn to blink in surprise.

“Mrs. Downs!” Parno called loudly, standing. The woman was at the door in seconds.

“Yes, milord?” she asked.

“Mrs. Downs, how was it you come by this position? For the Doctor’s enlightenment, please,” he added at the woman’s obvious surprise.

“Why, I saw it posted and applied for it, Miss,” Downs turned to the doctor. “Myself and several others were interviewed by the wives panel and I was selected. Have I erred in some way?” Downs looked worried now. Stephanie, her face red, shook her head as she tried to find some way out of the hole she had dug for herself.

“Not in any way, Maureen,” Stephanie managed to croak out. “I was simply. . .I was just curious. I am lucky to have you,” she added, “and thankful.”

“Thank you, miss,” Maureen curtsied slightly. “Will there be anything else, milord?"

"No, ma'am, thank you," Parno smiled, and she blushed in pleasure, returning to the house.

"Milord, I. . . ."

"I think I shall take my leave, good doctor," Parno said stiffly. "Should you be interested in discussing anything with me, you may call upon me at my office. I assume that Colonel Nidiad spoke to you concerning the hospital?"

"Milord, I… yes, he did," Stephanie nodded.

"If you decide to stay, then when you have a design that works for you, please bring it to the Colonel and he will see to it that the hospital is built to your specifications. If you need anything at all, please let the Colonel know. He will see to it. Good day, doctor," Parno bowed, stiff with anger, and started down the steps.

"Milord, I am sorry!" Stephanie bolted from her chair, coming to the stairway herself.

"As am I," Parno replied over his shoulder, stalking back toward the Headquarters building. "Good day, doctor."

Stephanie watched his walking away, silently cursing her tongue. She had assumed. . .and assuming was never a good thing for a doctor. Sighing, she retreated to the house.

It had been a long day. Perhaps tomorrow would be better.

# CHAPTER TWELVE

-

"Mornin' lad," Darvo greeted Parno. "What's eatin' at you this fine mornin'?" Parno scowled at the older man as he sat down at the table where Darvo was just starting his morning meal.

"Don't start on me this early," Parno warned, accepting a cup of hot coffee from a mess steward with a nod of thanks. He sipped at the warm liquid.

"Breakfast, milord?" the steward asked. Parno nodded.

"Please, Mister Gaines."

"Be up hot in a minute, sir," Gaines nodded, and scurried away.

"Y'know, lad, your mornin' manners are gettin' worse all the time," Darvo chided with a grin.

"Well, I'll work on that if it happens that I get the chance," Parno grumped. He rubbed his temple, trying to get rid of a headache.

"Bit too much to drink last evening?" Darvo asked, his face a mask of innocence. Parno frowned at him.

"No, I didn't drink anything. I went to bed mad and woke up with a headache."

"Ah," Darvo nodded in understanding. "Might want to see that new doctor. She's supposed to be a near miracle worker, 'corrdin' to Finn, and a right pretty lass, I'll. . .what?" Darvo broke off as Parno's frown deepened.

"The doctor was the reason I went to bed mad," Parno snorted. "Besides, coffee and a good meal will soon set me to rights." As he spoke, Gaines set a tray before him with ham, eggs, and potatoes. Parno smiled.

"Thank you, Mister Gaines. A feast fit for a. . .well, a Prince," he laughed.

"Thank you, milord," Gaines beamed, then departed. Darvo waited as Parno gave thanks, then dug into his meal with a gusto.

"So what happened with you and the doctor?" the older man inquired. "You didn't try to. . . ."

"No, I didn't," Parno looked indignant. "Give me just a little credit, Darvo, if you can spare it."

"Don't get lippy," Darvo shot back. "So what did happen? She seemed okay to me. A bit stiff necked, but then she had just endured a bumpy coach ride from Nasil."

"I went to see her after meeting with Pearl and then Wiggins," Parno said around a mouthful of breakfast. "She accused me of forcing Mrs. Downs to be her 'servant'. Was in the middle of dressing me down for it...and I didn't like it," he added, almost sulking.

"Did you explain -?"

"I did better than that," Parno grinned in triumph. "I had Mrs. Downs do it. Showed her," he muttered, stabbing at his food. "I told her to see you when she was ready to build her hospital, if she decided she wanted to stay. I don't want anything to do with that woman from now on, Darvo. You deal with her and see to it that she gets whatever she needs. If she stays."

"You think she won't?" Darvo asked, surprised. It wasn't like Parno to be so angry over a misunderstanding like this.

"I don't know," Parno shrugged, "or care, right this minute. If her attitude stays so piss poor, then she can go and be damned for all I care. We'll get someone else if she wants to go home, and be thankful for it."

"You know she graduated top of her class from Nasil School of Physicians, don't you?" Darvo asked, studying his charge with interest. "Not likely find another so smart as her, lad, willing to even come and take a look."

"We'll get by," Parno muttered.

"I'll see her after breakfast then," Darvo sighed. "See what she intends."

"Just keep her away from me," Parno ordered.

-

Darvo left the mess hall, heading to Doctor Corsin's residence. He shook his head in wonder. Despite everything that had happened as they worked to bring things together, Parno had taken it all in stride, never getting angry, or rattled. Now, one pretty woman comes to camp and he was stiff necked enough that if he fell, Darvo was sure the Prince would break somewhere.

"Every time I think I have that boy figured, he goes and changes on me," he muttered under his breath. As he approached the cabin, he saw Maureen Downs emerge, taking a seat on the porch. She stood again as Darvo made his way up the walk.

"Good morning, Colonel," she smiled. "What can I do for you?"

"Wanted to see was the good doctor up and about, ma'am," Darvo answered. "See what she was going to do about staying with us or not, and if so, what she needed doing."

"She's at breakfast, Colonel," Downs told him. "If you'll wait, I'll see. . . ."

"Maureen, who is. . .oh, good morning, Colonel," Stephanie said from behind the screen door. "Won't you come in? I was just eating my breakfast."

"Don't want to interrupt, ma'am," Darvo told her. "My business can wait until your meal is finished."

"Oh, don't be silly," Stephanie told him, swinging the door open. "Please, come in." Darvo paused only a minute before entering the small house. Mrs. Downs resumed her place on the porch as the two made their way to the small dining area.

"Please, sit," Stephanie waved to a chair opposite herself. "Coffee?"

"No thank you, ma'am," Darvo shook his head. "Just left the mess, myself."

"So, what can I do for you?" Corsin asked, returning to her meal.

"I just wanted to see had you decided whether or not you would be staying on with us, Doctor," Darvo replied. "And if so, what you might be in need of. We're ready to build, of course, if you already know what you need in the way of a hospital building." The young woman paused, looking at him.

"I don't know, Colonel," she admitted. "I'm afraid I put my foot in my mouth rather nicely with the Prince yesterday. He left here rather angry at me. I don't know that he wants me to stay."

"He does, if you want to," Darvo assured her. "He told me this morning to see that you get whatever you need and to start constructing a hospital as soon as you laid out how you want it."

"So he isn't angry with me?" Stephanie asked. Darvo fidgeted a bit.

"He is, isn't he?" she pressed, seeing the older man's discomfort. Darvo nodded.

"Aye, lass, that he is," Darvo admitted. "Your notion that he had forced Mrs. Downs to serve you left him winded. At the moment he wants nothing to do with you, unless it's absolutely needful."

"Oh," the young woman replied quietly. "I tried to apologize, of course, but. . . ."

"But he was mad, and kept walking," Darvo nodded. "I know the lad all too well, Miss. You hit a raw nerve within him with your notion of 'servitude'. Parno McLeod isn't one to engage servants at all, Miss Corsin. He allows others to do some things, like caring for his horses when he returns from a ride because his time is needed elsewhere, but when he's training, he does his own work. He takes mess, meals that is, with his men on most days. If they're out training, sleeping on the ground, then so is he. When they march, on foot, he goes as well."

"Really?" Corsin's eyes widened at that information. "But. . .he's a Prince of the Realm for God's sake! Why is he behaving like that?"

"He's a soldier, ma'am," Darvo pointed out to her, his own voice a bit stiff now. "These men, many of them, are outlaws, convicted criminals. Yet they are loyal to him to a fault. He's done more for them than anyone they've ever encountered, Royal or otherwise, and they respect him for it. They also respect him for sharing their hardships even though he's of no obligation to do so. He asks nothing of his men that he's not willing to do, or endure, himself."

"One of the arrangements he made when he brought these men here, along with their families if they had them, was that jobs here at Cove Canton would go to dependents of the soldiers on the post. Wives, children, what have you. Many of the soldiers have sons and they work in the stables, storerooms, and warehouses. Wives and daughters run the store, the canteen, and the recreation hall. All paid positions, ma'am, including the Board of Wives, which handles the selection process for jobs on the post."

"I know about that," Stephanie nodded. "Now, anyway. I didn't when I spoke so harshly. I'm afraid I let what others had said of Parno McLeod form my opinion for me, long before I ever received an invitation to come here."

"You aren't the first, nor likely the last, to do that, Miss," Darvo nodded, his look grim. "But if that's how you feel, then perhaps it's best you don't stay. I won't say we'll be better off, because I don't think we will. But if you can't be open minded, then it's likely best you don't stay. You won't last long here, anyway, with a poor opinion of the Prince. There's very few in this encampment who don't look up to him. They aren't likely to take kindly to harsh words about 'their' Prince, if you take my meaning."

"I. . .I didn't mean it that way," Stephanie blushed, "and I would never say anything about a member of the Royal Family in public," she said more forcefully.

"I wouldn't recommend saying it in private, either," Darvo cautioned. "Word travels. There are few secrets on an Army post." He leaned forward.

"We need you, or someone like you, Miss Corsin, This unit was formed to bear the brunt of any Nor invasion. Their casualties are likely to be horrendous should war break out. We need trained field surgeons and we need someone like you to train them, to show them things not normally taught that might help save the lives of our troopers and to promote good health here in the camp, for that matter."

"But we aren't at war!" Stephanie objected. "And we aren't likely to be with things so good between us and Norland. Aren't you really training for something that won't happen?"

"I'd like to hope so," Darvo admitted. "I've seen war, and would not like to see it again. But trusting the Nor isn't something that I can do, Doctor Corsin, nor can the Prince. It is our job to be ready for anything and that includes an attack by the Nor. If we failed to prepare and an attack did come, then we would be as guilty of treason as anyone who ever betrayed the throne. It's that simple."

Freeman-Corsin studied the Colonel for a long time, weighing his words against her own thoughts. While it seemed ridiculous that anyone would be thinking of war when relations between Soulan and Norland had never been better, the Colonel had a point. It was their job to prepare and be ready for such an event should it occur, just as it would be her responsibility to ensure that the men who defended the Kingdom had the best care possible. But, she had to consider how effective she could be here after she had so completely alienated the Prince. That had been no one's fault but her own, she admitted. Her mother's words came back to her then, 'just a high spirited boy, caught in a world that has no place for him'.

Like many high spirited men, Parno McLeod had his pride. Talking with the Colonel she could see that the stories everyone told about the youngest Prince, while probably true in themselves, meant nothing when stacked against his actions here. She herself certainly had no right to assume some of the things she had when speaking with him the day before.

If she returned to Nasil, she would simply continue her own practice, seeing rich and influential patients, treating people for various ailments, real and imagined. But if she remained in Cove Canton, she would have time to study more of the ancient art of medicine, applying what she knew, and what she could learn, where it would do a great deal more good. She would also be training field surgeons to care for wounded men in the field.

Everything she might do here would matter. She looked at Colonel Nidiad.

"I will stay, I think, Colonel," she said at last. "I'll run your hospital, and I'll train your surgeons, and care for your people."

"I'm glad to hear it," Darvo smiled. "We'll start on your building as soon as you are ready."

-

Within a week, the shell of the new hospital was standing. Parno had selected a good site for it, and Freeman-Corsin had seen no reason to change it. Prevailing winds would help keep the air fresh in the hospital and the slight rise would be good for drainage.

Darvo had kept the crews at it long and hard, wanting the building to be up well before the worst of winter hit. Another crew was beginning on a smaller building to be used by Professor Pearl to teach his engineering studies. His first class would be Parno's own Pioneer Company, men who would need experience in bridges, buildings, road laying, map making, surveying, and more. Once Pearl was finished with them, they should be able to do anything Parno required.

Hiram Wiggins required no building of his own, merely an office in which to work. His trade was helpful within the second week of arrival, as he warned Darvo of coming rain within two days. Fore-warned, Darvo had his crews work long hours the next two days, and when the rain hit, everything was covered, protected from the weather.

Darvo was forced to admit, things were looking fairly well, for once.

-

Parno was at his desk when Sprigs tapped on the door. Looking up, Parno waved the young man in.

"Courier message for you, sir," Sprigs informed him, laying the sealed message in Parno's hand. The Prince noted at once that the seal was Memmnon's.

"Thanks, Harrel," he nodded. As the secretary retreated from the office, Parno broke the seal. As he read, his face grimaced a bit.

Inside, Memmnon, in terse language, called him to Nasil to explain his recent expenditures and costs. Blunt and to the point, the message conveyed Memmnon's anger quite well, Parno decided. Sighing, he stood and walked outside. Sergeant Berry was standing just outside the Headquarters Building with two troopers from Parno's escort.

"Sergeant, we'll ride for Nasil on the morrow," Parno informed him. "Plan to stay for two, possibly three days. See to preparations for the trip. I want to be in the saddle at sunrise."

"Yes, sir," Berry saluted, then started giving orders to his two subordinates. Parno walked out to where Darvo stood supervising the building process. He saw Parno coming and walked a short way to meet him.

"I have to go to Nasil," Parno told him. "Memmnon wants an 'accounting' of the money I've spent so far. I knew this would come, of course, but I had hoped to be a bit further along when it happened. To have something to show, so to speak."

"Hospital will be done before you return," Darvo promised, "and it's a legitimate expense on a post this size as is the doctor and her staff. The school may be more tricky, mind you," the older man observed. "To say nothing of Roda Finn's gadgetry."

"I know," Parno nodded, "but I'm confident that Memmnon will at least give me a fair hearing. Whether he allows me to remain, that's something else again. I need a readiness report from you on the progress of the troops, to show that their training is on course."

"Ahead, really," Darvo nodded, "the men are actually far above where a similar unit of recruits would be by now."

"You seem surprised," Parno commented.

"I am surprised," the older man admitted. "Pleasantly so, mind you, but surprised none-the-less."

"Make sure that's in the report," Parno chuckled grimly. "I need all the help I can get."

-

"If I'm not on trial for regicide, I should be back in a week. Ten days at most," Parno said. Darvo looked up at his charge, scowling.

"That's enough o' that fool talk, lad," he ordered stiffly. Parno just laughed.

"Very well, old man," he chided in good humor. "Seriously, I think this is just going to be a simple meeting. Once I show him our progress I don't think Memmnon will have any serious objection to our operations here. We've justified most everything very well."

"Just don't get your dander up lad is all I'm saying," Darvo warned him. "You know they'll try to rile you. Master Feng, I'm depending on you to see to it that the lad minds his manners. What he has of 'em, at least," he added with a wicked chuckle.

"I shall, indeed, good Colonel," Feng grinned, eying Parno with much the same wicked look. "He shall be as tame as a lamb in the pens, I assure you."

"We'll see how likely that is!" Parno guffawed. He reached down to embrace Darvo's arm with his own.

"Take care, old friend," he said quietly. "I'll see you soon."

"Be safe, and good journey, lad," Darvo nodded, "and don't forget my daughter!" Darvo was finally ready for Dahlia to come to Cove Canton and Parno and his escort would bring her back on their return trip.

"I won't," Parno promised. He whirled his horse and nodded to Berry.

"Let's move out, Sergeant."

"Sir!" Berry saluted and bellowed for his scouts to head out. Three men headed out at a gallop, while the others followed along at a statelier pace.

Darvo watched them go, then headed for his own office. He had work to do before morning assembly.

-

Parno's trip to Nasil took only two days thanks to good weather. It was unseasonably warm with winter so near and their travel was comfortable. They exchanged mounts at a courier station near the half-way point. Parno had sent a good selection of horses to the station as soon as he could and provided them with two extra men to help care for them. The Regiment's horses weren't used by the couriers and were always ready for use. Parno had thought that if he ever needed to reach Nasil in a hurry, this was a good way to see to it.

They had passed the night at the station, making camp under the stars, then started toward Nasil the next morning on fresh mounts. By dark they were in Nasil, though both men and horses were worn down from the ride.

Parno and his detail left their horses at the Palace stables with instructions that the horses be seen to after the long ride. Berry and his men then headed to the Transient Barracks, while Parno and Cho Feng made their way into the palace and Parno's apartments there. Parno had not yet fully undressed for a bath when a messenger summoned him to Memmnon's office as soon as possible.

Parno had taken the message, then taken his bath, dressing in clean attire. Leaving Cho Feng behind, Parno made his way to Memmnon's office, valise in hand, wondering what he could expect.

-

"Have you any idea how much money you've spent?" Memmnon seethed in way of greeting.

"I'm fine, brother," Parno replied sarcastically. "Yes, it was a hard trip, but we managed to make it in two days. I had no desire to keep you waiting." Memmnon gaped at that a bit, then visibly calmed himself.

"You're right," the older Prince nodded. "That was uncalled for. A two day ride is fairly quickly."

"I keep horses at the courier station outside Cenevil," Parno shrugged. "We made camp there and came directly in today on fresh mounts. I received your message day before yesterday, well after noon. I departed at sunrise yesterday."

"You must be tired," Memmnon nodded. "Please, sit down." Parno nodded, taking his seat gratefully.

"I'm sorry I was so abrupt," Memmnon said, more calmly. "But you have been spending a good deal of money, Parno. I want to know why."

"I'm building a military post, Memmnon," Parno shrugged. "There's a good deal involved."

"I know that," Memmnon managed not to snap. "But the costs…what are you spending so much money on?"

"It's all here," Parno pulled a ledger from his valise and handed it over. "Every dime is accounted for, Memmnon. The post is entirely finished, save for two buildings. They will be finished before I return, weather permitting. Building materials, consumables, and of course payroll, are the top three expenses."

"How much is it costing to erect these buildings?" Memmnon asked.

"Nothing, save the material needs," Parno surprised him. "The men do the work, under supervision from carpenters and such. Any civilian labor is hired from the families that live on the post. Their houses were likewise built by the men."

"What sort of house did you build for yourself?" Memmnon asked with a snort.

"I didn't," Parno managed to say calmly. "There was an old house already on the grounds. I had the roof fixed, three broken windows replaced, and added a few furnishings as I hold most staff meetings there. My office is rather small," he added. Memmnon looked surprised, but nodded, continuing his perusal of the ledger.

"I have a hospital under construction," Parno continued. "I managed to get a young woman doctor, named Stephanie Freeman-Corsin, to attend the hospital. She is from here in. . . ."

"Who?" Memmnon looked up sharply. "Who did you say?"

"Doctor Stephanie Freeman-Corsin," Parno repeated.

"That's Physician Smithe's niece!" Memmnon almost shouted. "What in God's name is she doing on an Army Post in the middle of nowhere?"

"She's overseeing the construction of the hospital at present," Parno made the calm reply. "After that, she will begin training field surgeons and she will supervise the hospital as well."

"Parno, her family has served the Crown since Tyree!" Memmnon looked as if he would faint. "She's one of the most noted surgeons in Nasil, one of the best doctors in the Kingdom!"

"So I'm told," Parno nodded. "She came highly recommended," he added. Memmnon looked so aghast that Parno thought for a moment he'd be ill.

"Parno, I. . . ." Memmnon trailed off, unable to find words to sufficiently express his concern. His outrage. His disbelief.

"How did you manage to get her there," he finally managed.

"Just asked her to come take a look at the post and see if she would be interested in serving as the post physician. She studies a good deal of ancient medicine, as well, and I told her she would be free to pursue that study, so long as anything useful she found was shared with everyone. I think that was a major selling point, but I'm not sure of it."

"Parno, if anything happens to her -" Memmnon began.

"Like what?" Parno was puzzled. "I mean, her quarters are near mine, and there's a constant guard posted. Not to mention that the wives and children like her, which means the men like her. She's in less danger there than anywhere in the Kingdom."

"In a fort full of criminals?" Memmnon's voice was growing louder.

"They aren't all criminals, Memmnon." For the first time annoyance crept into Parno's voice. "And those that are wouldn't dare do anything that would result in their families being sent away. Some of them have it better than they ever have in their lives."

"What else have you done?" Memmnon asked, almost fearfully.

"I have engaged a number of civilian teachers, or instructors. One is an engineer, who is currently supervising the construction of a small school for military engineers. He will train my Pioneer Company, then, with your approval, he can start bringing others to Cove as well, training engineering officers in all manner of things. Bridge building, surveying, anything you like. Our ultimate goal is to establish a school where military engineers will be instructed in standard practices useful to military units on the move, or in camp. With military instructors who both have experience and have the advantage of Professor Pearl's training program."

"Really?" Memmnon showed real interest for the first time. "That's. . .that's not a bad idea, Parno."

"I thought not as well," Parno managed not to gloat. "As part of his salary, I have agreed to acquire permission for Professor Pearl to access any Royal Library for texts about ancient engineer practices and use the Royal Residence in any of the Provincial Capitals he travels to in order to do his research. Again, with the proviso that anything useful he gleans be made available to all."

"I admit, that's rather long sighted of you, brother," Memmnon said quietly. "What else are you doing?" Sensing that he might be winning Memmnon over, Parno went on, describing in detail the projects he had in the works.

"This Roda Finn," Memmnon asked, once Parno was finished. "What is it, exactly, that he's doing? I don't know if I caught the gist of it well enough."

"Basically, he's working on ways to make our artillery weapons more effective," Parno replied. "Through his own research, he has discovered an ancient formula to make a blasting powder, what he calls 'gunpowder'. It has explosive qualities that, if we can harness them, will make our weapons far more deadly and effective on the battlefield. You told me when you gave me this assignment that we must use every means we have. I'm pursuing that from every angle I can think of."

"So it appears," Memmnon nodded, clearly impressed. "I. . .I'm impressed Parno, really I am, but with all this time devoted to these things, what about your Regiment?" Parno reached into his valise again, pulling forth Nidiad's report.

"Here is a readiness report from Darvo," he said simply. "Darvo told me before he left that the men are actually ahead of their training schedule and doing quite well. That is especially true when you consider that we started with men who had not even had basic training. Most couldn't even ride a horse very well. Now, they can." Memmnon perused the report, noting that Darvo had praised the men for their hard work and the instructors as well. Never one to pull punches, he also noted that Nidiad had likewise berated certain areas of training that needed improvement and described what he was doing to correct the deficiencies. All in all, however, the report seemed more than satisfactory.

"Are you satisfied that I'm not wasting the Crown's money?" Parno asked finally.

Memmnon looked up at him.

"Yes," he answered after several seconds. "I admit, I didn't even conceive that you were doing so much, especially in so short a time. I was worried that you were just sitting there, milking the treasury."

"I have paid for a great many things from own pocket to avoid just such an accusation," Parno told his older brother quietly. Memmnon's eyebrows rose.

"Parno, that isn't necessary," he scolded. "I told you I would approve your expenses, so long as they were justified…and they are," he noted, laying Nidiad's report aside.

"Some things require hard money," Parno shrugged, not quite evasively. "Mine is all that I have, so I used it. I don't mind."

"Well, I do," Memmnon told him. "We are not a poor country, Parno, and I am not a skin flint. I expect you to be frugal, yes, but to me that simply means avoiding waste and getting the Crown's money's worth. You are clearly doing that."

"Thank you," Parno nodded.

"Let us continue this tomorrow, Parno," Memmnon stood, having noted how tired Parno seemed. "You've had a hard day's ride and the hour grows late. Get some rest, and come and see me tomorrow, when you've eaten. Fair enough?"

"Thank you," Parno repeated, standing. He was tired.

"I'll see you in the morning, brother."

# CHAPTER THIRTEEN

-

"It looks as though you've done a remarkable job so far, brother," Memmnon told Parno the next morning, having looked over the remainder of Parno's valise contents after sending the younger McLeod to bed.

"Thank you, Memmnon," Parno replied, pleased with the compliment.

"I admit, I'm curious to see what develops with this Finn person," Memmnon continued. "And I am . . .I don't know the right word for it, awed, perhaps, at the people you have assembled to help build your command. On a side note, I have noted those individuals that are assisting you and have sent a memo in my name to all libraries and to the residences in each capital that all possible assistance be rendered to them, or their agents or representatives. That should cover most anything they need. I have likewise prepared personal letters for each person named," Memmnon handed over a small sheaf of papers.

"I... I don't know what to say, Memmnon," Parno took the proffered letters. "Thank you doesn't seem to cover it."

"It's I who should likely thank you," Memmnon smiled. "I intend to look into this society myself. There are likely more of them that would welcome royal backing and the funding to continue their research. I had no idea that so much of what was lost before could possibly be reclaimed."

"Nor did I," Parno admitted. "There is one thing..." Parno trailed off, unsure of whether to continue. He had spoken to no one about this as yet and was unsure of himself.

"Yes?" Memmnon's eyebrows rose.

"Well, this may be a complete waste of time even to study," Parno admitted lamely. "But. . .the idea of sending messages by other means than courier is something that would benefit the Kingdom."

"Of course, it would," Memmnon snorted. "So would flying, if we could manage it."

"Well, I can't do anything about flying," Parno's face reddened slightly, "but I do have an idea about messaging." Parno briefly outlined his idea. He had thought about the idea for some time, spurred by the need for better communications for his 'weatherman'.

"Lights and towers, hmm?" Memmnon considered that. "The messages would need to be short, seems like."

"Well, perhaps," Parno agreed. "But what if there were a code established? Certain signals to cover entire phrases, things of that sort. I know I'm out of my depth here, but the idea seems workable, at least in theory."

"Have you spoken about this to your engineer?" Memmnon asked. Parno shook his head.

"Then do so," Memmnon ordered. "If he hasn't the time, then have him find someone who does. Someone who can think outside the norms. I agree, the idea at least merits study. See to it that it gets done."

"Very well," Parno nodded, wondering how to pay for that. As if reading his mind, Memmnon called his aide. As the man opened the door, a soldier of the House Guard entered, carrying a small strong box. The trooper sat the box on Memmnon's desk, then both aide and trooper were shooed from the room by the Crown Prince.

"This is for you," Memmnon said after the trooper and the aid had left. He raised the lid, showing Parno the contents.

"That's a lot of money, Memmnon," Parno stated, looking at the coins within.

"Some of it is to be used to replace your own money," Memmnon ordered, "and I mean that. I told you I would see to your needs. No more spending your own coin."

"Thank you," Parno smiled.

"The rest you can use as you see fit provided you keep a record of it. It's not a matter of trust, but of record keeping, understand. Now," Memmnon rose from his chair. "I know you have an errand or two to run and that you want to return as soon as possible. Please keep me informed of any changes and certainly let me know if anything useful turns up," he laughed lightly. "I also want to know when your engineer can start teaching our military. I'll have the first class ready to go as soon as he's ready. Another side note here," he added, "is to see if Doctor Freeman-Corsin would be open to a similar school for military surgeons. You might inquire with her about that."

"I'll see to it as soon as I return," Parno promised, cursing his luck that he would, indeed, have to speak to her again.

Memmnon hesitated for a moment before speaking again.

"You know that Therron expects you to fail," he said rather than asked. Parno nodded.

"I do not intend to share what you have told me with him," Memmnon said firmly. "I did not expect you to succeed either," he admitted, "but unlike Therron, I didn't hope for your failure. I simply expected you to sit on your hilltop and do nothing. I'm sorry about that," he added.

"No need," Parno shrugged. "I haven't exactly given you any reason to think otherwise."

"Be that as it may, now that I know you have it in you, I expect it to continue. I look forward to hearing from you. Speaking of which, you could include letters to me in your dispatches."

"Consider it done," Parno grinned, pleased for some reason that Memmnon would want to hear from him.

"I'll have this taken out to your horses," Memmnon waved at the chest.

"No need," Parno waved the idea away and heaved the chest up on his shoulder one-handed. Memmnon's face showed surprise.

"I train with my men," Parno shrugged.

"That must be some training," Memmnon noted.

"It is," Parno admitted. "Harsh and demanding and not very forgiving," he shrugged. "It has to be, in case you ever have need of us."

"Farewell, Parno," Memmnon smiled.

-

Outside, Parno delivered the box to Sergeant Berry with orders to place a guard on it, and procure a horse to carry it, though it would be only a small way. Before Berry could proceed, Cho Feng appeared, followed by a small carriage. Parno ordered Berry to place the chest in there instead.

"Have any trouble?" Parno asked Feng.

"No, actually, I did not," Feng replied, seemingly puzzled. "I told them you required a carriage and four horses and here they are. Good horses, too," he added. Parno looked them over, nodding in agreement.

"Well, we have a stop to make, and then we need to be on the road."

-

Dahlia Nidiad stood by watching carefully as Parno's men loaded her and her father's things aboard the wagon and into the carriage.

"How is my father, Parno?" she asked, turning to face him. The two had grown up together, and were more like brother and sister than anything else.

"He's cantankerous, obstinate, bull-headed, and hard to get along with," Parno grinned. "Same as usual, in other words."

"Oh, you," Dahlia slapped him playfully on the shoulder. "What's this about me being your cook?" She eyed him in mock crossness.

"Already have one," Parno sighed, "I had intended to place you on the rolls as my cook so you'd have a salary. You wouldn't have had to cook for me, just your father. I eat in the mess, usually, but, I had a house built for the two of you, so you can cook for him for free now," he teased.

"I wouldn't mind working, you know," Dahlia told him. "Not for you of course," she added playfully, "but there might be something I can do once I get there."

"I'm sure there will be if you want," Parno agreed, "and there's a hospital, too. You might work there as a nurse. Not for the men, but the women and children. You're more than smart enough to learn to be a doctor, you know, and there's a very smart female doctor in charge of the hospital."

"A woman? Really?" Dahlia considered that.

"Really. You can do, or be, whatever you like, so long as I can help it, girl. You know that."

"I know," she smiled. "I love you to, brother Parno," she teased, kissing him on the cheek.

"Yes, well, let's not ruin my reputation," Parno huffed. "I worked long and hard to get it…looks like we're ready," he added before she could respond. "You should make a walk through, make sure you've got everything."

"I hate to leave this place, to be honest," she sighed. "It's been home for a long time."

"It still is, so long as you want it to be," Parno assured her. "I left instructions it's not to be issued again without my permission." Dahlia awarded him with a brilliant smile.

"Now go and take a look, girl. We've a long way to go."

Twenty minutes later, the column was on its way to Cove Canton.

-

Edema Willows rode stiffly inside her carriage as it rocked along the Nor trade route north of Loville. The train had just passed through another of the small nameless villages that dotted the countryside. After four weeks on the road she was tired. She wanted to be home, where she could be comfortable . . .

Edema leaned forward, her eyes attracted to motion along the road before her. In front of their train she spied a large column of Nor horsemen heading for them along the road taking them south. They were in two columns and the lines seemed to go on forever. She frowned deeper as they met.

The men were unshaven, wet, and dirty. They had clearly been in the field, in this horrid weather, for many days. And yet…." something is out of place here", she thought to herself, looking over the line of troopers as they passed. "What am I seeing, and not realizing?"

Edema was a very intelligent woman, but the column was almost past before she realized what was. . .not wrong, she decided, but important. Despite the shape the men were in, and they were in bad shape, their horses and their weapons were in splendid condition. There was no knowing how long they had been in the field among the mud of the last week's rain, but they had maintained their weapons and horses as if on parade all the while allowing themselves to go to the dogs, she noticed. As the end of the column came and went, she realized that her count had been automatic. Just over one thousand horsemen had been in that column. A full regiment.

Her discomfort forgotten, Edema reached for her journal.

-

Edema would have been surprised to learn that the Tinker was watching the same column, though from more comfort. The traveler had taken a room in the small town through which the Willows had just passed without so much as slowing. The Tinker often took work here and the townspeople were, by and large, always happy to see him. They were curious when he showed up during this time of year, but, as he had told Parno, the explanation of a 'woman I must see' had been more than sufficient to allay any real concerns.

The truth was, no one cared why he was there. They were glad he was staying on a few days to fix various gadgets that had stopped working since his last visit.

The soldiers, however, that was something else again. They might well pay him a great deal of attention. Attention he didn't want.

So it was with a great deal of relief that he watched the column continue on out of the town, still heading north. He, himself, was about the head south after so long in the Norland country. All the better, he thought to himself. The more Nor troops he could see, and yet avoid, the better.

This was the eleventh time in the last two weeks he had seen a full regiment of cavalry on the road. Each time it had been a different unit, too. He would have wondered what they were doing, had he not been in a similar town three weeks past. As he had sat in the window of his rented room, he had watched as three full regiments had converged on the town, each from a different direction.

All showed signs of having been in the saddle for some time. Their meeting was not by chance, either, the Tinker took note. The next morning, the entire division, for such it was, mounted up and headed north as one.

Interesting.

It was time to go home, he decided suddenly, placing his small tally book into the hidden pocket of his coat. He had gathered a great deal of information for the Prince. Now, it was time to get that information home.

He would leave in the morning, he decided.

-

Edema noted that the train hadn't turned for the secondary road home as they normally would have. They had crossed back into Soulan two days ago on their way home. It had been a profitable trip, which always placed Edward in a good mood. When he joined her in the carriage that evening, she had asked him about the change.

"Oh, I thought we'd follow the Trades this trip home," he told her lightly. "Go through Nasil. The more I think about those bypass roads, the more I like them. Prince Parno's idea that I suggest them to the King or Crown Prince was a good one. I'm going to follow up on it."

"I had thought we wanted to get home as soon as possible," Edema had responded.

"We won't be more than a few days later than planned," Edward shrugged. "I've sent someone ahead to notify the house staff, if that's what concerns you, and," he smiled, "this way, you can shop in Nasil for Christmas. I thought you'd like that."

"It would be nice," she had smiled. Inside, however, she was disappointed. She wanted to place her journal before Parno as soon as possible.

"Don't worry," Edward saw the look on her face. "We'll be home in time to have things ready for Christmas." She smiled again, kissing him lightly, before lying back into her blankets.

Nasil. Wonderful.

-

Doak Parsons was concerned. No, he was worried, that's what he was. And so where the five men from his old gang that had accompanied him.

The small group had rode into Kent when they left Cove. There were still a few drive groups returning along the route and, as was the custom, Parsons and his men had often supped with the groups along the trail, contributing something to the fire, and receiving a safer place to rest in return along with company. The men sat and exchanged stories, laughing around the campfire.

They had frequented inns and road houses along the Trade Routes, and smaller roads as well, talking with all manner of people—always just passing the time while enjoying a drink and the warmth of a fire on a cold night.

Parsons had learned a great deal during the weeks he'd been on the trail. Most of the people he'd talked to didn't even realize he was questioning them. The same went for the men he'd selected to accompany him. They shot the breeze with trail hands, wagon handlers, traders, anyone who had or was traveling in the north. The men were all careful to exhibit enthusiasm for what the Nor were like and for the fact that the border was open.

"Wouldn't mind seeing it myself."

"Where's a good place to see, happen I can get up there, come spring?"

"Any bandits about? Army won't give us no hassle, will they?"

"Reckon there's any money to be made, was a man to head that way?"

These seemingly innocuous inquiries raised no alarms, or even interest in the people they spoke with, but the answers provided gave them a very good picture of what was happening.

Too good for their liking.

"Y'know, boss," one of them said softly as they rode away from their latest camp, "This is startin' to git scary." Parsons snorted, but said nothing. He had been scared for the past two weeks and nothing he had learned since had made him feel any better.

He was as sure as he could be that the Nor were preparing for war. Against who was anyone's guess, but it didn't take a genius to figure that Soulan was the likely target. If the numbers they had were even half accurate the Nor army was huge. Worse, it was well equipped and far better trained than ever before.

Even despite the fact that the Nor were buying huge numbers of cattle from the South, there was precious little beef to be had anywhere. People were literally going hungry with steaks on the hoof all around them. Something about that wasn't right.

Parsons made a snap decision then, reigning his horse in.

"We're headin' north," he ordered. While his official rank was Sergeant, to these men he was still just the 'boss'. They all nodded.

Parsons was mindful of his orders not to cross into Norland…and he wouldn't, but he would get as close as he could and see what was to see.

Prince Parno's hunch was looking more and more like it was right on the money. He wanted to gather as much information as he could before heading back. He still had some time and there was no sense wasting it.

-

The Willows arrived in Nasil just before dark. A courier had rode forward to prepare a place for their train and to secure rooms for them. Edema was thankful for a chance to stay in something other than their carriage. While nice, it was not made for such extended use, especially in cold weather.

Several of their horses were hard used by now and some of the men were looking a bit worn as well. Edward announced that three days would be spent in Nasil, with the train leaving for home at first light on the fourth morning. Everyone was glad to hear that.

A Royal courier arrived that evening with an invitation to dinner at court the next evening. Edward was delighted as this would give him the chance to suggest the changes to the roadways. Edema was glad he would have that chance, but begrudged every minute that it kept what she'd learned out of Parno's hands.

-

"That's an interesting suggestion, Duke," Memmnon nodded gracefully when Edward broached his idea about the trade routes.

"Well, it's not really my idea," Edward admitted, "it was your brother, Parno, who suggested I pass the idea along."

"Indeed?" Memmnon inquired, although Therron snorted in derision. "You see much of Parno?"

"He visits when he can," Edward smiled. "He's a very engaging young man. Edema is committed to finding him a wife, of course," he added, smiling at his own wife. "Says he should have someone to look after him."

"I pity the poor creature who weds him," Therron snarled darkly. "You say he visits you often?" he asked, glancing at Edema before returning his attention to Edward.

"Sometimes once a week, sometimes it's longer," Edward shrugged. "He is very busy, but of course you know that…and I am too, often. Sometimes I'm away when he visits so I don't get to see him as often as Edema, but he's graced us for dinner several times. A likable young fellow, to be sure."

"Indeed," Therron smiled. Inside, however, the wheels were turning. He eyed Edema Willows. Older, of course, but still a fine flower of a woman. So, little brother was visiting the Willows regularly, was he? Well, he'd see what he could do with that.

Memmnon, not having noticed the look on Therron's face, was still listening to Edward expound upon the importance of good roads to trade. The dinner lasted another hour before breaking apart. As the King took his leave, Therron McLeod gently took Edward Willows arm.

"Do you have the time to spare me for a conversation, Duke?" he asked politely.

"Well, I need to get Edema back to our rooms, milord. If not for that. . ."

"I can see that she has an escort from the House Guard, if that will suffice," Therron offered amiably. "I would really like the pleasure of your company for a little while longer. There is much for us to discuss."

And so it was that Edema found herself carried to her suite by members of the House Guard of Soulan while Edward stayed to 'talk' with Prince Therron McLeod.

She settled in and went to sleep before Edward returned. Doubtless still talking about his roads and bypasses.

-

Edema frowned to herself as the train set out from Nasil—on its way, finally, to Cumberland House. Edward had been rather distant since his 'talk' with Therron McLeod. He hadn't been rude, exactly, but cold. She wasn't sure exactly what the middle prince might have told him, but she couldn't imagine what bearing it could possibly have on her.

Probably told him that his roadway idea wasn't going to get any attention, she mused. Or that his taxes would be higher this year.

She would, she figured, find out soon enough. In the meantime she read through her journal again, adding notations that had escaped her initially. She wanted to have everything she could for Parno.

She was certain it was going to be important before it was over.

-

It was a weary column that pulled into Cove Canton three days after departing Nasil. Parno had not intended to push so hard but weather seemed to threatening and he had no desire to have Dahlia out in those conditions. As a result he had pushed his men and horses harder than normal. It hadn't been easy on Dahlia, either, but Parno had pointed out his reasons and she understood them. Her travel was far easier than theirs in any case and traveling faster meant that she would see her father that much sooner.

With darkness fast approaching, troopers from barracks were called to care for the horses, and to unload Dahlia's possessions. Darvo was on his porch when the carriage and wagon arrived and he hurried to embrace his tired daughter.

"Hello, my daughter," he whispered, nearly crushing her in a bear hug.

"Hello, father," Dahlia smiled. "I'm so very glad to see you."

"How was your trip? You look tired, pumpkin."

"I'm exhausted," the girl admitted, "but Parno wanted to push on because the weather looked to turn harsh. I'm glad we're here and we seem to have beaten the weather." She nodded to the west, where occasional flashes of lightning could be seen. A rare occurrence this time of year, but not unheard of.

"I have delivered your daughter, old man, safe and sound as promised," Parno walked up, smiling. Darvo growled slightly, but embraced his charge as well.

"Your trip?" he asked.

"Very well, in fact," Parno smiled tiredly. "I'll give you the particulars tomorrow afternoon, but suffice it to say that things are fine, at least for now."

"Why afternoon?" Darvo asked.

"Because you are not to report until one o'clock tomorrow afternoon, under penalty of. . .well, something ugly. Mucking stables comes to mind. I had a teacher once that told me mucking stables builds character as well as muscle." Darvo grunted, recognizing his own words.

"Thank you, lad," he replied gently.

"Bah," Parno waved his thanks aside. "With you out of the way, maybe I can get some work done." Darvo laughed at that, then placed an arm around his daughter.

"Come, daughter, I have had someone draw a hot bath for you and your bed is ready." Parno watched them go, then turned to head for his own bath and bed after ensuring that his men were seen to. It had been a long ride and he was tired.

He had a lot to catch up on tomorrow, and worse, he had to speak to "her" about Memmnon's idea. He'd need sleep for that.

-

Parno rose early and took breakfast with his men as usual. He had announced early on that there was no rank in the mess, so long as civility was observed. That included him. As a result, many of the men felt at ease enough to speak to him as if her were another trooper, something none of them ever thought about doing outside the mess hall.

Once he had eaten he dusted off his courage and started toward the hospital building to find Freeman-Corsin. He hated…hated…the idea of talking to her again, under any circumstance or for any reason. But, he admitted, Memmnon's request was very reasonable and after all Memmnon was doing for him it was little enough to ask him.

He liked the look of the building, he decided, approaching it slowly. It wasn't exactly what he had pictured in his mind. Indeed, it was actually better. An impressive structure that he hoped would inspire confidence in the men and their families.

He entered the building, mindful to stay out of the way of men still working to get the interior of the hospital finished. He found Stephanie Freeman-Corsin supervising the construction of what looked like a drainage system in a room off to itself.

"No, I don't want to leave it like it is," she was saying to the foreman. "This is an operating room, Mister Plank, not a common bath. Sterility and cleanliness are of the utmost importance in here. This drainage is a part of that and it has to be just as I asked for it to be. Understand?"

"No, I don't," the carpenter shook his head. "This drain is centered on the room, and large enough to provide adequate drainage for a room twice this size. I don't see why it's not sufficient."

"Because she said it's not," Parno said quietly from behind them. Plank whirled at the voice, a look of fear crossing his features briefly.

"If she says it has to be a certain way, then fix it that way," Parno ordered calmly. There was no mistaking the steel in his voice, however. "And, in the future, don't argue with the Doctor. She has complete control over this building and every aspect of its construction. If she wants a bare hole in the floor, then you give it to her, and don't question her about it. Now do you understand?"

"Of course, milord," Plank was falling all over himself now. "I'll see to it at once."

"Don't tell me," Parno ordered. "Tell her. She is in charge here. Period. If that's a problem for you, Mister Plank, then I'm sure we can find someone else for this project and let you get back to whatever you were doing before." Plank reluctantly looked to the doctor.

"I'll get right on it, ma'am," he promised, face reddening at the dressing down.

"Thank you," Stephanie replied stiffly, irked that it had taken Parno's interference to get the work done.

"May I have a moment of your time, Doctor?" Parno asked, his voice still calm.

"Of course, My Lord," she replied, a little stiffly. She walked to where he stood waiting.

"Please walk with me," Parno asked and started out the door. With no choice but to follow, Corsin did so.

"I had the situation under control, you know," she said in a huff, once they were outside.

"I'm sure you did," Parno nodded, "but I run this camp. Everyone had strict orders that whatever you wanted, you were to get, without question or complaint. That bears directly upon me, not you. I don't want him or anyone else, regardless of their position, thinking that they can ignore you at will, either because you're a woman or because you have no military ranking. Come to think of it, perhaps we should issue you a rank. Something appropriate. You will be commanding a large staff before this is over."

"I have never required any rank to do my job," Corsin replied stiffly.

"You've never worked in the military either," Parno pointed out reasonably, "and I have a request from the Crown Prince that will require you to have some authority now that I think about it."

"What sort of request?" Corsin asked warily.

"Prince Memmnon was quite pleased with the idea of someone of your caliber instructing our field surgeons," Parno informed her. "He asked me to appeal directly to you to consider a school here, on the Canton, for instruction of all the army's surgeons. Not all at once, of course, but whatever size class you feel would be possible."

Stephanie looked at him. Teach all of the army's surgeons? Her? Alone?

"My Lord, I don't know that I can undertake such a thing alone, let alone continue to oversee the hospital here."

"I don't intend for you to do it alone," Parno shook his head. "I don't think it's possible. I don't even know how many surgeons there are in the army to be honest. I know that there's one for every regiment, usually for every battalion…not to mention field hospitals, staff physicians, and so on. You'll need to recruit staff to help you teach them. If I may suggest at least one grizzled old field surgeon veteran…I doubt he can teach someone with your background anything about medicine, of course…but what he can do is impart to you what trying to care for wounded under combat conditions might be like."

Corsin considered that. She had absolutely no idea, whatsoever, of what such conditions would be like, that was certain. She couldn't very well teach them as if they would always have the secure, sterile facilities of a hospital.

"That seems like sage advice," she agreed finally. "I… I'll need a couple of days, perhaps a week, to work out a staffing plan and make sure it's adequate. As to class size, I'll have to know what help I'll have before I can plan that."

"Very well," Parno nodded. "I can inform Memmnon that you will do as he requests? It is a request, by the way," he added. "You need not do so, if you don't want to, but it would likely save a great many lives should we ever again find ourselves at war."

"Of course, I'll do it," Corsin replied at once, "with one proviso," she added suddenly.

"Yes?" Parno asked.

"That you forgive me my impertinence on the day we met, My Lord. I really am very sorry about that. I'm afraid I allowed the rumors about you to dictate how I perceived you. You deserved better than that and I should have done you better." Parno snorted in rye amusement at that and Corsin's face reddened.

"You owe me no apology," he surprised himself in saying. "As to the 'rumors', I fear they are all too true, in some cases. They do not call me the 'Black Sheep of Soulan' without due cause, Doctor. I'm hardly the sterling example of nobility." She actually laughed outright at that, her face losing its earlier color.

"I can understand that," she assured him. "Try being a doctor, and a woman. If not for my family's history of medicine and our connection to the Crown I'd be nothing more than an ornament on some nobleman's arm, Prince."

"You'd be a very beautiful ornament, at least," Parno shocked himself again with his reply. "Whereas I would simply be a brawling trouble maker." Corsin flushed in spite of herself.

"Then I'll teach your classes, Prince," she promised. "I'll try to have an idea of what I'll need, and what I can do, by the end of the week."

"That will be more than satisfactory, Doctor," Parno nodded. "I appreciate your time. I will let you return to your hospital." With that he walked on, leaving Corsin to watch him go, a new opinion of Parno running through her mind.

# CHAPTER FOURTEEN

-

Parno learned of the Willows' return by way of messenger. Edema's footman, Benson, had ridden over to the fort to deliver her message, inviting him for dinner the next evening. Parno had sent a reply that he would, indeed, be glad to attend. He informed Berry that he would need to be prepared to stay overnight and then set out to the store to gather some things to welcome the Willows home.

The next morning, he was in the saddle. It was cold and low-lying clouds created a thick fog along the roads.  By the time the small column was approaching Cumberland House, just after lunch, the day had cleared. It wouldn't warm up much, but the sun was shining.

Edward was out of the house when Parno arrived and Edema wasted no time in ushering Parno into the study and closing the doors.

"You were right," she said at once, going to the mantle and taking the journal she had kept during her travel. She presented the book to Parno, along with the map she had made careful notations on and a few sketches, including those of several men of the Wild Tribes.

"There's nothing to indicate what, exactly, they're up to, but their military is moving all the time…and they're good, Parno. Very good, from what I've seen. Their horsemanship is first rate, including their care of the animals. They look more like soldiers than ever before. Hard, well trained, capable soldiers."

"I feared as much," Parno nodded, taking the journal she offered him. He glanced at it briefly before placing it in his small shoulder bag. He would study it in more depth when he was back in his office. He wanted no one to know that Edema had done this for him.

"I'm in your debt, My Lady," he said quietly. "I will not forget it."

"There's something else," she said just a softly. "We had dinner in Nasil with the King and your siblings. Afterward, Therron asked Edward to stay. I don't know what he told him, but Edward has been in a funk ever since. Therron was particularly interested in the fact that you had often been a guest here." Parno frowned at that.

"I see no reason for that to be a bother to him," Parno admitted. "I would think that the fact that I'm out of Nasil would make him very happy."

"Don't take this lightly, Parno," Edema warned. She had decided not to tell Parno of Edward's small comments about how much attention she was giving the young Prince or vice-versa. "Don't underestimate Therron's hate for you. It's. . .it's almost palpable. Something one can almost touch."

"Oh, I know that," Parno actually laughed. "Of all three, his attitude toward me has always been the worst of the lot."

"This is different," Edema insisted. "I don't know what he said to Edward but I'm willing to bet that it was about you. In what way, I can't. . . ." She cut off as the door to the study burst open and Edward entered.

"Ah, Prince Parno!" Edward exclaimed. "How good it is to see you!"

"And you, Duke," Parno smiled easily, rising to take the Duke's hand. "Lady Edema was just telling me that you dined with my family on your return trip. I trust you had a profitable venture?"

"Fairly well," Edward nodded, his glance going briefly to his wife. Edema knew her breath was short. Edward had startled her and he knew it.

"Not so good as in the summer months, of course," Edward turned his attention back to his guest, "but still well worth the effort…and the cold," he gave a shudder. "How have you been?"

"Cold," Parno laughed, "though not so much as you, I suspect. It will soon be winter, though, without doubt. I suspect that there's snow on the wind, even now, the way it felt on the ride over."

"I was thinking the same thing, myself," Edward agreed. "I see you brought us yet another house gift. You know that isn't necessary, Milord."

"Perhaps," Parno shrugged, "but you and the Lady Edema have been very kind to me, Duke. It is little enough I can do to repay your hospitality. Tell, me, though, did you mention the roadway changes Memmnon whilst you were in his company?"

"I did," Edward nodded, "and I'll be delighted to tell you of the discussion over dinner. You are planning to stay the night are you not?"

"If you have no objection, that would be grand," Parno smiled. "I would love to hear of your travels. I'm especially interested in your news of trading from the north. I've given some thought to it, myself, if I remain here. Perhaps buying land of my own and raising horses. I'd like your advice, however, if you'd be so kind."

"Delighted!" Edward agreed at once. "Always happy to help an enterprising young man. Come, let's discuss all this over a table of good food, and then, perhaps, some brandy."

"That sounds agreeable." Parno followed his host's wave out of the study. As he left, Edema happened to glance at Edward. The look in his eyes made her breath catch. Edward smiled at her, but it wasn't a pleasant smile. More like a viper preparing to strike.

Dinner was far from enjoyable for her.

-

"What say we adjourn to the study, Prince Parno?" Edward invited as the servants cleared away the dishes.

"As you wish, Duke," Parno agreed, rising. Edema made as if to follow, but Edward's voice stopped her.

"Edema, dear," his voice was cold to her. "We won't bore you with talk of business if you'd prefer to retire." Unable to think of a reason to stay, she smiled.

"Of course, dear. Good night, my dear boy," she said to Parno, giving him a matronly kiss on his cheek. "It is good to see you. Your mother would be very proud of you, you know," she added.

"Thank you, milady," Parno said softly, bowing to kiss her hand. "Thank you for the dinner. It was lovely." Edema gave her husband a kiss as well as a brief embrace, then departed. As she went, the two men walked to the study.

"So, you are thinking of horses?" She heard Edward say before the door closed.

Going directly to her rooms, she thanked God that she had had the opportunity to give Parno the journal, maps, and sketched beforehand. Edward seemed determined to keep the two of them apart for some reason.

He cannot possibly be jealous of a boy barely nineteen, she told herself. He's just trying to show off, be a good, manly, host, that's all.

She was still worrying over it, however, as she prepared for bed. There was something amiss. She decided right then that she would tell Parno of Edward's comments. He needed to be forewarned in case Edward said or did something stupid. Or provoked the younger man into something rash.

-

Parno had spoken to Edward Willows for quite some time after dinner. In truth, he had considered the horse ranch before and, if things really were going to stay good with the Nor, then he might well make a good living raising and selling horses of good quality, both at home and in the north.

Finally the two men had retired. Parno would need to rise early and depart. He couldn't afford to be away from his command for too long at a time, even to visit the area nobility. If Therron was interested in Parno's time away from his post, it would be just like him to send someone from the Inspector General's office to check up on him. In the unlikely event that happened, Parno wanted to be on hand.

He was preparing for bed when he heard a soft knock at his door.

"Enter," he called, pulling on a robe that had been provided in the guest room. He was surprised to see Edema Willows walk into his room.

"What is it, Lady?" Parno asked, seeing the look on her face.

"Parno, I have to tell you something," she said at once. "It is possible that Edward thinks that. . .well, suspects that you and I are. . .well, you know." Parno's look told her that he didn't. At first. Slowly, however, comprehension dawned.

"Are you serious?" he asked, disbelief evident in his voice. "Why would he think that? Your devotion to him is obvious!" Edema smiled weakly at that.

"So, I thought," she agreed, "but certain comments he has made recently have made me wary and then there was that discussion with Therron in Nasil. His attitude took a turn for the worse after that." Parno sat heavily on his bed.

"You have been a frequent visitor here, Parno," Edema pointed out, "and I have doted upon you, I admit. I wouldn't have thought after all this time that Edward would have any jealousy in him, but I could be wrong. I... I hadn't planned to tell you this, but I've had an uneasy feeling about it since dinner. I felt that you should know."

"I... Edema I am so sorry," Parno said finally. "I never imagined. . .I mean, I know I'm not well thought of, but…"

"As I said, I'm not sure," Edema reminded him, "but I thought you should know."

"Thank you," was all Parno could say. Of all the stupid things!

"I must return," Edema told him. She placed a hand upon his cheek. "Dear boy, I am sorry to add to your burden, but I thought this best."

"You were right to tell me," Parno assured her. "I will take measures to ensure that this goes no further and I will not visit for a while, perhaps that will help."

"Perhaps, though I will miss your visits," Edema smiled sadly. "You are so like your mother." She kissed his cheek lightly, then was gone. Parno closed the door after her, never bothering to look into the hallway.

If he had, he would have seen a solitary shadow watching.

-

Parno rose early the next morning, slipping out of the house before the Willows' awakened. He roused his escort and in thirty minutes they were in the saddle. Parno left a message with the house staff offering his apologies for his early departure, citing the need to get back to his command and thanking them for their hospitality.

All the way back Parno was silent, thinking on what had transpired. So engrossed in his thoughts was he that he was already through the gates before he realized he was home. He gave his horse to one of the soldiers in his escort and started for his house. He was already on the porch when he realized that he had someone waiting.

"Morning, milord," the Tinker smiled easily.

"Hello, Tinker," Parno smiled automatically. "I wondered when I'd be seeing you again. Please, come in," Parno offered, opening the door. The Tinker followed him inside, careful to wipe his feet.

"Would you care for some breakfast?" Parno asked, hanging his coat in the hallway. "I haven't eaten yet and was about to have something fixed for me."

"That would be good, milord," Tinker nodded. "I suggest we eat in private, however," he lowered his voice, "I have a great deal to share with you." Parno took in the seriousness of the Tinker's voice and his stance and decided something.

"I'm not going to like this, am I?"

-

"I was right," Parno declared. "I don't like it."

"I'm sorry, milord," the Tinker shrugged, "but it looks as if you were right. The Nor are preparing for war so far as I can see. There's no way to know against whom, of course, but there is only one logical target."

"Us," Parno said it flatly and the Tinker nodded in agreement.

"Their numbers are. . .staggering, milord, to be honest," he went on. The traveling repairman was busy making notes on Parno's map. There were many, many marks already on it and the Tinker wasn't near finished. "Thousands of horseman. Not all cavalry, mind you, but all well mounted and with no small amount of skill. Their drills are sharp and their formations are strong. They have made vast improvements in that area."

"Wonderful," Parno murmured. "I suppose their infantry is equally as impressive." The Tinker stopped what he was doing and looked at the young Prince.

"Milord, I have either seen or heard of at least twenty-five different infantry divisions during the weeks I spent among the Nor. I have personally observed three of them in the field mustering their regiments and marching long miles, always in good form."

"Twenty -" Parno cut himself off with a choke. A quarter of a million men, possibly. All well trained and equipped. He had no words for that.

"A nation at peace with its neighbors has no need for such an army, milord," the Tinker said quietly.

"No," Parno agreed, "but one preparing to invade an unsuspecting neighbor does. This is what I feared," he almost whispered. "Are there any signs that they're preparing to attack soon?" he asked. The Tinker shook his head.

"No, milord. Many of these units are far to the north…or were…less than a fortnight ago, with no signs of preparing to move. They were in winter quarters, though their training continues. I believe they will wait until after the spring rains. It is the most likely course of action."

"I agree," Parno nodded. "I appreciate this, Tinker."

"I am happy to help, milord," the other man replied, smiling.

"I couldn't talk you into staying around here permanently, could I?" Parno asked. The Tinker shook his head slowly.

"I am not a soldier, my prince," he smiled. "This is not the life for me."

"I have plenty of soldiers," Parno replied. "I need someone who can gather information like this for me." The Tinker considered that for a moment.

"I am not a spy," he shrugged. "I can see what is to be seen, but that is all. Yes, I can often go where others cannot, because so many ignore me. That does not make me a good spy."

"I'm not really looking for a spy, in the true sense of the word," Parno told him. "But someone who can see, who can hear, and keep me informed is more valuable than a true spy. A real spy can't always be trusted."

"True," Tinker admitted. "I had planned to go further south for the winter," he said after a pause. "I usually go to the southern part of Flora. I have a few relatives there, and usually can find work to last me through the winter." He shrugged again.

"But, I can likely find some work here as well."

"You needn't find work other than what you need to keep you looking busy," Parno told him bluntly. "I'll pay you and provide for your expenses. You can stay here for a while," he added. "Truth is, there's enough 'work' to keep you busy right here for the next fortnight or so but it's up to you. I won't deny I could use your help but you've been a great help already." The Tinker studied him for several moments.

"I don't suppose you have one of those small cabins available?" he asked finally. "And room for my horses in your stables?"

"If I have to build one," Parno assured him. The Tinker smiled faintly, and nodded.

"Then perhaps I should stay," he said at last. "I would be going north again with the thaw. Perhaps you will have need of me then."

"I'm sure of it," Parno agreed. "Thank you."

"In the meantime," the Tinker smiled, "I will finish this map for you."

-

Parno rose early the next morning. He had slept restlessly, when he had slept at all. The news brought to him by Edema, added to what the Tinker had given him, had occupied his thoughts while awake and his dreams while asleep.

Washing, he dressed in a utility uniform and walked through the cold air toward his office. There was work to see to, of course, since he'd been away for two days and that would have to be done. While he was at it, at least part of his mind would continue working on the problem at hand.

So entrenched in his work and his worry, was Parno that Sprigs actually had to address him three times to get his attention. Looking up, Parno saw the young Lieutenant standing in his door.

"What is it, Harrel?" Parno asked. "I'm sorry, I'm a bit preoccupied this morning."

"A messenger from Cumberland House, milord," Sprigs informed him. Parno frowned. That would be bad news, he suspected.

"Send him in," Parno ordered.

"Milord," the man bowed deeply. Parno recognized the man as Edema Willows' personal footman.

"Hello Benson," Parno smiled. "How are you? Can I offer you some refreshment after the long ride over?"

"Beg pardon, Milord, but I haven't time. Mistress ordered me to see you at once and return. I am to wait only in case of a reply." Parno frowned at that and took the proffered letter. He opened it to find a few simple lines, apparently hastily written.

"Dear Parno,

It seems that Edward has a bit of jealousy in him after all.

He saw me leaving your room night before last and has decided that his honor is impugned. We leave at once for Nasil where he plans to lay his charge before the King. I wanted to warn you, for I know not what will happen.

Edema"

Parno read the short note twice, his face reddening as he did so. When he looked up, his eyes were fairly ablaze and Benson took an involuntary step back.

The Prince stood.

"Are they already gone?" he asked quietly, voice full of barely controlled fury.

"Possibly, Milord," Benson answered, "they were all but ready when the Mistress dispatched me on my errand. The Duke has decided that I am not to accompany the trip as usual." More bad news. If Edward had ordered Benson to remain behind there had to be a reason.

"Return to Cumberland House, Benson. If your mistress is still there, inform her that I have received her message and will see her in Nasil. She is to say nothing of our discussions until I arrive. Understood?"

"Milord," Benson bowed. When he straightened, his eyes were narrow and cold. "I trust that no harm will come to Milady?"

"You trust correctly, Benson," Parno nodded. "Harm may well come to someone, but it shall not be her. And, to put your mind at ease, she has done nothing wrong. I will tell you, in confidence and not to be repeated, that Lady Edema knew my mother. She has been kind enough, at times, to talk to me of her, tell me of her, as she died at my birth and I never knew her."

The look of suspicion left the older man's eyes and warmth returned. He nodded slightly. "I understand, Milord," he said, "and it will go no further by my lips." With that the retainer turned and departed. Parno walked to the door where Sprigs was waiting.

"Lieutenant, send for Colonel Nidiad, Colonel Willard, and Master Feng. Have my escort assembled, ready to ride for Nasil. Have my own mount prepared as well, please."

"Sir," Sprigs bowed slightly and went to send runners on their way. Parno walked slowly back into his office and looked once more out his window.

\-

"Lad, this is a bad move," Darvo said quietly. "It's best to wait and see what happens before jumping out like this."

"Punishment for adultery is quite harsh among the nobility," Willard offered from his own seat. "Waiting might place Lady Edema in harm."

"There is no adultery here," Parno ground the words out slowly, "and I intend to kill the man who says otherwise, regardless of who he may be. Edema Willows is like a mother to me, something I never had before I came here. She will come to harm only after I am no longer capable of drawing a sword."

"I'll go with you then," Darvo stood. "You can't. . . ."

"No," Willard said, rising from his chair as well. "I will go. You should remain, Colonel. If things do not go…well…you will need to be here. The Prince is well thought of among the regiment. They will respect you enough not to ride to Nasil and burn it down. I don't know that I could manage that."

"There will be no riding anywhere," Parno ordered. "This is my problem, my fight. Not the Regiment's."

"The men won't see it that way, Milord," Karls pointed out. "To them, you are one of their own. They will not take kindly to something like this."

"They will do nothing…nothing…to endanger their status as soldiers," Parno bit the words out. "This is a mistake and I should be able to correct it. Neither of you will go with me."

"One of us is going," Darvo said, and his voice brooked no argument. "I will accept Karls' judgment as a compliment and let him be the one, but one of us is riding with you—and that is final."

For once Darvo thought he had gone too far. Parno's eyes were bright as beacons along the coast and burned with a fury he had never seen in the young Prince. Darvo was not a fearing man, but, at that moment he realized suddenly that his young charge had, indeed, become a man to be feared.

Fortunately, Darvo was as important to Parno as Edema was. His eyes slowly fell from flaming to smoldering and he nodded silently.

"Work it out among yourselves, then. I leave in thirty minutes."

\-

The ride from Cove to Nasil was a hard one, at least in places. Descent off the Plateau was slow and the Rim, at least in some places, wasn't much better. The roads, however, made travel far easier than would otherwise have been the case.

It was a quiet Parno McLeod that rode at the head of the small column. His anger had fallen off at least partially. Instead of flaming fury, it was more of smoldering rage.

They stopped to make camp well after dark. Parno was loathe to push much harder, especially in the cooler air. Though it was not yet winter, winter wasn't far off. Occasional 'northers', bursts of cold air from the northern regions, would blow through on occasion and were capable of dropping the temperature by twenty degrees in a matter of hours.

Normally the ride to Nasil would take three days at a normal pace. Parno had debated on making the trip with remounts, allowing the small column to make much better time but he had decided against it, realizing that Edward and Edema Willows would not make the trip any quicker than he could.

The prince was seated near a small fire one of the men had built for him, staring into the flames and reflecting on his current situation. There was no doubt, at least in his mind, that it was his own reputation as a womanizer that had led to this difficulty. That and his own stupidity for spending so much time in Edema's company.

It had never once crossed his mind that his attentions, his presence, would cause a problem for her. He had been blissfully unaware of any tensions between the Willows and completely wrapped up in either learning more of his mother or collecting Edema's impressions about Norland. He cursed bitterly under his breath at his naiveté. He was a grown man. He should have thought about such things.

"What troubles you, young noble?"

Parno almost jumped, but managed to turn the motion into a simple turning motion, looking to where Cho Feng stood at the edge of the small fire's light. His robes were heavier than he usually wore and less flashy, but his face was just as intense as it always was.

"Master Feng," Parno nodded. "I am what troubles me." He continued, motioning for Feng to take the other chair near the fire, "My stupidity had led to this mess. My blindness, and carelessness."

"In what way have you caused this problem, young Prince?" Feng asked, taking the chair. "How is it that you are so responsible?"

"I spent much too much time in her company, Feng," Parno admitted. "She knew my mother, you see. Knew her and was with her when she died with me in her arms. I had never had anyone to tell me about my mother."

"I fail to see that this is an issue for doubt or guilt." Feng observed.

"I should have known that my spending so much time with her…around her…would lead to suspicions like this. I was blind to the danger even though apparently my brother Therron was not. I sense his fine hand in this. I have a poor reputation, you know, it is only natural that her husband would suspect something. Had he not, I'm sure that Therron whispering in his ear would have planted the seed, then watered it until it took root. Yet I failed not only to see it, but to even consider it. Thus…"

"Thus, you have decided that you are to blame," Feng finished for him. "Have you considered that the Lady has explained all this and the gentleman refuses to hear? Or to believe?"

"I'm sure she told him what was happening," Parno nodded, "but that's not the issue. It was my carelessness that led to his being suspicious in the first place. I failed to even consider the possibility. If I had, then I would have been more careful of how much time we spent together and of how it was spent. I am a fool."

"I have noticed, my young Prince, that you are very good at casting dispersions upon yourself."

"Well, I'm guilty of many things, Master Feng, but dishonesty isn't among them. I have, I'm afraid, earned most of the little titles I've been given over the years. I do chase women. I do drink, often to excess. I am prone to brawl, especially in public places. These are not the actions of a member of a ruling family."

"Indeed?" Feng's eyebrows rose as one. "I have known many noble families in my time, young Prince. Social behavior is not the true test of nobility."

"It isn't?" Parno grinned, in spite of himself.

"Not in the least," Feng replied. "A Royal Dynasty is both a blessing and a curse, young Prince. Dynastic families often give the people of a diverse land something to cling to—to believe in, if you will. Something greater than themselves or greater even than the people of that dynasty. True, some generations of every dynasty have poor rulers, but a strong and powerful dynasty can survive even that."

"The curse, on the other hand, is that the people of that land often begin to raise their leaders, their rulers, to a higher plane of existence than mere mortals can achieve. Physically, emotionally, and mentally you are no different from any other young man your age in good health. You desire the company of a woman, the taste, or perhaps the effect, of alcohol. You respond to challenges. Such things are natural and in a man not of a dynastic family they are considered normal."

"You however," Feng leaned forward slightly, "are not only the son of a dynastic king, but also a victim of a dysfunctional family arrangement. You have been told since birth that you are the cause of your mother's death. You have rebelled against your family since you have been old enough to do so. This is also normal. Were you the product of a peasant or commoner family, you would have simply left to make your way in the world absent the guilt that the other family members place upon you. Unfairly placed upon you, I might add."

"But you do not have that option, Parno." It was the first time Feng had ever called Parno by his name and it grabbed the Prince's attention.

"No, I don't," he agreed quietly.

"So instead, you rebel. A natural reaction. But consider this; had your family embraced you, as they should have, instead of ostracizing you, would that have affected your behavior? Would you, had you had the advantage of a loving home and family about you who cared for you, behaved in such a way as you say you are wont to do?"

"No," Parno replied, after a minute of careful contemplation. "Likely I would not. I would…"

"Would have sought to uphold the name of those who loved you," Feng nodded, "an admirable thing in any society. Denied that, you have acted as you have. So, while every man is responsible for his own actions, he cannot always claim to have power over those things that influence him." Feng stood suddenly.

"You have been a good student, Prince Parno McLeod. You are a good man as well. Better, I think, than you give yourself credit for. Remember that as you contemplate how culpable you are in this, or any other matter." Feng whirled, robes flying out, and disappeared into the night, leaving Parno staring into the fire once more with still more to think about.

-

The small party arrived in Nasil after dark on the third day of travel. They had made good time, but both horses and men were weary. Fatigue was evident in the blowing horses and slumped figures of soldiers.

Parno led them to the Royal Barracks where the horses were stabled. Then the entire troop settled into the transient barracks and collapsed as soon as they entered. Whatever happened on the morrow, they would face it after a good night's sleep.

# CHAPTER FIFTEEN

-

Parno McLeod entered the Palace with a small flourish. He normally dispensed with such things, but today, he had decided, was not a normal day. The prince had dressed in simple uniform and his sword rested at his side.

Several people working in the palace noted the sword with raised eyebrows. Coupled with the look upon the prince's face, the sword spoke volumes. Parno McLeod rarely carried a sword in the palace.

Parno rebuffed the chamberlain's attempts to stop him, pushing the man gently aside as he made for the doors of his father's private audience chamber. A look from Willard, who with Cho Feng had accompanied the young royal, silenced the servant.

Parno flung the doors open and walked into the room unannounced. His face showed neither surprise nor dismay at the sight of Edward Willows, standing before the king.

"Well, speak of the devil!"

Parno looked to the speaker, his own brother, Therron. Memmnon and Sherron were also there, Parno nodded grimly, having expected no less. His family sitting in judgment of him, as usual.

"Ah, my loving family, assembled to condemn me, no doubt," Parno smiled, his voice dripping with not only sarcasm, but condescension. For once, he was in the right and the feeling gave him new strength.

"Condemnation you rightly deserve, I might add!" Tammon McLeod snarled.

"Oh?" Parno replied. "And why is it that I deserve it, father?"

"For violating the wife of a Peer of this Kingdom!" Therron's snarl was, if anything, harsher than his father's.

"I see," Parno nodded, "and whose wife would it be?"

"You know damn well of whom I speak!" Tammon yelled. "Duke Edward has come before me to lodge a complaint against you. Because you are a member of this family, curse you, he cannot challenge you, thus he has used the only recourse open to him. Laying it before me!"

"I see," Parno repeated, eyes aglow. "Well, may I hear the charge, then?"

"Adultery," Memmnon told him, his voice subdued. "With the Duke's wife, Edema."

"I thought as such," Parno nodded, unfazed. He looked at Edward a minute, then strode to him. Edward flinched in spite of the presence of the King, but not quick enough. Parno's riding glove caught Willows first on one cheek, then the other, so quickly that no one had time to respond before the deed was done.

"Since you feel you cannot challenge me, sir," Parno's voice was deadly calm, "I shall challenge you. You have stained my honor and that of your Lady. I await your pleasure."

"You dare!" Therron rose from his chair. "Guards! Take the prince. . . ." Therron's voice broke off abruptly as Willard and Feng moved quietly to Parno's side. Therron looked at Feng with contempt, then turned to Willard.

"Colonel, you should think about what you are doing," he warned thickly.

"I have, Milord," Karls bowed slightly. "My Lord Parno is guiltless in this and my honor as his retainer demands that I stand by him." Therron's eyebrows rose at that, but he said nothing else.

"I am waiting, Duke Edward," Parno said into the silence. "I demand satisfaction for your slurs against not only my honor, but those of your Lady. A finer woman than you rate, sir. A woman loyal to you, and loving. You have dishonored a woman who is the closest thing to a mother I have ever known. For that, I will have your blood."

Breaths were heard all over the chamber at Parno's words. His words had been chosen carefully. Guaranteed to focus everyone's attention.

"What the hell are you talking about?" Edward stammered.

"I'm talking about using your blood to clean the stain of dishonor from myself and your lady," Parno said calmly. "Of course, knowing as I do that you lack the same courage with deeds that you claim with words, you may choose a champion to fight in your place. I would expect nothing less from such a coward, after all."

"Parno!" Memmnon called sharply. "You cannot. . ."

"Cannot? Brother?" Parno asked. "Indeed I can, Memmnon. This. . .gentleman, has stained my honor and that of a woman dearer to me than my own life with his accusations. The law clearly allows me to challenge him and I am required to do so, if I should regain my honor....and hers," he added, casting a venomous glance at Willows.

"Explain yourself, Parno," Tammon McLeod said quietly. For once his voice was subdued when speaking to his youngest son and lacking any sort of criticism. If anything, some noted, there was a look of sadness on the King's face.

"It is too late for explanations!" Therron shouted, on his feet once more. "The challenge has been laid, and must be. . . ." Therron broke off again as Tammon McLeod turned his gaze upon the middle son.

"Do not forget, Therron, who it is that rules here," the King spoke softly, but his words carried. Therron paled and took his seat. Tammon looked back to Parno. "I'm waiting."

"I was invited to the Duke's home some months ago for a harvest ball. There I met the Lady Edema for the first time in anything other than a court function. In the course of conversation, she mentioned that she had known my mother. Indeed, had been present when I was born. That she and the Duke had been friends of you and mother before you were even wed."

"That is true," Tammon nodded. "Lady Edema and your mother were very close."

"Lady Edema, at my request, told me of her," Parno said quietly. "Told me about my mother, something no one else had ever bothered to do—other than to lay her death at my feet, of course, which was something my loving family never missed an opportunity to do. She told me about how my mother lived, instead of her death, a death which was not my fault." He looked to Edward with nothing by contempt.

"She treated me with a kindness that I have rarely experienced, Duke. I do not expect you to understand, nor do I care if you do. Nothing has occurred between the Lady Edema and myself, except that she took pity upon me and told me about my mother. She also talked about your travels to the North. I have never been there and do not expect ever to go. Thus, through her eyes and yours, I have experienced the Nor lands." He turned to face his father, eyes bright with hate, anger, and disgust.

"And for that, this witless, gutless, fop, comes before you to accuse his wife, a loyal and loving woman, dedicated to him, of adultery. His lack of courage brings him here, to you, rather than to face me. Fine. I am here and I will gladly give him satisfaction. Who knows, he might even win. That would solve all your problems, father. Would it not?"

Tammon McLeod's face reddened at that and Therron leapt again to his feet. Before he could speak, however, Parno leveled his hate filled gaze upon the middle son.

"I advise you to hold your tongue, brother," Parno warned him softly. "I tire of your intrusion into a matter which is of no concern to you. Unless, of course," he added with a mocking smile, "you wish to be Duke Edward's champion. In which case, I would welcome your intrusion."

Therron McLeod's face flushed with fury but before he could answer a firm hand took him by the shoulder and pushed him into his chair once more. Therron jerked his head around, to see Memmnon's piercing gaze.

"Sit, Therron," the Crown Prince ordered. "This isn't any of your business, unless you do intend to champion Duke Edward's cause, which I must warn against unless you have some deep seated urge to die which I am unaware of." Therron's face flushed even deeper at those words.

"You think that impertinent whelp could defeat me?" he snarled in fury.

"I think that he would kill you if the chance presented itself," Memmnon smiled, almost mockingly, "and you seem determined to give him that chance."

"Enough," Tammon declared, his voice again not loud, but carrying. He looked to his youngest son.

"Parno, you will offer an apology to Duke Edward."

"I will not," Parno replied calmly. Sharp intakes of breath were heard throughout the room. Not even Parno had ever openly defied the King before.

"What?"

"I will not," Parno replied. "I have issued a challenge. As challenged party, he has the right to demand an apology, but I am not required to give it. He may call himself a coward and withdraw his claims, or he may answer."

"I am ordering you to apologize, Parno. I find that your behavior is not -"

"You cannot force me to do so, My King, and I will not yield in this matter," Parno was amazed at how calm his voice was. "The law is clear and even the hated son has the right to the law."

"Damn you, Parno," Tammon was furious. "Why must you always defy me?"

"Why must you always lack faith in me, father?" Parno shot back. "There is no pleasing you. No way to win for me. I have grown up without a mother and thanks to you, without a father as well. All of my life you, and they, have hated me and I have taken it. I will no longer yield. He may answer or withdraw his accusations as publicly as he made them. There is no other course of action open to him under the law." He looked calmly to Memmnon, who nodded slowly in agreement.

"He is correct, Father," the Crown Prince spoke slowly. "The law is clear."

"I will not allow this!" Tammon said loudly.

"It is not within the power of the king to deny the rights of the law to a citizen of the realm," Parno spoke evenly. "Had you given me even a shadow of confidence, showed any faith in me at all, and asked me to repudiate the charges, I should have done so. Unfortunately that is beyond your ability, My King. I am guiltless in this matter, as is the Lady Edema. There is no going back."

"You would challenge a man who is not a warrior, in order to regain your honor?" Therron baited.

"I have offered the Duke the option of choosing a champion is his stead, Therron. Are you offering to do so? You certainly claim to be a warrior. This offers you a chance to do something that your heart so greatly desires. Slay me."

Therron's face gleamed in triumph and he started to rise.

"No," Tammon declared. "There will be no royal battle, here. As the law requires, there will be justice. Duke Edward," Tammon looked to Willows, "you may choose yourself a champion or face Parno yourself, but your champion will not come from the Royal family. What is your answer?"

Willows turned to Tammon, face white and lips trembling.

"My Lord, you know that I am no warrior. How can I be expected to face Prince Parno in battle?" No one missed the Duke's furtive glance toward Therron McLeod, nor the desperation in his voice.

"Perhaps you should have considered that before you accused me," Parno said, his voice mocking.

"Silence," Tammon ordered. "Duke Edward, you have made harsh accusations, which have been answered not only with repudiation, which I might add agree with those of your Lady, but with a challenge as well. You must answer."

"I have no champion, Milord," Willows wailed. "My retainers are merchants and guards, not warriors! I have no one that I can call upon!"

"I will offer you my champion, Duke Edward," Therron said, his voice tinged again with triumph. "Do you accept?"

"Yes!" Willows jumped at the chance so quickly that neither Tammon nor Memmnon had the chance to intervene.

"Very well," Therron said, rising. "Parno, you will face. . .Enri Willard."

A gasp erupted from the room but Parno heard the strangled cry of anguish from behind him and his heart sank. He turned to look at a white faced Karls.

The room was silent as a tomb. Everyone there waited to hear what Prince Parno would say.

"I am sorry, Karls," he spoke where only Willard could hear. "I will withdraw, and offer the apology. You may leave my service, if you wish, with honor."

Willard's face was a conflicting swirl of emotions. He steeled himself and stood straighter.

"No, Milord," he said finally, his voice calm. "Enri is a big boy. He can look after himself. He has not yet accepted the challenge and perhaps he will not, but either way I serve you. I ask only, Milord, that if you can avoid killing him without endangering yourself that you allow him to live. If you cannot, I will understand."

"You assume that I will even win, Karls," Parno chuckled quietly. "Your brother is the holder of the King's Sword, after all."

"I have seen him fight, Milord," Karls shrugged. "I have also seen you fight. There is no doubt in my mind that you will succeed."

"Karls, I cannot face the brother of one of my most trusted retainers," Parno objected, placing his hand upon Karl's shoulder. "I cannot. Will not."

"Milord, if you withdraw now it will look like cowardice," Willard pointed out. "It will destroy your claim of innocence and leave you and the Lady forever stained by the charges of this coward. You have no choice but to accept and I will not leave your side."

Parno looked long and hard into Karls Willard's eyes. The young man was strong, with a spine of steel and the heart of a lion. Parno wondered what he had done to deserve the loyalty of such a man.

At the same time, it crossed his mind that once again his actions had placed someone close to him in the line of fire, even if indirectly. He had never imagined this. If his thrice damned brother had not interfered, the matter would likely have been settled quickly. Once again, his recklessness had allowed someone to mousetrap him into hurting a friend. He looked at Feng, who had been silent up to now, his look one of desperation mingled with regret and self-loathing.

"You are not at fault, here, Prince," Feng replied quietly. "There is no blame upon your honor. You must do what is right."

Parno sighed, his head dropping for a minute. Suddenly he reached out with both hands and gripped Karls tightly by the shoulder. He embraced the younger Willard, who returned it with equal fierceness. He released the hold and turned to face Therron.

"I accept."

The chamber erupted in noise as Parno whirled and departed, followed by his retainers.

-

One hour later, Enri Willard and Parno McLeod met upon the parade ground of the palace. The elder Willard was backed by Therron McLeod and Edward Willows. Parno was seconded by Cho Feng and Karls Willard.

"Milord," Enri smiled mockingly, with a bow just deep enough not to be insulting. "I am at your service."

"Time," Karls stated, his face showing none of the emotions swirling inside.

"Sunrise, tomorrow," Therron answered promptly. "Weapons?"

"Swords," Karls' answer was equally prompt, to the surprise of both Therron McLeod and Enri Willard. "Terms? Prince Parno is satisfied with first blood."

"Terms are mortal combat," Therron sneered. "Nothing less."

"At sunrise, then," Karls nodded. As the parties turned, the younger Willard stepped forward.

"I would have a word with my brother," he stated. Enri nodded. The other four participants of the formality withdrew, leaving the two brothers facing one another.

Enri Willard was tall, taller than Karls, and heavier. A long scar was faintly visible down the left side of his face, placed there long ago in a similar event. He smiled faintly at his younger brother.

"Appealing for mercy already, brother?" he asked lightly.

"My principal has no need of mercy, Enri," Karls replied calmly, refusing to rise to the bait.

"We shall see come sunrise, I suppose."

"You should withdraw," Karls said, his tone less formal now and showing concern.

"Withdraw?" Enri's voice showed his surprise. "Why would I do that?"

"Because he will defeat you, Enri," Karls told his brother. "You are no match for him."

"Did he ask you to appeal to me, brother?" Enri asked with a smile. "It is well known within the palace guard that Parno usually does his own fighting."

"He did not," Karls didn't quite snarl. "He offered to withdraw his challenge, offered it to me, not your benefactor. Not from fear, but for my sake. I told him he could not. That his honor demanded he continue."

"Offered to you?" Enri snorted. "Why?"

"Because I am his retainer and he is loyal to those loyal to him," Karls answered calmly. "He knew that his brother offered your services because of me. Among other reasons, I'm sure, but I was one of them. He was willing to forgo his honor and accept blame for wrongdoing that he is innocent of to spare me the conflict. I was also offered the opportunity to leave his service, my honor intact, if I felt the need."

"He is an honorable man, Enri," Karls continued. "One worthy of respect."

"Respect!" Enri Willard almost spat the word. "That witless fancy knows nothing of honor, nor respect. You dishonor our name by serving him and now you face your own brother at his side!"

"And you serve his, against him," Karls countered. "It seems we are both following the same pattern."

"After tomorrow, you will have no one to serve," Enri assured him smugly. "Perhaps I will offer a good word for you to Prince Therron. I'm sure you could manage a royal stable, somewhere. If the horses aren't too good, of course."

Karls sighed, wearily. He had hoped that his brother would listen.

"Your insults to me are meaningless, Enri," Karls assured his brother quietly. "We are finished here, it seems. I have asked the Prince, as a favor to me, to spare your life if at all possible. It is the best I can do."

"Spare me?" Enri's voice raised at that and several heads turned his way. "Why you insolent, ungrateful whelp! When have I ever needed mercy from an opponent?"

"You have never faced an opponent like him," Karls said sadly. "He will defeat you, Enri. You have no chance at victory, and little at survival." He turned to go.

"We'll see about that at sunrise!" his brother's voice followed him.

"I know," Karls answered over his shoulder. "I know."

-

Parno elected to stay in the palace that night, out of spite more than anything else he acknowledged to himself. Willard and Feng would stay with him as well. His apartments within the palace were roomy enough for the three. Willard had posted guards from the escort on the entrance to the apartments.

As the prince sat in the window seat overlooking the city, he sharpened his sword in the dying sunlight. Slowly, carefully, methodically. He was pleased with the blade already, but continued to slowly run the stone over the blade anyway.

Parno was glad that Darvo had not accompanied him to Nasil. He would not want his oldest and most faithful retainer to see what a mess his liege had made of what should have been a simple matter.

Once again the young prince berated himself, cursing bitterly under his breath. Why had he not foreseen how Therron would seek to trap him? Therron's presence should have been a warning to him, but in his anger Parno had ignored it.

Now he would face the champion swordsman of all Soulan in mortal combat. All over the bruised dignity of a Duke who was unworthy to bear the title. The blood of House McLeod had been strained too fine in Edward Willows. He was a coward.

Parno was certain that Therron had assumed that he would withdraw his challenge once hearing he would face Enri Willard. Withdraw in fear. Parno smirked in spite of himself at the thought. Therron knew too little of his younger brother.

No, he would not withdraw. Karls was right about that. If Parno withdrew the challenge and apologized, then both he and Edema would be stained for life. He himself could bear that well enough as he had done it all his life…but Edema deserved better and he owed it to her for the kindness she had shown him.

So tomorrow he would kill Enri Willard. Or at least injure him so severely that he might never again draw a sword. The effect on Karls Willard was difficult to ascertain. The younger Willard was tight lipped. He had not shared the subject of his discussion with Enri after the formals were observed and Parno had not asked.

Cho Feng entered the room, quietly as ever. Parno looked up at his teacher and laid aside his sword. He welcomed the distraction.

"Good evening, my Prince," Feng said.

"Evening, Master Feng," Parno nodded. "Have you enjoyed our stay so far?"

"It is a beautiful city, young noble," Feng nodded, "and the people are, if not friendly, not unfriendly." He smiled.

"Yes, it is a great city, I suppose," Parno agreed, looking out the window. "I suppose I am usually too bitter to notice that when I am here. I despise this place. I hate it as much as I am capable of hating anything."

"I understand," Feng replied. "One associates events with places and in the same manner. You have suffered greatly here, thus you cannot help but associate being here with being mistreated. It is natural."

"I guess," Parno shrugged. "I don't have your way of seeing things, Master Feng. I am educated, of course, but I have never had a talent for taking the wider view as you do. Darvo tried to teach me, of course, but a rebellious child rarely listens to even his most trusted adviser."

"Such can be said for many a ruler, Prince Parno," Feng chuckled. "Do not feel alone in that." The oriental weapons master hesitated for a moment, then asked,

"Are you prepared? Ready for sunrise?"

"I am," Parno nodded. "I wish it were not necessary, you know," he added.

"I do. I also know that the choice of champions pains you, as well. Karls Willard is a good friend and loyal retainer. Your offer was very noble. Most people in your position would not even had thought to offer at all."

"Well, every now and then I manage to do something right," Parno snorted. "It's rare, though. You should write the dates down when you see it."

"No one does right every time, Parno," Feng observed softly. "You blame yourself for much, but this was not your fault. I sensed during the meeting before your father that this was all planned very carefully."

"I'm sure it was," Parno nodded, "no doubt with Therron's oversight. Possibly even with my father's blessing, though I hope that's not true. Regardless, there is no denying that my stupidity is the root of this problem. I think, no matter what happens tomorrow, that I shall leave Soulan, Master Feng…for good." Feng's eyes registered surprise at that. Parno had often groused about his family, but it was always apparent that he truly loved his land and especially his people.

"And where will you go?"

"I don't know," Parno admitted. "Perhaps west. Maybe even south into the Latin Kingdoms. There are many places in the world I can venture and never return to this place, where I'm hated no matter what."

"You are not hated by everyone, Prince," Feng pointed out, "and you now have a regiment of soldiers to command. One that is very loyal to you as well."

"It's a farce," Parno snorted. "After tomorrow, it would not surprise me to lose that as well." He shrugged. "It's nothing I didn't expect."

"You seem to take great delight in expecting the worst, young noble," Feng said, his eyebrows rising. "I cannot help but wonder at that."

"Just being honest with myself."

"You automatically assume that you will fail, or, should you succeed, receive no recognition for that success."

"Well, that has been the pattern so far in life," Parno laughed quietly. Bitterly.

"I see," Feng nodded. "Your spirit is not in balance, Parno McLeod. Until you can regain that balance, your life will not be what you desire."

"Well, I'll put that on my to-do list, Cho," Parno said with a smile, "assuming I live that long."

"You will live," Feng assured him, turning to the door. "Your brother, Memmnon, is awaiting in the anteroom. He desires an audience with you." Parno looked up sharply at that.

"Send him in, then."

Memmnon walked into the room slowly, but steadily. He looked at Parno, still sitting in the window, examining his sword once again.

"Preparing, I see."

"Yes."

"It is not too late, you know. To back out, I mean. No one would blame you for not facing Enri Willard."

"I would," Parno said quietly. "I do not fear Enri Willard, Memmnon."

"No, I didn't think you did," Memmnon acknowledged. "You may be guilty of many things, Parno, but fear is not in you." Parno looked up at his brother, their eyes meeting.

"What brings you here, Memmnon? You knew I would not withdraw. Concerned for my safety, is it?"

"Hardly," Memmnon snorted, then realized how that sounded. "Not your safety, I mean. I am confident that you will triumph tomorrow." Now Parno's eyes registered true surprise.

"I am not a fool, little brother," Memmnon spoke calmly. "I am aware of your skill with a blade. Only the law forbidding your entry in competition has kept you from holding the King's Sword. Enri would know it, had Therron not blinded him to the fact." Memmnon crossed to an empty chair near his brother and settled into it.

"You know that Therron and Edward Willows set this up, do you not?" Parno said flatly. Memmnon nodded reluctantly.

"I think that Willows is nothing more than a dupe, honestly, Parno," Memmnon replied. "They were here, not long ago—the Willows. Therron took Edward aside and spoke to him in private. I didn't think anything of it at that time. Now, with hindsight, I see what must have happened." He paused for a moment, looking at his youngest brother.

"Parno, I want to tell you something," he said finally. "Things between you and I have rarely been any better than between you and the others. I know that and also acknowledge that the fault for that is mine. Over the past months, however, I have worked with you some closer as you built your regiment. I have come to respect you for that work and for the efforts you took on my behalf, on the family's behalf, in the Alma Province."

"Those were not the actions of a witless boy, playing at being prince. They were the actions of a Royal Son, loyal to his lord and land. Your statements this afternoon shocked father, I think. Therron, of course, is beyond any reasoning and Sherron and he share a brain, but father is isolated tonight in deep thought. I believe you may have hit him between the eyes earlier." Memmnon paused for a bit, choosing his words with care. When he finally spoke, his voice was quiet, but firm.

"I'm sorry, Parno, for the pain I have caused you. I'm ashamed, as well. My behavior was never that of a good brother. It was certainly not the behavior of a Crown Prince. I cannot undo the harm I've done, little brother. I can only go forward from today. I pledge to you, Parno, that I will never hold you to blame for the death of my mother, our mother, again. Nor will I treat with you in any fashion less than what you deserve." He stood abruptly, as if fearing he would lose the tight rein he was holding on his emotions.

"It is little enough, I know, to offer you for all the suffering you have endured over the years, but it is all I have. I hope that someday you can forgive me." With that, Memmnon turned without waiting for an answer and departed, leaving his brother still sitting in the window.

Parno would reflect, later on, that nothing his brother could have said would have surprised him more that those few brief words. To hear his brother acknowledge that he had treated Parno unfairly was surprise enough. To hear an apology, accompanied by a promise that it would not continue, was almost too much for the younger Prince. But for now, he was simply too stunned to say anything as his brother left the room.

It was several minutes before Parno returned to his sword, but return he did. Despite Memmnon's abrupt declaration there remained the matter of Enri Willard, Therron, and Edward Willows. Sunrise would come soon enough.

# CHAPTER SIXTEEN

-

The day dawned cool and clear in Nasil. Word of the 'contest', as such duels were known, had spread like wildfire and every noble within easy reach of the palace had hurried to Nasil, eager to see the show.

Parno arose well before sunrise and ate a small meal. Cho Feng assisted him with his armor, while Karls Willard stood by with the Prince's sword and shield.

Finally, as the first light of dawn began to creep over the horizon, the three made their way in silence to the inner courtyard.

-

"Gentlemen," the heavily scarred Sergeant of the Guard spoke quietly but firmly, "this contest is mortal combat. Each man is expected to acquit himself honorably as set forth in the Rules of Conduct. Any violations of that will be dealt with severely. I trust I make myself clear?"

Bran Holfurt had been the Sergeant of the Palace Guard for nearly ten years. He had held the King's Sword himself for seven years. As such, he was the judge and referee for such contests. He had little patience with weaklings, or with backstabbers.

"You do, Sergeant," Parno bowed slightly.

"Of course," Enri Willard almost snarled. The old veteran smirked.

"See that you do, gentlemen," he warned. "The contest will begin when I drop the flag. Each man will now go to his end of the court and brief his seconds. Luck to you both."

"It won't be a matter of luck," Willard sneered.

"Indeed," the old NCO nodded. Parno said nothing, but turned his back, walking to where Cho and Karls were waiting.

"Milord," Karls began, but Parno stopped him with a hand.

"I will do all that I can, Karls," Parno promised sincerely.

"I know that," Willard snorted. "I was about to direct your attention to the stands." Parno followed the nod, looking to where the crowd was thinner.

Therron sat with Sherron, to the left of the King. Edward Willows sat beside Therron.

But on the right hand of the King sat Memmnon McLeod, and with him was Edema Willows.

"One would think," Karls almost smiled, "that the Crown Prince is not in agreement with the Lord Marshall."

"One would, indeed," Parno nodded thoughtfully, then he turned his attention to business.

"Fight well," Feng said simply. Karls nodded his agreement and Parno smiled.

"I am indebted to you both, my friends," he said earnestly. "No man ever had better to stand beside him."

With that Parno whirled and walked into the court.

-

Tammon McLeod sat pensively, watching the drama unfold. Twice he had considered ordering the fight halted and dismissing the charges of Edward Willows out of hand. Memmnon had advised against it, however.

"If you do," the Crown Prince had warned, "then Parno is ruined. He will forever be followed by the charge that you acted thus to save him. Is he so reviled by you that you would do such? To your own son?"

Tammon had been angry at that, but agreed. Parno was, apparently, in the right in this instance and he deserved the opportunity to prove his innocence. But what chance did he have against Enri Willard? He voiced that concern to Memmnon during the discussion.

"Consider that Karls Willard asked of Parno that he, if possible, spare the life of his brother, the holder of the King's Sword," was all that Memmnon had said. Tammon had started at that, but Memmnon would say no more.

Tammon was still undecided about Therron's actions in all this and more to the point, what he, the King, was going to do about them. There was little doubt in his mind that Therron had worked devilishly hard to mousetrap Parno into this. In his anger the normally wary Parno had not seen, until too late, the trap laid for him.

The signal from the Sergeant brought Tammon back to the present.

-

As the flag dropped, Parno advanced casually onto the court. Willard did likewise and the two men met near the center.

Enri struck almost contemptuously at Parno, clearly expecting an easy victory.

Parno deftly turned the attack aside and struck back. Hard. Enri just barely managed to prevent from being skewered on Parno's blade and looked at the Prince in anger.

"Should take your swordsmanship more seriously, Captain," Parno said calmly. "Have to set a good example, after all."

Enraged, Willard set in with a purpose, unleashing a series of furious strokes that had overwhelmed more than one opponent in the opening seconds of such contests.

But not Parno McLeod. The young Prince parried each blow deftly—with his own sword in some cases—not even bothering to use his shield. With each block or parry, Willard simply became more enraged.

"Calmly, now," Parno chided mockingly. "Won't do for the Lord Marshall to see his Champion out of sorts, will it?"

"I'll kill you, you little piss-ant!" Enri Willard hissed.

"You'll try, I'm sure," Parno shrugged, at least as much as one could do so in the armor he wore. "So far, I'm not impressed."

Again, Enri Willard struck out with a flurry of blows. Again, Parno easily parried them. The crowd was beginning to murmur a bit, having half expected the contest to be over with in the first two minutes. It seemed, however, that this wasn't going to be the case.

Tammon McLeod shot a glance at Memmnon, who looked on, his face carefully neutral.

-

Across the way, Cho Feng smiled. He could not hear what was being said, but he recognized what the young Prince was doing.

"What is he doing?" Karls almost wailed.

"He is winning," Feng replied serenely.

-

"Why won't you fight?" Enri demanded, his breathing ragged.

"I am," Parno smiled. "I just fight differently than you do…and," Parno added, "I promised your brother I'd try not to kill you."

"He told me that," Enri snarled. "As if you could! You've yet to even make an attempt! Do you even know how to kill a man?"

Before Enri could add his smirk, Parno struck. His motions were swift, and timed, and Enri Willard could only barely parry them. The crowd's murmuring grew as the Prince struck again and again. Each time, the Lord Marshall's champion only barely managed to protect himself.

"How's that?" Parno asked finally, his breathing still as calm as it had been before the battle.

"You haven't touched me," Willard sneered, but his eyes now had a worried look.

"I haven't tried to, yet…but I will," Parno assured him.

-

"Parno is playing with him!" Tammon hissed to his oldest son. "Enri Willard is the most feared swordsman in the Kingdom and Parno is playing with him! Taunting him, if I'm any judge!"

Memmnon nodded, hiding a smile at the near pride Tammon's voice held for the youngest scion of the House McLeod.

"You knew he was this good?" Tammon demanded, almost angry.

"No," Memmnon admitted. "I knew he was better than Enri, but I had no idea how much better."

-

Therron's reaction was a bit different. His open-faced sneer of disdain had turned gradually to a look of mingled shock and anger. He had been certain that today would be the last he saw of his hated sibling. Therron had worked things just so the day before, trapping the younger Prince into a duel with Enri Willard. He had expected Parno to withdraw, leaving him stained forever with the charges against him. Enough to expel even a Prince.

Not only had he not withdrawn, he was, even now, making a fool of the Lord Marshall's Sword Champion!

"Milord?" Edward Willows said nervously.

"Silence!" Therron hissed, his gaze never leaving the court.

-

After twenty minutes of combat, Enri Willard was winded. Parno shook his head sadly.

"Not used to fighting a real battle, are you, Enri?" he taunted. "Not accustomed to having to work for it, are you?"

"I've never lost a contest," Willard managed to snarl, "and I won't lose this one, either!" With that, Willard lunged at Parno, both hands on his sword, the point aimed squarely at Parno's mid-section. Parno watched the blow coming and deftly sidestepped it. Before Enri could recover, Parno struck him at the base of his helmet with the pommel of his sword.

The elder Willard fell unceremoniously to the ground, head spinning from the blow. He immediately rolled, trying to avoid the blow he expected to his back. As he did so, however, he found himself looking up into the face of Parno McLeod, the Prince's sword laying across Willard's neck.

"Yield, Enri," Parno ordered softly. "I beg you. Do not make me slay you with your brother watching. You are fighting to defend a man who is unworthy of your service and who has laid false charges at the foot of the throne. Yield, I beg you, and let me spare your life. Soulan need's men like you."

Willard glared up at Parno for a moment, eyes clearing. He read nothing but sincerity on the face of Parno McLeod...and mercy.

Enri Willard had fought in many such contests as this one. So many, in fact, that he would have been hard pressed to place a number on them. In every one he had been triumphant and he had never offered, nor been offered, mercy of any kind.

Did that make him a better warrior than the young man standing over him now? A young man literally holding his life in his hands? Realization dawned on Willard then that it did not make him a superior warrior. He had been soundly beaten here today and Parno McLeod had every right, even an obligation under the rules of conduct, to take his life.

And yet, he hadn't. At least not yet.

"Karls was right," he grinned bleakly. "You are better than I am and you do have honor. I thank you for the chance to live, Parno McLeod. I'm honored by it, but you may as well kill me, Prince," he said finally. "My entire reputation, my career, is built upon my swordplay. If I yield to you, then I am done. My position demands that I -"

"That you die?" Parno looked aghast. "I think not, Enri. Your position demands that you fight. You have done so. It is not your fault that we meet here today. You are a pawn. A pawn of two men who planned to trap me into a fight I could not win, or see me dishonored. There is no fault in you for this. Nor blame." Parno leaned forward.

"Do not let them take your life and deprive your King of your service, Enri Willard. Do not grant them even a seed of victory this day. Yield in this matter and live to serve your liege another day."

Willard looked at Parno for a long moment, silent. Then his head lay back upon the ground.

"Sergeant," he called softly, and the grizzled NCO took the five steps that separated him from the combatants.

"Sir," Holfurt replied.

"I yield to Prince Parno McLeod, Sergeant." Holfurt looked to Parno.

"Terms of the contest are mortal combat, My Prince," he reminded him gently.

"As the victor, am I not entitled to spare a good man for another day?" Parno asked. Holfurt almost smiled. Almost.

"Indeed, you are, Milord," he replied. "Indeed, you are. Are you then, satisfied with the contest?"

"That remains to be seen," Parno said darkly. "I will not kill this man, however, to right the wrongs that have led us here this day. Make the call, Sergeant." Holfurt looked at Parno for a moment, no sign of surprise showing. He nodded, then turned to walk back to the podium before the courtyard throne.

Parno bent down, extending a hand to the beaten Enri Willard.

"Come, Captain," Parno smiled. "Fighting is dusty work. First drink is on me." Willard looked up at Parno, surprise evident on his face. Then, he chuckled softly, a faint smile playing across his weary face.

"I'll take you up on that, Milord," Willard smiled and allowed Parno to pull him to his feet.

-

"Your Highness!" Holfurt boomed. "Enri Willard has yielded in this matter, accepting the offer of Prince Parno. By the Rules of Conduct, Prince Parno is the victor. This matter is decided!"

"Very well, Sergeant," Tammon nodded. "Both parties will approach the bench."

Parno and Enri walked to the bench together, Parno helping a still rather unsteady Willard. Tammon looked at his son for a moment and Parno thought, just for a moment, that his father looked almost proud of him.

"In the matter of Edward Willows' charges against the Lady Edema, the throne finds in favor of the Lady."

"Edward Willows!"

Willows came forth slowly, his face pale.

"You have made grave accusations, Duke," Tammon rumbled. "Are you prepared to withdraw them as publicly as they were made? Your only other recourse is to now face Parno yourself," he added. Willows looked askance toward Therron McLeod only to find that the Lord Marshall had already gone. He looked back to Tammon.

"I am, My King," Willows almost trembled.

"Lady Edema," Tammon turned to look at Edema Willows. "Are you willing to accept this withdrawal?" Edema looked to Parno, who shrugged. She looked to Memmnon, who nodded gently and then to her husband, who looked stricken.

"If the charges are withdrawn as publicly as they were made, including an apology to my staff, then yes, Your Majesty. I accept." Finally, Tammon looked to Parno.

"And you?" he demanded gruffly. "Are you satisfied with this?" Parno almost snorted.

"I would prefer to have his head," Parno said easily and several gasps were heard from the crowd. "I'd ask for his bollocks, but he has none. I care not for any opinion concerning myself, thus I will allow the Lady's answer to be mine. So long as she is accepting, and held blameless, I will call this encounter closed."

"So be it," Tammon nodded, and again, Parno thought he saw the faint look of pride in his father's eyes. "Duke Edward," Tammon ordered, "you have amends to make, it seems. I'd suggest you get on with it."

Parno turned to see Karls and Cho Feng hurrying across the yard, both smiling.

"Well done, young Prince," Cho said when he reached Parno's side.

"Thank you, Cho," Parno murmured, conscious of the still present crowd and the talk racing through it.

"Thank you, Milord," Karls said earnestly.

"Not necessary," Parno assured him, smiling. "You are my dear friend, Karls. Whatever I can do for you, I shall. Always."

"I am glad to see you well, Enri," Karls said, venturing a smile. His brother returned it, albeit a bit weakly.

"Next time you offer me advice, little brother, I'll take it."

"Good," the younger Willard snorted. "About time, too."

"You can discuss that later," Parno smiled. "Right now, I owe the Captain a drink. And want one myself, now that I think on it. You two want to join us?"

-

The four men sat in Parno's apartments, gathered around a table. Parno and Enri Willard had both bathed and were wearing fresh garments. There was an open bottle before them, the level within it steadily dropping.

"I had no idea that you were so adept with a blade, Prince," Enri said, his voice not quite slurring.

"I told you," Karls objected to that, his own voice not quite steady.

"So you did," Enri nodded, "but I didn't believe it. Wouldn't have, had I not seen it for myself."

"I had a good teacher," Parno shrugged indifferently.

"Can't teach a man who hasn't the ability," Enri scowled, sounding somewhat like Cho Feng, Parno thought. "I've taught many a man to wield a sword, Milord. For them that haven't the ability, the "touch" if you will, no amount of training can make more than a fair hand with a blade. You are, without question, the finest swordsman in the Kingdom."

"I don't think that's the case," Parno rebuffed the compliment gently. "You were over confident, that's all. Were we to meet again, things would be different."

"I think not," Enri shook his head. "I gave you the best I had today, Milord. True, I was arrogant and careless at first, but not for long. Yet you stood that off with little or no effort. I might possibly last longer, were we to meet again, but the outcome would be the same. At least I hope it would be the same," he added with a laugh, "and not end with me skewered on your blade."

"I don't expect it to happen again," Parno said softly.

Enri nodded firmly. "Of that, you may rest assured. My father taught me that respect has to be earned, not given. You earned that respect, today, Parno McLeod," Willard said, raising his glass. "You are more worthy of your name, your heritage, than the brother whom I serve."

"Enri," Karls hissed. "You should not speak so!"

"I won't other than here," Enri assured him, "but I will not mince words tonight, little brother. Prince Parno spared me when he was under no obligation to do so and his brother sought to entrap him into a duel which he believed his younger brother was unable to win. Another man, someone with less honor, would have taken my life for spite." He looked back to Parno.

"I thank you, Prince Parno, for my life—and for a lesson in humility that was long overdue."

-

Parno made the short walk to the visitor's suite occupied by Edema Willows in silence. He was followed by Karls and Cho as they were about to set out on their return trip to Cove Canton. No doubt Darvo would be near frantic by now. Parno rapped lightly on the door. When it opened, Edema had obviously been crying. She wiped gently at her face.

"Come in, sweet child," she said softly. Willard and Feng each took places at the side of the door. Parno took two steps inside, then stopped at the sight of Edward Willows sitting at the table in the front room.

"My apologies, My Lady," Parno bowed slightly. "I did not mean to interrupt. I sought only to see after your well-being before I departed."

"Please, come in, Parno," Edema pulled at his arm. "Edward has something to tell you. He's already spoken to me. You should hear it," she added when Parno resisted.

He couldn't refuse her. Parno could never tell Edema Willows no. She was the mother he had never had. Slowly he walked into the room.

Edward Willows had the look of a beaten man, though no hand had been lain upon him. He had been drinking, Parno noted, but did not seem drunken. Edema sat beside him, Parno was surprised to see, and took his hand. Edward looked up at Parno, his eyes haunted.

"I. . .I'm sorry, milord," he managed. "I. . .I am a fool," he shook his head and lowered his gaze again. Parno frowned, something wasn't right.

"Edward, look at me," Parno ordered gently. Slowly the man looked back up.

"Tell me what it is that you have to say," Parno's voice was soft. "I daresay I already know, but to hear it from you might help." Edward looked at him for a moment, then nodded.

"Your brother, Therron," Edward told him, "took me aside when last we were here. He talked to me of you. He. . .he made some rather vile accusations, milord…and fool that I am, I believed them. Even when Edema refuted them to me, I still believed. Why would a Prince of Soulan lie, after all? To me, of all people. Who am I in the scheme of things? I'm a merchant that is wealthy, true, for Providence has been kind to me, but still just a merchant, Duke or no."

"Therron convinced you that I had, or sought to, seduce Lady Edema," Parno said it for him.

"He was very convincing, milord," Edward nodded, "and, as I said, fool that I am I believed it. When you visited our home and I saw Edema leave your room I know now that she was simply warning you of something just like this. She told me then, but I wouldn't believe her. Therron had convinced me you were the one I should watch, but it was him that betrayed me, milord. Not you." He stood slowly.

"I hope, Parno, that you can forgive me. I acted as I did on Therron's orders…or suggestions, I suppose, is a better way of putting it. The entire scene in the King's Chambers was orchestrated by him. I was but playing a part, the part of a fool."

Parno considered this for only a moment before speaking.

"Lay this aside, Edward," he said softly. "Put it from your mind and work to repair the damage between yourself and your lady that my family has caused you. I apologize for that. You were caught in a scheme to ruin me devised by my own brother and I gave you every reason to believe his accusations. Please know that I meant what I said. Your wife is dearer to me than my own life. The closest thing to a mother that I have ever had, but," he added, sadly, "I will visit your home no more, lest the idea continue to fester." Edema gave a small cry at that, but Parno shook his head.

"My presence has caused you enough pain, Edema. It has nearly ruined your marriage and could have cost you your husband's life. The fact that Therron manipulated this does not erase the fact that I made it possible with my behavior. Having a mother, even for a short time, was a blessing for me. I thank you for that kindness and will never forget it." He bowed slowly.

"I take my leave, now," he walked to the door. "I wish you, both of you, the best." With that he was through the door and gone before anyone could object. Once in the hallway, he finally allowed his anger to show through.

Suddenly, without need for thought, he started for Therron's apartments within the palace. His hand fell to his sword and his face was a stone mask. He had taken three steps before hands grabbed both arms.

"Milord," Karls whispered. "Think what you do!" Both Willard and Feng were smart enough to know what was on the Prince's mind.

"I have thought long enough!" Parno shot back.

"No, you have not," Feng told him. "There are bigger, more important things at stake than your idiot brother. Have you learned so little, Parno McLeod?"

The words had the desired effect and the Prince ceased to struggle. He looked at them both for a moment, then shook his head.

"Let's be away from here, while I can restrain myself." Both nodded eagerly, as ready to get clear of the palace, and the city, as was their liege.

Without further words the three of them headed for the stables to collect their horses. Parno didn't bother saying good-bye to anyone else. He knew they wouldn't care that he was gone anyway.

Inside, however, his burning fury cooled to a hard-shelled hatred of his brother. Yet, along with that feeling of rage also came the calming realization that his father, despite his open dislike of the youngest son, had not been a part of this. It seemed little enough to be thankful for, but Parno would take it. Take it and be glad for it.

For now.

# CHAPTER SEVENTEEN

-

Doak Parsons sat stoically near the south bank of the Ohi River, the natural border between Norland and Soulan. Through a glass he watched from the cover of trees as a Norland infantry regiment received instruction in boat use. Sailors manning the boats showed the men where and how to sit and how to man the oars.

Even as he watched, several of the long boats slid into the water and the soldiers in each began to row. Five boats, carrying a full company of infantry it appeared, made a brief crossing of the river, touching the south bank and then returning without setting foot upon Soulan Territory. The river had always been 'open territory', free to all. Thus, so long as the men didn't leave the boat, they had violated no treaty or law.

Lowering the glass, Parsons sat thoughtfully. No, no violation, but they were…very obviously practicing for just such an event. Raising the glass again, he observed the boats returning to the north bank, where the soldiers clambered out, replaced with yet another company and the process was repeated.

Again, no one set foot upon Soulan territory. Again, the boats simply touched and returned. This continued until each company had been across the river.

"Well, lads," Parsons breathed to his men, "is there any doubt now that the Nor are up to no good?" No one in his small party had an answer for that.

He didn't either. He carefully put the glass away and eased his horse away from the scene, followed just as carefully by his men. Once they were a mile or so from the river, Parsons increased his speed, heading south.

He needed to get back to Cove Canton. He had seen all he needed to in order to complete his mission. It was time to report back to the Prince.

-

Parno and his escort returned to Cove Canton eight days after leaving. He hadn't bothered to send a rider to inform Darvo of the outcome of the charges so he wasn't surprised to see the older man come storming out of the Headquarters building in full storm.

"I see that you are alive," he said testily. "May I assume that the problem is solved?"

"You may so assume," Parno nodded, dismounting. "Just a simple misunderstanding, Darvo." Karls Willard snorted loudly while Cho Feng smiled at his liege's knack for understatement.

"Well, what the devil happened!" Darvo demanded. "You could have at least sent word that the problem was in hand!"

"I did," Parno told him, blank faced. "A carrier pigeon was dispatched as soon as I arrived. Damn bird headed straight south, however," he continued, unable to hide a grin. "Birds don't care for the winter, you know." Karls laughed about that and even Feng smiled.

"Funny, funny," Darvo's face darkened. "Are you going to tell me what happened? Or will I have to beat it from your scrawny, worthless hide?"

"I tell you, the love, the respect, where does it go?" Parno shook his head sadly. "It's almost..."

"Damn you, you insolent, ungrateful whelp of a child!" Darvo bellowed and Parno finally laughed. He had succeeded in provoking the bellowing bull.

"Oh, relax," he ordered. "Everything is fine. Seriously. Okay?" he amended when Darvo's scowl didn't recede. "I admit, things between Therron and me aren't really that good at the moment, but hey! When have they ever been, right? It's just life as usual in the House McLeod!"

Darvo listened as his charge tried to put on a light air, but he'd known Parno too long. Raised the boy from a wee lad, just out of diapers. There was more to things than just a rift between himself and the Lord Marshall.

"I take it the question of adultery has been, for lack of a better phrase, laid to rest?" he asked.

"It has," Parno nodded, his voice darker now. More harsh. "It should not be raised again." With that, Parno entered the house, leaving Karls and Cho Feng to explain to the Colonel how things in Nasil had transpired. Darvo looked at the two of them for a moment, scowling when neither spoke.

"Well?" the older man asked testily.

"It was a trap," Karls told him flatly. "The Lord Marshall contrived to convince Duke Edward to lay the charges before the King in order to trap Parno into a duel...against my brother," he added. Darvo's eyebrows rose at that.

"Does your brother still live?" he asked, concern in his voice.

Karls smiled.

"Lives, and has a new respect for Prince Parno," he informed Darvo proudly. "Therron wanted the rules of mortal combat, but Parno, when he had Enri at his mercy, offered him his life to yield. Enri took it." Darvo nodded, not in the least surprised that Parno had beaten the Sword Champion.

"Indeed, there is much new respect in the city of Nasil for our young Prince," Cho Feng nodded, "but there is also a potential new problem," he added. "We had to physically restrain Parno from facing his own brother once the facts came to light, and the accusations have cost him his relationship with the Lady Edema, a relationship which was good for our liege. She doted upon him as his mother would have and treated him as a son. There is a black mood about Parno right now."

"I feared as much," Darvo sighed, shaking his head. "There will be no peace for him so long as Therron McLeod is allowed to continue his plotting."

"He almost ceased to be able to plot," Karls told him, his voice edgy with concern. "Had Cho and I not been with him when he discovered what had happened, I have no doubt that Therron would now be dead and Parno in dire trouble, if not dead himself."

"I'm glad you were there," Darvo told them both. "Rightfully it was my place, you know."

"No more so than ours," Feng reassured the older man. "We all have sworn to protect him, Colonel, and it was for the best that you remained here. Colonel Willard is correct in that, had things gone other than they did, you were the sole person who might have prevented a response from the men in this camp. They are very much enamored with the Prince."

"True," Darvo allowed. "I can only wonder, though, how the Lord Marshall will respond to this latest setback."

"If the mood of the King is any indication, Therron will have to be very careful, at least for a while," Karls said thoughtfully, "and Crown Prince Memmnon is well aware of the problem. I think, for the time being at least, the Lord Marshall will not be acting against Parno, not openly at any rate. I know not what he may try or be able to accomplish under the table."

"He's a snake, never doubt," Darvo told them darkly, "and full of hate for the lad. We'll have to be watchful, make no mistake and that includes Parno himself. He's prone to act rashly when his dander is up."

"Then we must ensure that he is not allowed to take any action that may endanger him," Cho told the other two men. "Too much is at stake."

"What?" both men looked at him questioningly. Cho simply shrugged.

"We will know, soon enough, I suspect," was all the explanation he offered.

-

Parno sat in his study, gazing out the window.

He had been lucky, he reflected. Therron had set a very neat trap for him and he had blundered right into it, blinded by his anger. Had he not been so skilled with a sword, thanks to Darvo Nidiad, then he might well be dead or maimed this very moment.  His only other option would have been to withdraw his challenge, leaving both himself and Edema forever tainted by the accusations Edward Willows had lain. He frowned deeper at that. Therron had nearly ruined the Willows' marriage in order to get at Parno and had caused them great pain. Parno would accept part of the blame for that, as he had given no thought to how it would look for him to spend time with Edema. The novelty of someone treating him well outside of Darvo had blinded him to any problems that might arise from his actions.

"Am I always to be an unthinking, rash, idiot boy?" he wondered to himself. He would never allow others to see his indecision, save for his three closest friends, Darvo, Karls and Cho. He almost laughed at how close he and Cho Feng had become. The man had a few short months ago been a prisoner and Parno a Prince. A black sheep prince, to be sure, but a prince none-the-less.

Fate does have a way of making us laugh, he chuckled mentally, but I must settle with Therron for this. His actions cannot be allowed to go unpunished. As his dark thoughts pervaded his mind, his eyes fell upon the blanket covered map. His frown grew still deeper.

There are bigger, more important things at stake than your idiot brother, Cho had said to him just three days ago.

Does he know what I know? Parno asked himself. Cho Feng had an uncanny— some might say unnatural—ability to know things he shouldn't know. He always seemed to know what was on Parno's mind. Had he, somehow, picked up on Parno's concern for the Nor? There was no way to know.

But seeing the map had turned his thoughts away from Therron and back to the problem he had been working over when Benson had arrived with Edema's note not even two weeks ago.

Rising, he uncovered the map. He opened a locked drawer at his desk and removed Edema's information and the Tinker's notebook. Slowly, carefully, he began to compare the two sources of information, making more notations on the map and in his own notebook.

Within a few minutes, he was lost in the numbers, descriptions, and other information contained there, leaving behind, at least for now, the troubles with his brother.

-

"My Lord?"

Parno looked up from his notations, seeing Harrel Sprigs at his door. He stood casually, covering the map.

"What is it, Harrel?" he asked, smiling.

"I'm sorry to bother you, milord," Sprigs said quietly. "It's just. . .well, sire, it's long past dinner and I was beginning to worry." Parno glanced at the window and noted that it was dark outside. He had worked for how long oblivious to everything?

"That's fine, Harrel," Parno assured him. "If you don't take care of me, then who will?" he smiled and Sprigs beamed at that. Harrel Sprigs had come to the regiment as a volunteer not long after the fort was opened. When Parno had spoken to the young man, he was surprised to find that Sprigs was not only a law-abiding citizen, but also a very educated young man.

Parno had seized upon him as a secretary almost at once. The young man was not impressed with that idea as he had wanted to be a soldier. He had specifically chosen this regiment because it had promised to be a tough unit and one that only a few would be able to make. To mollify the young man, Parno had persuaded Cho Feng to take Sprigs under his wing, so to speak. As a result, Sprigs, for all his scholarly ability, was one of the best fighters in the regiment. Cho had instructed him in several forms of hand combat as well as the sword. He had also, unbeknownst to Parno, charged Sprigs with protecting the Prince when he was engaged in something that would distract him from looking after himself. For that reason, Sprigs training was far greater than even Parno had known.

The result was satisfactory for all concerned. Parno had an able and educated secretarial assistant that could accompany him into the field when the need arose and Sprigs had learned more about the martial arts than anyone else in the regiment. Thus, the triumvirate of Nidiad, Willard, and Feng had a man close to the Prince at all times, both ready and able to defend the Prince's back, should they not be present.

All in all, a most satisfactory arrangement for everyone.

"I think I will retire," Parno told his lieutenant. "It's been a long day, anyway, and in truth I'm not hungry. Thank you." Sprigs bowed slightly and left the doorway. His own quarters were there in the main house and he headed for them. Parno blew out the lamp on his desk and slowly went up the stairs to his own room, his mind still full of numbers, locations, and threats.

His dreams were filled with them as well.

-

Doak Parsons pushed his men and his horses harder than he normally would have. Partly it was his hurry to get what he'd learned into the hands of Parno McLeod but just as important was the fact that the Prince had expected him to return to Cove Canton in six weeks' time. He'd been gone seven weeks already.

While he knew that Parno would allow him some leeway, he didn't want to use any more of it than he had already. He had been justified in what he'd done, he knew. Their observations along the Ohi were proof enough of that. But there was something else at stake. Something that Parsons himself was surprised to find was important to him—the young Prince had trusted him—and not just with money, either, but with something important, a job that had needed doing. Parsons found himself not wanting to let the young scion down and it had been a long, long time since Doak Parsons had worried about disappointing anyone. Anywhere.

"Doak," Harry James almost whispered from behind him, "the horses are about done in. We're gonna have to stop for a while. For them, if not for us." Parsons eased his pace, glancing at the men around him. Many were slumped in the saddle, obviously exhausted. The horses were foaming, not a good sign this time of the year. Harry was right. They had to stop.

"All right," Parsons agreed, reluctance in his voice. "We'll make a camp here. Start again at first light. I think there's an Army post a few miles east of here. We'll see if we can trade mounts there."

Hating every second that it cost him, Doak Parsons dismounted and helped his men care for their trail weary mounts. No one even bothered making a fire, so tired were they. Munching on trail biscuits and drinking water from their canteens, the men fixed their bedrolls and were soon fast asleep.

All, that is, except for Doak Parsons who lay awake, staring at the few stars visible through the tree tops overhead.

-

Morning brought more bad news.

"These two are done for," Harry shook his head sadly. "They can walk on their own, but not carry any of us." The two horses in question were obviously lame. Parsons didn't bother to question James' opinion. He was, if anything, an even better horseman than Parsons himself. If he said they were done, then they were.

"All right," Parsons sighed. "There's a small town near here. I'll head over there with a couple men and see can we find a few horses we can buy."

"Buy?" James couldn't help but grin.

"Yes, buy," Parsons wasn't amused. "We're done with that and don't forget it. None o' you," he looked at the men around him. "We got a chance, here, ta git clear o' the name o' being horse thieves and highwaymen and I don't aim to foul it up. You all want to go solo, head on out. But, you stay with me, you do what I say. Just like always. Got that?"

"Ease up, Doak," one of the others said softly. "We ain't leavin' out and we ain't gonna screw up. We'uns all taken a vote, 'n decided this was what we was for. You ain't the only one what wants a fresh start, ya know." Parsons looked at them all for another minute, then nodded, satisfied.

"Sorry," he told them. "It's just important, that's all."

"We done seen them Nor just like you did, Doak," Harry nodded. "We know what's to stake here. We ain't gonna abandon ya, nor the Prince neither, comes to that."

"Good," Parsons finally smiled. "Harry, you stay here. You're in charge till I get back. Stay off the trail, and outta sight. Poole, Conny, you're with me. Let's see can we git us some new horses." Silently the men gathered the mounts, lame ones included, and headed out. The other three men remained, guarding their camp.

Parsons cursed the lost time but knew there was no help for it.

He was still cursing later than day when the small patrol was finally on its way again. Damn wranglers, he cursed under his breath—and they call me a horse thief!

-

Once more Parno was staring out the window of his study. He had broken his routine today, staying inside rather than walking the camp as usual. So far he didn't think anyone other than Sprigs had noticed.

His eyes went back to the map before him. He didn't know what to do. Well, no, he knew what to do, he just didn't know of a way that he could do it, not without everything he'd gathered being summarily dismissed simply because it was he who had done it.

He wondered, idly, where Doak Parsons was. Had the thief simply taken his money and ran? Parno doubted it. True, it was possible. Anything was. But he held out hope. He had felt, rather than known, that Parsons was worthy of the trust he'd placed in him, that the man was simply waiting for an opportunity to prove his worth.

He likely didn't know it himself, Parno allowed, but the Prince had given him the chance to redeem himself and be useful and that meant something to him.

Parno would have to wait and see if his trust paid off. Meanwhile, he had a decision to make. He was tired of warring with himself over what to do. It was time to let the others in on his secret. Rising, he walked to the door of the study. When he opened it he found a soldier standing there, not quite on guard, waiting to act as a runner.

"My compliments to Colonels Nidiad and Willows and to Master Feng," he said to the waiting courier, "and would they join me in my study as soon as practicable?" The runner bowed, then hurried out the door to find the men in question.

Parno returned to his desk, waiting patiently.

-

"Lad, what is all this?" Darvo asked as the three men sat in Parno's study. They had waited patiently as the young Prince had ordered Sprigs to assume the guard on the door himself and post others outside. He had also closed the curtains, forcing him to light several lamps.

"How far are we as a regiment from being combat ready?" Parno replied with his own question. The look of shock on their faces would have been comical was the situation not so dire.

"Technically we're as ready as any new regiment can be," Darvo admitted reluctantly. "I'd prefer a good bit more time in drill and weapons training to be honest, but they can fight well enough now. Why?"

"Because I think we'll have need of them all too soon," Parno told him flatly. "What I'm about to show you does not leave this room, understand?" When he had received nods from all he walked to where his map sat on an artist easel. Pulling the blanket from it, he stood back to let them see.

"It is my belief, based on the intelligence you see on this map, that the Nor are planning to attack us with overwhelming strength. Probably as soon as the spring rains have ended."

"What?" Karls almost leaped to his feet, rushing to the map. Darvo rose slower and approached the map at a more dignified speed. Again, Cho Feng remained motionless, his face a mask.

"Where'd you come by all this, lad?" Darvo asked five minutes later, still studying the map.

"From talking to people who have been traveling in the north, thanks to the new trade agreements," Parno said quietly. "From listening," he shrugged. "People talk, Darvo."

"So they do," the older man nodded, "and sometimes it's just that. Talk."

"Sometimes," Parno nodded, "but this is too many people, and too much talk, to ignore. We're facing a serious threat."

"Who else knows this my lord?" Karls asked.

"No one knows about this," Parno indicated the map. "I suspect that anyone who has the eyes to see knows what is on it if they're paying attention at all."

"How certain are you of this information, lad?" Darvo asked, his voice betraying both skepticism and concern at the same time.

"Some of it is absolutely certain," Parno replied confidently. "The sources in red are confirmed by more than once source. The green by trusted sources. The blue are rumors…or rumors of rumors." Darvo nodded, pleased that Parno had used common sense in his gathering of information.

"Lots of red on this map," Karls noted, "and a good bit of green as well."

"Yes," Parno sighed, "there is. Too much."

"What do you intend to do with this, lad?" Darvo asked. Parno shrugged.

"I don't know," he admitted. "That's why I'm showing it to you. I'm open to suggestions. I don't know who I can give this to that won't throw it aside simply because it came from me." Darvo grunted in agreement.

"We need to have eyes in the north," Karls offered. "Someone who can move about and see if. . .what?" He broke off at Parno's uncomfortable look.

"I've already done that a bit," he admitted, "and that cannot leave this room, ever. If my father or Therron found out I had asked people to go north looking at the Nor army there's no defense I could mount that would save me."

"True," Darvo nodded. "Well, I suggest that you keep at it, then," he shrugged. "If this is even partly accurate," he gestured to the map, "then the Nor Army is quite a bit larger than it should be in time of peace."

"It's not just larger," Parno told him, sitting for the first time since entering the room. "It's better equipped and better trained than at any time in its history. Including," he added softly, "in cavalry and mounted infantry."

"Their horsemanship is a joke," Karls scoffed. "Always has been that I've ever read."

"For the most part," Darvo spoke with the voice of someone who had fought Nor cavalry. Long ago, anyway.

"Not anymore," Parno told them. "They have hired..."

"What does WT mean?" Karls asked, then looked abashed. "Sorry, milord," he apologized, realizing that he had interrupted.

"Wild Tribes," Parno ignored the intrusion. "The Nor have imported tens of thousands of horses from the West and hired members of the Wild Tribes to teach them how to employ them. Care for them. How to be trained as cavalry."

"What?" Darvo was stunned. "How sure are you of that?"

"Very sure," Parno replied firmly. "Absolutely sure. Wild Tribesmen have been seen in large numbers and in the act of training Nor horsemen. Fact, not guess," he added.

"Lad, that's very bad," Darvo said into the sudden silence. "It's always been our Cavalry that has made the difference in the past. If the Nor can counter that, then. . . ."

"Then they may well defeat us," Parno nodded. "Especially if they attack by surprise, when readiness is at an all-time low and we're thinking we're on good terms, for once."

"Good Lord!" Karls exclaimed softly. "They'd roll right over us!"

"That's what I'm afraid of," Parno admitted. "Now you know why I'm asking for your input."

"You know not how to proceed," Feng spoke at last. "You seek our council for that." Parno nodded in silent agreement. Feng looked at the other two men for a moment, then rose.

"You risk being ignored because of your status," he agreed, "and once ignored, the hope of convincing anyone that the threat is real is likely lost." Again Parno nodded.

"Then there is only one course for you to follow," Feng shrugged lightly. "You must continue to gather information while preparing this regiment for combat. Only when you have overwhelming evidence can you approach your brother, Memmnon."

"Memmnon was the one I was thinking of," Parno admitted. "He will at least listen, before throwing me out."

"And yet, this action creates another problem," Feng continued, as if Parno hadn't spoken. "Wait too long and the time needed to prepare will not be available. Reveal your secret too early and risk being ridiculed, and the warning lost. An elegant quandary, to be sure."

"So how do I decide when to go and speak to Memmnon?" Parno asked. The other three sat silently, pondering the problem. Finally, Darvo spoke.

"I would estimate that the Army would need a minimum of three months to transfer to a war footing without alerting the Nor that we know they're up to something," the seasoned veteran observed, obviously thinking hard on what readying the army would entail. "There's training to be stepped up, supplies to be gathered—any number of things. And," he added, frowning, "it will be difficult to do some things quietly. Field rations, for instance, will require large numbers of cattle to be slaughtered for jerky, tons of flour for field biscuits, and we can forget such items as parched corn, that late in winter. There simply won't be enough grain for it."

"And then there's the horses," Karls added, also thinking hard. "Forage will be difficult to come by in the early spring. Grass won't be available for grazing in any large quantity and hay will be gone—used up during the winter. The horses will also be coming off lean times in some cases as garrison commanders try to stretch their stores."

"The Quartermaster Corps will definitely have their work cut out for them," Darvo nodded in agreement, "and then there's leather. Saddles will need to be re-worked, reins and rigging re-strung. All that takes leather and in large quantity as well."

"Weapons, scabbards…hell, even boots," Karls shook his head. "I mean, there are literally hundreds of items we take for granted in peacetime that will become vital in war. And while we're at war, getting those items will become more difficult than in peacetime. Getting them to the men who need them even more so," he added.

"Agreed," Parno nodded, his gloom growing. "Even if we started now we'd be hard pressed to be fully prepared in time, and starting now, except for us, is not going to happen. There's no way I can think of to convince Memmnon, let alone my father, with only what I have now."

The others fell into silence again, mulling over the few options they had.

"Perhaps someone else could present this information?" Karls offered. "Someone that the King would be more inclined to hear?"

"That's what Memmnon's for," Parno told him. "If I can convince Memmnon then he can probably convince Father, providing he doesn't turn a deaf ear once he knows it came from me originally, and that's the problem," Parno continued darkly. "Anyone we approach about this will eventually have to admit where they got their information. Finding someone who can talk to the King won't in and of itself help us."

Karls nodded in understanding and set back again.

"Without risk, there is no gain," Feng said finally. "Taking your information to your brother is a risk. He may not even believe it himself. The only solution is to work to erase any possible doubt of what you believe you know to be the facts. How you present this information to Prince Memmnon may have a direct bearing on whether or not he accepts it as true, and upon how he, in turn, approaches the King with it."

"I have one more patrol to hear from," Parno told them at last. "They are overdue, even now. It may be that they won't return."

"Parsons?" Darvo asked. Parno nodded.

"I asked him to take five of his men and nose about—here in Soulan only," he added. "Find and talk to people who had been to Norland recently and see what they could glean from them, without revealing the why, of course."

"Parsons is the kind of man for that work, right enough," Darvo surprised Parno with that. "I know he's a criminal but men like him, they keep their word. If he's overdue he may simply be following a lead or a hunch. He could also have fallen victim to foul play or an accident," he added with a shrug, "life is uncertain, lad, for all of us."

"I know," Parno nodded, hiding his relief that Darvo, at least, agreed with his own assessment of Parsons. "I'm hoping to see him soon."

"Then I suggest we wait and see what he has to say," Darvo said firmly.

"For how long?" Karls asked. "We need to set a time frame for when we must act on this, regardless. We can't wait too long for the reasons we mentioned and for others as well."

"One week," Parno said firmly. "If he isn't here in one week then I will assume that he isn't coming back. After that, I'll take what I have now and ride to Nasil. I will lay the entire thing on Memmnon's desk. Once I've done that, I've done all that I can." He stood.

"Meanwhile we must begin preparing this unit for war. We have a head start over everyone else. Don't waste it."

-

Three days later a weary and saddle sore Doak Parsons led his men through the gates at Cove Canton. The guards were shocked at the bedraggled look the men wore and the horses looked as if they would be useless as mounts in the future.

In truth, that was possible. Once they had secured re-mounts Parsons and his men had rode as far into the night as they could and broke camp well before dawn the next morning. That pattern had been followed for three days running. All of them, men and horses alike, were at the end of their rope.

"Never thought I'd be glad to see this place as I am right now," Harry James commented tiredly as the six men rode into the gate.

"True 'nough," Parsons muttered tiredly. He was filthy and exhausted. They all were. He dismounted and rummaged into his saddlebags for the book he'd used to keep his notes together, handing his reins to James.

"See to the horses," he ordered. "Then fag out. All of you. You've earned it." The men nodded dully, walking their mounts toward the stables. Parsons watched them go for a moment, then turned.

To find himself face to face with Parno McLeod.

"I see you finally remembered where we were," Parno said, eying Parsons closely. "You look about done in," he added. "I'm glad to see you back."

"I'm sorry, milord," Parsons told him. "We. . .we went a might further north than I'd planned and we had some horses play out on us. We made best time we could, just wasn't good enough."

"I said I was glad to see you back," Parno reminded him. Parsons grimaced.

"That may not last, you see what I got ta tell ya."

Parno nodded and turned to the nearest trooper. "Have Colonels Nidiad, Willard, and Master Feng report to my quarters at once. My quarters, not my office, understand?"

"Milord," the soldier bowed slightly and hurried off. Parno turned to look again at Parsons.

"C'mon," he ordered. "I'll get you something to eat. Something hot." Without another word he set off to his house on the small rise overlooking the inside of the fort. Parsons followed him, also without a word. Sprigs hurried from the Headquarters building to join his liege.

"We'll have visitors momentarily," Parno told him without preamble. "Inform the cook I'll expect hot food as soon as possible and a hot bath ready to be drawn after the meeting," he added, glancing at Parsons. "See to it that the Officer of the Day knows that the men who just came in are excused duty for the next two days and that they're fed. Have a warm bath waiting for each of them as well, then return to the house. I'll need you at the door, once more." Sprigs nodded in acknowledgment then hurried to obey.

"I take it you bear bad news," Parno said calmly to Parsons once no one was in earshot.

"I'm 'fraid I do, sir," Parsons agreed tiredly. "Mite worse'n bad."

"I suspected as much," Parno nodded. "You've made sure your men will stay quiet? Everyone else will know soon enough."

"They know not to be runnin' their mouths," Parsons agreed. "Not even to each other. They'll do what they's told."

"I have no doubt."

-

"So, there it is, milord," Parsons finished. It had taken him over an hour to relay what he had heard and seen himself to the assembled command staff. There had been questions, of course…some he could answer, some he couldn't.

"We'll keep you no longer, Mister Parsons," Parno said softly. "There's a hot bath waiting and a new uniform."

"Thank you, sir." Parsons chuckled.

"Told you it was unseemly, man o' yer station callin' me sir," he reminded Parno. The Prince smiled at that, and nodded.

"So you did, Lieutenant," he replied. Parsons was so tired it took him a minute to realize that Parno had called him. . . .

"I ain't hardly officer material, milord," the former thief said quietly.

"I think I can decide that," Parno rebuffed him lightly, "and you are as of now Lieutenant Parsons. You and the men who followed you here will now be separated from your current assignments and formed into a scout detail. We'll discuss that later, however. For now, get cleaned up and get some rest."

Parsons regarded the young Prince carefully for a moment, then saluted slowly.

Once it had been returned, Parsons left the room. Darvo chuckled, despite the gravity of their predicament.

"You've made a lifelong friend there, lad," he told Parno. Karls and Feng both agreed.

"Be that as it may, we now have another source of information to add to our map," Parno replied. He slowly uncovered the map and the four of them spent the next two hours adding Parsons information to the map, then compiling the various reports into one.

Standing back, they studied their handiwork. They didn't admire it, just made sure it was complete.

"Lord Above," Darvo broke the silence at last. The others nodded mutely.

"This is bad," Karls Willard spoke and the others laughed darkly at his understatement.

"So, what now?" Darvo asked, turning to Parno. The Prince studied the map for a while longer. Finally, he sighed, turning to face his friends.

"I will ride for Nasil on the morrow," he told them.

"Want me to go along?" Darvo asked. Parno shook his head.

"No, none of you are going. Not this time," he added, as they all three began to protest. "We can't afford it. I may be gone for ten days or more. All of you need to use that ten days to continue training our men and preparing our stores," he added. "There's no time to lose. This regiment was designed for something just like this," he reminded them. "To blunt a massive Norland assault. We're considered expendable."

"I don't want our men unprepared for battle. If they're thrown into a grinder like that only good training and better discipline can ensure that at least some of us survive."

The three men in front of him nodded their agreement. They'd never expected this.

"I'm sorry," Parno told them all. The weight of their lives as well as the others suddenly forcing him down. "I never thought that something like this might happen. This was supposed to be a nice, calm garrison post." Darvo snorted.

"No such thing in this army, lad," the veteran told him. "That's the lot of soldiers, Parno. You train for something you hope never happens. Then, when it does, you wish it happened somewhere else. It's no different for the men in the Nor ranks, I assure you."

"I suppose not," Parno agreed. "Well, all of you have work to do and I have a visit I need to make."

-

Parno hated coming here.

It wasn't that he didn't like Roda. He did. The fussy little man was a constant source of amusement.

He was also dangerous.

Some of the 'concoctions' that he came up with were spectacular...even moreso when they 'concocted' unexpectedly.

"Hello, Prince," Roda smiled, seeing Parno walk into his workshop. "What beings you out on such a cold day?" Parno looked first left, then right, very carefully while replying.

"I need to speak with you, Roda," Parno told him. "In private." Roda nodded, and led the way toward his personal office, shouting instructions to his two assistants as he went.

"Carl, you damned buffoon, put that down! Carefully, you idiot!  Unless you want to spread yourself all over the valley. Billy, you half brained ape! How many times do I have to tell you never touch that!"

"Sorry Professor," the two chorused, eyes rolling. Parno almost smiled but the effort was just too much for him at the moment. As the two men entered the office, Roda took a chair and motioned Parno to another.

"What can I do for you, milord?" he asked. "Bear in mind, that the time we spend here is directly proportional to the possibility that one of those cretins will kill us," he added.

"We will be swift," Parno assured him. "I wanted to know how your weapons research is faring."

"Very well, at the moment," Roda assured him. "I believe I've solved the problem with the mines and will start testing them in another day or so but I still need to tweak the design a bit so that we can make them in large number."

"The ballista rounds?" Parno asked. Roda frowned.

"They work," he admitted, "but they are more unstable than the mines, milord. At least once in twenty, or perhaps twenty-five shots, they explode prematurely. Once on the delivery system itself. Had there been an actual crew they no doubt would have been killed."

Parno nodded, disappointed.

"Is there any hope of making them work better? Reducing the risks?" he asked. Roda shrugged.

"Perhaps, milord. I am experimenting now with a system similar to that of the mines. I don't know that it will fire correctly as yet. It's just in the planning stages."

"Trebuchet rounds?" Parno asked.

Here Roda smiled.  "They perform wonderfully," the inventor enthused. "Far outdoing my original estimates, in fact."

"And we can use the same rounds for the catapults?" said Parno.

"Yes, yes, I told you before that would work," Roda agreed irritably. "Why?"

"As of today, your experimenting takes a back seat to production," Parno ordered without answering the question. "I want as many of the mines, catapult and trebuchet rounds as possible. I want people working on them every possible minute. Do you understand?"

"No, I don't," Roda looked confused. "Why would you. . . ."

"I don't need questions, Roda," Parno told him flatly. "I have given you your head since bringing you here. Now I need you working on something I need and need badly. I'll send a work detail up here later today to start digging you new bunkers...safe places to store the weapons as you ready them…and a guard force to ensure that no one gets too interested in what you're doing."

"How many of them can you make in the next three months?" Roda blinked like an old owl at that.

"I. . .I don't know, milord," he replied honestly. "It will depend on how quickly we can get a means of mass production set up and, you understand, there are inherent dangers in hurrying this sort of thing."

"I do," Parno nodded. "Proceed as quickly as is safely possible, Roda," he ordered. "I want as many of those particular rounds ready as quickly as is safely possible."

"Milord, is there a problem of..." Parno halted his line of inquiry with a raised hand.

"You know all you need to know for now, Roda," Parno told him sternly, though not unkindly. "You don't want to know, anyway. Trust me. Just see to it that things are moving. Whatever you need, I'll see to it that you get it. Understand?" Parno seldom took on Royal 'airs' here or anywhere for that matter, Roda knew. When he did, it wasn't wise to argue.

"I will get right on it, milord," Roda promised. "I'll begin laying out new bunkers now so that the work crew can start immediately."

"Excellent. Make no mistake, Roda," Parno told him, looking the inventor directly in the eye. "The work you do, and are about to do, is vital to the kingdom. In ways I cannot yet tell you. Trust me and work well, work safely, and above all else, work swiftly."

Roda sat motionless for a few seconds after Parno departed. There was only one thing that could necessitate the need for the weapons he crafted here. Soulan was going to war.

But with who? They were at peace with the Nor and there was no one else. Yet Parno had been most insistent, almost desperate, and certain that Roda's inventions would play an important part in protecting the kingdom. He shook himself.

Regardless of the reasons, Roda had his orders from Parno McLeod himself and Roda owed Parno his life and much more besides. He rose from his chair and scurried out of his office.

"Carl, you moronic imbecile! Bring the strings and come with me. Get the hammer and some stakes! Billy, you're coming too. I can't afford to leave you in here unsuperv… don't touch that you idiot!"

-

Parno was in the saddle before sunup. Berry and his men were with him and no one else. The trip would be a hard one.

"Snow on the wind, milord," Berry commented as they made their way down the road slowly in the growing light.

"I know," Parno nodded. "No help for it, I'm afraid. We have to get to Nasil."

"We'll get there, milord," Berry promised.

There was no more talk as everyone concentrated on the road. Riding in poor light was treacherous enough without distractions. Parno was concentrating on the road with only part of his mind, since he was also thinking about what he would say to Memmnon once he reached Nasil.

Would Memmnon at least hear him out? Probably, Parno judged. Would he believe him? Possibly. Much of that would depend on how convincing Parno was in his explanation.

"What will I do if he doesn't believe me?" the young Prince wondered. "And what will happen if he doesn't? Will I be removed from my position? Punished in some way? What can they really do to me, anyway? I'm already basically ostracized. There's not much more they can do to me, save banish me, and if they do that then at least it won't be my problem anymore."

Even as that thought occurred to him, he shook it off, angry at himself.

"Of course, it will still be my problem", he chided himself. "This is my home. My people. My friends in some cases, though there's all too few of those. Whatever happens, I can't just walk away, washing my hands of any obligation."

He almost stopped the trip at that. Maybe waiting was better. Waiting and gathering more information.

No, Darvo had been quite clear about how much time, minimal time, the Army would need to prepare for an invasion the size of the one the Nor were apparently planning. Three months at a minimum and they hadn't much longer than that now. They had five months at the very outside, depending on how strong the spring rains were and when they relented.

That's all the time we have, Parno thought bleakly. Once that's done, the Nor will attack us in greater strength than ever before and with an army better equipped and trained than ever before in their history.

No, it had to be now. There was no choice.

-

The trip was difficult to say the least. They had been in saddle most of the first day when the snow began falling, and it fell swiftly.

"Likely be this way until we're off the plateau, milord," Berry told him. "I don't know that we can get down today. Not before dark."

"We need to if we can," Parno ordered. "I don't want to risk the men's lives but as long as we can proceed, we will. We cannot afford to be caught out here, Sergeant. Not like this. Once we're down, we'll likely still face rain, but the snow and ice will be gone. If we can make it off the mountain then we'll stop at the first inn we come to and stay the night."

Berry nodded and sent a man ahead to scout the way.

The going was slow and, in some cases, treacherous. More than one time a horse and rider fell. One horse had to be put down, his leg broken in two places. The rider had managed to escape injury, for which Parno was thankful. They had brought a few remounts for just such an emergency and one was immediately pressed into service.

The small column pressed on.

Finally, just at dark, they reached the trail leading off the mountain. Berry eyed the snow-covered roadway with no small trepidation. Parno sat beside him, considering for only a moment before giving orders.

"We're going down," he ordered. "We have some light and the road is a good one beneath the snow. Let us go now and we'll stop as I promised. We cannot delay and be caught in the weather." Again, Berry nodded and the small column began easing its way down the mountain.

-

It was long after full dark when the weary group of men rode into the small village of Cenevil. Berry knocked at the door of the inn, waking the owner.

"Who are you?" the sleepy-eyed owner demanded.

"My name is Parno McLeod," the Prince himself said, appearing out of the snow. "My men and I need lodging and food for ourselves and our horses."

"O… of course, milord," the owner was instantly co-operative. "Please come in. I'll have my man awakened to see to your mounts."

"We can do that ourselves, milord," Berry spoke softly. "Won't take a bit." Parno nodded and stepped into the inn.

"I don't know that I have rooms for…" the owner began, but Parno stopped him.

"If you haven't enough rooms we'll sleep on the floor, near the fire. We will require breakfast well before dawn, as we need to be in the saddle again at first light. Will that be a problem?"

"No, milord," the inn owner replied, "and I'll have something going for your men in just a moment." Parno nodded and took a seat by the fire. He almost felt guilty, warming this way, while his men were…

"Milord?" Parno started awake at the touch on his shoulder. He looked up to see Berry looking down at him in concern.

"Are you all right, milord?" the sergeant asked. Parno nodded.

"I'm sorry, Sergeant," he said, standing. "I was more tired than I realized."

"No need, milord," the big sergeant smiled slightly. "There's a room prepared for you at the top of the stair, sir. We'll bunk here for the night."

"I'll stay here with you," Parno replied, but Berry was shaking his head.

No, milord," he said softly. "There's not a man here will think less o' you for takin' the room. Do so. Let us worry about down here." Parno looked at Berry for a moment, then nodded wearily and made his way to the room.

He was asleep as soon as his head hit the pillow.

-

The remainder of the trip was easier only in that the opposition was rain rather than snow. The Trade Route wasn't far from their first night's stop and they were on it, galloping east, less than two hours past sunup. Another stop that night put them near Nasil.

"We'll be there before dark tomorrow, milord," Berry promised.

Parno nodded.  It wouldn't be long now and then he'd have to face Memmnon.

The easy part of this trip was almost over.

# CHAPTER EIGHTEEN

-

They arrived just before dark, men and horses exhausted. Royal stable hands took the horses at once while Berry took his men to the transient quarters. Parno made his way into the palace, carrying his valise. Inside was everything he had managed to gather.

He hoped it was enough.

He walked directly to Memmnon's office where a guard told him that, yes, the Crown Prince was still in his office, but had asked not to be disturbed. Parno simply stared at the guard until, after ten seconds, the guard murmured; "Wait here, milord," and disappeared inside. He was back in five seconds.

"The Prince will see you, milord," the guard announced. Parno nodded and walked inside.

"Hello, Parno," Memmnon smiled as his younger brother entered his office. "What brings you out in such bitter weather?"

"Memmnon," Parno nodded in greeting. "It is business of a most urgent matter, I assure you. Else I would still be by my fire." Memmnon's face lost its smile.

"What is wrong?"

"I have something to tell you, Memmnon," Parno began softly, "and you aren't going to like it."

-

"You set up your own spy network?" Memmnon almost goggled. "Parno, that is not your province!" Memmnon wasn't angry, exactly, but he was dismayed. His younger brother had worked hard to establish himself. The duel with Enri Willard had impressed even their father, not to mention the onlookers who had gathered for the occasion.

This threatened to undo everything the younger McLeod had accomplished.

"No, I didn't," Parno replied evenly. "I haven't a single spy. All I have done, brother, is ask questions. Many, many questions and the answers have disturbed me a great deal."

"Questions of whom?" Memmnon demanded.

"People traveling the Nor lands," Parno told him. "People who have seen the changes taking place in Norland. People who have done business there, traveled there, even lived there for a time in recent months." He leaned forward.

"Memmnon, it is my belief, my fear, that when the spring thaw comes, the Nor will attack us in overwhelming strength. With greater numbers and better training than ever before. If I am correct, then we must begin preparing…now…for that contingency."

"Father will explode when he sees what you've been doing, Parno," Memmnon warned. "You must know that. All the progress you've made could be lost."

"I know that," Parno nodded in sad agreement, "but what else can I do? I can't simply set by, knowing what I do, and say nothing, Memmnon. If I'm right, then we face the gravest threat in several generations. If I'm wrong," he shrugged.  "If I'm wrong, then I'm no worse off than when I started."

He leaned back, then, as if talking had exhausted him.

Memmnon studied his younger sibling for a time, turning over what had been said in his mind. Parno had known the risks of divulging his thoughts and still had done so. Not to help himself, obviously, since even he knew that this was likely to spark another round of contentions between the King and his youngest offspring, not to mention Therron.

No, he had done it because it was his duty as he saw it to present his information. If he was correct then the people of Soulan faced a grave threat, and that was as right as any words ever spoken. Always it had been the Southron cavalry that had made the difference in any war between them and the Nor. If that advantage was now gone and the Nor had built and trained a large army...

"Show me what you have, Parno," Memmnon said suddenly, and felt a sadness at the relief on the younger McLeod's face.

"He was afraid I wouldn't listen", Memmnon thought. "That no one would listen."

"Let's look at your information, and see what we can see." Memmnon said.

-

An hour later they were still looking and Memmnon's concern for his younger brother had now turned to concern for the entire kingdom.

"My God," he breathed as Parno finally finished tallying the intelligence marked on his closely guarded map. "Parno, this is. . . ." Memmnon trailed off, looking up at Parno's bleak face.

How long has he lived with this? How many weeks has he labored under this strain?

"You've done well, Parno," Memmnon said firmly. "No matter what anyone else says, this is excellent work. I've never seen better." Parno smiled tiredly.

"I'm glad to finally have someone to show it to," he admitted. "I have worked and labored for a great long time, growing increasingly fearful with each passing week. I was afraid…"

"That I wouldn't listen?" Memmnon asked kindly.

"No, I felt sure that you would give me a fair hearing, Memmnon," Parno told him, "but I did fear that no one else would and that the threat would be ignored."

"Well, I can't speak for the King," Memmnon told him, "but I intend to speak to him at once. Why don't you wait here? Rest a bit and warm by the fire. I will come for you once I've spoken to Father." Parno nodded tiredly, watching his brother go.

"And now we'll see", he thought bleakly. It was a good sign that he had at least convinced Memmnon.

"If anyone can get through to him, it's Memmnon", he thought. "If he takes his time and doesn't mention me until it's all on the table, then there's a chance…"

Parno felt a hand upon his shoulder, shaking him gently awake. He started, his eyes snapping open to see Memmnon looking down at him. He hadn't even realized he was asleep.

"I was more tired than I realized", he thought to himself.

"I hated to wake you," Memmnon smiled. "You looked so peaceful. I have spoken to father and he wants to see you. Now."

"Very well," Parno sighed, rising to his feet. "May I inquire as to how things went?"

"They were. . .interesting," Memmnon replied cryptically. "Let us hurry."

Parno followed his brother through the hallways to the King's apartments. Parno knew the way but had gone there only on rare occasions. Tammon had never been someone Parno wanted to visit and Tammon had rarely invited him anyway.

As they approached the doorway, two guards snapped to attention.

"Your sword, milord," one of the guards spoke softly, indicating Parno's sword. "You must leave it here." Parno frowned, eying Memmnon's own blade.

"That isn't necessary," Tammon's voice spoke as the door opened. "Never make such a request again," he added, and the guard paled.

"Come in, both of you," Tammon ordered, and the two brothers entered the King's apartments. Tammon waved them to chairs near his great desk where the map and information that Parno had given Memmnon lay spread.

"Parno," Tammon said evenly, "Memmnon has laid this before me and has been very convincing, yet I must tell you, this is beyond your purview. You had no authority to do such a thing."

"I am aware of that," Parno replied evenly.

"Good," Tammon nodded. "As it is, however, I am glad that you did. Where it not for you we would as yet be unaware of this threat. Likely our first indication would have been when the Nor hordes came across the border. Thank you."

Parno blinked at that, but nodded, holding his tongue. Tammon smiled softly.

"I know that surprises you," he said softly. "I have come to regard you in a different light, of late, my son."

Again, Parno nodded, not knowing what to say. Tammon's face lost its almost smile, apparently having expected more from Parno in way of reaction, but rather than pursue it he took his own chair.

"I will shortly summon Therron to look at this, as it is his responsibility to prepare our defenses. I wanted to discuss this with you first, however, as you are the one who has gathered this information...but I want to know something beforehand. Is this," he waved to the information spread before him, "one of the things you were discussing with Edema?"

"Yes, my King," Parno replied formally. "It is."

"I see," Tammon nodded gravely. "Then I owe you an apology as well as my thanks, and that of the Crown," the elder McLeod said formally.

"I did only what needed to be done," Parno shook his head. "There is no need for either." Tammon regarded his youngest son for a moment, then nodded.

"Let us turn to the issue at hand, then."

-

Therron, of course, did not react as well.

"He had no right!  None!...to do this," the 'Marshall' said vehemently, his face red as he waved to the map and information on the table. "I insist that he be removed from his post as..."

"That's enough," Tammon McLeod said quietly, his gaze boring into Therron. "I have already pointed out that this is beyond his purview and he has admitted it. I will point out, once, that this subject is closed now and for all time. Do not raise it again."

Therron's attack lost its power at that. Tammon McLeod wasn't known for his patience, or forbearance.

"This issue at hand," Memmnon took over casually, "is how prepared are we and what must we do to ensure that we are as prepared as possible for this eventuality? As Lord Marshall," Memmnon managed to keep his words from sounding scornful, "that is your purview, brother. So, speak."

"The Nor war making capability is a farce," Therron snorted at once, almost a knee jerk reaction as he was still glaring at Parno. "If they attack, we will destroy them. Our cavalry..."

"Will be outnumbered," Tammon said evenly, "and against better opponents than they have ever faced."

"Nor cavalry is a joke," Therron scoffed.

"And would you make that same statement in regards to the Wild Tribes?" Parno risked speaking.

"What?" Therron asked, nonplussed at the change of subject.

"The Nor have acquired horses from the West," Tammon grated, his patience with his middle son nearing an end, "and trainers as well. Thus, their cavalry will not be quite as humorous as you may believe."

"From the Wild Lands?" Therron looked as if he'd eaten something spoiled. "Are you sure?"

"Yes," Parno nodded. "Over a dozen different sources have relayed to me that Wild Men are training the Nor cavalry on mustangs brought in great numbers from the Wild Lands…and they have been doing so for at least a full year."

"In what numbers?" Therron asked, his temper cooling rapidly.

"At least twelve divisions—divisions, Therron—that have so far been positively identified," Memmnon replied evenly. "Divisions that number roughly eight thousand each."

"Twelve divisions," Therron was aghast. "That's a near two-to-one advantage over us," he breathed, "and if they are well mounted and well trained. …"

"They are," Parno assured him, "and the army is massive, Therron. Nearly half a million men, if the numbers are anything like accurate."

"How likely is that?" Therron regained some of his composure at that opening. "These people you've talked to, how versed are they in studying and identifying…"

"One of them is a former Soulan Cavalry leader who now owns a large ranch in the western part of the province," Memmnon answered for Parno. "As such, I must assume that he is at least capable of distinguishing good horsemanship from bad and good horse flesh as well," he added.

Therron's attack flagged again as he sat back in dejection.

"Well?" Tammon asked testily. "Are we prepared for such a war?"

"No, My King, we are not," Therron admitted. The words almost dragged from him. "We cannot possibly withstand such a force, at our current levels."

"How long to prepare for the invasion, then?" Memmnon asked, "and what are their likely avenues of attack?"

"Their best route is to simply force a crossing over the Ohi and come straight down the Kent plains and into the Tinsee valley," Therron rose, pointing to the map. "It's almost a natural invasion route and gives them forage if they time their attack right."

"As to how long?" Therron looked bleak. "We have twelve divisions of infantry, seven of cavalry, and two divisions of heavy infantry. Even with the Militia," Therron shrugged, "we'll have less than half their numbers."

"And the Militia will not be able to withstand such an attack," Tammon pointed out.

"Not likely, no," Therron agreed.

"Then we have a great deal of work to do, it seems," Tammon rose from his chair looking far older to Parno's eyes than when the youngest Prince of Clan McLeod had walked into the room.

"I'll order increased training in the southern regions at once," Therron nodded, "where the weather is more accommodating than here. We will commence training everywhere as soon as possible, however."

"We'll need more men," Memmnon said softly. "We'll need to raise several new divisions. I'll see to the preparations for equipping them."

"We'll muster the militia once a week, as well," Therron offered. "Increase their training regimen and bolster them with new recruits. It's faster and more efficient than raising a new division from scratch."

"How many Militia divisions can we muster?" Tammon demanded.

"Two from each province, Milord," Therron replied at once. "Their numbers will likely be low as we have been at peace for so long. I will see to new training and to a few new officers for their officer corps. Experienced officers. When the time comes," he added, "it may be that you will need to inform the Provincial Governors that the Militia will be commanded in the field by others, whilst their own commanders remain at home."

"That will not go over well," Memmnon pointed out.

"Tell them," Parno suggested, "that their command staffs will be needed to rebuild the Militia's taken into Crown Service and that you would not want to entrust such a job to anyone other than the men who had raised the Militia you were now depending on to bolster our defense against invasion. That there is no one else better for the job."

"Not bad, for a rogue," Tammon smiled, the twinkle in his eyes removing any sting from his words.

"Thank you, I think, My King," Parno smiled in reply, and was rewarded with the first laugh he could ever remember hearing from his father.

"Let's be about it, then," Tammon ordered. "We haven't much time."

-

"Are we all in agreement, then?" Tammon McLeod looked around him. For three days the King, his sons…all of his sons…and his top generals and advisers had poured over maps and reports. All of the men Tammon had called in on the problem had looked at the information that Parno had accrued and eyed the young Prince with renewed interest, almost respect. Parno returned their nods impassively. He knew better than to allow their acknowledgment to convince him he was now in favor with anyone.

The decisions made were hard, Parno conceded. Soulan's army was divided into five Army Corps. The base for each Corps was two infantry divisions and one cavalry. In most cases the infantry were mounted, riding to the battlefield, but then dismounting to fight on foot. The 2nd Corps, based in Loville, would likely bear the brunt of any Nor attack, thanks to the three bridges there spanning the Ohi River. Right now those bridges were part of the new spirit of cooperation, carrying goods back and forth in trade agreements made by the Norland Ambassador.

In time of war those bridges would become invasion routes. As a result, 2nd Corps was somewhat heavier than most, with an additional cavalry division and one 'heavy' infantry division. That division was specifically trained and equipped to make assaults on fortifications or to repel that same kind of assault from behind fortifications.

The 3rd Corps, in Shelby, guarded the bridge over the Great River, the sole remaining bridge that spanned the mile-and-a-half wide river. It, too, had an additional cavalry division and another heavy infantry division—the only such infantry divisions in the Soulan Army. The Kingdom of Soulan had never launched a war of aggression, thus the need for such formations was limited to defensive preparations.

That left the Militia divisions. Each of Soulan's six provinces were required by law to maintain two divisions of Militia, both to aid in suppressing any bandit activity and to support the Army in time of war. This tradition was so old that no one, including the House McLeod, knew it's origin. Parno supposed it had been a decree of the House of Tyree, the founding House of the Dynasty of Soulan, of which the House McLeod was directly descended.

The provinces had one division each of mounted infantry and cavalry. The decision had been made early on to absorb the various militia into the existing divisions within the standing army. Units would be added by brigade so that they could fight as a unit and their colors would see no break in service. Twelve divisions meant thirty-six brigades, plus what little artillery and support services each maintained.

Kent Provincial Militia units would simply be absorbed by the 2nd Corps. The men would be fighting on familiar ground and defending their families. It made little sense to send them away and many would likely object anyway.

Tinsee's Provincial Militia would be added to 1st Corps, stationed just outside Nasil itself. The 1st Corps was primarily responsible for the defense of the heartland. It would fall to them to stop any invasion that made its way that far south.

The Misi forces would be used to patrol the banks of the Great River in their province. Their border was, by far, the longest along the River.

In the Alma province, their forces would join General Herrick's 5th Corps in Moble. To him would fall the immense job of patrolling the expansive shores of the Gulf of Storms and defending those shores. A division of the Flora province would also aid him in that task.

The remaining Flora division, and both divisions of the Gera province would take the field with General Freeman's 4th Corps, stationed in Lana. Their area of responsibility would include patrolling the Sunshine Coast and in aiding in the defense of the heartland should the need arise.

"Do not forget the heartland," Parno said quietly amid the silence, "specifically, the Gap of Cumberland. It is a likely invasion route. If they can succeed in tying down our forces in the field, a large force coming through the Gap would be virtually unopposed." Therron snorted at that.

"The Gap has few trails that would support such a force," the Lord Marshall replied, disdain evident in his voice. "It would take over a week for mounted units to even reach it, let alone their trains and artillery."

"A good sized cavalry force, living off the land, could wreak havoc once loose in the heartland, Therron," Parno pointed out, his voice still calm. "We ignore that threat at our own peril."

"The Nor will never get that far," Therron predicted airily. "Davies will stop them and if not, I will take 1st Corps and personally run them into the ground."

"And if 1st Corps is needed elsewhere?" Parno asked, careful to keep any challenge out of his voice.

"Where?" Therron asked derisively. "The Nor will attack across the Ohi as they always have and we will crush them as we always have," he added, looking to the Generals around the table for support. One by one they nodded their agreement.

"That is the most likely route," one voiced their opinion.

"It is foolhardy to expect the enemy to continue to make the same mistakes," Parno said calmly. "We must assume that they will learn from their history, just as we teach from ours. We cannot afford to leave the Gap undefended."

"Your opinion has been noted...and dismissed...Parno," Therron almost sneered. Parno looked to his father, who nodded in reluctant agreement. Memmnon's face betrayed little, but Parno could see he was unhappy with the way Therron was managing things. Parno shrugged finally.

"As you wish, brother," he said simply. He had tried. He couldn't force them to see what he, himself, saw.

"Does anyone else have anything to add?" Therron asked. When no one else spoke, the Lord Marshall looked to the King.

"With your permission, Sire, we shall begin posting the orders."

"Very well," Tammon nodded after a brief pause. "That will be all for now, gentlemen." The generals departed behind Therron. The middle son sneered slightly at his younger brother as he departed, but Parno refused to rise to the bait. Once they were alone, however, he looked again to his father and his oldest brother.

"Do not neglect the defense of the Gap," he said one last time. With that said, he left the office himself. He wanted a drink and something to eat. Perhaps, he reflected, that would calm the uneasy feeling that Therron was leading them to disaster.

-

The next day as Parno was preparing to return to Cove Canton a thought stuck him. Leaving his escort with orders to continue their preparation, he made his way back to his father's office. There he found his father and both of his brothers pouring yet again over dispositions and training orders.

"Hello, Parno," Memmnon smiled tiredly. "I thought you would be in the saddle by now."

"I will be shortly," Parno assured him. "I realized as I was preparing that I had forgotten to ask which corps my unit will be assigned to."

"What?" Therron looked up sharply at that.

"Where will my unit be serving?" Parno repeated. "I didn't think to look with everything we. . . ."

"Serving?" Therron looked aghast. "Nowhere! That rabble of yours will be useless in the war that's coming. Stay at home and let your criminals continue to play at soldier. If they do well, we might use them as baggage guards for real troops."

Parno's face flushed deeper and deeper as Therron's disdain for his men and their ability became more clear with each word.

"Therron, I hardly think that's called for," Tammon said softly, but firmly, "and Parno's unit was formed for just such a time as this."

"They haven't had enough training to be of any use," Therron waved a hand in dismissal, "and they aren't soldiers in any case, just a loose bunch of rabble held together by promises and threats. They'll fold at the first sign of trouble."

"They are at least as well trained as many of the youngsters you'll be committing to battle from the Provincials," Parno grated, "and the shirkers and no accounts have long since been weeded from the patch. They are good men and good soldiers."

Therron's snort of disdain made his opinion know of Parno's statement. Parno ignored him, looking to his father and his oldest sibling.

"Is that it, then?" he asked, voice trembling with fury. "Good boy, Parno, run along now? After all that work and expense, my men and I are considered worthless?"

"I'd not agree with that," Memmnon assured him, glaring at Therron. "It's true, they haven't the experience that many of our units have, but as you say, neither do our younger recruits."

"Those younger recruits are all volunteers!" Therron almost hissed. "And loyal, law-abiding citizens, I might add."

"Therron," Tammon's deep voice rumbled across the argument. "Is it your professional opinion that Parno's men are sub-standard? Or is it your opinion of your brother that powers your argument?" Therron looked nonplussed for a moment.

"It is true that I have no love for my brother, sire," Therron said after a brief pause, his voice respectful, "but in this case, no. That has no bearing on my decision and it is my decision to make. His men are not equal to the task."

"And how would you know that, considering you've never laid eyes on..." Parno broke off at the raised hand of his father. Tammon's eyes, however, had never left Therron.

"Therron, I'll ask you once more and I suggest you take great care in how you address me," a warning timber crept into Tammon's voice. "What reasons, what proof do you have, that Parno's men are not capable of serving in combat?"

"I have had someone watching the progress of their training, Sire," Therron replied bluntly, ignoring the gasp of outrage from Parno and a withering frown from Memmnon.

"According to my man," Therron went on, "my brother's project has not come to fruition as yet and is unlikely to do so. He has frittered away his time playing with noisy toys and diddling. . . ."

"I'll kill you if you finish that," Parno growled low in his throat, his hand resting on his sword.

"Silence!" Tammon roared. "I have a kingdom on the verge of war! I have no time for squabbling children!" He turned to Therron.

"If you were about to say what I think you were," he warned, voice dangerously soft, "then I'll remind you that trial by combat, against a champion of your choosing, decided that matter. If you raise it again, you do so at your peril. I trust I make myself understood?"

"Yes, sire," Therron forcibly kept himself from retreating under his father's hard gaze. "I meant only that he has wasted the time given him and has not seen to adequately training his men. I did not mean to imply anything outside of that. His men are not capable of sustained combat operations. I doubt they would last out the first day without deserting to a man."

Tammon McLeod considered his middle son for a long moment, looking directly into his eyes. To his credit, Therron managed not to look away from the piercing gaze. Nodding suddenly, Tammon turned to his youngest son.

"I am inclined to take Therron's advice in this, my son," he spoke slowly, "and it is his decision, as Lord Marshall of the Army."

"Sire," Memmnon began, only to be silenced by a raised hand.

"I have made my decision," he said stonily. "I am sorry, my son," he told Parno. "Perhaps if you had used your time more wisely..."

"Don't," Parno cut his father off, his voice thick with emotion. "Don't finish it, Father. It is your right to make the decision, but you base it on deliberately false information. That, too, is your right," he almost spat.

"Since I am not needed, I will take my leave," he bowed stiffly, fury threatening to erupt from every pore. "Luck in battle, Father. Brothers." With that Parno turned to leave.

"Parno!" Tammon called out to him. Parno stopped, but did not turn.

"Do not think of this as an indictment upon you," his father told him. "Rather, it is..."

"It is most certainly an indictment on me," Parno grated, refusing to turn back, lest his brother gain some satisfaction in the tears of rage that threatened to spill from his eyes. "You, yourself, have said, 'had I used my time more wisely'. That is indictment enough and nothing less than I should have expected. Farewell, and

Godspeed."

Without another word, Parno McLeod walked away.

-

"Parno!"

Parno heard Memmnon's voice as he mounted his horse. For a moment he considered simply ignoring it and riding on, but Memmnon had been good to him, of late. He felt compelled to look back.

"What is it, Memmnon?" he asked coldly.

"I am sorry, Parno," Memmnon told him, voice ringing with sincerity. "That wasn't right."

"And as the purveyor of King's Justice you stood by and said nothing in my defense," Parno's voice was still frigid. His tone and the look on his face said something else. As my older brother, and someone I had come to trust, you failed to aid me when I was wronged.

"There was nothing to be done," Memmnon protested, though not heatedly. "It isn't my place."

"You could have defended me," Parno told him. "You know that I haven't wasted my time and that my men are far better prepared than many of Therron's. As to that, were you aware of Therron's spy?"

Memmnon's silence was answer enough. Parno nodded.

"As I thought. What a fool I have been, thinking that matters between us were improving. Things haven't changed so much after all, have they?"

With that final dig, Parno whirled his horse and spurred it on its way, taking him away from Nasil…and his family.

# CHAPTER NINETEEN

-

When Parno returned to Cove he went directly to his house, allowing the orderly to see to his horse and gear. He was still in a foul mood, even after three days of hard riding. The men of his escort had recognized that mood and word soon spread throughout the cantonment; the Prince was angry.

Darvo had known from the look on Parno's face and the way he carried himself as he stalked to his residence that his liege was aggravated in the extreme. He collected Karls Willard and the two of them headed over to see what the problem was.

As they entered both were surprised to see Parno sitting at the table in his study, drinking. Parno seldom drank these days.

"What do you want?" he demanded, voice surly.

"We're fine, Milord," Willard replied drily, "and how was your trip?"

Parno eyed him hostilely for a moment, then snorted in somewhat angry humor.

"My trip was wonderful," Parno oozed sarcasm. "My family, happy to see me as always, made the visit even more so. Practically fawned over me. Quite embarrassing, really."

"They did'na believe you, then?" Darvo asked, concern in his voice. Parno had convinced him that something was happening.

"Oh, they believed me," Parno assured him, rising to his feet. He walked over to the window, gazing out at the camp.

"Then what's the problem?" Darvo asked, when Parno didn't volunteer any more.

"The problem," Parno hissed, "is that there's a traitor among us." He flung the glass in his hand at the fireplace, sending a shower of slivers into the pit.

"What?" Willard was stunned. "You mean in the capital?"

"I mean here!" Parno retorted savagely. "My brother, the Lord Marshall, has a spy in our camp, or nearby. He has told my father that we haven't 'used our time wisely' and that our men 'aren't capable of serving as a line unit'."

"Based on that information, and his undying love for me of course," Parno added snidely, "his Eminence, the Lord High Marshall has determined that our unit is 'unsuitable for use in the coming conflict' and the King, and the Crown Prince, have concurred."

"That's absurd!" Willard protested. "Our men are at least as ready as the Militia units that will be thrust into the fighting! And better trained and equipped, at that!"

"Funny, that's exactly what I said," Parno smiled bitterly. "But then, those Militia recruits are all 'law abiding volunteers', not criminals and apparently they're more competently led."

"Lad, let's don't be hasty," Darvo started, but Parno waved him off.

"Don't start with me, Darvo," he warned. "Not today. Even if you're right, this isn't the time. Not while I'm mad."

"Very well," the older man nodded after a brief pause. "In that case, we need to set about trying to find our informer and get rid of him."

"I've thought of little else, I assure you," Parno nodded, "but where do we start? Is it one of the men? Someone Therron promised a full pardon to if he informed on us? Is it a sutler? Someone in town? Everyone has the potential to be his informer, Darvo."

"Well, there are a few we can rule out," Karls stated. "Starting with us and Cho Feng." He paused for a moment, looking at the floor.

"It's very possible that one of the men in my original company is the traitor, Milord. They would be acting under orders, mind you, and not selling us out. Still, if I find out it is one of them, I'll have his guts for lanyards."

"None of that," Darvo admonished at once. "We can't go off half-cocked. And," he added, "since the Lord Marshall has already told you of the spy in our midst, it's possible that he's gone, or that he won't be reporting anymore, and you can't punish a man for acting under orders from the very highest military authority in the land, short of the King himself," he eyed Willard. "That's not fair to the man following orders."

"So we just let it go on, then?" Willard demanded, almost challengingly. "This is just the kind of thing that could destroy the morale we've worked so hard to establish!"

"No, we look for the source," Darvo told him, "but we do it quietly. If word of this reaches our men they may well start looking at each other in a new light. We've managed to build a good regiment here, despite all my worries to the contrary. I don't want the camaraderie they've established between themselves, and us, destroyed by what might even be a lie."

"What?" Parno and Karls echoed one another.

"Have you considered, lad, that Therron said that just to make you look for his spy? Destroying your unit in the process?" Parno's look of shock was answer enough.

"I thought as much," Darvo nodded firmly.

"But Memmnon knew of the spy as well," Parno told him, remembering the final exchange between himself and his oldest brother.

"Did he?" Darvo asked. "Or did he know only that Therron assured him he had someone keeping an eye on you?"

Parno blinked hard at that one. He had not considered anything like that at all.

"See then," Darvo managed not to smirk. "We don't know that we truly have a spy among us, only your brother's word, and forgive my saying so, milord, but if your brother the Marshall told me the sun rose in the east, I'd want to see it myself, first."

Parno broke out laughing at that, though Willard wisely remained silent. When Parno finally calmed his laughter he walked over to Darvo and embraced the older man.

"Ahh, Darvo, my oldest and dearest friend. What would I do without you?"

"You'd stay in trouble and be on the run most of the time," Darvo assured him, returning the hug tightly. "Why do you think I've stayed with you all this time, lad?"

"Thank you, my friend," Parno said sincerely. He dropped his hands to his side.

"Well, then," he looked at both of his seconds. "Since we're not even sure there is something to do something about, I want our training regimen increased and I want our storehouses full as soon as possible. Make sure our horses are in good shape and that our saddlery and tack are as well."

"I want everything in our inventory ready for war as soon as possible."

"I thought we weren't to be a part of. . . ." Karls started to object.

"I've never been very good at following orders, Karls. You should know that by now," he smiled. "We'll not be attached to any of the Corps, true, but that doesn't mean that we won't be fighting." His face turned serious.

"This isn't going to be like the previous wars, my friends. The Nor will hit us hard, with numbers we can't begin to match. Before our land and people are safe again, we'll have need of every fighting man and every weapon we possess."

-

Parno struggled to maintain his decorum.

"I'm sorry, what?" he asked.

"I asked if you would dine with me this evening," Stephanie Corsin repeated, smiling nervously. "You do eat don't you?"

"Of course I eat!" Parno replied, only realizing afterward that she was baiting him.

"Well, then have dinner with me tonight," she said again. "I want to celebrate. The hospital is officially finished, as of an hour ago."

"Really? That's good news indeed," Parno said earnestly.

"I didn't expect you to be quite that enthused," Stephanie smiled sweetly. "You are full of surprises, Prince." Parno realized that he'd almost slipped. She would know soon enough, of course.

"Well, I'm glad to see that things are progressing," he covered himself lamely, "and now with the construction finished that should leave time for assembling an adequate staff for training," Parno tried to smile encouragingly.

"Never let up, do you?" Stephanie sighed.

"I can't afford to," Parno said without thinking. The woman eyed him closely for a moment.

"Is something wrong, Parno?" she asked quietly. "You've been very. . .tense, for lack of a better word, for weeks. Is there something I can do to help?"

"Finishing the hospital helps," Parno again smiled, putting more effort into it. "And, though I can't credit why you would ask, I'd be delighted to dine with you."

"Thank you," she rewarded him with another smile. "I'll expect you to call at seven this evening, unless that is not a good time."

"Seven it is," Parno nodded. "I'll be there."

-

Parno was hungrier than he had thought…or else the food was extremely good.

"Mrs. Downs is a great cook," Parno said around a mouthful of beef steak. It was so tender one hardly needed a knife to cut it and the morsels threatened to melt in one's mouth.

"I'm glad you like it," Stephanie smiled, "and I'll have you know that I cooked this wonderful repast, Parno McLeod, thank you very much."

"You did?" Parno froze. "Uh, it's um, good."

"You don't have to act so surprised," she feigned hurt, "I can cook you know."

"You sure can," Parno agreed. "I haven't eaten this good in. . .well, I don't know, exactly." Stephanie's laughter rang across the room and Parno felt warmed by it somehow.

"Thank you, My Lord," she bowed lightly. "A high compliment."

"Soldier food isn't always appealing, I admit, but it's always filling. At least here it is." he added laughing.

"I've seen the care you take with your men, Prince," Stephanie said more seriously. "They are very lucky to have you."

"Remind them of that next time it's March Day," Parno chuckled.

"I've seen that," the doctor frowned slightly, "and treated the blisters that arise from it as well. Tell me, it is really necessary to push them so hard?"

"It is if they are to be able to do it when it counts," Parno shrugged. "By doing it now, over and over, then they'll be able to should a time come when they have to do it and also manage to arrive to where they are going while they are still in some condition to fight if need be."

"It always comes down to that, doesn't it?" Stephanie said softly. "Fighting."

"Well, they tell me that's what an Army is for," Parno grinned slightly. "That and absorbing tax money," he added, laughing a little.

"I had no idea how expensive it was to maintain an army until I came here," she admitted. "It makes me wonder why we do it with things so peaceful."

"Training an army takes time," Parno said guardedly. "If you wait until you need to train one then it's generally too late."

"I hadn't thought of that," she admitted. "Do we need one?"

"We might," he nodded. "Anything can happen over time."

"What is happening?" she asked. Parno stopped eating now, giving her his undivided attention.

"I see now why you asked me to dinner," he joked, his grin robbing the words of any sting.

"I invited you to share my celebration," Stephanie didn't quite huff, "but I'm not blind. I've seen the flurry of activity around here. Most of the older soldiers are grumbling slightly. Something about 'winter camp rules' and the like. Apparently winter time is considered 'down' time for most soldiers."

"For those already trained," Parno nodded, choosing his words with care. "These men are doing well but their training isn't finished so we have to keep working. Once the training is complete then we can slow down to something akin to maintenance levels. Allow the men to keep their conditioning, keep up their training, but not have to push quite so hard."

"Stick before carrot?" she grinned.

"Something like that. So, are you satisfied with how the hospital turned out?"

Talking about the hospital allowed Parno to keep the discussion away from the preparations for the rest of meal. Finally, Parno rose.

"I thank you, Lady, for a fine evening. I must take my leave, though. It has been a long day and will be another tomorrow." He moved to the door and she followed.

"I understand, My Lord," Stephanie replied graciously. "Thank you for gracing my home."

"It was in every way my pleasure," Parno smiled. Suddenly, she stood on her tiptoes and kissed him lightly.

"Mine too," she flushed at her forwardness. "Goodnight, Parno." With that she closed the door, leaving a stunned Parno McLeod on the porch.

-

"Draw!"

Winnie Hubbel watched with eyes like those of a hawk as the company before her—Archery Company "A"—drew their bows yet again. They had been at it for over an hour.

"Hold!" Captain Gregory Franklin ordered. He was the commander of the company, but he was taking his cues from Winnie today.

The girl sighed as she watched a few of the men. Their arms were starting to tremble ever so slightly. It could be fatigue, she allowed, but the truth was, these men were not yet conditioned properly to using a long bow for extended periods of time.

Archery wasn't as easy as it looked. Drawing and holding the bow took strength, but more than that it took proper conditioning of a particular set of muscles. Muscles that most people didn't use on a regular basis.

Hence, this exercise. Three times each day, each company held an hour drill where the archers simply drew their bows, held them for fifteen tics, and then eased them back into position. There was a ten tic break between each draw. The work was demanding, but it was paying off.

When she had started this program only three weeks ago, not a single man in "A" Company had been able to complete the hour. Now all but a handful could and that handful were improving each day.

"Release!" Franklin ordered, and the men, almost in unison, eased the strings back to the battery, or rest, position. She nodded as each one released a held breath as he did so.

"You're doing well, Captain," Winnie said softly. "I'll be back, likely. Headin' ta check on t'others." Franklin nodded, not allowing her words to distract him from his count.

"DRAW!"

Satisfied that things here were going well, Winnie started across the grounds to where Archery Company "C" was training. Unlike companies A and B, these men were shooting and it was part of her job to make sure they were learning and performing correctly.

She shook her head at that, a slight smile coming to her face. Here she was, a seventeen year old girl, working as a training instructor in an army camp. Could life be any more ironic?

Women didn't serve in the army. Legends told of a time when they had, before the Dying, but that was all they were. Legends. Winnie didn't believe them and she didn't want to be in the army, regardless. She knew her limitations. As an archer, she was one of the best around. In fact, only her father, of the men around her, was better.

Thinking of her father, Winnie frowned slightly. He was supposed to be training these men, with her assisting him. Yet, for the third straight day in a row, Whip Hubbel was nowhere to be found.

She knew where he was, of course. Whip never hid much from his daughter. He was 'up on the hill'. Without thought, her gaze drifted to the collection of buildings on the small rise north of the fort. Even at nearly a mile, some of the buildings and towers were visible.

No one much knew what went on up there. The few that did flatly refused to comment and asking too many questions of them drew unwanted attention from Parno McLeod himself…and no one wanted that.

But despite the secrecy, everyone knew that something was going on up there. Odd rumbles, some that literally shook the earth beneath her feet, were not uncommon. On more than one occasion fire had broken out in the small compound 'up on the hill'.

Winnie shook her head again.

Not my job, she told herself firmly, and that put the ironic smile back on her face. She had a job.

And Company C was waiting.

-

It might have amused Winnie Hubbel to have been with her father at the moment or at least to have seen what he was doing.

"I don't trust this here gimmick o' yers, perfesser," Hubbel's voice was skeptical.

"Trust isn't an issue, my good archer," Roda Finn assured him. "All I need for you to do is fire this arrow," Finn held up the arrow, "into that clay jar," he pointed downrange, "so that I may observe what happens. I assume you can hit the jar?" Roda baited.

Hubble's face contorted slightly.

"At this range?" he scoffed. "Could like as not throw the arro' inta it," he informed Roda Finn.

"I wouldn't recommend that," Finn warned. "There's a reason why you're shooting from behind this barricade. Oh," he added, having been turning to go, "and do remember to drop behind the barricade as soon as you let fly. Very important, Master Archer. Very important." With that the fussy little man waddled to his own barricade.

Which, Hubbel noted, was several yards behind his own. Shaking his head, Hubbel raised his bow, knocking the arrow into place. He didn't know what was so special about this arrow, anyway. It wasn't especially well made, though it did have a chipped flint arrowhead. It wasn't done very well, Hubbel noted, being too blunt and still too thick, but it would fly straight enough for this.

Hubbel let fly, watching the arrow heading downrange. Suddenly, he remembered Finn's warning and dove down to the ground.

Narrowly escaping injury.

The clay jar exploded as the arrow pierced its side, flinging small metal objects of all description in every direction. Hubbel felt and heard the impacts on the barrier in front of him.

"Yes!" he heard, and looked up to see Finn dancing…or trying to dance. Hubbel almost laughed until he remembered the explosion.

"Are you tryin' ta git me kilt!" he roared, coming up from the ground in a flash of anger.

"Oh, tut," Finn waved away the much larger man's anger. "I told you, get behind the barricade. Perfectly safe there. And look!" he pointed downrange. "Look what your arrow did!" Curiosity won out over rage and Hubble looked downrange to where the jar had been setting only to see that the block of wood it had been perched on was gone, as was a good hunk of the dirt below it. Likewise most of the small shrubs that had been around it were gone as well as the scarecrows dressed in armor, which Hubble had really wondered about.

"Great Day!" was all the grizzled bow master could manage, looking at the damage.

"Indeed, indeed," Roda Finn was pleased. "Of course, very few, if any, among the Prince's soldiers will have your skill, so using the longbow won't be possible. However, I should think that a cross bowman with some skill should be able to put a flint tipped dart into that jar at, what? Say, fifty steps?" Hubbel thought about that for a moment, then nodded.

"Shouldn't be any trouble," he agreed finally. "Not for a man with a steady eye and hand."

"Wonderful!" Finn enthused, hastily scribbling notes in a small journal. "Thank you, Master Archer, for your assistance in this."

"Wasn't like I's given a choice, Finn," Hubbel growled. "Prince said ta me, 'go up on the hill and help out Roda Finn'."

"Yes, I know," Finn nodded, eying the archer speculatively. "Still, never hurts to let someone know how much you appreciate their help and I do appreciate it. There isn't another archer in this entire organization who could do the things you're doing with that bow." Hubbel nodded, slightly appeased at the commentary on his skills.

"What now?" Hubbel demanded.

"We need to do it again," Finn admitted. "Several times, in fact. I have to make sure that this wasn't a fluke and then make sure that the device works every time before we can start making them in any quantity."

"I'd say it works, right enough," Hubbel nodded.

"Once," Finn reminded him. "That isn't sufficient. It has to work every time, or at least as close to every time as we can possibly get it," he added, frowning. "Some will fail, of course. It's inevitable, given what we're working with, but I haven't figured out anything better at this point. Of course, you being the expert, you may see something I don't. Do you see a way to make this better? Easier?"

"Not just at thuh moment," Hubbel admitted. "Whatcha call that thing, anyhow?"

"A mine," Finn smiled. "Not a true mine as the ancients reckoned such things, of course, but as close as I can come. For now," he added.

"Be a fine thing, man could make somethin' as that fer a arra'," Hubbel mused, looking down at his bow. "Couldn' be suh large, o' course. But sumthin ta, you know, make folks yonder," his head nodded to the north, "think twice. Know what ah mean? What?" This last came as he glanced at the inventor, only to see him staring back, eyes wide.

"Great ghosts!" Finn cried happily. "That is a remarkable idea, Master Archer! Simply remarkable!" Finn ran off immediately toward his workshop.

"It is?" Hubbel asked Finn's back. Then louder, "Hey! Is we done here or what?" When there was no answer, Hubbel shook his head sadly and followed the eccentric inventor into the workshop.

Warily. He paused at the door just as he'd seen the Prince do the first time he'd brought Hubbel 'up on the hill' and then only after an oath that Hubbel had thought was about to include his daughter's virtue not to speak of what he was about to see.

Once he'd had a look at Roda Finn's workshop, though, Hubbel had seen the absolute need for such secrecy. Finn was irritable, fussy, hard to please or to even tolerate, but the things he could do, that he could make happen, were nothing short of extraordinary.

Satisfied that his life was in no immediate danger, (couldn't be sure of that, of course, but it looked clear for now), Hubbel walked into the shop. Finn's two assistants were crowded around the little man, watching as he hastily drew designs on a piece of parchment.

"Why not use a fuse," the taller one, Billy was his name, wasn't it? was saying. "Just light it up, then fire it off."

"And if it burns to quickly?" Carl, the other one, demanded. "Or blows out in flight?" Hubbel walked over to the table as the two argued, looking at the paper. It was a diagram he noted, and it looked an awful lot like an. . . .

"Is that a arra'?" he asked cautiously. Finn nodded without looking up.

"That it is, Master Archer," Finn told him, still scribbling furiously. "As I said, it's a remarkable idea. One worth study."

"You plannin' on puttin' that. . .that stuff," he pointed toward the field outside, "on a arra'?"

"Yes," Finn nodded, looking up. "Why so surprised, Master Hubbel? It was your idea, after all."

"I did'na mean to do sumthin' o' this sort!" Hubbel snapped. "Thing be like ta blow a man's head or arm off!"

"Oh, tut," Finn waved the objections aside. "Not at all. Well," Finn paused, calculating. "Well, probably not, anyway," he said finally and went back to work. Carl and Billy were still arguing over the best way to make the thing work.

"I still say that a fuse. . . ."

"Hey!" Hubbel's booming voice stopped the two in mid word. "Stop yer yammerin' a minute and help out, 'stead o' just runnin' off at the mouth, like." He looked down at Finn.

"Lookie here, Roda," he said firmly. "Ah ain't a firin' that thing if'n it's already lit. Period." Finn looked up at him.

"Then what?" Roda demanded. "You have an idea?" That caught Hubbel off guard.

"Well, I ain't. . . ." He trailed off suddenly, as an idea did come to mind.

"Then we'll just have to work with what we. . . ." Now it was Finn who trailed off as Hubbel took up a pencil and started scratching on the same paper as Finn was using.

"What are you. . .?" he stopped as Hubbel's sketch took shape. When it was finished, he looked up at Finn.

"How's 'bout that?"

-

"Very well, Roda, I'm here," Parno said warily. "What did you want?" Parno was nearly exhausted. There were a thousand and seventeen things to do every day as they worked to prepare the regiment for war. Coming here meant that at least a hundred of them would go unfinished today.

"I know you're busy, milord," Finn nodded, with none of his usual sarcasm. "It's just. . .well, you needed to see this. It may change your plans somewhat." With that, he nodded to Hubbel.

"Anytime you're ready, Master Archer." Hubbel, standing again at the forward barricade, nodded, and turned.

"Roda, I've seen your mines," Parno protested tiredly. "I know they work, that's why I asked you to make so many of them. . . ."

"I know, milord," Finn said agreeably. "And we're set to start producing them soon. Day after tomorrow, perhaps. But this. . .please to duck, milord," he added, pulling Parno down with him.

"Firin'!" Parno heard Hubbel yell. Two seconds later he heard a smaller explosion than one normally heard when visiting Roda Finn's playground. He rose, cautiously, and glanced around, careful to expose no more of himself than needed to see.

"What happened?" he asked, a worried tinge in his voice. "Did it. . .misfire?" Parno almost gulped out. Misfires, as Roda called them, were the worst, the absolute worst thing that could happen here. . . .

"No, milord," Finn was standing. "There was no misfire. Come and see." With that, Roda joined Whip Hubbel and the two of them started off down the range. Parno hurried to catch up.

"So what happened?" he demanded. "I came up here, Roda, because you told me you had something new that I needed to see!"

"See, then," Roda smiled, his arm sweeping to the target area. Parno looked, seeing one 'scarecrow soldier' blown in half, and the rest. . .he looked again. The one was dead, had he been a soldier, that was evident and the 'soldier' to either side was also wounded…or dead, depending.

"What was that?" he asked. "You did this with one arrow?" he demanded of Hubbel. The archer nodded, smiling.

"Did at that, muhlord," came the reply. Parno looked at the damage again, then back to Roda.

"Okay. Show me."

Finn produced another arrow from Hubbel's quiver and handed it to Parno. He took it hesitantly, knowing from experience that anything in Finn's shop, possession, or vicinity could explode without warning at any time. He examined it carefully.

The arrow looked quite unremarkable at the rear. Knock, flights, good straight wood. As it neared the front, however, Parno noted that there was no arrowhead. Instead, the arrow swelled a bit, and ended in a blunt, flat, tip. Similar to a nail.

"What is this?" he demanded.

"Ah. . .we don't, that is we haven't thought of a name for it, seeing as how we just sort of cobbled it together."

"Then what is it?" Parno repeated.

"Well, it's an explodin' arro, muhlord, to be simple 'bout it," Hubbel saved Finn from further embarrassment. "Reason it looks so odd, we needed sumthin' that would force thuh flint inta thuh powder, oncet it hit thuh target." Parno looked at the man stupidly for a moment. Then his eyes widened.

"You mean to tell me that you can make arrows like this?" he was almost beside himself. "Arrows that almost any of my archers can use, without killing himself or someone next to him?"

"Ah, yes, milord," Finn nodded. "That's. . .that's essentially the case. Design still needs some adjustment, of course, so that we can produce them in large numbers, but. . . ."

"Roda, you're a genius!" Parno exclaimed. Finn's blush of pleasure was interrupted by the clearing of a rough throat. He looked at the large archer next to him and then hurriedly back to Parno.

"Milord, it was Master Hubbel who came up with this idea," he told the Prince hurriedly, "and with the design that makes it useable," he added. "All I did was build it as he drew it."

"Thank you, Whip," Parno smiled at the big man. "This. . .this is a great help to us. A very great help, I think. I want as many as we can get. Don't slack on the other things, mind you," Parno warned. "I'll get more help, if needed but I want as many of these as can be made before. . ." Parno caught himself but the other two simply nodded.

"We git it," was all Hubbel said. Finn nodded.

"Good. I have to get back," Parno said, returning the arrow to Hubbel's hand. "This is marvelous. Make me hundreds of them, Roda. Hundreds!" And with that the Prince was gone, leaving the other two men watching after him.

"Think he liked it," Hubbel nodded firmly.

"So, it would appear."

-

One week after his return from Nasil Parno had assembled the members of his 'staff' for a dinner at his quarters. He was reluctant to tell anyone what was happening before it was absolutely necessary, but already people were commenting about the increased training regimen and the need to get so many items organized, repaired or replaced. New boots, spare uniforms, reworked saddles—the list was endless. There was no way to hide the fact that the regiment was outfitting for something.

As stewards cleared away the dishes, Parno looked around the table. Doctor Corsin was there, along with Jason Pearl. Darvo, Karls, Cho Feng, and Roda Finn rounded out the 'council'.

Parno considered again the words he would use. Soon, he would have to inform the rest of the regiment, certainly the officers of the battalions and companies who would lead the men into battle and help spur their training. Better, he had decided, to share what he knew with those now seated at the table now. He needed their input, their advice, and most of all, their support.

With the stewards work done, they departed, leaving the assembled diners to their wine and ale. Parno took a drought of his own mug, then tapped lightly on the table with his knuckles to attract everyone's attention. Conversation died out as the assembly looked in his direction.

"I suppose you are wondering why you're here," he smiled slightly. "I wish we had done this more," he admitted. "I've had a very pleasant evening. Truth be known, however, there is an ulterior motive." Everyone was paying attention now.

"Intelligence has been presented to the Crown that indicates the Nor will attack us in great, perhaps overwhelming, strength—as soon as the spring rains subside." He knew no way to soften the blow, so simply dumped the information before them. Startled gasps, sharp intakes of breath, and shouts of exclamation rounded the table only after five seconds of stunned silence.

"Quiet down," Parno raised his hands. "Quiet down!" As the furor decreased, Parno waited for everyone to settle before continuing.

"I know this is a shock," he said quietly. "It was to me as well." That wasn't quite true, but no one needed to know that. "With things going so well in recent months, no one was expecting something like this. As it is, through hard work, we have some warning. While we could all wish for more, let us be grateful for the time we have to prepare." He stood.

"All around the realm, every military command in Soulan is preparing for war. They aren't aware, except at the command level, that that's what they're doing, but they are. And, so are we." He saw a few heads nod as the dots began to connect concerning the last week of flurried preparation.

"I have asked all of you here tonight as my friends, my advisers, and as citizens of this Kingdom," Parno continued. "There is much to be done in the coming months to prepare this regiment, indeed, this post, for the coming war."

"My Lord," Corsin asked hesitantly, raising her hand.

"You aren't in school, Doctor," Parno replied, though he smiled to rob the words of any sting. "Say what you have to say." Corsin still flushed slightly, but managed to smile.

"How certain are we of this?" she asked bluntly.

"Absolutely," Parno replied just as bluntly. "The evidence presented to the Crown was irrefutable. The Nor have been preparing for war all along. Their diplomatic outreaches of the past two years or so were simply the final preparations of the implementation of the plan."

"What are we to do?" Pearl asked, looking worriedly around.

"We are to prepare to defend our Kingdom, Professor Pearl," Parno said calmly. "Your work, indeed, the work of everyone here at this table, has just become ten times more important that it was a week ago. This is not just a problem for the soldiers, but for those of you who support them as well. We need you now, more than ever."

"I take it that not everyone is aware of this problem?" Roda asked.

"No, and that is how it must stay, at least for now," Parno replied. "I know that many of you will be tempted to tell others, especially loved ones, about this. I ask you not to, not yet. If word were to leak out that we are aware of their plans, they may choose to strike at once. If that happened, they would bowl over us with little effort."

Again, startled gasps rounded the table. No one had expected to hear that from a member of the ruling dynasty.

"I know," Parno nodded, "but their efforts on the diplomatic front have been very successful. Our readiness and preparedness are at an all-time low. We need this quiet time to strengthen ourselves so we can be as prepared as possible when the attack comes."

"If we are successful and the Nor take note when spring comes, then perhaps they will deem the attack to be too risky, too costly, to pursue."

In truth there was exactly zero chance that would happen, but the civilians didn't and  couldn't know that. Parno decided that little white lie wouldn't hurt anything.

"And so, I ask you to turn your attention to what we need, here and now, to be prepared for what is likely to come. I want each of you, in turn, to review your area of expertise for us all, outlining problems, shortages, preparations, anything that might be important. There is a great collections of minds at this table. Use it. Doctor Corsin, I'd like you to go first. How prepared are we, for example, to care for mass casualties? Will our current stores allow for that? And our medical personnel?" Corsin stood.

"Well, milord. . . ."

The meeting turned technical at that point. Comments sparked other comments and the occasional argument while the talk continued well into the late evening. As the evening began to wane, Parno called their attention.

"I've given you a great deal to think about," he told them. "Let us retire and face this problem tomorrow with clear heads. Remember that this information is not to be repeated outside this room." The assembled guests rose and began to leave. Doctor Corsin hesitated, waiting for everyone else to leave. When they were alone, she turned to him.

"How sure, really, are you of this, My Lord?" she asked, hesitantly.

"Please, call me Parno," the prince told her, though there was no smile. "Everyone who was seated here tonight does so."

"Very well, M. . .Parno. How certain?"

"Completely," he told her. "There is no doubt." She nodded, dumbly. For a moment she looked weak, even seemed to waiver a bit on her feet. Parno reached out to take her by the arm, steadying her.

"Are you all right, Doctor?" he asked, concern in his voice. She smiled weakly.

"If I am to call you Parno, then the least you can do is call me Stephanie."

"Are you all right, Stephanie, then," Parno asked again, a hint of a smile at the corners of his mouth.

"I. . .I don't know," she admitted. "I never once imagined that. . .I mean, things were going so well. What has happened to change all that?"

"It hasn't changed," Parno shrugged. The two sat back down. "The Nor have never had any peaceful intentions, Stephanie. This entire charade has been but with one purpose, to blind us to the coming storm until it was too late."

"Have they succeeded?" she asked bluntly. Parno studied her for a moment, then shrugged again.

"Possibly," he admitted. "I won't lie to you; the danger is very great. The Nor Army is vast and much improved over previous forces they have fielded against us. They have made allies, for now at least, of the Wildmen of the western territories." Corsin's eyes betrayed her fear at that. Wildmen were the bogey men used by all parents to keep their children in line. The stories were only partially embellishments.

"What will we do?" she wondered aloud.

"We will fight," Parno said simply. "Defend this land and its people. To the last man if needed. We can do nothing else."

Corsin looked at him closely, as if seeing him for the first time. She nodded finally, her own courage seeming to take strength from his quiet certainty.

"I'm sorry, Parno," she stood suddenly. "I have imposed upon you. Please forgive me. Just the worry of a woman, I suppose."

"Nonsense," he rose as well, accompanying her to the door. "We all have the right to be worried. Man, woman, makes no difference."

"Thank you," she smiled again. Gathering her shawl, she started outside.

"Wait," Parno said suddenly, before he thought, "and I'll walk you to your cabin."

"That isn't necessary Parno," Stephanie replied.

"I know," he smiled, taking his own jacket and ensuring that Sprigs knew he would be out, "but I want to. Besides, I promised Memmnon that I would make sure nothing happened to you."

"You did?" she asked, as the two walked down the portico steps.

"Oh, yes," Parno chuckled. "I thought he was going to fall into a fit when he found out you were here. Apparently, you are very highly thought of in Nasil. I got quite an earful from him about ensuring that you were safe and secure here among my nest of criminals." In spite of himself, Parno heard the bitterness creep into his voice.

"Ah," Stephanie said softly. "You and your family aren't really close, are you?" she asked.

"No," Parno replied bluntly. "I thought for a moment we might at least draw closer, at least Memmnon, my father and I, but it was not to be. There will never be any familial feelings between my family and myself."

"I'm sorry, Parno," Stephanie said softly. "That's not the way it should be."

"So, I've heard," he responded lightly. "So, I've heard. At any rate, the fact that you were here was quite a shock."

"I'm sure it was," Stephanie's voice held a trace of scorn. "Only my mother supported my decision to come here. Everyone else had the usual, 'you're a woman', 'no business on such a post', 'talents wasted', and so forth."

"So why are you here?" Parno asked. There was no hint of challenge, just simple curiosity. "There's certainly no reason you shouldn't be, if that's what you desire, but what made you come here? And stay?"

"It's worthwhile," came the instant reply. She looked up suddenly. "And so are you." Parno blinked at that, not knowing what to say. Suddenly, they were at the Doctor's door.

"Well, I am safely home, Parno McLeod," she grinned, "and I thank you, kind sir."

"My pleasure, Lady Corsin," Parno grinned crookedly. "Goodnight, Doctor."

"Good night, My Lord." Again, before he could act, or react, she stood on her tiptoes, kissed him lightly, then fled inside.

"I've got to be quicker," Parno decided.

# CHAPTER TWENTY

-

Time flew swiftly. Too swiftly, it seemed to Parno McLeod, as he worked and worried over his regiment. Time was running out. Already there was a hint of spring in the air. Parno watched the calendar with trepidation as the days wound toward the coming of the new season.

Spring. The time of renewal.

The time of war.

By the first day of March the rains had begun and with them came warmer air. Unstable air. Storms battered the mountain and training was limited in those days. Parno bemoaned every lost minute, but there was nothing to be done.

And when the rains ended, the Nor would come. He was sure of it.

The only bright spot in his bleak outlook was that Roda Finn's 'factory' was making weapons every day. Including the wonderful 'exploding arrows' designed by Whip Hubbel. Even Darvo had been impressed.

"'That thing will make us able to do more than we ought with our numbers, lad'," the grizzled veteran had said after seeing a demonstration. "'With weapons like that, along with the other things Finn has developed, it will mean that a smaller unit can do the same damage as a bigger one and more impressively, as well'," he added. There was something to be said for intimidation, after all.

Parno agreed that Roda Finn's weapons would enable the regiment to do more damage than any other unit their size or even twice or five times their size.

But there were still only so many soldiers and so many weapons, as well. Once in battle, Parno feared they would use them up quickly and then be overrun.

"'May well happen," Darvo nodded in agreement when Parno voiced his concern. "But we'll do a sight o' damage 'fore that happens, lad," he had grinned and Parno found his mentor's calm demeanor rubbing off on him.

Cho Feng had agreed.

"'My people have used similar weapons for many generations," he had informed Parno one evening as they sat around the table, discussing how best to use the weapons. "The shock factor will be invaluable in the first battle. After that, the damage done physically will still be considerable."

Parno hoped he was correct. He knew and knew deep in his soul that Soulan wasn't ready for the storm that was coming. He almost laughed at that thought, gazing out his window as yet another lightning bolt hammered the earth from above.

Therron's disdain of his men had angered Parno but as the time drew near the younger Prince began to see that disdain in a different light, one that would allow him to act on his own.

Despite his repeated warnings, Parno's father and his older brothers were ignoring the threat posed by the Gap of the Cumberland. Parno had spoken to Doak Parsons about the trail through the Gap, since the former outlaw had used it on his return from the Ohi River. Parsons answers had chilled the younger man.

"'They kin use it, milord," Parsons had assured him. "Not be easy in some places, I grant ya, but it can be done. 'Specially if'n they all come a horseback. Moving anything heavy through there'd be a might hard, but a few stout men with axes, breakin' trail fer'em, and they're down to the Gap in a week. Ten days, at most, assumin' they start out from Loville, was we to lose the bridges'.'"

Parno rubbed his face, trying to scrub away the fatigue that the constant strain of work and worry had left him with. He was exhausted.

"Now is as good a time as any to get some rest," he decided. Which made him think of his men. They had worked very hard over the last two months and a bit more. They needed rest as well. He called for Harrel Sprigs.

"Milord?" the young Lieutenant entered a moment later.

"My compliments to Colonel Nidiad. I want the entire regiment on limited duty. Guards to be maintained, regular duties performed, but otherwise, rest and recuperation for the men."

"Yes, milord," Sprigs bowed, then departed to deliver the message. When he was gone, Parno returned his gaze to the window and to the storm that raged outside.

"That's all I can do, for now," he said to himself. "We'll have to make do." With that he headed upstairs for some rest of his own.

Soon enough, he knew, there would be no rest for anyone.

-

Therron McLeod was also watching the storms. Rain had been falling in Nasil for just over a week, keeping Therron from being able to move about much at all. He disliked not seeing things for himself but there was no point in slogging about in the mud.

Just as there was no point in trying to force men to train in it. The cold rains of March would simply leave many men sick, and some dead, of pneumonia. He wanted every man available when the time came.

Well, not every man, of course. Parno's men would be of no use. Therron felt a momentary twinge at the lie he had told his father. He didn't have a spy in Parno's camp, in truth. The thought had never occurred to him. And why waste someone on such a job when Therron already knew the truth? There was no way that Parno had taken that riffraff and turned them into a fighting unit. None.

Therron felt a familiar anger course through him at the thought of his youngest brother but fought it down. There was too much to do to worry about Parno just now.

And, if things went as he planned them, the youngest McLeod sibling wouldn't be a problem anyway, once all was said and done.

Therron wasn't blind, nor was he a fool. He knew that his father was sick and had been for some time. Which meant that Soulan would soon need a new leader. One with the stamina and backbone to defend it against the Nor.

Someone like him.

Memmnon was the Heir, of course, but if Therron could defeat the Nor then he would gain a considerable following among the nobles of the kingdom. He already enjoyed the support of the army. With enough of the nobles in hand, Therron, as the hero that had saved Soulan from the Nor, would be in a position to force his will upon father and brother alike.

He didn't relish the idea, of course. No true McLeod would. But facts were facts. And the fact, as Therron saw it, was that he would simply make a better, stronger King than Memmnon would. He held no personal animosity toward his older brother. He and Memmnon had always gotten on well enough. They had their disagreements, as any brothers did, but they were always settled amicably enough.

No, it wasn't personal. It was his duty. That was how Therron thought. How he had convinced himself of the rightness of his actions. He should be King because he was better suited for the job. Not because Memmnon wouldn't be a decent King, but because Therron would be a better one.

And Soulan needed a better king in times like these.

Therron felt a wry smile cross his lips at the thought of the Norland Emperor actually helping him, Therron McLeod, seize the throne of Soulan. Without the threat of war, Therron's plans would have taken a great while longer to ferment and the risks would have been far greater.

But the Nor had given him a great gift in deciding to go to war with Soulan. Therron himself would lead the army to its final victory and then be heralded a hero when the Nor were beaten back across the Ohi, their tails between their legs.

Yes, Emperor Bane had done him a great favor. Too bad he'd have to repay it by destroying his army. Therron continued to watch the rain pelt his window, his mind swirling with thoughts of being the victorious war leader and the King of Soulan.

-

It would have surprised Therron to no end had he known that, one floor below him, Memmnon stood watching the same rain and thinking about the fact that his brother, Therron, was plotting to seize power from him at the first opportunity.

Memmnon acknowledged that he, himself, was partly to blame. So wrapped up had he been in other things that he had often neglected the nobles around Nasil and around Soulan at large. In that vacuum, Therron had taken the opportunity to win many of them over to his 'side'.

He also controlled the Army. An army they needed whole and hearty to defend the realm, not divided by the removal of their Lord Marshall on what was practically the eve of war. Memmnon sighed, rubbing his eyes in an attempt to fight off a coming headache.

Why, he wondered, didn't he just give Therron what he wanted? Let him have the throne. Memmnon had seen by now that the problems of the position far outweighed any benefits and there were problems, Memmnon knew. He, himself, didn't desire power, it had simply come to him. It was his duty and he had accepted it. He had seen, first hand, that being King would not be the great experience that Therron seemed to think it was.

For Therron, there was only the power. The right to do as he pleased once he was installed as King. He either didn't see the inherent problems Soulan faced or simply didn't care.

Or, Memmnon allowed, perhaps he did see them and simply believed that he could handle them better than Memmnon could, or even Tammon for that matter. Either way, Memmnon was certain that Therron was plotting to take the throne. Possibly by force.

As fate would have it the Nor had given Therron all the room he needed to make a peaceful case for his ascension to the throne over Memmnon. If he could defeat the invasion and drive the Nor back across the Ohi then he would be a hero, a strong, steadfast defender of the people. Someone that no one would object to being King.

The problem was that Therron simply wouldn't make a good King. He didn't have the temperament for it, for one thing. Therron was apt to lash out at those around him, to treat people with a high and heavy hand that many found to be too much. Had it not been for the King's ever watchful eye Therron might have been in more trouble than was normally the case.

Even so, Memmnon knew this was a problem he would have to face sooner or later. Tammon was in no shape to deal with his quasi-rebellious son. Memmnon would have to do it for him and do it in such a way as not to upset the balance of the army. They needed to be focused on defending the Soulan people from the Nor, not on supporting one brother over another for King. Looking out once again at the rain, Memmnon began working on a way to make all that happen.

\-

It would have surprised both brothers McLeod in the palace that night to know that, whilst they plotted around each other, their father was sitting next to the fire in his private chambers, considering the problems facing him.

Including a son that Tammon was convinced meant to seize the throne of Soulan at his first opportunity. The old man sighed wearily, his hand rubbing along his temples.

Never, in the ageless history of Soulan, had the throne been 'taken'. Never. Peaceful ascension to the throne by the legal heir was simply taken for granted. To do otherwise was unthinkable.

Tammon shook his head slowly. To have it happen under his rule. What had he done to deserve that? Even as the thought came to him, he snorted.

You've done nothing, he told himself, and that's the problem. You've simply made your will be so, and that's that. Now you have a son that is bordering on being out of control and power hungry on the eve of what might be the greatest war in the history of Soulan. Some King you are.

Tammon shook off those thoughts. Richly deserved though the self-recrimination might be, it wasn't helpful. It didn't solve his problems. Of course, at this juncture, nothing would solve his problems.

Therron ran the army and Tammon needed the army. He needed them ready to repel the coming invasion and protect the kingdom. If they succeeded it would be with Therron at the helm, rather than himself, which would make Therron's power grabbing that much more acceptable to some.

The key to everything was the war. If they lost, then Therron wouldn't be a hero, but there also wouldn't be a kingdom to assume control of. If they won, and Therron survived. . . .

The King's thoughts trailed away at that dark idea. He had considered having Therron meet with some 'accident' or other. The problem was that if the word ever got out, then Tammon would have helped destroy the very thing he had sought to protect. The peaceful succession of power.

I should have let him fight Parno, Tammon thought darker still. Had I known how good the boy was with a blade, I might well have insisted upon it, could I have seen this in the offing.

But this wasn't Parno's fight and, the King reflected, the youngest Prince of Soulan had suffered quite enough at the hands of the royal family. No, this was Tammon's fight. A problem of his own making.

One he desperately needed a solution for. One that wouldn't ruin his family…or his kingdom…in the process.

\-

The rains were beating down along the Ohi River as Lieutenant General Gerald Wilson watched from horse back. His men moved along the trails just a few miles north of the river. Trails that had been cut, then hidden, months ago. Trails that led into prepared camping areas within easy gallop of the jump off points for his invasion of the south. His assault force, the men who would cross in the navy boats, were already in position several miles both up and down river from Loville. They, their naval comrades, and their boats were carefully hidden, just a few hundred yards from the river, alongside their camps.

The men he was with now were part of the force that would assault the bridges themselves. Taking those bridges was, as always, the key to everything. With those three bridges in hand the Norland Army's supply route and line of communications would be secure. Guarded by hand-picked men so that this time there would be no cavalry 'dash and attack' to cut their supplies and leave the invasion force to whither on the vine.

Wilson smiled as he thought of that. This time, things would be different. The force opposing him was much smaller than his own. Once across the river, Wilson was more than confident that his army would crush the Soulan 2nd Corps. With that done, the heartland would lie open to him, with only the 1st Corps in Nasil itself to oppose him.

True, there were problems to deal with. The rains, thus far, had been heavier than he had hoped and the river was rising rapidly. Once the rains had subsided, the river should fall just as quickly, however. With the naval boats and personnel, the height of the river shouldn't matter anyway but Wilson wasn't accustomed to trusting in fate. He worked very hard to anticipate any problems he might encounter and devised plans to counter them.

For instance, what if the Soulanies discovered his army marshaling for an attack and attacked first? That wasn't likely, of course. Soulan had never launched a war of aggression against Norland, or anyone else for that matter.

Still, he couldn't simply disregard the possibility. Which was why he had quietly and carefully increased the garrison at Loville to a full brigade. While they could never stand against the Soulan Army alone, they could hold long enough for Wilson to get there with the bulk of his army.

Then there was the possibility that his advance would outpace his ability to resupply. This time of year there would be little or no foraging. He didn't mind taking from the Soulan people to feed his own men but they wouldn't have even a fraction of the supplies he would need here at the end of winter. That meant that his men would be dependent upon the wagons rolling across the bridges to keep them fed and equipped.

He had hundreds of wagons, divided into three separate commands. One would always be on its way south to him, while the other was either returning or loading for its next trip. However, the further south the invasion force went, the longer those trips would take and the more vulnerable they would be to attack. He had designated an entire cavalry division to safeguard the wagons and the routes they would take. He disliked giving up that much fighting power, but what use would the extra men be if he couldn't feed them or their horses?

There was also the remainder of the Soulan Army to consider, along with their militias. If the naval feint to the far south didn't work, then he could end up facing the combined strength of three Soulan Army Corps, all well trained and well led. That force, while still nominally smaller than his own, could well be enough to stop his advance, or at least slow it to a crawl.

The militias represented a separate problem all on their own. If they failed to link up with the main Soulan Army after the attack well-organized guerrilla attacks on his rear areas could wreak havoc with supply and communications. They might not be able to prevent his army from re-supplying, but they could damage his ability to do so at will or when most vital.

Wilson shook his head. He had tried to think of everything and had others working on the problems as well. They had counters prepared if the need were to arise. He'd have to trust that their plans would work. There was only so much one man could do and he could only be in one place at the time.

"Message from Loville, milord," a courier rode up, handing a rain drenched dispatch bag to him. Wilson nodded, taking the bag. An aide used a cloak to shield the paper as Wilson read.

Good. The troops in Loville were in place and none the wiser. Also, the garrison commander had received a dispatch from the southern boat force that they were in place and all was in readiness. The original dispatch was included and Wilson decided he would look at it later. He returned the forms to the pouch and handed it to his aide.

"Let's get into shelter," he ordered, and turned his horse toward the house he was using as a headquarters. His men followed without comment, glad to be getting out of the rain.

"So, General, what do you think?" a voice next to him asked quietly. Wilson turned to regard the speaker.

Brigadier Charles Daly had attached himself to Wilson's command at the 'request' of the Emperor. Daly's kinship with the Emperor allowed him some leeway in how he addressed Wilson and into what matters he could inquire. So, despite his dislike for the man, Wilson had to allow some leniency in how he addressed the near royal.

"I think we're in readiness, General," Wilson told him. "When the time comes we will be able to complete our mission. Missions, I should say," he added.

"Good," Daly nodded. He knew that Wilson didn't like him, but didn't care. He was here to make sure that the Emperor was aware of everything that was going on. Daly had his own staff, including Imperial couriers. They would ferry dispatches directly to the Emperor. Dispatches that would not go through Wilson so the Commanding General would have no way of knowing what Daly was telling the Emperor.

Wilson spurred his horse slightly, moving out at a faster pace than before. He felt a headache coming. It seemed that the Soulan Army might not be his only opposition.

-

Far to the west and south, Lieutenant General Jackson Andrews, commanding the Norland 2nd Field Army, was in a similar situation…including the rain, which wasn't a real problem for him.

Andrews was tasked with attacking across the Great River, into Shelby. He would be using boats as well, though his men would be using somewhat larger rafts, rafts that, in theory, would enable his men to carry their horses across with them.

Andrews also had the added problem of coordinating with Norland's 'allies', the members of several of the nearer Wild Tribes. Andrews detested the Wilds and their barbaric customs as well, but he could not, would not, deny that they had done wonders in training the Nor cavalry…and they were fierce fighters.

The Wildmen were savages with no regard for human life at all, including their own. To them, there was only the fight. They didn't think along the lines of conquering and holding land. Instead, theirs was a nomadic way of life. They fought for the pleasure of battle, taking whatever they could from whomever they attacked. Their practices of mutilating corpses of fallen foes left Andrews with a queasy feeling in his stomach, especially when he remembered that, if all went according to plan, he and his men would be at war with the Wildmen in less than two years.

He put the thought aside, however, for now. That was a long way away. Today there was only Soulan. The hated Southrons.

Andrews' attack wasn't a feint, exactly, but it wasn't the primary attack, either, which meant that his force wasn't as large as Wilson's. Having the equivalent of two divisions of Wildmen cavalry added to his fighting force was hardly an imposition, even with their repulsive ways and it would give him the opportunity to study them in battle, he mused. Something to take advantage of.

In the meantime, he had his own preparations to see to. His men were almost two miles away from the bridge, easily out of sight of even the most powerful glass. Only a handful of his own men were near the bridge, himself included, and the Soulanies were accustomed to seeing the Wildmen along the western bank of the Great River, coming and going.

Lifting his glass, Andrews studied the bridge once again from the cover of trees. It was a large span, in essence two bridges built as one great bridge. A marvel of engineering from a time long past, before the Dying. Such a thing would be all but impossible now, he knew. That was the one reason that no one had ever tried to destroy the bridge itself. It was irreplaceable, and therefore valuable, to everyone.

Today it was an objective. One Andrews meant to take if at all possible. If he could establish a good bridgehead on the eastern bank and keep it supplied then his part of the war plan was assured. True, he'd like to do more than that, and he would if the opportunity arose, but his primary goal—his only goal, in fact—was to seize the bridge and threaten Shelby, tying down the Soulan 3rd Corps.

He could do that. He would do that.

With that thought, he turned his full concentration back to the bridge.

-

Major General William Brasher leaned over the map table in the small house he was using as his headquarters, committing to memory the route he would take and the alternates, should the primary route be blocked.

His job was the riskiest of the entire operation in some ways. His men would strike deep into the Soulanie heart land, alone and unsupported. Speed was the essence of his plans and yet he couldn't simply strike out with nothing but his horsemen.

Because of the time of year and the likelihood that his men would not find sufficient forage Brasher had to have a baggage train. He would need hay and feed for his animals and food for his men. There was no way around that.

Because of that need his column would advance much slower than he wanted. Speed was essential to his success. He had to take the Gap and pass through it before Soulan could mount a strong defense.

It was true that his force was strong enough to overwhelm whatever garrison happened to be placed there if need be. It was the delay that would be problematic. If the Soulan forces put up much of a fight then it might take a day, or even two, to get past them and get his force reformed. That was too long. He had to get through quickly. Much depended on his force reaching Nasil as quickly as possible.

He had considered placing his supplies on horseback, but the plan simply wasn't workable. He hadn't the horses to spare or not enough to make a difference anyway. Sighing in defeat, he accepted the fact that he would have to depend on his 'pioneer' units. Roving ahead in small wagons with axes and saws, the pioneers would widen the roads where necessary to allow his wagons through. They should be able to outpace the wagons, considering that the initial roadways would need no work. It was only when they began to reach the mountains that the roads would pinch off into something more like trails than actual roadways. By the time his wagons made it that far the pioneers should have already made a dent in the problem.

If they hadn't he could always execute them as an example to the next unit he sent forward. Brasher was known for his ruthlessness. Feared for it, some would say. No one wanted to serve under his command, but those who did always managed to do a better job than their peers in other commands as they were 'more highly motivated' in Brasher's words.

Brasher was the youngest Major General in the Norland Army and intended to be the youngest Lieutenant General in the next campaigns. He was determined that he was destined to do great things.

And nothing would stop that. Nothing.

-

"'Pears the rains are at an end, lad," Darvo commented on the third day with no rain. Today was sunny, and a bit windy. Perfect weather for drying the saturated soil.

"So, it does," Parno nodded in dismay. "It'll be time, soon."

"Aye, that it will," came the calm reply. Parno turned to look at Darvo.

"It's time we told them," he said simply. Darvo nodded.

"Sound the assembly, trooper!" he called across to the bugler. The young man started at that, but placed his horn to his lips and played the call.

As the men fell in by companies, Parno looked at his command. Twelve companies in all, plus the artillery command and the support company, consisting of farriers, armorer staff, drivers, and others whose presence made it possible for the soldiers to fight. Willard called the assembly to attention, ordered the roll called, and then placed the men at parade rest. He nodded to Nidiad, who walked up to the small podium.

"Lad's," Darvo's voice boomed across the parade grounds, "there's something you need to hear. It's important, so listen good. I warn you now, what you're told here today doesn't leave this camp. I want that understood by everyone. Anyone as does repeat it, I'll see hanged…and I mean that."

"Word will spread right enough, 'fore long," he continued, "but that decision ain't for us to make." He turned to Parno, who nodded. As he stepped forward his men erupted into a cheer.

Despite himself, Parno smiled. He raised his hands and the men grew quiet again.

"I can see that my decision not to have a direct role in your training has paid off," he joked, and the men laughed aloud through their ranks. Parno waited for the laughter to die off before continuing.

"Men, in all likelihood, we'll soon be at war," he said bluntly and watched a ripple run through the assembly. "I know that things with the Nor have looked promising for a long time. Apparently, they were too promising. Everything that's been accomplished over the last two years or so has been with the intention of making us let our guard down."

"I won't go into how someone figured this out. It took long hours of hard work, I'm told, and not a little sweat and blood, to see behind the veil at what the Nor are planning. My personal best guess is that the Nor will launch their attack within two weeks of the end of the spring rains. They'll want dry ground to march on and they'll want the rivers and streams to be as empty as possible, and it appears that the rains are near their end," he added, lifting his hands to point toward the blue sky overhead.

"We have until then to be ready, not just as a unit, but as a kingdom. We can't do much about the Kingdom," he smiled, and was rewarded by a few chuckles. "No one there much listens to me anyway," he added, which drew outright laughter.

"I know a bit about being an outcast," Parno told them. "I know what it is to have only the worst expected of you and to have the good things you accomplish thrown out with the trash. I know," he told them, grinning, "what it is to be the Black Sheep in the family." The men before him erupted in cheers again, some even clapping.

The men of the Regiment knew that their prince was a black sheep, all but ostracized by the Royal Family of which he was part and they cared not at all. Not only did they not care, they took great pride in the fact.

"You've made me very proud in the last few months," he told them suddenly. "You've worked hard. Harder in these last months as we tried to prepare you as best we can for what's coming. You are as ready as we can make you. Better trained, better equipped, and more prepared for what's ahead than any other unit of the Soulan Army." He paused for a second, then continued.

"There was much opposition to this idea, as you all know by now. Much of that opposition still exists and I was given command of this outfit because I am much like you. The outcast. The Black Sheep."

"In the weeks and months ahead, you will likely have the opportunity to prove these detractors wrong. I want you to remember when you are facing combat, all the malicious things that have been said about us as a unit. Remember every insult, every derogatory remark, every slight and slur. Remember them and the anger they made you feel, and still make you feel! Just as I do!"

"Use that anger! Use it to stiffen your resolve and strengthen your arms." Suddenly a feral grin appeared in the young Prince's face and more than a few returned it.

"Use it to kill our enemies and make them fear the name Parno's Company!" Parno shouted suddenly, angrily. "Make them fear the Black Sheep of Soulan!"

The men of Parno's Company were still cheering when their Prince, their Black Sheep, left the podium. Darvo gave his young charge a feral grin, nodding in admiration and respect. The work was finished.

Now all that remained was to see how well it had been done.

-

Late the next afternoon a new flag appeared in the camp. No one knew where it came from or who had procured it. Rumor was that several of the men in the unit had gathered wives and daughters and had it made in record time.

Everyone agreed that the flag was unique...even impressive in its own way...and that it was a fitting banner to be flown over this camp. This camp and no other.

The flag was emerald green in color. On the upper right-hand corner was the seal of House McLeod. On the Upper Left was the symbol of the Soulan Army. It was the center of the flag that attracted, and held, everyone's attention. Centered in the emerald banner was a sheep. A large, imposing, black sheep with claws and fangs that dripped blood, and with eyes that were as red as rubies.

Parno's Company now had a battle flag. When the time came, they would follow that flag and their commander into any battle. Anywhere.

And that time was coming all too swiftly.

# CHAPTER TWENTY-ONE

-

After days of worrying and watching, expecting a Nor invasion force to appear opposite his position on the Ohi river at any moment, General Bryce Davies, commander of Soulan's 2nd Army Corps, was relaxing. He was enjoying a day on the lake with his wife and family, playing with his grandchildren. Life had been good to him, he knew. Five good children, three strong sons and two beautiful daughters and they had graced him with eight grandchildren so far. Grandchildren who were delighted at seeing 'papa' again, after his long absence.

He watched and laughed as the children frolicked around the water, yelling for him to come and join them. He decided to take them up on the offer and rose from his chair, removing his shirt. He had taken two steps toward them when he heard someone else shouting his name.

He frowned, looking around for the source of this interruption. Someone would pay for ruining this good day. Suddenly, he began to shake to and fro, as if the earth itself was moving beneath him. Oddly enough, his family didn't seem to notice. He was about to ask them if they had heard…

"General!"

Davies woke abruptly, sitting bolt upright in his bed. His aide, Major Randall Brimley, was standing over him, hand still on the general's shoulder where he had been trying to shake his commander awake.

"General, sir! The Nor! They're coming!"

Davies was on his feet before the major could finish his warning, grabbing his boots. He had slept in his clothes, as was his habit these last several days.

"What strength?" he demanded. "And where?"

"Here, sir," Brimley informed him breathlessly. "They're trying to force their way across the bridges!"

Davies didn't wait for more information.

"Have our men turned out?" Davies demanded, stalking out of his tent. Dawn was less than an hour away, the eastern sky already glowing with the impending rise of the sun.

"Yes sir!" Brimley assured him following. "Colonel Pierce had the watch, sir, and heard the commotion as the Nor got into position. He had an entire regiment up behind the barricades before the Nor got started. As soon as the attack began, the artillery opened up on the Nor positions across the Ohi."

"Excellent," Davies nodded. Trust Nelson Pierce not to be caught napping. "Let's see what our 'friends' from the north are up to, then, shall we?" Without waiting for an answer, Davies swung into the saddle of his waiting horse and set out for the battlefield, followed by his ten-man escort.

The ride was a swift one. Davies believed in being where he could see what was happening and his tent was less than a mile from the bridges. The three bridges across the Ohi at Loville were the weak point of his defense. Left from before the Dying, these bridges were the only remaining way across the Ohi for wagons and heavy equipment. When he arrived his first impression was not favorable.

"They're crossing in boats," he muttered to himself. "Under cover of darkness." Colonel Pierce appeared out of the darkness, his face grimy with sweat and dirt.

"We can't hold them, sir," Pierce told his commander bluntly. "There's just too many of them. We're holding the bridges, for now, but it's a near thing at times, and they're crossing up and down stream by boats. Thousands of them."

"Thousands of troops?" Davies asked, considering this news.

"Thousands of boats, sir," Pierce corrected. "With anywhere from ten to twenty men per boat. There's no way we can contain that sir. Sooner or later they'll have enough men above or below us to trap us against the river."

Davies was stunned. They had planned for boats, of course, but only for raiding parties or as part of an all-out assault against the bridges. The Nor, it seemed, had bigger plans for their boats.

"You see no way to contain them?" he asked Pierce.

"I'm sorry, sir," Pierce shook his head. "They're about to put more troops across the river in boats than we can muster against them—and they're pressing the bridges hard. Very hard, sir. I just don't think we have the numbers for a static defense. In the field where we can maneuver?" He shrugged. "Then we may have a chance to contain the attack."

"Do you have any estimate of their numbers? Any feel for the pressure?"

"If I had to guess I'd say we were facing better than fifty thousand troops here, sir," Pierce didn't blink. "That's counting the boats. As for how many may be behind? Waiting for the bridges to fall?" Again, the shrug. "I don't know."

Nelson Pierce was one of Davies' brightest, and hardest fighting, brigade commanders. There wasn't an ounce of back-up or give in the man, Davies knew. If he thought their position untenable, then it likely was. Davies pondered for a few minutes, considering his options. Finally, he nodded.

"Very well, Nelson," Davies spoke calmly. "Hold for a few more minutes, if you can, and give me time to get the command organized for a retreat. We'll form a mobile line behind you, giving you and your men time to withdraw and get mounted."

"Yes, sir," Pierce nodded. He hesitated as if weighing whether or not to speak.

"Yes?" Davies asked.

"Hurry, sir. I doubt we'll be able to buy you much time."

-

As the most likely unit to face the Nor in any attack, 2nd Corps was one of the heaviest in the army. Most Corps in the Soulan army contained two infantry divisions and one cavalry division, along with attached artillery, quartermaster, and other support units.

2nd Corps was much stronger. Davies had at his command three infantry divisions, two cavalry, and one 'heavy' infantry division, troops specially trained and equipped for the hard combat associated with making or repelling assaults. His command had been further supplemented with three divisions of militia, but those units were spread out in penny packets, watching likely crossings along the Ohi, and scouting rural, sparsely populated areas where the Nor might erect assault bridges across the river.

Thus while on papyrus his unit was strong enough to contain even a determined attack, his strength was depleted by the various tasks he had to perform. His regulars had also been pressed into some of those same duties. As a result, he had scarcely three divisions to oppose the Nor onslaught.

While the Nor faced him with twice that many, at least.

Once his command was rejoined things would be different, he told himself. With his command unified against the Nor, his men would be able to withstand their assault.

But in order for that to happen, the men involved in this attack had to withdraw in good order, preserving their remaining strength for that better day, and they had to accomplish that while taking as much of their equipment and supplies with them as they possibly could.

With that in mind, he began barking out the orders he hoped would bring that about.

-

Colonel Pierce watched cautiously as the attack against his force holding the bridge barricades seemed to intensify. Until now, the Nor had been content with keeping up a steady pressure against the entrenched troops around the bridge. Flights of arrows had wounded hundreds of his men despite their protective environs and a steady fire of flaming artillery projectiles had started a number of fires.

His men had been able to extinguish the fires, but the cost was heavy. While they were fighting the fires, his men were exposed to the seemingly endless waves of archery fire. The brigade entrenched around the bridges was slowly melting away.

"Sir, there's a large force moving up on our western flank," a breathless runner appeared out of the smoke-filled gray of early dawn. "Captain Sands says that a number of the boat landings appear to have mated up and are moving on his redoubt in considerable strength."

"What does he consider. . .considerable?" Pierce asked, almost laughing as he heard the words aloud.

"Around five thousand, sir, in this group," the runner informed him. "There are signs of others behind them. Torch lights, lanterns and what have you. No way to judge what's behind them, or how many." Pierce nodded, noting the light. The sun would soon rise fully as dawn gave way to full day. What would the coming light reveal?

"Advise Captain Sands to hold his position for now," he ordered the runner. "We need to buy as much time as possible for the General to get things organized."

"Sir," the man saluted and hurried back to his Captain. Pierce watched him go, hoping the young man made it.

"Sir!" another runner rode up, leaping from his horse. "Captain Early reports a large enemy force approaching the eastern redoubts! And his position is taking light artillery fire as well!"

That did it, Pierce decided. The Nor were now across the Ohi in sufficient numbers to make his position untenable. He motioned for his aide and a courier.

"Inform General Davies," he ordered the courier, "that I intend to withdraw fighting, starting roughly fifteen minutes from now. We are about to be cut off. Staying here will not stop the Nor advance." The courier nodded and hurried off. Pierce turned to his aide.

"I want the wounded loaded, ready to go, in ten minutes. I want no one left behind. Understood?"

"Sir, I don't see how they can -" the young man started, but Pierce cut him off.

"I don't care how they do it! Just get it done! They have ten minutes. Take the reserve company to assist in loading. GO!" He shouted when the young man seemed to hesitate.

The aide went. Pierce turned to the runner from Early's position.

"You heard my orders?" The man nodded.

"Then inform Captain Early." Pierce dismissed the man, waving a nearby runner to him.

"Ride to Captain Sands redoubts and inform him to be ready to pull back in fifteen minutes. Go!" The man was off. Pierce wasted no time, instead ordering more runners off to his company and battalion commanders.

He didn't want to lose any more of his men than the fate and fog of war would take from him.

Soulan would need them all. Soon.

-

"Pierce is about to fall back," Davies told his assembled staff. "He can't hold the bridges and his brigade will soon become enveloped by troops that crossed by boat."

"Tell him to hold to the last!" Brigadier General Ran Howard demanded. "We can organize a counter-attack and still. . . ."

"Ran, we're beat," Davies told him quietly. Howard was a good man, but he was too apt to sacrifice men under his command in the name of honor, rather than reason. "We can't win this battle and that's a fact. Since we can't, there's no reason to sacrifice Pierce and his men in a futile gesture. We'll need every man before this is over, Lord knows."

"But we can't just abandon our. . . ."

"We aren't abandoning anything!" Davies snapped. "And I don't have the time, the Kingdom doesn't have the time, to stand here debating it. Now I've given orders and I expect them to be carried out! Understand?"

"Yes, sir," Howard nodded, all business. He didn't like it, but for all his misguided notions, Howard was a good soldier and officer.

"Now, I want 2nd Brigade mounted and the 1st Cavalry Brigade standing by to give Pierce and his men time to get their wounded to wagons and get mounted. After that, I want the entire 2nd Cavalry Division in position to screen our movement. Support them with our best mounted archers. Any questions?"

No one had questions.

"Then get moving. We're out of time."

-

Across the Ohi Lieutenant General Gerald Wilson, the commander of Norland's 1st Field Army, watched from a tower built for that very purpose as the vaunted Soulan Army scattered in apparent confusion. He turned to his Chief of Staff.

"We're going to do it, Charles," he gloated. "We're going to trap them against the river and destroy one of Soulan's best Army Corps on the first day of the war!"

"Perhaps, sir," General Charles Daly replied, examining the far shore through his glasses, "but they are still fighting and our casualties have been higher than expected." He lowered his glasses and faced his superior.

"Far higher."

Wilson fumed inwardly at the laconic reply, but held his tongue. He'd chosen Daly as his Chief of Staff due to his kinship with the Emperor. It wouldn't do at all to toss him from the tower in a fit of rage. Something Wilson was known for.

"Casualties were to be expected," Wilson waved away the comment with a hand. "This is one of Soulan's best units and it is led by one of their best field commanders. Expecting him to simply roll over and let us walk across the bridges unopposed is unsound thinking but our enemy's position is tactically untenable. Our victory is assured."

"Not if he withdraws," Daly replied, still watching the battle. "If he manages to elude destruction and withdraw with the bulk of his command intact, then half of our primary objective will be lost." He lowered his glasses once more and turned to look directly at his commander.

"The Emperor expects us to destroy this Army here. Today. If we do not. . . ." Daly trailed off, leaving the consequences of failure hanging unsaid.

"He won't withdraw," Wilson scoffed. "Davies has too much pride for that. He will stand with his command until the last man and die before surrendering. It's his way."

"Very well," Daly shrugged, and turned his glasses back to the bridges. He stood quietly for a moment, examining the events just across the river.

Suddenly, wave after wave of mounted horsemen appeared in his view. As Daly watched, half of them dismounted and formed a shield wall in front of those who remained on horseback. Daly almost smiled as he switched his focus to the bridges.

Sure enough, the Soulan troops manning the bridge barricades were falling back, covered by a few last artillery rounds and flight after flight of arrows. The Soulan General had saved his men, and their arrows, for this moment.

"I think you may want to see this, sir," Daly commented over his shoulder. He managed not to smile as he spoke. He didn't even sound too smug.

-

"By the unit!" Pierce called loudly, then waited. Soon he heard his command being echoed up and down his line.

"Fall back!" he yelled, and half his men withdrew at a run for one hundred feet, forming a new line. As men fell wounded, others grabbed them. Those who died were left behind.

Pierce walked slowly back to the new line, knowing his men were watching him. It was important that he not look rattled. Hearing what sounded like a covey of birds overhead, Pierce smiled. He looked up in time to see a second flight of arrows, thousands of them, sail overhead. General Davies had promised him cover, and he'd delivered.

"Second rank READY!" he cried over the din of battle. As the new line settled in, those remaining on the line prepared to leave.

"FALL BACK!" Pierce ordered, and again the call was echoed over the field. The second rank turned tail and ran for the shield wall. Pierce watched in grim satisfaction as his men managed to withdraw in the face of such overwhelming numbers, mindful of their comrades, helping their wounded brethren. It pained him to see so many laying on the ground, beyond any earthly help.

That's war, he thought darkly. It's costly.

As his men continued to pull back, Pierce followed, walking calmly. He arrived at his horse, held by his aide. He swung into the saddle, followed by the aide. There were five men around him as a guard.

He waited until his men were all mounted. He was proud of them, sitting there calmly. They'd held out against staggering odds for almost an hour and left many of their friends on the field of battle, yet they were still strong. They were still willing and able to fight, but they were done for today.

There would be another day, however, and another, and another. Pierce wondered for a second how many of them would still be alive at war's end. He was glad he didn't know, he decided. Better that way.

"By column!" he ordered. "Move OUT!"

The Army of Soulan's 2nd Corps was retreating for the first time in memory.

Pierce knew it wouldn't be the last time. This wasn't like previous invasions by the Nor. They weren't sloppy, disorganized bumblers as the histories had always portrayed them. Either the histories were distorted or this time the Nor were ready.

Pierce didn't know which was worse.

-

War would come to more than just 2nd Corps today.

General Roland Raines rode along the defenses of the Great River Bridge in Shelby, surveying the handiwork of his troopers. When warning had reached him from Nasil that the Nor and the Wildmen had struck a deal of some sort, he had immediately gone to work strengthening the aging defenses along the Great River.

Shelby was a teeming river port, the largest inland part in all of Soulan. Both imports and exports passed through the dock on almost any given day, but it was long since there had been a credible threat to the mighty city and Raines admitted, if only to himself, that the fault was at least partly his own.

His men had worked steadily for the past weeks, strengthening, rebuilding, and adding to the defensive line. This bridge was the only link between Soulan and the Wild Lands of the West. It was one of only a handful of bridges across the Great River that remained from before the Dying and had once been a major trade route according to historians.

To Raines, it was an invasion route. One that his men had worked diligently to plug. True, a determined enemy with sufficient strength might still force his way across it, but the price would be horrible. Raines' artillery was well placed and already zeroed on the bridge. Any force that tried to force such a crossing would find the going difficult, and costly.

He didn't know if that would be enough, but Raines also had other problems. While the bridge might be all but impassible to an enemy army, the river was another matter. Boats could easily transport enemy troops to the Soulan shore and there wasn't much he could do about it. He had been granted one division of Militia, one each from Tinsee and Misi provinces. Thankfully both had been cavalry divisions and he had placed both of them to patrolling the shores north and south of his position in Shelby, on guard for any attempted crossing.

But those troops could only monitor so many miles of shore and there was a lot of shore. The enemy could easily cross over deep in Misi province, or north of him, into the upper Tinsee. If they managed to gain a foothold then Raines would be forced to weaken his defenses at the bridge to try and smash that beach head. To the north the terrain was on his side and there simply weren't all that many places for a successful crossing in large numbers.

The south, however, was another matter. For hundreds of miles the river rolled along Misi's western border, with few bluffs or other obstacles to stop them. Local militias had been alerted to watch for signs of crossing but, again, there was only so much that could be done by so few men.

Raines sighed, rubbing his temple as all these thoughts threatened to erupt into a headache of gargantuan proportions. His companion noticed this action and frowned in concern.

"Sir, are you alright?"

"Yes," Raines nodded. "I'm fine Billy. Just thinking on how many things could go wrong…and how little I can do about it."

"I understand, sir," Colonel William 'Billy' Booth nodded. As Raines' Chief of Staff, Booth was both younger and of lower rank than most of his contemporaries. Chief of Staff for a Corps Commander was generally a Brigadier's post.

Booth was one of the smartest younger officers Raines had seen in nearly a generation, however. The younger man hadn't minded taking the job without the rank and Raines was glad to have him. Booth was not only smart, but a talented tactician, and good strategic thinker.

"Let's head back to headquarters," Raines said suddenly. He was tired and his headache wasn't easing any. After weeks of worry and waiting, it was a wonder his head didn't ache constantly, or that an ulcer hadn't eaten his stomach completely.

"Of course, General," Booth replied and nodded to the escort's commander. The troopers fell into trail, following at a respectful distance, but close enough to intervene if a threat appeared.

"You're still worried about boat crossings, I take it?" Booth asked once they were on their way. Raines nodded.

"Yes. It's the one thing we can't exercise at least some control over."

"Sir, we've done all that can be done," Booth reasoned, "and the cavalry are wearing out their horses keeping the river banks patrolled. We've established watch posts all along the banks as well."

"I know," Raines sighed again. "I swear I think if they'd just do something, I'd feel better. The damn waiting is what's difficult."

"I agree waiting is hard," Booth replied, "but I'd rather they didn't attack at all. Not here. We'd be hard pressed as you said to contain them once they establish a foothold and while we're fighting that one, they might well just launch another one."

"I've thought of that as well," Raines nodded. "I've decided that if there is word of any river crossing, the cavalry will have to deal with it. We may send one mounted division as well, if needed, but I want at least two divisions here in Shelby at all times. They can cross the river in boats easy enough, but they'll have to supply any army that gets across, and that means they'll need the bridge."

"They can forage off the land, sir," Booth pointed out.

"Up to a point," Raines nodded. "But we'll be burning crops and what not as we go if we're forced into a retreat. If there's nothing for them to eat, they'll have to try and resupply them. The River Squadron, once it knows where the beach head is, can help interdict those supplies by boat. No," Raines shook his head, "they need this bridge to mount a successful campaign."

"We'll hold it, sir," Booth's voice had quiet confidence.

"I think so," Raines agreed, "but what damage will be done elsewhere while we do?"

Booth had no answer for that and the two rode on in silence.

"I want you to compose a request for the Marshall," Raines spoke quietly as they neared their headquarters. "In the event that war breaks out and there is an attack on us here in Shelby, I want General Herrick's Corps to assume responsibility for defending the Misi province if the Wildmen or the Nor force a boat crossing of the Great River."

"Yes, sir," Booth scrawled a few notes in his field book. "But, sir. . . ."

"I know," Raines interrupted. "They are unlikely to move his Corps, but there's always a chance.  We cannot hold the bridge and be responsible for so much territory. We simply don't have the manpower."

"Herrick will have his regulars, along with at least two Militia divisions. He will be able to effectively patrol the Misi province along the Great River. We'll continue to patrol the river north of Shelby."

"I'll see to it, sir," Booth agreed. His voice betrayed his thoughts on the subject.

"If they don't, Billy, then we'll do the best we can," Raines shrugged. "But I'm not at all sure that will be good enough."

-

Later that day, Booth knocked hurriedly on Raines' door.

"Sir," Booth looked pale. "Our scouts report movement along the far shoreline."

"What sort of movement?" Raines asked, rising, and reaching for his belt.

"Horsemen, sir," Booth informed him. "They're just watching for now, it appears."

"Let's have a look."

Raines' horse was waiting, along with his escort. He and Booth mounted quickly and headed for the observation tower near the bridge. Their mood was pensive, to say the least, and no one spoke.

Upon arrival Raines practically leaped from his horse, leaving it to his escort to secure the animal, and hurriedly climbed the stair to the tall observation deck. The Captain on duty saluted stiffly when he saw Raines appear.

"Carry on, Captain," Raines threw a sloppy return of the salute, "and mind that the Nor may have us in their glasses. No more saluting."

"Sorry, sir," the young Captain replied, shame-faced.

"No worries, Captain," Raines smiled. "What's the situation?"

"We've seen movement along the shoreline, sir," the Captain pointed unobtrusively, "and there is now a rather large contingent of troops near the far end of the bridge."

Raines nodded and bent his head to the glass.

Sure enough, he easily spotted the body of troops. At least a brigade he decided after observing them for a few moments. He frowned. The enemy troops were milling about rather carelessly, taking no precaution whatever to avoid being seen.

"Colonel," Raines spoke to Booth without turning. "Send runners immediately to all field commands. Two runners per command in fact, on different routes," he added. "Be on guard for river crossings. At this time the troops on the far shore appear to be designed to keep our attention focused on them, and nothing more."

"Yes, sir," Booth scribbled furiously.

"Have Brigadier Simmons report to me here, at once," Raines ordered. Simmons commanded an independent Cavalry Brigade. Not assigned to a division, Simmons took his orders directly from Raines.

"I'll see to it, sir," Booth nodded, and hurried down the stairs. Raines looked at the Captain.

"What's your name, son?"

"Emmett Wilson, sir! 2nd Recon."

"Well, I hope you don't mind my company for a while, Captain Wilson."

"Glad to have you with us, sir. Coffee?"

-

Brigadier Alan Simmons reported to the tower within fifteen minutes. Raines was looking through the glass as the younger general made his way up the steps.

"You sent for me, sir?" Simmons asked.

"Yes," Raines turned from the scope. "I want you to send heavy patrols north and south of our position, along the Great River. There's a brigade, at least, of enemy troops across the bridge from us at this time, but they aren't making any attempt to disguise their presence, nor to organize an attack. I don't like that."

"I see," Simmons said thoughtfully. "I'll send one regiment in each direction, with a third ready to ride at once, if that suits your needs, sir."

"That's fine," Raines nodded, pleased. "I want them to patrol at least ten miles out. I'd prefer that they spread out a bit and perhaps make cold camp at the end of the patrol while establishing a few listening posts along the way. Can you see to that? Some of the local militia should be most helpful with that."

"I'll detail a company of militia with each patrol, sir," Simmons nodded, thinking furiously. "That should allow for several posts, and runners for each."

"Very well, General. You have your orders."

"Sir," Simmons stiffened, but did not salute, then hurried back the way he had come.

Raines turned back to the glass, eying the far shore once more. Hearing boots on the stairs, he turned to see Booth rejoining him, along with several runners.

"Messages away, sir," Booth informed him.

"Good. Send a message to Nasil, if you will. Two couriers, well mounted, and different routes. Inform the Lord Marshall of the following." Raines quickly outlined his actions so far.

"And reiterate my request for General Herrick to move into Misi in support. If my hunch is right we'll need all the help we can get."

"Sir!" Captain Wilson called. "Movement on the bridge!" Raines spun quickly, laying his glass on the bridge.

"They're burning the far barricades," Raines murmured. "Pass the word, no firing without my order. They're trying to goad us into revealing our artillery positions. Keep them under observation, Captain. If we don't respond, they may well try to continue working forward."

"How far do we let them get before we fire, sir?" Wilson risked asking.

"We'll see," Raines replied. Turning once more to Booth he spoke quickly.

"Add this to the message and get the runners away as quickly as possible. I have a feeling this is the beginning." As Booth hurried on his way, leaving the runners for the General, Raines turned his eyes once more to the bridge. Smoke plumes were now clearly visible to the naked eye.

How far indeed?

-

By the noon hour, enemy troops had worked their way a third of the way across the bridge, burning and wrecking the barricades that Raines' men had labored to erect. The job of those barricades was to slow an attacking army. With a third of the way now cleared, Raines had a decision to make. Sighing, he turned to the waiting runners.

"Order Brigadier Foss to prepare his artillery to engage, but hold their fire until I give the word, then return here," he ordered the first. As that man hurried on his way, Raines turned to another runner.

"Inform Brigadier James he is to take two companies of archers, another of crossbow men, and two companies of swordsmen onto the bridge. Have the archers engage the enemy burning party at maximum range. He is to avoid creating a major engagement. His objective is to slow, or stop if possible, the destruction of the barricades. If the enemy flees, he is not, repeat not, to pursue, but to return to our lines. Repeat that." The runner rattled of the orders exactly. Raines nodded.

"Off with you, then."

In minutes the first runner was back.

"Brigadier Foss reports ready to fire, sir. He also stated that the enemy are very close to one of his preplanned target zones. The maximum range, he admits, but doable. He can engage on your orders."

"Very well," Raines nodded. He turned his glass to the bridge, where James' was starting across the bridge. He was not surprised to see James himself in the lead.

"Damn that headstrong boy," he murmured to himself. Quincy James was Raines' nephew, son of his older sister. He was proud of the lad, to be sure, but he had to learn that he no longer commanded a regiment, but a full brigade of men. The days of his leading from the front were supposed to be past.

As Raines watched James led his chosen men along the narrow walkways left in the barricades for just such an occasion, James halted his men behind one of four major strong points along the Soulan side of the bridge, points designed to allow the Soulan troops to make a stand along the bridge itself. Raines saw the archers make take their positions.

On James' order, a flight of arrows launched from the line, lofting toward the enemy troops. Some fell short, a few even went long, but the majority of them fell in among the enemy troopers. Raines watched as the Nor and their Wildmen allies reacted in consternation. Busy with their destruction of the barricade, they hadn't noticed James and his men approach.

"Enemy runner on the bridge, sire," Captain Watkins reported, pointing. Raines looked for himself and nodded.

"Business will pick up, now, I'd wager."

As he and Wilson watched, the enemy troopers formed a ragged line and their own archers readied. Before they could fire, however, another volley from James' men caught them. This one was better placed and hit the enemy before they were organized. The effect was almost instantaneous. Several dropped, hit by Soulan arrows. Others bent to help fallen comrades. Still others turned to retreat. A few stalwart lads lost arrows of their own, but without knowing exactly where the Soulan troops were, they landed off the mark.

James' third flight landed then and even the stalwart among the enemy had had enough. Grabbing their wounded, the enemy troops ran for their side of the bridge. Raines noted that several were left behind, such was their hurry to escape another volley.

James loosed one more salvo, then ordered his men back, following his orders, but the Nor along the shoreline had spotted them. Just as the last of the men were leaving the position, Nor catapults lofted several rounds, including flaming pitch. Raines watched helplessly as the pitch and boulders fell where his nephew had only seconds before been standing. Smoke obscured the view and the General was forced to wait and see the results of the enemy fire.

After what seemed an eternity Soulan troopers emerged from the smoke, hurrying back to their own lines. Several men carried fallen comrades across their shoulders whilst their fellow soldiers covered the retreat. Raines was pleased to note that the men did not appear rattled, nor in a rout. They were simply following orders. Being under fire had not broken them.

Finally, Raines saw his nephew emerge from the smoke, a Soulan trooper thrown across his own shoulder, accompanied by two swordsmen. James' face was covered in soot as was his uniform, but he appeared uninjured.

"Thank God," Raines murmured. He didn't relish having to inform his sister that he had 'allowed' her favorite son to be killed or injured. He watched as the small unit made its way back to friendly lines then sent a runner to order James to report to him at the tower.

Minutes later a soot-covered Brigadier James, still smelling of sweat and smoke and a bit out of breath, arrived on the floor of the tower just under the observation platform. Raines had commandeered the room for this meeting.

"Brigadier James, reporting as ordered, sir."

"You idiot," Raines snarled, eyeing his nephew with a jaundiced eye. "I didn't mean for you to lead the attack." James, unrepentant, merely grinned.

"I chose to interpret the orders loosely, sir."

"Yes, well," Raines broke eye contact. "Just bear in mind if you will, for the future, that I'm the one who will have to face the wrath of your mother should you get your fool self killed!"

"Sorry, sir," James said contritely. "I admit, that didn't enter into my decision making."

"Well, it was well done in any case. Casualties?" James usual enthusiasm dampened some.

"Seven killed, fifteen wounded. Two of those probably won't last the night out. Pitch got them." His eyes spoke volumes and Raines nodded. He knew what pitch could do to a man.

"I'm sorry about your men, Quin," Raines said softly, using James' childhood nickname. James shrugged.

"Fortunes of war, sir," he replied philosophically. "We'll lose a lot more before this business is finished."

"I'm afraid that's truer than you know," Raines agreed. "Well, see to your men and yourself. There's still plenty of light left. The Nor, or the Wilds, may try again."

"I admit, I was a bit let down in the Wildmen," James told his uncle, head tilted to one side. "I thought they'd stay and fight after all I'd heard of them. Maybe we're worrying about nothing where they're concerned."

"Perhaps," Raines nodded, "but let's not assume anything of the sort for now. Soulan hasn't been at war with the Wildlands in over a century and that was a brief, though bloody, encounter. Back then they were ferocious warriors and would sooner die in place than surrender or retreat."

"I won't take them lightly," James promised. "With your permission?"

"Granted. Go take care of yourself, Quin."

# CHAPTER TWENTY-TWO

-

Memmnon had taken a break from looking over the weekly reports from his Chief Constables. With war in the offing he had ordered all of his regional and Provincial Marshals to be on the lookout for anything that might indicate subversive or enemy actions in the Kingdom. If the Nor were planning to attack, then there was no reason to believe that saboteurs and spies wouldn't be a part of their war plan. Soulan certainly made use of them.

As he walked along the courtyard he noticed a flurry of activity near the inner gates. Curious, he headed that way.

"Milord!" a sentry called, seeing the Crown Prince heading his way. "Urgent courier from General Davies, milord! The Nor are attacking in strength at Loville!" Memmnon hastened his step at that, hurrying to the exhausted courier who was just now dismounting from his horse. The man faltered, almost falling, before another sentry grabbed him. The courier's horse was also done in, foam flecking its coat, and its tongue hanging.

"Call for the Sergeant," Memmnon ordered. "Have this man and his horse seen to at once," he instructed, taking the courier pouch from the rider.

"Aye, Milord," the sentry acknowledged. "Sergeant of the Guard! Post One!" Memmnon ignored the bustle behind him as he headed for his father's office, ripping open the envelope as he went.

The sentry's words were true, he noted. General Davies had come under attack before dawn, two days ago. He read as he walked, noting the details for later. He grabbed a passing soldier.

"Find the Lord Marshall," he ordered. "Have him report to the King's private office at once."

"Aye, Milord!" the soldier saluted, then ran off in search of Therron McLeod.

Memmnon resumed his walk, still reading. Davies was retreating, he was startled to read. Citing a hopeless tactical situation and a determines attack by overwhelming numbers, Davies had decided to abandon the defenses and engage the Nor on open ground. It was his hope that the Soulan Army's familiarity with the ground and superior horsemanship would give him a better advantage against the Nor horde now flooding across the Ohi.

He was also requesting immediate reinforcements. Memmnon sighed at that, knowing that the only force capable of reaching Davies in time to matter was the 1st Corps, stationed in Nasil. The only force in position to protect the heartland.

Memmnon found his father pouring over a map with one of his chief military advisers. While Therron was the Lord Marshall, Tammon was King and the Ultimate Authority in Soulan.

"Father, there is news from General Davies," Memmnon spoke quietly. Tammon looked at him for a second.

"Clark, excuse us please," he spoke to his companion. A former Marshall of the Army, Clark was one of Tammon's most trusted people.

"Of course, milord," Clark left the room, closing the door behind him.

"The Nor have crossed the bridges at Loville," Memmnon said without preamble. "Davies has fallen back, choosing to fight in the field rather than be enveloped trying to hold the defenses. The Nor," Memmnon continued, passing the report to his father, "used boats to great effect, apparently. They managed to put several thousand troops on our side of the Ohi and used them to try and flank Davies as he fought to hold the bridges. They only just escaped."

"He should have been more aware!" Tammon growled, taking the offered report and reading through it.

"There's no telling how far up and down the river the Nor launched their boats. Davies had patrols all along the Ohi, Father," Memmnon pointed out. "It was his forethought that kept his entire army from being destroyed in place. As it is, the 2nd is still an effective fighting force, and are in the field, defending the Kingdom."

Tammon read on in silence, ignoring Memmnon for the moment. As he read, some of the scowl left his face. Finally he nodded, looking up from the report.

"You are right," he agreed. "According to this, there were some two hundred thousand enemy troops either directly engaged with Davies or waiting to advance when the bridges fell. He did well to save his command and withdraw in an orderly fashion."

"He has requested the 1st Corps assist him," Memmnon pointed out. "Since moving General Freeman south, the 1st is the only army left to defend the heartland."

"And we have no choice but to move them to Davies' assistance," Tammon sighed. "He is too heavily outnumbered to engage them in an outright battle. I'll have Therron. . . ." He broke off as Therron chose that moment to walk in.

"You summoned me, Father?" he asked, breath ragged from running.

"No, but it's good you're here," Tammon replied, handing over the report. "The Nor have struck Loville."

"I had someone fetch you as soon as the word arrived," Memmnon said quietly. Therron frowned at the word 'fetch', but turned his attention to the report.

"Davies retreated without even attempting to hold the bridges!" Therron almost spat. "I'll have him relieved at once!"

"If you'll read a bit further," Tammon spoke coldly, "you'll see that he managed to save his army from being completely enveloped and destroyed by a force several times his own size." Therron, red faced from the rebuke, returned to reading. When he was finished, he looked up, calmer.

"I was wrong, Father," he admitted reluctantly. "Davies has done well, it seems."

"Indeed," Tammon frowned at his younger son. There were times when he doubted Therron's ability to cope with the traditional duties of the second son of the realm.

"I shall lead 1st Corps to his assistance, myself," Therron declared, straightening. "Together, we can easily withstand the Nor."

"Easily?" Memmnon couldn't help blurting out. "Therron, did you notice, during your perusal of the report, that Davies is facing a force estimated at a quarter of a million men?" Therron's face went red at that.

"Need I remind you, brother, that this is my area, not yours," he declared loftily, and Memmnon's own face went red at that.

"Need I remind you, brother," Memmnon snarled, "who it is that will one day rule?"

"Quiet!" Tammon snapped. "I have told you before, I have no time for squabbling children! The very Kingdom is in danger and the two of you are arguing over who is more important!" Both men fell silent. Tammon turned his eyes to Therron.

"It is time for you to realize that you are not the ultimate authority in this Kingdom, Therron," he grated. "As Crown Prince, Memmnon has the right to question any decision you make and I should not have to remind you that I have the right, and the power, to make decisions with or without your input. If I do need to remind you, then perhaps you should not be Lord Marshall of my armies. Understood?" Therron paled at that, nodding.

"I meant no disrespect, Sire," he spoke carefully. This wasn't the time to rock the boat. Not yet.

"As it is," Tammon sighed, "I see no alternative but to allow you to take 1st Corps into the field and march to Davies' assistance. But Therron, I warn you now," the King's voice turned colder, "listen to General Davies, and seek his counsel before acting. He is a seasoned veteran and has far more experience in these matters than you do. Understand?"

"I do, Father," Therron assured the King.

"Then make ready," Tammon ordered him. "Take 1st Corps and leave as soon as possible. Today, if practicable. You need to be in the field with Davies as soon as possible. We cannot allow the Nor to gain a sizable foothold in our Kingdom."

"By your order, sire," Therron bowed and left. Memmnon watched him go, eyes still glowering. Tammon did not miss that look.

"I know he is troublesome," Tammon said gently. "But he is good at what he does. I fear you'll need to watch him closely, though, once I am gone." Memmnon looked startled at that. Tammon rarely spoke in such a way. The King chuckled.

"I am not so young as I once was, Memmnon," he explained. "There will come a time when I am no longer able to rule. Either death or infirmity will decide when that is. Once that day is here, then the responsibility will be yours. You can, of course, replace him when that happens. If you do, then I advise you to choose his replacement with care. Much of the army will be loyal to Therron. Do you understand what I'm saying to you. Son?"

Memmnon nodded, an icy chill spreading down his spine. His father had seen it also. No wonder he had looked so haggard, of late.

"I understand, sire," he spoke quietly.

"I hope so," Tammon sighed heavily. "If he becomes too troublesome, I may have him replaced myself before that time arrives. That might be better in all honesty," the King mused. "Trouble is, we cannot afford to replace him now in the midst of a war, and if he is successful in repelling the invasion, then his popularity will soar." Tammon sat heavily into his chair. Memmnon realized with a start that his father looked far older than he had just three months ago.

"Don't trouble yourself with what may one day be, Father," Memmnon told him, forcing a smile to his face. "You have more than enough to deal with as it is. Therron and I have always worked together and we will continue to do so. Don't waste your worry on that."

Tammon smiled tiredly and nodded.

"I think you're right," he replied. "I am tired, Memmnon. I think I'll rest a while. But call me if I am needed."

"Of course, Father," Memmnon nodded and left the office, ordering Tammon's aide to see to the King. As he walked toward his own offices he couldn't help but think on what he'd just said…and heard.

Memmnon knew, then and there, that one day he would have to deal with Therron. Even if Soulan managed to survive this latest Nor onslaught, and that looked questionable to say the least, would the Kingdom survive a war between himself and Therron?

Hours later, watching Therron march out ahead of the vanguard for 1sts Corps,

Memmnon still had no answer to that.

Later in the day, Memmnon McLeod walked along the concourse of the palace grounds, hands locked behind him, eyes fixed on some point only he could see. His discussion with the King concerning Therron had left him unsettled.

There had never been a coup in Soulan, not in its long history. The house McLeod descended directly from the House Tyree itself, the founding dynasty of the Kingdom of Soulan that had ruled for over two hundred years alone. Soulan had been fortunate in that, while it had sometimes had incompetent leaders, it had never had a bad one. The people were treated fairly and the law was the same for all, regardless of social status. This, in itself, was a legacy of the House of Tyree.

But now, Memmnon was forced to admit, there might indeed be a problem in the offing. Therron was becoming more and more open in his defiance and not just where Memmnon was concerned, either. He also appeared to be testing his personality cult against the King himself.

In any other time he was sure that Tammon McLeod would have long ago dealt with Therron. The threat of war looming, and now upon them, had prevented it and left Therron is a perfect position to make a claim that he, rather than Memmnon, should sit upon the throne of Soulan.

Memmnon sighed. His hands moved to massage his temples as the problems threatened him with a headache.

Atop everything else was the status of the King's health. Tammon had not been well for some months. He blamed it upon old age and a wild youth, but Memmnon, as Crown Prince, knew the truth. More than once the Royal Physician had warned Tammon that his health was slipping. Not to the point that he could not rule…not yet, at any rate.

But the pressures of rule were enough by themselves. The war had made it worse and, Memmnon acknowledged, Tammon's own ire at Parno had complicated it. Memmnon shook his head again.

Parno. He had never been the problem. As an older and hopefully wiser man now, Memmnon could look back at how he and the others—the entire palace—had made Parno's life hell. He had known nothing but hate and misery his entire life. Was it any wonder that he was a rebel? If he was to be treated as a bastard child, then why not act like one? There was surely nothing to be lost, was there?

And yet it was Parno who had stumbled onto the Nor plot to invade Soulan. Parno who had trekked through the harsh winter to bring the information he had gathered, knowing as he did so that his actions might see him treated even worse than before.

Parno loves this land and its people, Memmnon thought to himself. Perhaps it is he who should be King and neither myself, nor Therron. He shook his head yet again.

That wasn't possible, of course. Parno was third in line but he would never be taken seriously as a ruler. Thanks, yet again, to the way his family had treated him his entire life.

We have done that, he thought bleakly. The memory of Parno looking to him for help when Therron and the King had told him his men were not good enough to defend the realm came back to him. The look of a little brother looking to his older brother for help. Something anyone should have... but Parno never has, Memmnon though sadly. I've denied him even that. Yes, his father had treated Parno poorly, blaming him every waking hour for the loss of the Queen. Unfairly, to be sure, but still a fact, and Memmnon had done the same. All of them had.

"How could we have done that?" he asked himself. "How could we be so cruel as to blame a child for being born? Are any of us fit to sit upon the throne?"

Nothing could change the past, Memmnon acknowledged bleakly. He had reached out to Parno in recent months and Parno had responded. Hesitantly at first, of course, but who could blame him? And when Parno had found the Nor plot who was it he had trusted with it?

His older brother upon whom he thought he could, at long last, depend. "And then, I abandoned him when Therron had dismissed Parno's work with his regiment," Memmnon thought.

True, Memmnon didn't know if they were ready for battle. But was anyone? He did know that Parno's men had to be at least as well prepared as any of the militiamen who were, even now, fighting against the Nor invasion.

His refusal to fight for Parno had hurt the youngest McLeod. Something that wouldn't have been possible if Memmnon himself hadn't been trying to bridge the gap between them. A gap created by his own doings, Memmnon acknowledged. Now all that work was destroyed. He had seen that much in Parno's eyes as he left Nasil that day.

Parno would not be so foolish as to place his trust in Memmnon again, the Crown Prince knew. Nor in anyone else inside the palace…and why should he?

Why should he, indeed?

"Milord?" Memmnon heard suddenly, and turned to see a member of the House Guard coming toward him.

"Milord, the King has asked to see you," the guard informed him. Memmnon nodded in reply and started back toward the palace itself. He couldn't change what was past and he had a bleak future in which to try and change it now.

-

"You summoned me, Father?" Memmnon said quietly, entering the King's office. For weeks now this had been the center of the Soulan preparation for war and it now served as a command center. Maps adorned the walls, tables, and even the King's desk.

Tammon nodded wordlessly, handing over a message form.

Memmnon took it, noticing at once that it was from General Raines, Commander of 3rd Corps in Shelby. Shelby, home of the sole surviving bridge across the Great River.

As he read, Memmnon was both dismayed and heartened. Dismayed to discover that the Nor, supported by the Wild Tribes of the Westlands, had attacked in force across the bridge.  Heartened by the news that Raines was, at least for now, holding fast. In his closing remarks Raines asked again for additional mounted units to patrol the great expanses of shoreline in order to prevent enemy boat crossings.

Considering that the Nor had used boats to great effect at Loville, the request was not unreasonable.

"I suppose we should have expected it," he said flatly, laying the dispatch upon his father's desk.

"Yes," Tammon nodded, gazing out the window of his office. "We should have and here is something else we should have likely thought of," he sighed heavily, handing over yet another report. Memmnon took it warily and began reading.

This report was more chilling, if anything. It came from General Freeman, Commander of 4th Corps in Lana.  It read that a Soulan fishing vessel had encountered a large fleet of ships in the Eastern Sea. A very large fleet. General Freeman was of the opinion, based on the report of the Captain of the fishing vessel, that this fleet, now sitting some thirty miles off the Sunshine Coast, carried an invasion force. He had dispatched a pair of frigates to try and maintain contact with the fleet, shadowing it. Another ship acted as a courier for them.

"Wonderful," Memmnon sighed, taking a seat dejectedly. "Yet another army, just sitting off the coast, waiting and watching for a chance to land somewhere."

"Indeed," Tammon nodded, still looking out his window. "There is little choice, of course, but to order Freeman to move his Corps south so as to be in a position to interdict this invasion force, should they try to come ashore."

"They may not try to," Memmnon replied, "and there may be no troops aboard those ships, father," he added.

"Possible," Tammon nodded absently. "That thought had occurred to me as well as I waited for you to arrive, but we cannot afford to make such an assumption."

"We can send our fleet out to meet them," Memmnon suggested.

"And we will," Tammon agreed, finally turning to look at his oldest son and heir, "but our fleet is not yet assembled entirely and their ships outnumber the Savannah Squadron. By a rather large margin, if this count is even close to accurate. I have no doubt that our fleet will give a good account of itself, but I do doubt they can stop it. Hurt it, yes. Stop it, no." Memmnon was shocked at how poorly his father looked. Bad news atop bad news, along with the instability wrought by Therron, was taking its toll on the King of Soulan.

"We can order the Sunshine Squadron to join them," Memmnon offered. "It will take some time to order the move and more still for them to make it, but it can, and should be done. As soon as possible. Perhaps," Memmnon mused, "the two can catch the force between them."

"I agree," Tammon sighed. "We have no choice, really. I have also considered having the Southern Squadron moved around the Key Horn and up to support them. It would take time, however. Time we may not have."

"It would leave the Gulf of Storms uncovered," Memmnon commented, "but how likely is it that the Nor will have two such fleets?"

"How likely was it they would assemble an army of five hundred thousand and make an alliance with the Wild Folk?" Tammon retorted, though there was no heat in his words. Memmnon nodded.

"True," he admitted. "We cannot take anything for granted."

"And we cannot ignore this threat," Tammon nodded. "Prepare the orders at once. I would like it very much if our fleet can join forces and coordinate their attack. Make sure that is in their orders. Also, order Freeman to prepare to move his forces south. We must try to determine where the Nor are likely to try and come ashore and place Freeman nearby. If we happen to catch them in the act of landing their men we could destroy that force before it can make a significant impact upon the war."

"I will see to it at once," Memmnon nodded, rising. Tammon looked up at his heir, his face drawn.

"It may be that you will not have to bear the burden of Rule after all, my son," he said softly.

"Nonsense," Memmnon scoffed, with more confidence that he felt. "We will defeat them, Father. We may lose ground for a while, but ground can be retaken. We will be the victors in the long run."

"I fear the run may be very long indeed, Memmnon," the King said wearily. "Very long indeed."

-

Lieutenant Colonel Bret Chad watched in dismay as a seemingly endless stream of Nor troops poured across the countryside of his native land. He had long since stopped trying to calculate the numbers, leaving that chore to his aides. Instead, he tried to figure a way to impede the flow of enemies into his homeland.

Chad's 12th Mounted Infantry, Kent Militia, was in the field when the invasion had begun. A messenger had located them less than two days after the start of the war, but by the time the regiment had been able to return there was little they could do.

2nd Corps, comprised of three infantry and two cavalry divisions, along with the bulk of the Kent militia's two mounted divisions, was steadily falling back on the Tinsee Valley, unable to stop the onslaught of invaders.

In fact, they were struggling to merely slow them. General Davies was hard pressed to keep his Corps from being enveloped as they fought to slow the enemy advance. He had dispatched messengers to Nasil requesting assistance, but no answer had yet been received.

Unable to link up with the rapidly retreating 2nd Corps, Chad had instead been shadowing the invading force, trying to determine their intentions. His mind raced as he looked for some way for his force to make an impact.

Realistically he knew their odds were slim. True, they could simply launch an attack on the enemy flank, but Chad knew that the 12th would simply melt away under so many enemy troops…and Soulan would need all the troops they had before this war was over.

"They aren't fighting as they have in the past," Major Tom Hildebrand, Bret's second in command commented quietly. "Everything I've ever read in the histories indicates that the Nor. . . ."

"I'd say that we can forget the history books, Tom," Chad replied darkly. "They also indicate that Nor cavalry is a joke, at best." His hand swept the land before them, where well-ordered Nor cavalry units were moving, "Do they look inept in any way?"

"No, sir, they don't," Hildebrand shook his head. "What are we going to do?"

"What can we do, Tom?" came the dejected reply. Chad took his hat off and rubbed a hand across the top of his head. "We have seven hundred men, total. We'd last all of ten minutes against that lot. I won't throw away the lives of our men in a futile gesture."

"I wasn't advocating that, sir," Hildebrand replied. "But our messengers haven't returned as yet, and. . . ."

"Beg pardon, sirs," a young lieutenant interrupted, "but there's something you should see."

"What is it, Morely?" Chad inquired gently. The lad looked shaken, but then they were witnessing an invasion of their homes. Everyone was shaken. Stories at the dinner table about what great-great-grandad had done in the last war were no match for experiencing things first hand.

"A large body of this force is breaking away, sir," the young officer informed him, "and heading this way."

Chad and Hildebrand followed the young man to the top of the next ridge where both men gasped. A large body indeed.

"Looks like several thousand of them," Hildebrand said softly.

"Right at fifty thousand, sir," Marly informed him. "All mounted but only about half are true cavalry, it seems. The rest appear to be mounted infantry. They have a large supply train forming to their rear," he pointed. Both men switched their glasses to the area, where dozens of wagons were forming into a train. Sharp eyed cavalry surrounded the train.

"Dividing their attack force," Chad murmured. "Why would they do that?" he wondered aloud.

"Everything we've gotten back so far indicates they're pushing General Davies hard. Very hard, in fact," Hildebrand commented. "Why take that pressure off?"

"Why, indeed," Chad nodded in agreement. "Let's see where they go."

By dawn the next morning it was clear where the Nor were headed.

"They're going for the gap," Hildebrand said firmly. "With 2nd Corp reeling the way is open and by now, sir, 1st Corps could already be on their way to reinforce them."

"Then the 4th Corps will have to come up from Lana to stop this outfit," Chad noted. "Very well, then. Let's get messengers ready to ride. I'll draft the message at once and have aides copy it. I want two messengers each to 4th Corps, Nasil, and General Davies."

"Meanwhile," he turned to Hildebrand, "I want eyes on this column at all times. That won't be easy since they'll have a screen out. See to it that our men are prepared and warn them to take no chances. At this point we need information, not heroes."

"Sir," Hildebrand nodded, and left to carry out his orders.

"Send for my aide, Corporal," Chad ordered.

-

Parno McLeod stalked from one end of his porch to the other, stopped for a moment to allow his angry gaze to linger on the horizon, then whirled to stalk to the other end of the porch. This ritual was now a common sight in Cove Canton. Since his return from Nasil where he was informed that he and his men wouldn't be needed to combat the impending invasion, Parno had been in an ill mood even at the best of times. At less than the best of times, it was much, much, worse.

Knowing that the Nor were planning to attack just made it worse. Parno was being forced to sit idly by as his whole kingdom struggled to prepare as quickly as possible for the pending invasion. With their own preparations already made, there was little to do in Cove Canton…so he stalked, and he worried, and he fumed. Perhaps not all the time, but enough of it that everyone knew not to bother him when he was like this.

"Lad, you're wearing a hole in that porch, you know," Darvo Nidiad's voice floated to him from below. Okay, almost everyone.

"I'll have another built to replace it, then," Parno snorted angrily, without missing a stride. Stalk, pause, whirl, repeat. Stalk, pause, whirl, repeat. It was almost a dance, Nidiad decided. Wouldn't do to say that, of course.

"Lad, there's no sense in working yourself into a fit over this," Nidiad was becoming exasperated himself. Parno had been in this funk for weeks. It was well into spring and his Prince's anger had abated not one whit that he could see.

"I'm trying to work myself out of a fit," Parno shot back. "I'm mad as hell and I don't want to be around anyone while the potential for me to make an ass of myself exists…and so long as I'm mad, the potential exists."

Nidiad didn't reply to that, seeing the sense in what Parno was saying. It was a twisted kind of sense, but sense nonetheless.

"Rider approaching!" a call from the camp's gate announced. Several men headed that way, including the Officer of the Day. The camp expected a messenger any day now with word that Soulan was once again at war with Norland.

Parno descended the steps off the porch and he and Darvo began walking that way. Parno saw Captain Hamm confer momentarily with the courier, then wave him on. The courier handed the reins of his horse to a nearby trooper and accompanied the Captain to where Parno and Darvo stood.

"Milord," the courier bowed, offering Parno a dispatch envelope. "My Lord Memmnon's compliments, sir." Parno snorted lightly, but took the envelope.

"Get yourself a meal, lad," Darvo ordered the courier. The man bowed again and set off for the mess. Meanwhile, Parno quickly read the dispatch.

"Damn it!" Parno swore loudly, slapping the envelope against his leg. "Read this," he told Nidiad disgustedly.

"They're moving 4th Corps to the south?" Nidiad blurted, reading the dispatch.

"To counter a possible coastal landing along the Sunshine Coast," Parno nodded. "Leaving nothing in the heartland."

"'This move is based on intelligence that a large fleet of enemy vessels has been observed some thirty miles off shore, effectively maintaining station off our coast'," Darvo quoted. "They're moving the entire Corps on what might happen?"

"That's what it says," Parno almost spat. "All my warnings of protecting the heartland. . . Why didn't they bring 5th Corps east from Moble?" Parno wondered.

"If this force goes around the peninsula and hits the Gulf Coast, 5th Corps will have to stop them," Darvo replied, though Parno knew that. He studied his young liege closely.

"We need to be cautious," Darvo warned quietly. "We need eyes in the field, lad. Someone keeping an eye on what's happening about. We're only a two, maybe three-day ride from the Gap of Cumberland."

"Don't I know it," Parno agreed. "Very well. Find Karls. Let's get around the map table and see if we can get this sorted out."

-

An hour later, the three men responsible for leading the Regiment were finishing their planning when another rider was announced. Parno, Karls, and Darvo walked out onto the porch once more as a breathless rider made his way to the steps below. He bowed shortly and presented his pouch.

"My Lord."

"Have you any word, son?" Darvo asked, as Parno opened the pouch.

"Nors are across the Ohi, sir," the courier replied shakily. "In great numbers. Word has reached the Capital that a force from the Wild Lands is attempting to force the bridge over the Great River at Shelby. Again, in great numbers, sir." Using horsemen to ferry messages was the quickest way to communicate but in this case, the second dispatch had arrived before the first.

The war had already begun!

"Great Kingdom," Darvo breathed. He ordered the young rider to get some food then looked at Parno.

"You were right, lad. The Nors have made an alliance with the Wild Folk."

"It's worse than that," Parno told him, tossing the pouch to his mentor. "2nd Corps is already retreating and General Davies is asking for 1st Corps to come to his assistance. He reports that the overwhelming numbers are too great to stand against without 'substantial' reinforcement. 1st Corps, according to this," he pointed to the letter, "is already on the way to him."

"And the 3rd is engaged with the Wild Folk," Karls muttered. "With the 4th going south, maybe already moving south, that leaves the Heartland completely vulnerable to attack."

"Long planning went into this," Darvo agreed. "They're hitting us in too many places at once and with greater numbers than we can hold off."

"If they manage to get a force on the coast before 4th Corp can get into position. . . ." Karls began.

"And if they hit the Cumberland?" Parno demanded. "They can cut straight through to Nasil and control the entire Tinsee Valley! After that it's just a matter of isolating and eliminating individual forces. We'll be beaten."

"Why would they come through the Cumberland when their attack on the west is going so well?" Karls protested. "It makes no sense."

"They know that the closer they get to Nasil, the harder the fighting will be," Parno told him, "and the flat lands favor our cavalry, despite their improvement in that area. They've already managed to lure 1st Corps out of Nasil and have forced the King to reposition 4th Corps farther to the south." Parno broke off, his eyes growing distant.

"What are you thinking, lad?" Darvo asked softly.

"That those ships are a ruse," Parno looked straight at him. "They're empty. There's no attack force landing on the shores. Those ships only have one purpose and according to the message we received not an hour ago, they've already accomplished that mission."

"But if they aren't empty, then. . . ."

"Then 4th Corps, and the 5th, will be there to stop them, won't they?" Parno shot back. "While how many Nor troops flood through the Gap?" He looked at Karls.

"What's at the Gap?" he demanded.

"There's an old fortress there, of course," Karls stammered, caught off guard by his Prince's sudden fire. "A brigade of militia is stationed there but may well have sent the bulk of their forces west by now."

"Perfect," Parno nodded, looking again off into the distance. Suddenly he turned to his two subordinates.

"I want this entire regiment ready to ride by morning. War footing. Remounts, rations, everything. Understood?"

"Lad, we've no orders...." Darvo broke off at the look on his Prince's face.

"Ready…by…morning." Parno bit each word off.

"Aye, Milord," Darvo dipped his head, and he and Karls set out.

-

Colonel Chad watched in dismay as the Nor vanguard continued to make better time than he'd thought possible.

"At this rate they may well reach the Gap in less than a week," Hildebrand commented from his side. "Certainly, less than two."

"We've got to slow them down," Chad agreed. "But how?"

"There are several bridges that we can destroy," Hildebrand pointed out. "That won't stop them, of course, but…"

"But it might slow them down," Chad nodded. He'd been thinking on that as well. "But slowing them isn't going to be enough. Once that lot," his hand swept toward the general direction of the invader's advance, "hits the Gap, they'll have a clear field before them."

"There's the fort at the gap, sir," Hildebrand pointed out. "Might take them a few days to…"

"They'll just bowl it over," Chad snorted. "There's nothing there but a token force, anyway. The bulk of the troops stationed there were sent west to General Davies, according to our last report."

"We can bolster them with our own men," Hildebrand said softly. Bret turned to look at him.

"If it comes to that, we will," he told his second, voice firm and unyielding. "But that won't help much. We have to get someone. . . ."

"Beg pardon, sirs," Marly spoke, walking up to the two men at a quick pace. "There's a rider, sir. Dispatches," he added, offering the courier envelope to his commander.

Chad opened the dispatch, and began reading. "Damn it!" he swore suddenly.

"Sir?" Hildebrand looked at him.

"1st Corps is already in the field, on its way to support Davies!" Chad almost spat out. "There's no one left in the region to stop this lot and they won't even know of them for another day, at least. There's no way for our riders to reach them before then."

"Officer's call, Mister Morley," Hildebrand told the lieutenant. "All company commanders, their seconds, and senior NCO's. Fifteen minutes."

"Sir," the younger man saluted, and scurried away.

"We'll have to get working on those bridges today," Chad muttered, "and start making our way to the Gap. There's no one else."

"Sir, begging your pardon," Hildebrand said hesitantly. "But there is one other post near the Gap."

"What?" Chad turned, looking at his second. "Who?"

"Milord Parno's, sir," Hildebrand told him. "The prison company."

"Great," Chad snorted. "That's a big help."

"It's better than none at all," Hildebrand pointed out calmly, "and Lord Parno is fairly skilled, make no mistake. For that matter, his second is Darvo Nidiad."

"Ah," Chad nodded, remembering the older man. "A good man, Darvo. But I can't see what good a bunch of prisoner's can do and that's leaving aside Lord Parno's somewhat lack luster reputation." Chad was a loyal Soulander, but Tom Hildebrand was a friend and Chad spoke openly and honestly to him, whatever the subject.

"His reputation is that of a fighter, sir," Hildebrand reminded him, "and, if I may? Lord Parno was involved in a duel, a sanctioned event, in early winter last year. He was the winner. Decisively so, I might add."

"So?" Chad replied with a raised eyebrow. "Dueling is nothing like commanding in the field. Or fighting in the field for that matter."

"Normally I'd agree, sir," Hildebrand nodded, "and my opinion of Lord Parno was much the same before the duel, I admit. But it wasn't so much the duel, sir, as the opponent."

"And who was that?" Chad asked, on the edge of becoming annoyed. It wasn't like Hildebrand to beat around the bush like this.

"Enri Willard."

Chad gaped at that. The Playboy Prince had defeated Enri Willard?

"You're joking."

"No, sir, I am not," Hildebrand shook his head. "Defeated him in open combat, and even though the contest was mortal combat, Parno, as the victor, chose to spare Enri. Rumor has it that he told Willard that Soulan needed men like him."

"Well..." Chad considered that. He looked off into the distance toward the oncoming enemy. At this distance there was little to see other than dust but if one looked long enough, he could see the long columns winding around the narrow lanes and catch the glimpse of light reflecting on metal, banners waving.

"Very well," Chad replied after a moment. "Send a courier to the Prince, suggesting that he and his Forty Thieves might want to move to the gap. Though if he has any sense, he'll run the other way."

"He won't run," Hildebrand said firmly. "If he didn't run from single combat against Willard, he won't run from anything."

"More's the pity," Chad shook his head. "We'll need men like that to survive this as a kingdom." And no one will survive this, he thought darkly, looking once more at the horde of Nor troopers.

No one.

-

They had worked through the night.

Every hand was pressed into service. Soldiers were helping in every area under the watchful eyes of those who knew what had to be done. The hustle and activity of Cove Canton proper was increased by the frantic work being done on The Hill.

"Be careful with that!" Finn had screeched more than once as the not quite stable liquid he called "nitro" was loaded carefully onto specially prepared wagons. Beakers hung in tufts of cotton cloth, allowing them to swing when the wagons jarred. Not too much, of course, as swinging into each other could prove just as disastrous as hitting the wagon boards.

"Where did that name come from?" Parno had inquired as he watched the work with no small trepidation.

"It's what the ancients called it, milord," Roda had answered. "I gleaned the formula from a very old text. Very old," he frowned. "Likely the last of its kind, I fear. I have had copies prepared and the original is now in your safe." Parno had nodded at that, glad to know that Roda was thinking ahead.

Now as the sun began to rise in earnest, Parno looked over the column. Soldiers were literally sleeping in the saddle as they waited in formation for the word to move out. Wagons, artillery, supplies…Parno went down a mental checklist of items as he rode the column once more. He couldn't afford to miss anything. He stopped short as he passed an ambulance.

"What in the blazes of hell do you think you're doing?" he demanded sharply.

"I'm going with the column," Stephanie Corsin replied calmly. "You'll have wounded if you fight a battle."

"The hell you are!" Parno almost screamed. He managed to keep his voice to a moderate bellow, but he was aghast at even the suggestion. "You get this ambulance out of the column right now, mister!" he ordered the driver. Before the man could move, however, Corsin's small hand covered the driver's.

"Stay where you are," she ordered calmly, never taking her eyes from the Prince. "We. . .I…am going. I am a doctor and the best one anywhere around. It's useless for me to stay here when there will be men I can treat, and perhaps save, where you are going. The decision has already been made, milord."

"I make those decisions, Doctor!" Parno managed not to growl, "and there is no way I'm allowing you to accompany us to the Gap. I won't tell you again to move this wagon," he directed that at the driver.

"You may step down," Stephanie turned to the driver, taking the reins. "I won't ask you to disobey the Prince's orders." She turned back to Parno.

"I can drive myself." Parno was about to launch into another fit until he looked at the doctor's eyes. She was determined. Scared, yes. But determined.

He sighed.

"It's no place for a woman, Stephanie," he tried to reason with her, "especially a woman of your upbringing and station." Corsin snorted at that.

"I've heard that all my life, Parno McLeod!" she shot back, her voice carrying. Neither were aware of the crowd they were drawing, "And I never have liked it. Nor have I let it stand in my way. Now, this wagon is ready to roll. You're holding up the column, standing there arguing!"

"They'll make a fine couple when they're married," Darvo Nidiad whispered to Cho Feng as the two sat watching.

"Indeed," the oriental nodded. "I believe that Parno has met his match."

"We're ready, lad," Darvo called out, riding up from where he'd been watching. "On your say so." Parno realized that Darvo was giving him a chance to save face. He wasn't going to win. He turned back once more the Stephanie Corsin.

"When I say it's time for you to leave, you leave. I'll have your promise of that, right now, or I'll have you confined until we're gone." His voice was flinty and Stephanie fought to keep from wincing.

"I promise," she replied.

"Let's get moving, then," Parno ordered at once. Darvo nodded, then motioned to Karls Willard. The younger man galloped to the front of the column, issuing orders as he went. A dozen company commanders yelled out orders. Then, finally, the column was moving. The going was jerky at first as the long line shook itself down but within minutes, things were moving nicely. Doak Parsons rode up.

"You sent for me, milord?" the older man asked. Parno nodded.

"Take your men and scout ahead," the Prince ordered. "Make sure that the road is clear and there are no obstacles. We can't afford any delays." Parsons nodded and was gone, galloping to where his men sat waiting. Parno turned to look at Darvo.

"Let's get moving."

# CHAPTER TWENTY-THREE

-

"Sir, there's a column approaching!"

Colonel Brian Landers looked up from the report he'd been reading.

"A column?" he asked worriedly. "From where?"

"The south, sir," his aide assured him. "Regimental from the look of it, though they have a sizable train."

"Thank God," Landers breathed, rising to his feet. Since the message from Lieutenant Colonel Chad, Landers had been on pins and needles expecting an attack at any moment. Having stripped his command to a bare minimum to send reinforcements to General Davies, Landers had only one regiment of regulars and two under-strength battalions of Militia to hold this area.

On paper, with no real attack expected, that had looked like more than enough to garrison the small fortress and keep sufficient patrols out to prevent raiding parties from roaming at will.

In the face of a full Corps of enemy soldiers, however, it looked like spittle on a hot stove eye. Gone before you noticed it.

"Any idea who they are?" Landers asked, hooking his sword belt around his waist and heading to the open door.

"Not as yet, sir," the aide replied, "but the lead banner appears to be from the House McLeod."

"Good God!" Landers was stunned. "Sound assembly at once! Have the Officer of the Day and Sergeant of the Guard meet me at the gates!"

As the aide scurried away, Landers wondered what any member of the Royal Family would be doing here, especially in the face of the impending destruction of the small fort. He hurried to the gate, finding the requested men already waiting for him.

"Make sure we're in good shape," he ordered the day officer, who nodded and returned to his work. He'd already been doing just that, having been interrupted by this needless summons.

"I want the sentries sharp," Landers ordered the Sergeant of the Guard. "See to it yourself. We don't want anything sloppy with a member of the Royal Family along."

"Yes, sir," the Sergeant replied, hurrying to inspect his posts.

Landers walked just outside the gate and nervously awaited the arrival of the column.

-

Parno was exhausted. He and his men had made good time but they were paying for it, both personally and in horseflesh. Twelve horses had already been put down and sixteen more were limping along behind the main column, lame. The men slouched in their saddles, haggard and weary.

Three wagons had also lost wheels and would have to follow as soon as they could. Thankfully, none of them were the wagons carrying Roda Finn's wizardry. If they had been…

Don't even think it, Parno shook his head tiredly. Had that happened, then there wouldn't likely have been much of a column left.

"What is it, lad?" Darvo asked from his side. He'd seen his liege shake his head.

"Just thinking about something useless," Parno smiled tiredly. "One of those 'what-if' things. Are you as tired as I am?" he asked.

"Probably worse," Darvo admitted. "I'm a wee bit older than you are, laddie," the older man winked. "Though if not for Feng's 'conditioning', we'd not have any of us made it. Not this fast."

"You have all done well," Feng put in from just behind Parno. He looked disgustingly fresh.

"We're all worn dry," Parno agreed. "Well, most of us," he added, looking at Feng in mock disgust. "But a good hot meal and night's sleep will set us right. We'll have a titan's work ahead of us tomorrow."

"That we will," Darvo agreed.

"I'm wondering what kind of reception we'll get from the Fort's commander," Parno admitted.

"What do you mean?" Karls Willard asked from Parno's other side.

"Well, I'm not really in the chain of command, you know," Parno told his subordinate, "and I'm not supposed to be here, either."

"You're a Prince," Willard said stiffly. "You can be anywhere in the Kingdom you wish…and you have a regiment of fighting men to back you," he added.

"We're here to fight the Nor, not our own people," Parno chided good naturedly, "but thanks." Willard snorted, but said nothing.

"Colonel Landers isn't a bad sort," Darvo supplied. "He's not a real lion, if you know what I mean, but he knows his duty and does it. I expect he's ready to fight if needed."

"I expected nothing less," Parno assured him. "I meant how will he react to my being here? It's tantamount to removing him from command, you know."

"If the Nor strike here, he'll be glad he's not in command," Darvo predicted.

-

Landers frowned as the column drew close. Troopers sagged in their saddles and their formation was loose and sloppy. Not what he'd expect to see from a royal regiment.

The haggard column drew to a halt near the gate and three riders approached, a fourth trailing slightly behind. Landers was shocked to see that the fourth man was foreign looking.

He placed his attention on the other three, all wearing the uniform of the Soulan Military. The uniforms were dusty, with collars open. The three men drew reign less than twenty feet from the gate where Landers stood.

"Colonel Landers?" the youngest asked, giving Landers a start. He'd assumed that the older man, the colonel, was in command.

"Yes," he replied. "And you are?"

"My name is Parno McLeod," the young man smiled tiredly. "This is my regiment. We'll be bivouacking with you for a time. I hope that doesn't present a problem."

"Of course not, Milord," Landers gasped out. "We had no word of your coming, I'm afraid."

"That's because we're not supposed to be here," Parno told him bluntly.

"I see," Landers replied. "I. . .I confess that I hoped you were here to reinforce the post, milord. We've had dispatches from the field that a large body of Nor are heading this way."

"Is that a fact?" Parno asked, eyes twinkling. He looked to the older man, who frowned, and then to his younger subordinate, who smirked. Parno turned back to Landers.

"How long before they arrive, do you think?" he asked, seemingly unconcerned by the news.

"Less than a week at best," Landers told him. "There is a militia unit in the field, the 12th Kent Mounted Infantry, keeping tabs on them, slowing them where they can."

"Excellent," Parno smiled. "Best news I've had all day, in fact." Parno dismounted, followed by his men.

"Colonel, I need you to assign men to care for our horses and I'd like your mess to prepare a good hot meal for my men. We'll bed down to recover from our little trip and tomorrow we'll start preparing a reception for our visitors from the north. Will that be a problem?"

"Not at all!" Landers assured him, turning to the Sergeant of the Guard. "Turn out the 8th Mounted at once. Have them see to Lord Parno's horses and baggage train then. . . ."

"We'll see to the train, Colonel," Parno interrupted politely. "No offense, but there's some things in there that require special handling. Something your men aren't trained for."

"But they will be, soon," he added, smiling. "Very soon, indeed."

-

"That's the last of it, milord," Roda Finn reported quietly. The trip had worn on the fussy little inventor, but his eyes were still sharp. "I've got some of Colonel Landers' men working on a bunker for the explosives. Should be ready by early morning, tomorrow."

"So long as we don't get blown up," Parno nodded tiredly. Most of his men had already been dismissed to eat, bathe, and rest. He looked around.

"I've asked Colonel Landers to post his best men on guard around the wagons," he assured Roda. "Their orders are to keep everyone at least one hundred feet away, including themselves…best we can do for tonight. Now get something to eat, my fussy friend, and rest. You look like hell, Roda," he added with a smile.

"You don't look any better, milord," Finn assured him. "You should rest, too. We'll need you sharp when the time comes."

"I intend to," Parno promised. He turned to the men still with him. Sergeant Berry was standing not far from him.

"Get some food and some rest," he ordered. When Berry hesitated, Parno chuckled.

"I'm safe enough, here, I think," he told them. They all looked somewhat shamefaced. "It's okay, and I appreciate it, but we've got a man's work ahead of us starting dawn tomorrow. You need to be ready for it. Now go."

The men stiffened to attention and turned away. Parno watched them go, catching sight of Cho Feng approaching as the men left.

"You look well, Master Feng," Parno commented dryly. "Just another ride in the country, aye?"

"I am accustomed to hardship," Feng smiled benignly, "and this wasn't much of a ride. I was disappointed that the men seemed so fatigued," he added with a frown. "Perhaps I should increase my training regimen."

"I think the time for training is long since passed, my friend," Parno laughed softly. "Starting tomorrow, we see if the training has paid dividends."

"It will," Feng assured him. He looked at his liege with shadowed eyes. "You think you are ready for this?"

"I have no idea," Parno didn't bother to lie. "I guess I'll have to be."

"You know that many of your men will likely perish, if not all of them," Feng told him softly. "You must be prepared for that, Parno. Should you live, you will carry the guilt of their loss with you for all your days, I suspect. You cannot do so." His eyes narrowed.

"It will cloud your judgment and your thinking. A good commander," Feng continued, "must be a paradox of thinking, Parno. He must look after his men as he would his family but, conversely, he must be ready to sacrifice any or all of them should his duty require it. You have grown close to many of your troopers. When the time comes, will you be able to order them to their deaths?"

Parno looked at Cho for a long time, considering. Would he? Would he be able to order so many men, his men, hand-picked by himself, into a fight where some, if not all of them, would perish? The thought wasn't a good one, and it weighed on him.

"It is one thing to train for war, my son," Feng said softly. "It is another thing, entirely, to face that war. The men you have selected and trained, men who have helped you in this endeavor, will face death at the hands of your enemies under your command. You will face it as well, though I am confident you will survive. This despite your tendency to rush head first where the battle is hottest."

"What makes you so sure I'll make it?" Parno scoffed. "Because I'm a Royal? That's no protection from death, Cho. You know that. For that matter, I may freeze in the face of the enemy, or even run if things turn bad enough." Parno shrugged. "I've never been in this situation. I have no idea what I'll do when the time comes."

"You will do well, Parno," Cho assured, a sad timbre in his voice. "You will come into your own when the battle is joined."

"Just make sure you do not lose yourself in that battle." With that warning, Feng whirled and walked away.

Parno just shook his head. He was too tired to try and make sense of Cho's riddles tonight.

-

Morning dawned clear and a bit cool over the Gap. The post was bustling with activity already as the garrison troopers went about their normal activities. They moved a bit quicker this morning, however, knowing that a member of the Royal Family was on the post and that the Nor were approaching in large numbers.

Parno stretched as he rose from his blankets. Landers had been scandalized that the young scion intended to sleep on the ground alongside common soldiers and had been somewhat vocal about it.

"'I can't have you sleeping outside, for God's sake!'" Landers had almost screeched. "Milord," he added hastily. "'What will the Lord Marshall say?'"

"'Considering that he and I despise one another, you may well get a promotion from it,'" Parno had smiled. "'These aren't common soldiers,'" he had added. "'They are some of the best trained fighting men in the kingdom…and I always share my men's hardships, Colonel. I always have.'" That had ended the discussion.

Now, as Parno eased the stiffness from his bones and muscles, he noted Landers already on his way over. Parno waited for him, accepting his breakfast tray from one of his men. The soldier offered a small greeting, then moved a good twenty feet away, where he stayed. Parno sighed, shaking his head a bit, and dug in. In the distance, the Black Sheep were going through their morning ritual of Cho Feng's exercises.

"Milord," Landers spoke as he approached. "Might I interrupt your meal?"

"No interruption, Colonel," Parno assured him, wolfing down his food. He was hungry. "Have a seat and tell me what's on your mind."

"The Nor are on my mind, milord," Landers assured him, taking the proffered camp chair. "We may have a week at most before we see them on our door and I haven't the slightest idea how we're to hold them. I've sent warnings to Nasil, but have received no answer as yet."

"You know the strategic situation?" Parno asked around a mouthful of steak. Landers nodded bleakly.

"Then you know that there's no help to send at the moment…I think," Parno kept eating as he spoke, "…that the naval force is a ruse, Colonel. I don't think there's any invasion force on those ships. They're just there to force the King to reposition men that would otherwise be sent north to the front or even west to the battle on the Great River. But those are threats that must be honored, since I may be wrong," Parno noted. "Thus, there are precious few assets to deploy here. We may be all there is."

"We can't possibly hold so many troops at bay here, Milord," Landers objected quietly. "We won't last a full day."

"Yes, we will," Parno corrected him. "We have no choice. If the Nor get through the Gap then we lose the heartland and probably the war. I do not intend to allow that to happen, Colonel."

"Then what do we do?" Landers asked.

"I have a plan, Colonel," Parno assured him. "I want you and your second to ride the area with me and with my seconds. We'll scout the ground, you knowing it best of course, and begin constructing barricades—earthworks and the like, to help hold the Nor at arm's length. We'll also prepare a second line of defense, and a third if time allows."

"We'll construct the same for the artillery. Prepared positions, secondary and tertiary positions. Our final line will be along the fort itself. We will hold for as long as possible and if need be until the last of us falls. If we don't then this war is lost." Parno stood, leaving his tray on the chair he vacated.

"Let's have a look at the land, Colonel, and then get the men to work."

-

"This is actually better than I expected," Darvo commented as the command group rode the Gap, eying the terrain for defensive features.

"I agree," Karls nodded. "We can make a real stand here, milord."

"I think so," Parno replied. "Colonel, I want men working along this line," he pointed to the spot where the Gap began to narrow into the hillside. "I want spike trenches, earthen ramparts, and roofs over the trenches with firing slits for archers, ballistae, and any other direct fire weaponry."

"I want the trees beyond cleared for at least three hundred yards. Take what lumber you need for the barricades and leave the rest to impede our visitors."

"Three hund. . . ." Landers almost choked. "Milord, that could take days!"

"Best get started then," Parno ordered. "I want your men evenly divided between this initial line of defense and the free fire zone." He turned to Karls.

"I want our men working on the second line here," he indicated a small, though sharp, rise along the ridge. "I want our trenches on this side, but with cut-through slits to allow them to withdraw without exposing themselves to enemy fire. Consult Roda Finn and Captain Lars about where the artillery needs to be placed and make sure the positions are properly prepared. See to it as well that he has enough help to set up shop back from the front…well back from the front," he added ruefully. He turned to the rest of the group.

"Colonel Nidiad will be in charge of the overall construction," he informed everyone. "He has far greater experience in these matters than I do. No offense to you, Colonel Landers, is intended."

"None taken, Milord," Landers assured him. Darvo had been right. Landers wasn't afraid to fight, he was simply overwhelmed by the approaching storm.

"Good then," Parno smiled. "Darvo, once the work is finished on these lines, I leave it to you as to where the third line shall be, so long as the fourth is anchored on the fort…and the fort's exposed walls beefed up."

"You say that as if you aren't going to be here," Darvo frowned.

"I'm not," Parno's face was neutral, but his eyes twinkled.

"Where will you be, Milord?" Karls asked in confusion.

"I'm going to take my 'escort'," he raised an eyebrow at Darvo over that, "and go have a look at this Nor horde for myself. I'll meet up with Colonel Chad and see what his thoughts on the Nor are. How they're advancing, how they look and act, I want…" What Parno wanted was cut off by a chorus of stunned objections.

"Out of the question!"

"Milord, that's preposterous!"

"Absolutely not, lad!"

"Gentlemen," Parno said quietly, raising a hand to stall their objections. When they had quieted, he continued.

"I intend to have a look," he stated firmly. "It's important to know what kind of troops we're facing and I want to make sure that the Nor are heading in the right direction. It may be necessary for Colonel Chad to tweak them on the nose, a bit, in order for us to get them where we want them."

"Where we want them?" Landers was shocked. "I want them gone! No offense, milord," he added quickly.

"I want them gone as well, Colonel," Parno chuckled, "but they've come a long way looking for a good fight. I'd hate for them to go home disappointed." He looked at the men around him each in turn.

"Make no mistake, gentlemen. This may well be the deciding battle in what promises to be a long, ugly war. The Nor are not fighting as they have in the past and their army is tough, disciplined, and well trained. We aren't going to rout them and send them running for home so easily. Not this time."

"The only way we win is to kill so many of them that they realize the cost is simply too high to continue," Parno told them grimly. "And Colonel," he looked at Landers, "I know you're concerned. So am I. But we have a few very nasty tricks up our sleeves that will rock the Nor on their heels, I believe. Not to mention buy us precious time."

"Don't forget that this force was broken off from the attack against General Davies" Parno pointed out. "Without their support his Corps may well be able to hold, or even take the offensive, without the aid of 1st Corps. If that's true then we may have help soon." He watched as understanding dawned on the faces around him.

"But we cannot, we will not, count on, nor expect, that help," he emphasized. "Every plan we make will be made with the assumption that we will have to fight with what we have. That means two things, in particular."

"First, we must conserve our strength. What we have may well be all we'll have, period…thus the defensive structures I've just ordered. Secondly, we have to bleed this enemy army as hard and as much as possible. This won't be one of those grand battles where awards are won and tales are born. It will be an ugly, bitter, dirty brawl, possibly to the last man."

"The cost of failure is too high, so failure is not an option." He looked at them all once more, seeing that they understood. Satisfied that they did, he nodded.

"Then let's be about it."

-

"Lad, you had'na ought to do this," Darvo said yet again as Parno prepared to depart. Parno looked at him.

"I have to see," he said simply. "I need to see what's happening. What they're doing, how they're acting. It might be a help when they arrive here to know how they're trained."

"I'm taking Berry and his troop with me," he assured the older man, "and Lieutenant Parson's men as well. They might prove useful." Darvo snorted, but nodded in agreement.

"I'll be back," Parno said gently. "I'm just -"

"Going to have a look, I know," Darvo waved his hand disgustedly. "Mind you remember, without you…here…to bolster the troops, we'll like as not be finished 'fore the first day's out. Don't let that slip your mind."

"I won't," Parno slapped the older man's shoulder lightly. "See you in a few days."

Parno took enough time to pen a letter to Memmnon, explaining the situation to him as Parno knew it to be and then handed the letter to Sprigs. The young lieutenant hurried to find a courier to carry it at once to Nasil.

Ten minutes later Parno and his small column headed north, himself and Cho Feng in the lead.

-

"We are being watched, my Prince."

Cho Feng's warning was given quietly, his voice carrying only far enough to be heard by his young liege. Parno nodded and turned slightly in his saddle, addressing the troop of men trailing him.

"Be on your guard," he ordered softly. "But remember, the men around us are probably ours, so let's not shoot them." Soft chuckles drifted up through the ranks as the word was passed. Hands drifted to swords and safeties were removed from already loaded crossbows. They had been on the trail for two days, riding as hard as they dared. Even now, Parsons and his men were out, scouting the fringes on both sides.

"I think they are trying to decide who we are," Feng observed. "They are cautious."

"I don't blame them," Parno nodded. "They've been in the field for over a week or more. I'd imagine they've all grown eyes in the back of their heads by now."

"Indeed," Feng smiled. Parno suddenly drew up, raising a hand to halt his small column.

"Show yourselves!" he called loudly. "My name is Parno McLeod, of Soulan."

"Thanks be to God!" he heard a voice call from somewhere in the woods. "Move forward, lads," the voice ordered. Five men emerged from the woods, cautiously despite the call from Parno. A grizzled older man approached Parno and bowed.

"Master Sergeant Gris Buford, 12th Kent Mounted Infantry, Milord," he spoke softly. "We are guard post number seven," he indicated his men.

"Good work, Sergeant," Parno smiled. "We only noticed you a few minutes ago."

"You shouldn'a noticed us at all," the sergeant looked pained. "Beggin' pardon, milord."

"Most wouldn't have," Parno agreed. "You and your men are very good. I need to see your commander, Sergeant. Can you have a rider escort us there?"

"At once, sire," Buford nodded, turning. "Peterson! Escort the Prince to Colonel Chad's Command post!"

"Aye, Sergeant," a young trooper came forward. "This way, gents, if you please," the young man indicated a narrow trail. Parno nodded to the Sergeant and followed. Just inside the woods again, Peterson stopped long enough to mount his horse.

"Follow me, milord," the young man spoke quietly. "The Colonel's about a half mile distant, or at least his tent will be," he added. "Colonel's like to be out watching the Nor. Likes to see for himself, you know what I mean."

"I do," Parno hid a smile. "That's why I'm here."

Parno's small column followed the young trooper along the trail in single file.

Nice place for an ambush, Parno thought. The Nor would string through here in much the same fashion as he and his men were. A few well-placed bolts would drop many of them, the men laying the ambush mounted and gone before the Nor could react.

The column broke into a small clearing a few moments later, where some few tents were scattered about. Parno looked around the encampment, liking what he saw. Only the barest necessities, ready to pull down and be on the move in minutes. Either Colonel Chad had been a good commander prior to the invasion or he'd learned on the fly in a hurry.

Either one spoke well of him, Parno decided. As they approached the camp Peterson halted to answer a challenge.

"Halt and identify!" a voice called from their front.

"Trooper Peterson, with Prince Parno McLeod and party," Peterson replied calmly, his voice softer than the challenge. He turned to Parno.

"Wouldn't do for the Nor to hear me say that, sire."

"Good job, Trooper," Parno complimented him and the young man blushed at the praise.

"Advance for Recognition," a new voice ordered. Peterson led the column into the camp itself where a Major was waiting.

"Major Hildebrand, sir," Peterson saluted. "Prince Parno McLeod, by way of Post Number Seven."

"Good job, Trooper Peterson," Major Hildebrand returned to the salute. "You're relieved and may return to your post." Peterson saluted again and turned his horse.

"Pleasure to meet you, milord," he murmured, then was gone, back the way he had come.

"Welcome, milord," Hildebrand stepped forward and bowed. "I must admit we're relieved to see you…or anyone."

"We can dispense with the amenities, Colonel," Parno replied, dismounting. "Glad to meet you," he extended his hand. Hildebrand took it in surprise.

"I wanted to see what you fellows had turned up around here," Parno spoke pleasantly. "I understand you've been shadowing this force for several days."

"Just under a week, milord," Hildebrand nodded. "We're working to slow them down where possible and to gather all the intelligence we can about their movements, command structure, and column."

"That is outstanding!" Parno exclaimed. "Excellent work. I'd like to see them for myself and I'd also like your opinion, and your Colonel's, on what you've seen so far."

"Of course, milord," Hildebrand had to work to hide his surprise. "The Colonel is in the field at one of our forward observation posts. The Nor have camped early today, we think because of the threat of rain."

Parno nodding. He'd seen the clouds gathering and wondered if the rain would be a help or a hurt. True, the Nor might slow their advance, but how would rainfall affect the preparations at the Gap? He didn't know—and that worried him.

"As soon as you're ready, then, Major," Parno ordered. Hildebrand nodded, calling for his horse. Soon after he was leading Parno and his men forward. The column wound along a well-worn trail, halting at the base of a small rise.

"We'll have to leave the horses here, milord," Hildebrand informed him, dismounting. "I'd suggest leaving most of your men behind, as well," he added. "It's a small post and movement will attract attention." Parno nodded and turned to his men.

"Wait here. Master Feng and I will climb to the post and see what we'll see. Don't worry," he added with a grin at some of the sour looks. "You'll see plenty of them before we're through." Dry chuckles answered that as the men dismounted and, without being ordered, set guard posts. Hildebrand watched without comment.

"We're ready, Major," Parno turned back to Hildebrand. The major nodded and led Parno and Cho up the rise, using footsteps and handholds recently carved into the hillside and its landscape. As they neared the top a man wearing the uniform of an Army Colonel appeared overhead, leaning over.

"Tom, what in blazes?" Colonel Chad asked, seeing his second in command climbing up toward him. "I thought I told you I didn't want the both of us up here at the same…"

"Sorry, sir," Hildebrand smiled, slightly out of breath, "but Milord Parno wished to see you and asked me to guide him here." Chad stiffened at that, and quickly extended a hand to assist his second over the crest of the rise. Once Hildebrand was up, Chad turned to assist the Prince only to find him and an Oriental looking man already upright.

"Pleasure to meet you, Colonel," Parno smiled, extending his hand. "I've heard good things about you and your men. Well done."

Chad took the hand without thinking, trying not to beam at the praise. "I must say, Milord, you made good time. We didn't expect you for at least a week."

"Expect me?" Parno looked puzzled.

"I sent riders to your post, milord, informing you of the situation. They couldn't have reached you before today, though," Chad continued, frowning as he did the math. "How did you get here so quickly?"

"I just looked at a map," Parno shrugged. "This seemed the most likely spot for a brawl so my men and I rode up to see what we could find."

"Just rode up -" Hildebrand murmured, then cut himself off.

"Sir, I don't think you realize what it is we're facing here," Chad said cautiously. "There are some -"

"Fifty-plus thousand Nor, yes?" Parno asked. "I spoke with Colonel Landers at the Gap. His men, and mine, are currently working on fortifications to hold the Nor at bay. I came up to meet you and get a look for myself. I want to get a feel for how they operate. Maybe get an idea of how they react."

"Of course," Chad stammered, surprised. He cast a glance at Hildebrand who was struggling to keep a straight face. His eyes, though, burned with the phrase 'I told you so'. Chad nodded in agreement to the unspoken dig, then turned back to the prince.

"We've been trying to determine those things, milord," he admitted, "and we've had some success. We know how they react to sabotage, since we've destroyed several gorge bridges. Some of those hollows. . . ." he shook his head. "If we'd only had the manpower to lay an ambush with them packed in tight, trying to turn."

"I understand, Colonel," Parno patted the man's shoulder lightly, "and trust me, when they reach the Gap, we'll make them bleed. In the meantime let's have a look, shall we?"

-

"They're moving faster than I'd hoped," Parno admitted. He looked at the sprawling camp before him. Thousands of pinpricks of light marred the landscape as the Nor made camp, lit fires, and settled in for the night. Parno had observed their guards being set. They were disciplined.

"We've done what we could to slow them, sire," Chad defended himself, taking Parno's comment as criticism. Parno looked at him in shock.

"Good God, man, I'd say you've done bloody marvelous!" he exclaimed. "You've managed to slow them several times and kept them from breaking free of observation. What more can be expected of you in the face of these odds?"

"Thank you, milord," Chad murmured, relieved that Parno hadn't been disparaging his efforts or those of his men—and perhaps a little shame faced for thinking it.

"Don't thank me, Colonel," Parno grinned sloppily. "I'm afraid I've got more for you and your men to do. I want these bastards hounded every step of the way from here to the Gap. Come morning, I want you to select your best company to keep..."

The talk went on long into the night. When it ended, Chad was smiling for the first time in two weeks.

-

"Your thoughts?" Parno asked as he and Cho Feng sat around their fire.

"He is a good man, and an able commander," Feng replied.

"I meant about my plans," Parno sighed. He knew Feng knew what he'd meant.

"They are ambitious," Feng looked at him. "Perhaps too much so. But if they succeed, then perhaps not."

"You think I'm reaching too far, then?" Parno pressed.

"I think you reach too far for the men you have available," Feng corrected. "Your plans are not inadequate, Parno. Your manpower is."

"It's all I have, Cho," Parno shrugged helplessly, "and we've got to slow them down. Darvo and the others need at least five or six days to prepare. At most, right now, they've got three, perhaps four days. After that, the Nor will be on our front."

"I know," Cho sighed. "I did not say you were wrong, young Prince. I said you haven't enough men."

"What should I do, then?" Parno asked. "What part of the plan should I leave out in order to make the rest more likely to work."

"I do not believe that you can make any better preparations," Feng told him bluntly. "I simply want you to be prepared for some things to fail and for Chad's men to pay the price for that failure."

"You told me I had to know when to sacrifice," Parno replied just as bluntly. "If this isn't a time for that then when would the time be? If they hit the Gap before our preparations are complete, then all is lost." Cho surprised him by smiling.

"You have learned well, young Prince," he said, rising to his feet. "I am proud of you. I will retire now, I think," he straightened his robes as he spoke. "I look forward to seeing you in battle, My Prince. I look forward to seeing you come into your own."

"What. . . .?" but Feng was already retreating to his blankets.

"Tomorrow, young prince. Tomorrow will be soon enough."

-

Parno's plan was simple, but not easy. Chad had called his company commanders together before dawn, issuing new orders. Some of them had looked stunned, but others, older and wiser, perhaps, than their counterparts, had grinned wolfishly, nodding in agreement. As the meeting broke up Chad cornered Captain Hiram Johnson who had drawn the hardest and most dangerous assignment.

"Ram, you and your men will be on the spike from now on," Chad told him. "You know your orders. It is vital, vital, that you not loose contact with the Nor. We have to know where they are and what they're doing at all times."

"I won't let you down, Colonel," Johnson assured him. "My boys'll get it done."

"You'll likely have casualties," Chad warned.

"They're soldiers," Johnson shrugged. "They know that. So do I. No matter what happens, we'll keep tabs on them. It will be easier than what the rest of you have to do," he added with a grin. "Shovel work ain't no fit way for a horseman to earn his pay."

"True," Chad nodded, returning the grin. "Still, if the Prince's plan works…"

"Indeed," Johnson nodded, "and I think it will. He's a fighter, that one."

"I believe he is," Chad agreed. "We'll know soon enough."

"Have a beer waiting for me," Johnson shook his Colonel's hand, then headed to his command. Chad watched him go.

"Never easy, is it?" Parno McLeod's voice drifted to him. Chad turned to see Parno standing just outside the firelight.

"No, milord, it isn't," Chad shook his head as Parno walked forward to be nearer to the fire.

"You and your men have done well, Colonel. No one could have expected better, nor done better."

"Thank you, milord."

"We'll win this war, Colonel," Parno told him firmly, "but the cost is sure to be high. It's already high, I'm willing to state, though I've no word of casualties from the front lines."

"It's dirty little battles like this one, though, that will ensure that our Kingdom, our people, survive. So long as our people survive then whatever happens to me I can accept."

"I don't mind what happens to me, so much, milord," Chad shrugged. "I accepted responsibility for my men when I gained this position. My life is secondary to that responsibility. It's the lives of my men I think of when I worry."

"Don't you think your men feel that same way about you?" Parno asked. "About protecting their lands and families? We don't have the market cornered, Colonel, on dedication to service. Our men know what's at stake as well as we do." Parno's face hardened slightly.

"And that will be the difference in this war, Colonel. Our enemy is fighting for conquest and power, and Lord knows what. Our men are fighting for their lives, for the lives of their loved ones, and for their homes."

"That's the men who will win this war, Colonel," Parno told him. "Men who aren't afraid to sacrifice themselves in order to defend what's dear to them, and that includes me." He grinned.

"It's no secret that I'm not well liked by my family. You needn't look so shocked, Colonel. I know that the entire kingdom knows. My siblings have seen to that," he almost spat. "So I'm not exactly out here fighting for my family."

"Then why are you here, milord?" Chad blurted. "I mean, you don't have to be here! You could be safe in Nasil, or anywhere!"

"I'm here fighting for my people, Colonel, and for a land that I love. My people, our people, will not ever see a day of slavery and servitude so long as I can do anything to prevent it. I owe them that."

"Why?" Chad was puzzled.

"Because of who I am," Parno answered simply. "With privilege and power comes responsibility, Colonel. I was raised, despite my ostracizing, as a Royal. I like to think I've earned everything I've ever gotten, including a few beatings I'd soon forget," he added with a lopsided grin. "But the simple fact is that I had more opportunities to do well than most small towns ever see combined."

"There's a debt for that. One of honor. So no, I can't be in Nasil or anywhere else while my land, my people, are suffering."

"You are full of surprises, milord," Chad shook his head. "Forgive my saying so."

"Nothing to forgive," Parno waved away the apology. "I don't stand on ceremony, Colonel. Never have. I also have a few loyal retainers who remind me near daily that pride goeth before the fall, so to speak. Between them they manage to keep me from taking myself too seriously."

Chad laughed outright at that. He was surprised by the Prince's disposition. Most 'nobles' he'd known, let alone a member of the current ruling family, would never join an outfit like his in the field, sleeping on blankets under the stars and fighting the enemy as closely as this one appeared willing to do. It gave him a surge of hope, discovering that such a man existed in the ruling class of his homeland.

"I'm very glad you're here, Milord Parno."

"You know what, Colonel? So am I."

# CHAPTER TWENTY-FOUR

-

Parno McLeod couldn't remember ever being more exhausted than he was when Fort Cumberland came into view. He reigned his horse in, raising his hand to halt the movement of men behind him, examining the land before him.

Colonel Landers' men had succeeded in clearing the field of fire that Parno had requested. The land between him and the fort was marked with stumps and with fallen trees. Parno was pleased. The fallen timber and the stumps would simply make it that much more difficult for the Nor to approach the Gap and there was no way around it. The Nor had to have the Gap for their plan to work.

And they wouldn't get it, so long as Parno and his men could draw breath.

"Rider coming, milord," a trooper noted. Parno's eyes caught the movement and tracked it. There were actually three riders, he saw. As they drew near Parno recognized Darvo and Karls, along with a trooper he didn't know.

"Welcome home, lad," Darvo smiled as he reigned in beside Parno's horse. "It's good to see you."

"Same to you," Parno smiled tiredly. He shook hands with Darvo and Karls. "How are the preparations coming?" he asked without preamble.

"We're all but finished," Karls grinned broadly. "We'll be finished sometime tomorrow, in fact. The main thing we lack is completing the reinforcing for the Fort's exposed walls. All else is in readiness."

"Good," Parno nodded. "Because we should be seeing the Nor no later than morning, day after tomorrow. Could be here by first light tomorrow, though I think we've slowed them down enough they can't make it that quickly...save for a scouting party, perhaps," he added.

Parno had been in the field for five days and was bone weary. Colonel Chad's men had performed brilliantly for him, though they had suffered for it. While one company had screened the Nor, keeping tabs on them, the rest had been hard at work laying traps, digging pits, and setting small ambushes. While the casualties the Nor suffered were a mere drop in the barrel, the time it had cost them was what had been important.

Twice they had forced the great column to stop and evaluate its patrols. Each time that had bought most of day in precious time for the men at the Gap to finish their defenses. Parno was relieved to see that the time had not been wasted. Colonel Chad's men had suffered several casualties in the process of buying that time.

"Darvo, this is Colonel Chad," Parno introduced the 12th Mounted's commander to his mentor. "Colonel, this is Colonel Darvo Nidiad, commander of Parno's Company." Willard and Cho Feng exchanged grins at the name, but remained silent.

"Pleasure to meet you, Colonel," Chad spoke quietly but with confidence. He and his men had proven themselves again and again over the last two weeks. He had no need to feel intimidated.

"And you, Colonel," Darvo shook hands with Chad warmly. "Thank you for looking out for our wayward leader," he grinned, nodding toward Parno.

"More like he's looked after us," Chad assured Darvo. "You've done well training him."

"Took more than me to accomplish that," Darvo laughed.

"Yes, well, now that all that's out of the way," Parno cut in, "let's get inside the lines, shall we? These men are tired and deserve a good rest. Karls," he looked to his third in command, "I want a company mounted and ready to ride as soon as possible. One company of Colonel Chad's men are still out, screening the Nor. I want them relieved by fresh troops before dark. See to it, if you will."

"Of course, milord," Willard nodded, and turned his horse.

"Karls," Parno called out and Willard turned.

"I don't want you leading it," the prince smiled. "I'll need you here when the time comes."

"Aye, milord," Willard nodded, wondering how the prince had known his plan to accompany the troops.

"You looked a little too eager," Parno answered the unasked question. Willard smiled and nodded again, then set off to roust out the required company. Parno turned to Chad.

"I want a squad of your best men to remount and head out with the new company. I know they're tired, but they can return with Captain Johnson's company. I just want to make sure that the hand off goes smoothly and happens before dark."

"I'll see to it, milord," Chad nodded and turned to discuss that with Hildebrand.

"Let's get into the fort," Parno ordered. "I want a troop of Lander's men with ours as well. Men familiar with the ground and the trails here about. I don't want our men fumbling about on unfamiliar ground."

"Good thinking," Darvo nodded. "I'll see to that. You see to yourself."

"I think I'll take that deal." Parno replied.

They rode on toward the fort in silence.

-

Parno left his horse with the farriers of his own command, with orders to see to all the horses as they came in. He went next to his tent, gathered clean garments, and went straight away to wash the dust and grime of several days from his body.

Thus refreshed, his next stop was a good hot meal which Lander's had ordered prepared for all the men under Chad's command. Landers approached the prince as he sat on a wagon's end board to eat.

"How was your trip, milord?"

"Tiring," Parno smiled. "But informative. I think we've got a better than even chance of frustrating the Nor commander. He isn't, at first glance, a very inventive thinker. We'll have to see if it stays that way, of course," he cautioned.

"Can you make sure that Colonel Chad's men have the chance to clean up and get them bedded down? If there's fighting tomorrow, I want to keep them out of it, if possible, but they should be rested just in case. I'd prefer they not be assigned any duties for at least tomorrow as well."

"Already taken care of, milord," Landers smiled. "They've been in the field since the war started. A few days before hand, in fact. I've made arrangements for them to have two days of rest and refit, enemy plans permitting."

"You're a good man, Colonel," Parno said quietly.

"I get by," Landers smiled. "I'm a fair administrator, milord. That's all. I've never been a particularly good soldier, I guess. Too much of a stickler for the rules. Of course," he chuckled lightly, "I've lost much of that, these last weeks."

"I think we all have, Colonel," Parno assured him, "and don't sell yourself short. You're a good soldier and a good commander."

"Thank you, sir," Landers tried not to beam too much at the praise.

"What's our count, by the way?" Parno asked, eating his food with a relish. It was his first hot meal in several days.

"We're mustering just under five thousand men at present, milord," Landers informed him. "Not counting Colonel Chad's command. Several Militia and Home Guard units have reported here during your absence. We've had a fair number of retired or former soldiers report here looking to serve. I've formed them into an auxiliary unit for now."

"It seems like you have things well in hand, then," Parno finished off his meal. Rising, he left his tray on the wagon board. "I think I'll get some rest, Colonel."

"Milord," Landers rose, looking at the young prince. "There's been no decision made on who will command tomorrow, nor on an effective chain of command as yet. This is my post, but in light of your presence. . . ." he trailed off expectantly.

"I'll be in command," Parno assured him. "I want you to command your normal forces, Colonel, and be available to me for input. Darvo will be my second, while Willard commands the Sheep. Chad will retain his command of course. Should Darvo and I both fall, command will rest with you and with Colonel Chad."

"Both of you know what's at risk, here, Colonel. Both of you are good men. If I pass, I expect you to give a good accounting of yourselves in my absence."

"We will, milord," Landers nodded gravely. "I look forward to serving under your command." With a nod of respect, Landers turned and departed. Parno watched him go, wondering if the Colonel resented being usurped.

"He is glad you are to lead the defense," Cho Feng said softly from behind him. By force of will Parno managed not to start, turning slowly to face his teacher and friend.

"Think so?" he asked. "I admit it looked that way to me. Not that I blame him. I don't really want to be in command either."

"It is the way it must be," Feng shrugged. "Your destiny is upon you, Parno McLeod. Time for you to become the man you are meant to be."

"You keep saying things like that," Parno complained. "and never explaining them. If you know so much about what I'm supposed to do, why aren't you telling me?"

"It isn't my place," Feng shrugged philosophically. "Each man follows the path Destiny lays before him, or he flees from it. You have chosen to follow. The rest is in your hands, Parno."

"Tomorrow, day after at the latest," Parno sighed, "we'll be attacked by a force at least ten times our size, Cho Feng. I didn't choose that. My men will likely be slaughtered before any real help gets to us, and once we've fallen, the Nor will flood into the heartland and the war likely be lost. I didn't choose to be at the center of that."

"Yes, you did," Feng replied. "You didn't have to come here, Parno. You aren't even supposed to be here," he added, grinning. "Yet here you are because you see it as your duty. Your responsibility. That was your choice."

"So it was," Parno sighed wearily. "At any rate, if I don't get some sleep, I won't be much good tomorrow. Goodnight, Cho."

"Good night, My Prince," Cho bowed. "Sleep well." He watched as Parno walked toward his blankets.

"Sleep well," he repeated to himself. "You will surely need it."

-

Parno was shaken awake before dawn.

"Milord," Sprigs looked as he'd only just been awakened himself. "Milord, Captain Jerrolds' company has just returned. The Nor are approaching."

"What?" Parno worked his way out of his warm blankets and began dressing.

"Captain Jerrolds says that the enemy began a heavy push a few hours ago, milord," Sprigs explained, helping Parno with his gear. "Apparently their commander, knowing how close they are to us, decided to simply absorb any further casualties as the price of doing business and simply pushed his men forward as quickly as possible."

"Captain Jerrolds predicts that we'll see the Nor shortly after sunrise."

"Damn it," Parno muttered. He'd hoped for late today at the earliest. He hurried toward the forward command post, situated along the second line of defense. When he arrived, Darvo, Landers, and Chad were already there. He met Karls Willard coming in as well.

"Morning, milord," Karls smiled. "Looks like it's that time."

"So it does," Parno nodded. He walked up to the command group where Captain Jerrolds was in the process of giving his report. All the men stiffened as Parno walked up, but he waved it aside.

"We've no time for that these days, gentlemen. Tell me the situation."

"We were keeping an eye on the Nor, milord," Jerrolds told him quietly. "We had managed to ambush two of their patrols, killing all hands in each." He reflected for a moment. "In hindsight that may have been what pushed them to this."

"About five hours ago, not long after midnight, the entire camp rousted. Heavy patrols screened the van and flanks in company strength. We clashed with the leading van troops, but they had ready support and we were forced to withdraw."

"Once we had reformed, and that took perhaps twenty minutes, I searched for a way to impede their progress but there was none, milord. Their flank security was tight. Not just horsemen, but also foot soldiers and also, I think every scout that they have that is worthy of the name is out, screening around their advance."

"I am sorry, milord," Jerrolds finished quietly. "I have failed."

"No, you haven't," Parno smiled encouragingly, "and your actions did slow them, at least some. You weren't there to fight the horde on your own. Just to keep an eye on them and I doubt your attack on their patrols sparked this advance. Something like this is in keeping with their current strategy."

"Make us think they're bumbling around in the dark then suddenly, when they're in knife range, they strike. Don't worry, we're ready for them."

"Aye, milord," Jerrolds looked slightly less crestfallen.

"See to your men, Captain," Darvo ordered. "You'll be in the reserve for today so that you can rest and regroup." Jerrolds saluted and moved away.

"Estimates on when we'll see them?" Parno asked at once.

"According to Jerrolds' information, they're still about ten miles distant, give or take," Landers replied, looking at a map. "At their pace, especially with the terrain worsening and with darkness still upon them for another three or so hours, I don't think they can make it before two, perhaps three hours after sunup. Even then it won't be all their forces, just the van."

"And they'll be some fatigued, I'd guess," Darvo put in. Chad nodded.

"That they will," he agreed. "My men and I noted that the last few miles getting here was worse than most all the terrain we'd operated in during our time in the field. It's rough going and they're at it in the dark. I don't see how they can keep organized without the light of day to see by."

"We must assume they can," Parno disagreed. "I'm not questioning your judgment, Bret," he smiled, "but we can't afford to think like that. Let's always, from this minute forward, assume that if we can think of it, they can do it. We're far less likely to be surprised that way." Darvo Nidiad studied his former ward proudly and nodded.

"Alright, then," Parno sighed, still rubbing the sleep from his eyes. "Let's get the artillery set. Darvo are the mines in place?"

"They are," Darvo frowned. He wasn't a fan of Roda Finn's gadgetry, "and marked as you requested."

"Then I want the sharpshooter company on the line, but in reserve. We'll use the mines first, I think."

"Mines?" Chad asked, confused. "As in, mining?"

"As in explosives," Parno smiled. "Something our resident genius cooked up for us. Literally."

"Is that the disagreeable little man we built that bunker for?" Landers asked.

"Yes, he is somewhat hard to get along with, I'm afraid," Parno smiled. "but he means well. He's just not used to being around so many people and it's his inventions, the work he'll do in that bunker, that will help us survive this battle. So try and allow him some leeway if you can."

"This I have to see," Landers murmured. Chad looked interested, however.

"Explosive," he sounded out the word. "That isn't anything new in mine country. Gases are released from the ground all the time that a spark can set off, but to be able to control when and where something explodes. . . ." He trailed off, weighing the implications.

"Indeed," Parno grinned. "We're about to put that theory to the test, I'm afraid." Parno looked at the sky. Still a while till dawn.

"Gentlemen, return to your units and make sure your men are fed and ready. We'll likely have a while before our next decent meal. I want five runners from each unit sent here to the command post. Men who will know where you are should I need to send a message. My own men will have left from center on the main line. Colonel, have your regulars take from center right and place one militia battalion in reserve, between the first and second lines. Have the other battalion man the second line in the event of a breach. Have the smaller units who have come in during the week organized on their flanks, under the overall command of the Battalion commander for now. If we have time we'll organize those men into one unit later today and establish a proper chain of command. Karls, I want Parsons and his men out in front of us, watching. They're to withdraw at the first sign of the Nor and are not to engage. Questions?" There were none. "Let's see to our preparations, then," Parno ordered.

"Milord," Landers, Chad and Willard all echoed, saluting. The men eased away, heading for their various commands. Parno looked at Darvo Nidiad.

"If I've missed something, now would be an excellent time to bring it up."

"You've done well, lad," Darvo smiled. "It's too bad -"

"Yeah," Parno sighed softly. "It is. But we'll give a good accounting of ourselves at least, and if we can hold them long enough perhaps Memmnon, or Father, or even Therron, can come up with a way to stop this lot."

"Best get some breakfast yourself, Parno," Darvo ordered. He rarely used the Prince's first name like that and Parno looked at his old teacher carefully.

"It's been a grand thing, watching you grow into a man, lad," Darvo placed a huge hand on the younger man's shoulder. "It's been my honor to teach you."

"Thank you, Darvo," Parno smiled, "but don't make it sound like a eulogy just yet. We might win, you know."

"Aye," Darvo nodded, looking toward the tree line where the Nor would emerge, "and even if we do, one or both of us may not see it. No sense leaving things unsaid, lad. Off with you, now," he added, shooing Parno. "Eat. See to your plans. I'll watch things here for you."

"Okay, pa," Parno laughed and had to duck a large fist as it whistled through the air over his head.

"Ungrateful, insolent whelp!" Darvo's bellow followed a still laughing Parno into the dark.

-

The first Nor troopers appeared roughly three hours after sunup. A cavalry battalion, from the looks of it, emerged from the tree line already formed in a ragged line of battle. Observers higher on the ridges above the gap had spotted them minutes before and everyone was in place.

Parno watched the enemy horsemen as they milled around at the tree line, looking at the earthworks surrounding the Fort. The Prince smiled at their consternation. They'd likely been expecting to find some troops guarding the pass, but not this.

"Surprise," Parno smiled, looking at the enemy through his glass.

"Orders, milord?" Darvo asked.

"Nothing yet," Parno ordered. "Pass the word, my orders remain unchanged. No one fires until I give the word. No sense letting them see how few of us there are until we get a chance to bleed them some."

"Aye," Darvo nodded and sent runners on their way. Parno continued to watch the enemy horsemen. After nearly ten minutes a small party of them began to move cautiously forward, waving a white flag.

"Seems our neighbors want to chat," Parno smiled at Darvo. For some reason that Parno could not explain he felt good. Alive. Blood was coursing through his veins so strongly that he could almost feel it. The air he breathed was clean, invigorating.

"Seems so," Darvo nodded. "I'd not let them get close enough to see anything," he advised.

"I won't." Parno moved forward to the front line and gave an order. A flaming arrow arched through the air, sticking deep into the ground near the approaching riders.

"That's far enough!" Parno called. "Say your bit!"

"In the name of the Emperor of Norland and by order of Major General William Brasher, 3rd Norland Field Army, you are ordered to lay down your weapons and surrender yourselves to the rightful rulers of this land!" The words boomed across the open field and was met with a chorus of derisive hoots and jeers all along the line.

Parno laughed, waiting for the noise to die down.

"I think you've your answer, right there!" he called back. "You and your men are invaders in our land. Turn back now, and live. Stay, and we'll put you to the sword!"

A mighty cheer rose from the ranks at that answer, Soulan Troopers clanging sword and shield to make even more noise. The enemy captain seemed at a loss. After a moment of bickering among his own men, he tried again.

"Your King has deserted you!" he called. "You've been left here to die, alone. Unaided. See reason, and surrender! There's no need for bloodshed if you will accept the rule of the Emperor of Norland!"

"Our King," yelled a voice from down the line before Parno could speak, "has sent his son to fight you! And he'll soon be kicking your ass all the way home to your bloody emperor!"

If the cheering before was loud, it now became deafening. Men all along the line took up the same chant.

"PARNO! PARNO! PARNO!" The chant rolled off the hills around the Gap, bouncing back in endless waves of echoes. Parno, caught off guard by it all, didn't reply to the challenge.

"Lad," a smiling Darvo Nidiad shook him. "Need to tell these lot off," he nodded to the Nor party. Parno nodded.

"Leave this place and never return or face the consequences! No more parley, no more talk! You want our weapons, then come and take them!"

The Nor party whirled their horses and headed back to their own, unable to gallop due to the stumps and trees that had been felled but left. Parno watched them go, laughing.

"Well, that'll put a bee in their bonnet, I'd say." He turned to Darvo. "I don't think that bunch will try to attack us on their own, but make sure that my orders are understood. I don't want someone tipping our hand on nothing more than a raiding party."

"They know, lad," Darvo assured him, "and they're ready."

"I figure we've got an hour, maybe two, before we see the rest of their division. The whole outfit won't be far behind that."

The Soulan troops settled in to do what all soldiers spent the largest part of their time doing.

Waiting.

-

Parno's time estimate was fairly close. One hour and forty-five minutes later the bulk of a Norland cavalry division was either in the edge of the clearing or just inside the woods. Men both mounted and afoot could be seen in and out of the edge of the woods.

"I think they're going to try and attack," Darvo commented, "at least it looks like it."

"I agree," Parno nodded. "Division commander is either under orders or trying to make a name for himself." He turned to the runners behind him.

"Have all archers stand to," he ordered. "Normal rounds only for the artillery. In fact," he smiled, looking over the barricades toward the tree line. "Have Captain Lars loft a few of the heavy blocks at our friends in the tree line. Just to let them know that we don't like them." The artillery runner grinned and took off at a run.

Parno watched the enemy horsemen forming for an attack, obviously working out among themselves the best way to navigate the wasteland of downed trees and standing trunks left in the cleared area. Even as they debated, the Prince heard the 'thunk' of trebuchets firing and looked over in time to see the large stone rounds being heaved from their slings in the general direction of the distant tree line.

He smiled as the Nor panicked trying to get out of the way of those giant stones, some succeeding, others not so lucky. Screams from both men and horses drifted across the field as the stones hit home. Nor troopers fought to control skittish mounts and commanders fought to control now skittish troopers.

"Not going like you thought, eh, fellas?" Parno murmured to himself. Before the Nor could recover, Captain Lars had another salvo on the way, and another behind that. As the third salvo landed the Nor retreated into the tree line, having sustained several casualties without drawing a drop of Soulan blood in exchange.

"Cease fire!" Parno called and heard the order relayed. He turned to Darvo.

"I think we've discouraged them from trying to take us by themselves. I don't know that I wanted that, to be honest. I'd rather they had hit us and perhaps we could have smashed that one unit before their main army closed up."

"They may try again," Darvo replied, still watching the tree line through his own glass. "It may be that they simply pulled back to make their plans under cover of the trees."

"True," Parno nodded. He looked to the sky. Not yet noon. It promised to be warmer than usual today. He hoped it stayed that way. Even better, he hoped for no rain and a strong southerly wind. That weather pattern might come in handy before the fight was over.

"Call me if anything happens, or if they re-appear," he ordered. "I need to talk to Roda Finn."

"Aye, milord."

-

"Hello, milord," Roda smiled as Parno walked into the inventor's 'bunker'. "How goes it?"

"So far, so good," Parno shrugged. "Roda, I need to run something by you. Have you experimented much with fire throwing?"

"You mean pitch and the like?" Roda frowned. Parno nodded.

"Some," Roda allowed. "It's very unpredictable, milord, and dangerous to use, both to the equipment and the men."

"I know," Parno agreed, "but how far could a trebuchet, or even a catapult, hurl the flaming pitch?"

"Well," Roda looked thoughtful. "That depends on the weight of the pitch, milord. If we used cauldrons of some sort I'd think that we could loft the load two or even three hundred yards, at least. Though with trebuchets we'd loose a good bit of pitch as the cauldron would tumble. Not to mention the increased risk."

"Could we loft a heavy, flaming cauldron four hundred yards with a catapult?" Parno asked.

"I'd have to work that out, milord," Roda replied cautiously. "It's a combination of things. After a certain weight the cauldron's weight would be more of a hindrance than a help. Also, the strength of the catapult would have to be figured into the equation along with any wind." Roda was already running the figures in his head.

"Work on it, Roda," Parno ordered. "I need to be able to throw the pitch at least four hundred yards…any further would be a bonus, but I need at least four hundred yards."

"I'll find a way, milord, if there is one," Roda promised, scratching on a piece of papyrus, already working the equation.

"I'll leave you to it, then."

-

It was after the noon hour when the Nor struck. Parno suspected that a single division of the Nor Army was facing him so far. He had wondered if the commander would risk an attack alone or wait for his General and the bulk of the army.

The answer came when a line of screaming horsemen erupted from the woods, running their horses as fast as possible in the terrain Parno had left for them.

"Wait for it!" Parno called and the order echoed up and down the line. Every man on the line was armed with a longbow or a crossbow. The crossbowmen were all expert shots, while several of the long bowmen were as well. The others were swordsmen, men at arms, even lancers and pike-men, all of whom had cross trained on the longbow for just such occasions as this.

Parno estimated the enemy force at two thousand men in the first wave. He had near that many bowmen on the first rank alone. He wasted a second to hope that the Nor General commanding the rest of the army would attack in such piecemeal fashion.

When the Nor were within easy bow-shot, he nodded to Darvo.

"LET FLY!" the older man bellowed. The Soulan troopers stood and loosed already nocked arrows at the oncoming enemy troops.

Men and horses alike screamed as arrows found their marks, piercing armor and skin. Many horses collapsed in a tumbling heap, which in turn often tripped up other horses behind or beside them.

A second volley followed, and then a third. Nor troopers fell in droves and the attack faltered. A fourth volley sent them into a retreat, leaving their wounded on the field.

"HOLD!" Darvo called. A sporadic final flight of arrows flew toward the retreating Nor, as archers heard the call too late to prevent their arrows from flying.

Parno waited patiently as runners from each unit arrived with their reports. Darvo grinned broadly.

"No casualties, lad," he informed the waiting Prince.

"This time," Parno nodded. "We won't be that lucky again."

"Like as not," Darvo agreed, "but we hurt them badly. I'd say they lost a good twenty percent of their force."

"I agree," Parno replied. "If there wasn't fifty times that number coming up from behind, I'd even feel confident."

There was nothing to say to that and Darvo held his peace.

"I don't think this lot will try that again," Parno said after a moment. "Do you?"

"Hard to say," Darvo hedged. "If their losses made them angry then they just might. But if I was their commander, I'd not attack this place again unsupported, knowing that I had such a large force at my back and on its way."

"If there are any Nor wounded close by and you think it prudent see if we can gather some prisoners. We might gain something useful from them."

"I'll take a look, and see," Darvo promised.

"I wonder if their Army Commander will launch an attack today?" Parno mused, looking to the sun. The light was going to be fading soon.

"It depends," Darvo shrugged. "If he's over confident in his numbers then he may well attack. If he's a cautious soul he'll want to wait for full light before launching his attack, especially when he sees what we've done to that bunch," he nodded toward the tree line where the Nor had taken refuge.

"I'd like to think that he'll wait, but we can't count on it," Parno decided. "I want the sharpshooter company deployed as we planned. Their orders are to remain unengaged unless the wall is breached. Their job is to make Roda's 'toys' work."

"Aye, milord," Darvo nodded. "I don't trust t. . . ."

"Everything he's shown me so far has worked," Parno cut off the coming objections. "And I know you don't like it, but we're fighting for our very existence here, Darvo, and if Roda's work saves even one of my troopers, then I'll take it."

"Aye, milord," Darvo agreed, albeit reluctantly, "and I do hope they work, lad," he added. "I just don't expect them to."

"We'll see what we see," Parno shrugged.

-

Parno was walking the line when the first determined attack came.

With perhaps an hour of sunlight left the Prince had allowed himself to relax, just a bit. He toured the forward positions, complimenting his men on a job well done. Morale was high and Parno cautioned them all that such an easy win wouldn't likely happen again. Somber looks had matched his own as his men nodded. The Black Sheep, as Parno's own regiment had taken to calling itself, had realized some days ago that they weren't likely to survive.

But they were fighting for their families and their land…and for the man who had given them a second chance at life. Not only that but he had provided a better life for their loved ones, come what might. They were as ready as they could be.

The other units were similarly determined. They knew what was at stake and were grimly determined to do their utmost to hold the Nor at bay for as long as possible. For the Kent men it was vengeance for whatever horrors the Nor were, even now, inflicting upon their land and their loved ones. For the rest, mostly Tinsee militia, aside from Colonel Landers regiment of regulars, it was to prevent what was happening in Kent from happening to their own farms and families.

In each case, whatever their motivation, the men were ready.

Just as Parno was about to return to the small command post along the second line of defense, lookouts up and down the line raised the alarm.

"To arms! Action front!" This call was repeated up and down the line and men hurriedly left whatever they had been doing to take their places along the line. Parno hurried up the steps at one berm for a look at the enemy, only to be dragged down again by one of his own troopers.

"Beggin' yer pardon, milord," the trooper grinned. "Kinda attached to ya nowadays. Soon as not be losin' ya, if'n ya don't mind." Parno grinned back.

"I'd as soon not have you lose me, either, Greer," he replied. "I'll just head back to the Command Post and have a look from there."

"Fine idea, milord," Greer agreed. "Hurry along, now, 'fore these Godless heathen get within bow-shot." Parno shook his head at the carefully disguised order and ran for his own position. He arrived to find Darvo looking through his glass at the tree line.

"They're deploying their artillery, lad," the older man smiled slightly. "Have to bring 'em out o' the woods to set up. Makes for easy pickin's, they're not careful." Parno nodded and turned to the artillery runner.

"My complements to Captain Lars and could he see about making life difficult for his counterparts?" The runner stiffened and took off at a dead run. Lars would need no more instruction than that, Parno knew.

"They'll be forming to attack, likely inside the tree line, lad," Darvo warned. Parno agreed.

"We're ready, I should think," Parno mused. "I wonder how far into the tree line." He gauged the distance with his eyes, trying to detect movement inside the darkening landscape across the battlefield. Nothing.

"Wait for them, lad," Darvo advised. "They may intend only to try and batter us some with their artillery. If they can get the range before nightfall, they might well take shots at us all night."

"I imagine Lars will discourage that," Parno grinned. As if fulfilling a prophesy, they heard several thunks from along the line as Lars' men lofted their first salvo. Parno raised his glass, looking down range for their impact zone. He was not disappointed. Two enemy catapults were hit outright, smashed to bits and their crews killed or maimed. A trebuchet was knocked off its carriage and the other rounds, while missing their true targets, did kill several Nor artillery men and some of their carriage horses.

A second salvo was on its way as soon as Lars saw his men were on target. This salvo struck none of the enemy artillery, but again managed to create havoc by falling among the crews and their draft animals. Screams of both man and beast once again echoed across the hills of the Tinsee landscape.

Lars continued his barrage for several minutes, sending the solid shots rolling across the Nor positions. Finally, with over half his pieces either damaged or destroyed outright and casualties mounting, the Nor artillery commander withdrew, abandoning much if his equipment.

"Cease fire!" Parno ordered and runners relayed the orders to the gunnery stations. Cheering once again erupted along the line as the Soulan troopers taunted the Nor across the way. Parno allowed himself to smile slightly.

Let them enjoy it while they can, he told himself. It will be otherwise soon enough.

Parno and Darvo watched the wood line for most of an hour until the darkness enveloped them entirely, preventing them from seeing. Finally, Parno sighed. It was doubtful that the Nor would attempt an all-out attack in the night over the treacherous terrain to their front.

He and his men had bought one day, at least, for Soulan. One precious day in the life of his kingdom.

Tomorrow would be another day, however. Another day entirely.

-

The various commanders gathered around Parno's small fire later than night, elated over the day's events. Parno quickly snuffed that elation.

"We've had a good day, yes," he agreed, "but that was nothing. A few artillery salvos and one broken attack by fewer men than we actually had on the line…and that by one over eager cavalry commander. Make no mistake, gentlemen, this was the easiest day we're going to have in this battle."

The assembled men grew somber at that, realizing that Parno was right. It was one thing to allow the rank and file to celebrate such an easy victory. Quite another for men who knew better to allow themselves to be fooled.

"I expect the Nor to make a determined attack, in force, come dawn tomorrow," Parno told them. "During the night I would not be surprised to see their scouts attempt to close on our lines. That's why I ordered the fires lit."

One hundred yards out from the line, almost a third of the way to the Nor position, small bonfires were burning in the night. Scouts had slipped over the lines at dusk, lighting the pyres that had already been stacked for just that purpose. Others were left unlit, on the hope that there would be a need for them the following night. If they survived, of course.

Another line burned closer, only fifty yards out. Parno hoped that these fires would allow his lookouts to spot Nor scouts or spies attempting to creep up on his lines while also destroying the enemy's night vision. It might not work but there was nothing lost in trying, he reasoned.

"Come morning, I want the men ready to go one full hour before dawn. That means mess has to commence early. I want to try and get them a hot meal since lunch is likely to be a slab of beef on dry bread—if we have time for anything." The others nodded, agreeing.

"We'll leave the lines as they are for now," Parno continued. "Colonel Landers has used his time this afternoon to organize the smaller units and the volunteers into a battalion sized unit. Major Kender," Parno indicated the newest addition to these command meetings, "is senior, and has assumed command of the unit. They will man the second line tomorrow." Kender nodded, having already received his orders earlier.

"We'll be pressed hard tomorrow, gentlemen, unless I am sorely mistaken," the young Prince warned. "Expect a hard push right off. In his position, I would seek to simply overpower us. He has numbers on his side and he knows it. If they can hit us in succeeding lines they stand a better than even chance of overpowering us."

"In the event that the front line is compromised, archers will withdraw first, followed by swordsmen and pike-men. Captain Lars, if we're threatened with a line breach, your men will have to move the ballistae at once or we'll lose them. In the event they can't be saved, I want them destroyed or disabled in place. The last thing we need is to have them used against us." Lars nodded, already having worked out a plan to save his front-line weapons. All the other artillery was safely behind the second line.

"Should we lose the first line," Parno went on, "then holding the second line at the end of the day is vital. We lack the strength to retake the first line. If it falls then the Nor will have a better chance of getting their artillery into the battle and that could well decide the battle against us. So we try to hold the front line as best we can. But," he warned, emphasizing his point with an extended finger, "not at all costs. We will not sacrifice our men to hold that line." He looked at each man in turn before continuing.

"You all know the likely outcome of this battle. If we were anywhere else then I would advocate moving into the field and trying to contain the Nor with ambushes, raiding attacks, and other delaying tactics. But the simple fact is that this is the only viable choke point for us to use against them. Once through the Gap, the Nor can attack in any direction they want and we would be powerless to stop them."

"So, we hold here, gentlemen. To the last man. We hold as long as possible, buying as much time as possible for the King to send a force sizable enough to contain this threat and then drive them back."

The assembled commanders all nodded their agreement. By now, no one in the Fort doubted that this was a last stand.

"When I was learning to be a soldier," Parno said suddenly, "part of my studies included ancient military history. There are numerous accounts of men in our same position. Fighting in terrain just like ours against overwhelming odds. In most of those accounts, the smaller commands managed to last at least three days. I expect no less from us. We can give Soulan three days in which to rally to this threat. Three priceless days that might well mean the difference between our people surviving as a free Kingdom or living the rest of their days and those of their decedents as little more than slaves."

"Anything else we can give them is a bonus," Parno smiled. "It won't mean much to us, but when this war is over and we are victorious then the historians will remember us. They'll point to the stand we make here and say that here Soulan's sons showed their true colors. Their true spirit."

"Make our people proud, gentlemen," Parno concluded, standing. "Give them something to remember. Something to rally around. They may well need it before this war ends. See to your men."

The commanders saluted and broke away, heading to their various commands to make sure of their preparations. Darvo remained behind, conferring briefly with Karls Willard before the younger man hurried off to their own unit. Cho Feng, who had remained silent on the fringe of the group, closed in now near the fire and took a seat.

The three men sat in silence for a time, each gazing into the fire, lost to his own thoughts. Finally, Darvo broke the silence.

"You spoke well, lad," he rumbled softly.

"Just words," Parno shrugged. "It's all I had to give."

"Many times," Cho spoke, "the words of a leader are all his men need in order to give more than even they themselves knew they had, my Prince."

"It still seems weak," Parno shrugged again. "I'm asking them to fight and die to hold this piece of ground. Words seem cheap compared to that."

"You're asking them to fight and die for their people, lad," Darvo corrected.

"If we weren't fighting here, we'd be fighting somewhere else. At least here, where the terrain helps even the odds, we have a chance to accomplish something with that sacrifice."

"I agree," Cho nodded. "This is a good place and you have no choice but to fight, Parno McLeod. Even if your own character did not demand it, you would still have no choice but to fight somewhere, if you were to survive. As the Colonel said, at least here in this place you have the chance to fight effectively."

"In the end, it won't matter," Parno said glumly. "All of these brave men will be dead in a few days and the Nor will be into the interior. After that?" Parno shrugged once more, helplessly. "I don't know if we can win the war once they have a formation that strong behind the lines."

"Then we have to make sure that they don't make it behind the lines with that strength intact," Darvo said firmly. "We make them bleed, here and now. So that when we do fall they are nothing more than a shadow of their former selves. So weak that even a Militia division will be able to destroy them in the field...and so full of fear at what a mere five thousand have done to them that they'll tremble before a large force."

Parno nodded at that. Darvo's words mirrored his own thoughts along that line.

"Well, I'm for bed," he said suddenly, rising again from his chair. "I expect tomorrow to be a hard day and a long one. Wouldn't do to face it with less than a few hours of sleep at least."

"Agreed," Darvo stood as well. "Goodnight, lad. Master Feng."

"Sleep well, Colonel," Cho smiled.

"Night, Darvo," Parno echoed. As the Colonel walked away to his own blankets, Feng eyed Parno closely.

"Do not let your worry concern you, Parno," he said softly. "You will do well and your men will not let you down."

"I'm not concerned with that," Parno chuckled, albeit without humor. "I'm more worried about letting them down."

"You will not," Cho assured him. "Rest, young Prince. I will watch for you."

"Cho, thank you. For everything," Parno said earnestly. "Without you, I could never -"

"Do not believe that," Cho cut him off. "I may have helped you, yes, but you would have found a way. You do not have it in you to do less. Now sleep. Tomorrow and its worries will be upon you soon enough. Do not borrow those problems for tonight. Sleep."

"Very well," Parno managed to smile. "Goodnight, Cho."

"Sleep well, young Prince."

# CHAPTER TWENTY-FIVE

-

Parno was awake long before dawn. He bathed and dressed quickly then walked forward to the Command Post. He saw that civilian volunteers and kitchen workers were scurrying back and forth with the breakfast meal for those men on the main line and nodded in satisfaction. He took a similar bowl from a passing steward and wolfed down the hot oatmeal, surprised at his hunger. Darvo Nidiad appeared out of the darkness, his visage illuminated by the dim battle lantern in the small enclosure.

"Mornin' lad," he said gruffly, voice still stiff with sleep.

"Morning, Darvo," Parno smiled in reply. He felt better with a few hours of sleep and a full belly. "Sleep well?"

"I'm getting too old to sleep on the ground," the older man grumbled.

"You've gotten spoiled, living the good life down in Cove, that's all," Parno jibed.

"It's too early for your sass, lad," Darvo warned. Parno laughed at that.

"Okay, old timer, I'll cut you some slack. For now," he added. Darvo glowered at him a moment then turned his attention to his own bowl of oatmeal.

"This ain't bad," he murmured, chewing in satisfaction.

"Sticks to the ribs," Parno nodded. "I'm glad they were able to get the men fed."

"You ordered it done, lad," Darvo chuckled. "It wasn't a suggestion, far as they were concerned."

"As long as the men get fed," Parno replied absently. "That's the main concern. Any news overnight?"

"None that I've been made aware of," Darvo shook his head, "and the lookouts and scouts report all quiet, so far. I think the fires kept them away, after all."

"I hope so," Parno breathed. "Do you think the Nor will wait for full light?"

"No idea," Darvo shrugged. "I would, but that bunch don't seem to think as we do and they seem far too willing to sacrifice their own men. I don't like that much."

"I noticed that myself," Parno agreed. "Though it doesn't really bother me. Every man they waste is one less to send against us."

"True. But it doesn't speak well of the man in charge. If he's that brutal to his own, what can our people expect?"

"All the more reason to fight like demons," Parno replied firmly. "Might be a boost to our men to think along those lines." Before Darvo could reply, a runner appeared out of the dark.

"Captain Mathis' compliments, milord, and he believes the Nor are preparing. We cannot see, as yet, but the noise carries in the stillness."

"Very well," Parno replied. "I'm going to take a look," he told Darvo. "Or a listen, as it were. Pass the word to all commands to be alert." Darvo nodded and turned to the runners. Parno followed Mathis' runner back to the front. He found Captain Mathis leaning over the parapet, straining to see or hear anything.

"Milord," he said softly, seeing Parno below him. "Sorry to bother you but I think it's soon to be show time."

"No bother at all, Captain," Parno grinned. "I was wondering how I'd pass the time." Mathis grinned slightly as Parno eased up beside him. "What have you got?"

"Listen carefully, milord," Mathis replied. Parno listened, ears straining. The faint sound of metal striking metal came from before them.

"Hear that?" Mathis almost hissed. "Been a bit of that now, last few minutes at least. I've heard voices as well, though not loud enough to make out any words. They're gettin' ready, I'm sure of it. The fires have burned down low enough that our visibility is the lowest it's been all night, too." Parno looked then to the fires he'd had set. They had, indeed, burned down to mere embers during the night.

"Good work, Captain," Parno told the man. "Keep a sharp lookout. I've already had the word passed to be alert. I'm going to go see if we can do something about the light."

"Milord," Mathis nodded in reply, never taking his eyes off the terrain before him. Parno made his way swiftly back to his post, sending a runner off to collect Captain Lars. Lars was in the command post in less than three minutes.

"Milord?"

"Captain, we're hearing some light noise to our front," Parno told him. "I'd like you to loft a few pitch cauldrons over, preferably in the same area as you engaged their artillery in yesterday. Might lob a few stones over, as well. Just for variety."

"Aye, milord," Lars grinned. "I'll see to it. Take about five minutes with the pitch."

"Send the pitch first," Parno added. "I'd like to see what they're doing, if we can." Lars nodded and left for his post on the run.

"Likely preparing for a dawn rush," Darvo commented.

"Yes," Parno agreed. "That will give them a full day to press any advantage they gain. I don't intend to give them that advantage if I can help it."

The two men waited in silence. Lars estimate was right on, as slightly less than five minutes later, Soulan catapults launched six half-barrels of flaming pitch in the direction of the Nor lines. Parno watched the flaming liquid spread as the barrel hurtled through the air, landing in various places along the battlefield. The barrels struck home seconds later and the resulting fire illuminated the area.

A line of Nor horsemen had formed up in the open area, preparing to attack. Behind them were at least five lines of infantry, geared for a heavy assault. The pitch barrels fell right into their midst.

Parno watched in fascination as the pitch struck, the flaming, heavy goo sticking to anything it touched. Men began screaming as their skin burned away. Horses bucked and writhed in pain, breaking up the cavalry formation. Enemy troops ran screaming among their brethren, bright, horrible beacons in the dark. Panic began to spread among the Nor and commanders worked to control and contain it.

Large boulders followed the pitch, landing in front of the Nor, rolling, bouncing, and tumbling into the mass, crushing men and horses alike. Parno continued to watch, the entire action bathed in the eerie light of flickering flames and shadows. Finally, the Nor commanders gave up trying to maintain their formation and ordered their men to charge. Moving troops would not be a target for such ponderous weapons. Parno nodded. He would have done the same.

"READY!" Darvo bellowed across the line and the call was answered and repeated along the line. Archers nocked arrows. Swordsmen drew their blades. Safeties were removed from crossbows and ballistae. Parno turned to the nearest runner.

"Order Captain Moore to prepare his sharpshooters," he told the man. "He is to fire at the mines when the second line of infantry approaches. The second line. Understand?" The man nodded.

"Go!" The man ran off into the dark.

"I hope they work," Darvo murmured. Parno didn't reply. He hoped they did too. He turned to another runner.

"Have the archery battalion fire three volleys of standard arrows, followed by one volley of the Hubbel arrows. Understand?" The man nodded.

"Go!" Parno ordered once again. The runner set out at a dead run.

"Good plan, anyway," Darvo commented. "If they work, it'll break their back, I'd say."

"I'll take what I can get," Parno agreed. He watched intently as the horsemen drew closer. They were unable to gallop, due to the rough terrain. With the fires from the pitch back-lighting them they made excellent targets. When they were one hundred yards distant, Parno looked to Darvo and nodded.

"LET FLY!" Darvo bellowed suddenly, and the air was filled with arrows. The lighting was poor but it was apparent from the screams that some arrows found their mark. Parno heard the ballistae fire, followed by more screams from men and horses.

"War is hell on horses." The thought came to Parno's mind suddenly. He had just killed more horses than most farms ever owned. He shook the thought off. There was no time for sentiment. Not now.

Another volley of arrows was in the air and the cavalry line staggered under this barrage. Closer now and with dawn threatening in the east, the Soulan bowmen were finding it easier to find their targets. Another volley followed and was joined by the slower ballistae. Nor troopers continued to fall, but those who remained continued forward doggedly.

Lars catapults joined the fray as the horsemen entered one of his preplanned fire zones. Once more large stones rolled among the Nor, crushing men and horses alike. The carnage was unlike anything Parno had ever read of…and still the Nor kept coming. What did it take to stop them?

Suddenly the world seemed to explode. So intent on the cavalry, Parno had failed to notice that the Nor infantry was still approaching. Captain Moore, however, had never taken his eyes from the dim shapes that represented his targets. As the dawn's light had grown he was able to see the 'targets' his men were to shoot at. The very instant that the second line of Nor infantry crossed the line visible only in Moore's mind, he lowered his hand. One hundred cross bows, fired by the best shots in the whole regiment, twanged in near unison.

Their bolts reached out, seeking not Nor flesh and blood, but rather simple containers that looked very much like small stones. In reality, the thin vessels were filled with a mixture of Roda Finn's exploding powder, surrounded by iron balls. The bolts were tipped with flint, making them spark when they struck the eggshell thin pots. The spark ignited Roda's powder in a small explosion, which sent the iron balls streaming outward in all directions.

Right into the massed lines of Nor infantry.

Each mine had two bolts assigned to it. Of the fifty mines targeted in the first volley, seven failed to ignite. Three more were missed entirely, their intended bolts hitting enemy troops or horses that blundered into their path.

The remaining forty ignited as Roda Finn had promised. The result. . . .

Parno gaped at the ragged holes left in the Nor line. Not only had the mines staggered the second line, the exploding canister rounds had also inflicted terrible damage on the leading rank of Nor infantry. Men were felled by the dozens in some places and were either dead or dying.

"Mother of God," Darvo whispered in awe. Parno could only nod in agreement. He had never imagined destruction on this scale. For a moment he felt almost sick at the carnage he had just ordered. He shook it off, however, reminding himself that the Nor had brought this on themselves.

"They're still advancing," Parno said in disbelief. "What does it take to break them?"

"I think they're more afraid to go back than they are to go forward, lad," Darvo commented. "I doubt that failure is something this General suffers more than once."

"There has to be a breaking point," Parno murmured.

Nor archers were now firing on the move, sending ragged volleys into the Soulan lines. Though many fell short or embedded into the breastworks, others found targets. Parno's men began to fall, victims of Nor archery. Frustration gripped Parno. Would the Nor simply roll over them first thing?

"Easy, lad," Darvo's voice reached out to him. "It's early yet and our casualties aren't that serious as of yet. We're doin' fine, so far."

"But they're still coming!" Parno exclaimed.

"So we stop them the hard way," Darvo shrugged. "We can muster almost as many men as they can cram into the Gap against us."

"And they have thousands more behind!" Parno argued. "We don't!"

"Patience, young Prince," Cho Feng's voice was almost melodious. Parno whirled to see Feng standing beside him, face serene.

"Men are lost in battle, Prince," Feng said calmly. "It is a fact of war and nothing you can do will change it. You must lead. There will be time for worry after the battle is won."

"And if we lose?" Parno challenged.

"Then there will be no need for worry," Cho replied philosophically. Before Parno could fire a rejoinder at that the battlefield exploded again, albeit less forcefully. Parno looked on as the first flight of Hubbel arrows landed amongst the Nor. Oddly, the smaller projectiles seemed to have more of an effect upon the enemy troopers than had the mines. Confusion reigned within their ranks as the Nor soldiers looked around them in panic at fallen comrades and shredded lines. It was too much. As regular arrows continued to rain down upon them, their ranks broke and the survivors began moving to the rear.

The fifth and final rank tried to stop them, but the men in front had faced too much horror in the dawn's early light. They were shot. Terrified beyond reason, they ran for the rear as fast as their legs could take them, ignoring orders from their superiors. When the fifth rank moved to stop them, the survivors ran them over, or ran them through, if that's what it took to escape the carnage of their failed attack.

The Soulan troops added to the rout with flight after flight of arrows, ballista bolts, and artillery fire. Parno finally recovered and ordered a cease fire.

"CEASE FIRE!" Darvo bellowed down to the runners and the cry was relayed down the line. A ragged cheer went up from the front line as Soulan troopers watched their enemy flee in disorder.

"How about that?" Darvo grinned. "Roda's gadgets worked, after all."

"Indeed," Feng nodded.

"So, they did," Parno observed, calming visibly. He looked at Darvo and Cho, a bit shame faced.

"Sorry about that," he murmured. "I sort of panicked, I think."

"No," Darvo. "You didn't panic. You did allow the fact that things didn't go as you planned to rattle you, but that's not the same thing." Ever the teacher, Darvo was almost lecturing.

"I shouldn't be in command," Parno whispered. Darvo and Cho shared a look.

"You think anyone else could lead this lot?" Darvo demanded. "These men are fighting because you're in command, lad, and you're doin' well. Cho?"

"I agree," Cho nodded. "This is your first battle, Parno. No amount of training can prepare you for the real thing. You handled yourself well. Forget your doubts and concentrate on the task before you."

Parno considered that for a moment. His confidence slowly returned as the words of his advisers sank in. True, he had been thrown out of sorts by the Nor's determination in the face of a spirited defense, but, he reasoned, he had a good battle plan and it had worked. He knew now how hard it would be to stop them. Next time, he'd be ready.

Darvo and Cho Feng exchanged a grin as they watched their young leader work through all this in his mind. They saw him slowly regain his confidence, his trust in himself and his ability.

"Okay, then," Parno finally said. "Let's find out how badly we're hurt, and see if there's any damage to the fortifications." He turned to the artillery runner.

"Tell Captain Lars I want one salvo of the special ballista rounds ready for the next attack. On my order only," he added. The runner bowed quickly and went on his way.

Parno turned to the next runner. "Inform Captain Moore we'll use the next wave of mines during the next attack. I'll let him know when to fire once I see the Nor formation."

"Milord," the runner saluted, and took off for the front. Parno looked around.

"Have I overlooked anything?" Parno asked.

"Not that I can see," Darvo smiled. Cho merely shook his head.

"Well, then. I guess we wait and see."

-

Across the way, Major General William Brasher, 3rd Norland Field Army, Commanding, seethed with fury as his best division was routed by the rabble behind the breastworks to his front.

Nothing had gone according to plan so far. First his men had been hounded and shadowed by Soulan cavalry. Every attempt to break contact with them had failed. When he increased the strength of his patrols and screens, the enemy had simply vanished then attacked his sentry posts again at night. His men had walked headlong into ambush, after booby trap, after stake pit. His force had bled all the way to the Gap.

Only to arrive and find row after row of barricades, earthworks, and spiked trenches manned by more Soulan troops than should have been in the entire area. The Commander of his vanguard division had launched an attack late in the evening only to be repulsed with heavy loss. His artillery chief had brought his weapons forward, intending to deploy them and batter the enemy fortifications down, only to be hit with a vicious counter-battery fire that had wrecked almost a third of his artillery train.

Now his best infantry division, screened by one of his better cavalry brigades, had just been decimated with what he could only describe as witchcraft! He viewed the battlefield through his glass, seeing the bodies of his men lying crumpled in heaps. He had lost more men in this one engagement than General Wilson had lost in the entire battle of Loville…and Loville had been a great victory!

"We have to hit them again," he said to no one in particular. "Order the Second and Third Divisions to prepare at once. Second to lead, third to follow right behind." Aides ran to deliver the necessary orders, leaving their General to his foul mood.

Brasher eyed the fortifications across the field, looking for some kind of weakness. He was still looking when his next two units began to form up inside the tree line.

"I will destroy this Fort and then move on to complete my mission," Brasher promised himself. Failure carried a heavy penalty in the Norland military. He would not pay that price.

-

"Milord," a runner gasped, having made his way from the front lines in record time. "Colonel Landers' compliments and the Nor are forming for another attack. Just inside the tree line."

"Very well," Parno nodded. He turned to the runners behind him.

"Advise all commanders. The Nor are preparing another attack. Expect a stronger rush this time. Archers to engage at maximum range. Artillery to engage as soon as the enemy emerge from the tree line." The runners all hurried away, taking the warning to their respective commands. Parno sighed, bringing his gaze back to the front line and the field beyond it.

"They'll hit us harder, this time," he predicted. "We've lost some shock value, I guess, with the mines and the Hubbel's. Regardless, the damage will still be there."

"Maybe," Darvo allowed. "But, as you say, the damage will still be there."

"I hope it's enough," Parno observed. "We can't just let them walk over us the first day. We have got to hold this place for as long as possible."

"Everyone knows that, lad," Darvo replied gently.

"I know," Parno sighed. "I keep repeating it hoping to make it happen, I guess."

"Stranger things have happened," Darvo grinned.

Further conversation was cut off as bugles sounded from across the field and Nor infantry began emerging from the woods. Forming their lines as they came, row after row of Nor left the tree line, heading for the Soulan lines. Parno watched in dismay as the count climbed higher and higher.

"They're going to try and carry our line by pure weight this time," Parno decided. He turned to the artillery runner again.

"Tell Captain Lars to prepare a salvo of special rounds, catapults only, and stand by for my order before firing. After that, special rounds every third salvo until further orders, moving one rank to the rear with each salvo, when possible."

"Aye, milord," the runner acknowledged, heading for Lars' command post.

"How many of those things have you got, lad?" Darvo frowned.

"Not near enough," Parno admitted. "Roda is working to ready more of them, but it's a time-consuming effort and not a little dangerous," he added.

"Bear in mind you don't want to expend everything today if we can avoid it," Darvo warned.

"We have to stop them or it won't matter," Parno shrugged helplessly. "I'm seeing at least two divisions in line against us this time. Five to one odds even if we had the entire force on the line, which we don't. We've got to cut the odds."

"I don't disagree, lad," Darvo assured him. "Just bear in mind, we'll need these fire weapons of Finn's tomorrow as well, in all likelihood."

"We'll worry about tomorrow when it gets here," Parno said calmly. "Our goal for today is to get to tomorrow."

"So it is, laddie," Darvo chuckled.

The two of them watched in silence as the Nor's second attack wave moved closer and closer. There was no cavalry screen this time. The Nor General was apparently smart enough to know that his horse mounted units were of little use in this terrain.

The first salvo of artillery rounds lofted over their heads, landing amid the leading ranks of Nor. Once again heavy stones rolled over the advancing legions, crushing men beneath their weight as they bounded along. The second salvo launched before the first stones had stopped rolling.

Archers from behind the line began once again to loft arrows, with every third salvo being the Hubbel arrows. Nor troopers fell in increasing numbers.

How many men have I killed so far? he wondered. The idea of killing so many men, even his sworn enemies, was a dirty feeling. One he doubted he'd ever be clean of again. The Nor, meanwhile, continued to advance. Parno turned to his artillery runner.

"Begin special rounds and fire the special rounds off the ballistae as well," he ordered. The young man nodded his understanding and took off to the front. Parno turned his glass back to the advancing Nor. The leading ranks were now well within one hundred yards of the front line. He lifted his hand and caught Captain Moore's eye. The Captain watched and when Parno dropped his hand he ordered his men to fire once more.

The explosions ripped through the Nor troops once again. Before the enemy could recover, Lars dropped the first round of exploding catapult rounds in their rear ranks. The result was mass confusion but it worked against Parno this time. The enemy, realizing that the fire was behind them, rushed the earthworks to their front.

"Have the 8th Mounted stand by to engage any breakthroughs," he ordered a runner. The 8th Mounted Infantry was a Tinsee Militia Battalion. Parno had stationed them in reserve behind the front rank of barricades.

"Artillery is having a good effect," Darvo noted. "They aren't stopping, but their follow on units are taking a beating." Parno eyed the Nor lines himself, nodding in agreement.

"We'll see what effect. . . ." Parno's words were cut off by a thundering explosion to his front. A billow of smoke was rising from one of his own ballistae, and men could be heard screaming in pain.

Parno knew at once what had happened. One of the ballista rounds had detonated on the carriage. Looking at the scene, Parno was shocked to see an area some fifty feet long that was now unmanned. Worse, the fortifications were damaged.

"Order the 8th Mounted to move in and seal that hole!" Parno yelled at the nearest runner. The startled trooper took off in a burst of speed, leaving Parno watching and hoping the message arrived in time. He turned to the near breathless artillery runner.

"Cease fire on all special ballista rounds!" he ordered. Again the runner took off, noticeably slower than earlier.

"Send up the replacement artillery runner," Parno ordered Lieutenant Sprigs. Sprigs hurried to obey, while Parno turned to survey the ground before him.

The remainder of the ballista rounds had launched correctly, landing among the front and following ranks of the Nor advance. While not so strong as the catapult and trebuchet rounds, they were loud and caused some damage. Still, their effect wasn't worth another episode with a bad round.

"Lad, they're going to hit the wall this time," Darvo told him.

Parno nodded. "I know. It's up to the men, now."

Parno could only watch as his men rose to battle Nor troops who had managed to make it through the hell Parno had created to attack the fortifications. Crossbow bolts, arrows, and pikes descended on the Nor who still came doggedly forward.

One smart Nor commander had seen the ballista incident and noted that the line in that area was quiet. He had led what was left of his regiment and the one behind him, now devoid of its commander, to that spot on the wall. The Nor reached the line just as the 8th Tinsee Infantry arrived.

The Nor were pouring over the wall as the 8th began to arrive and the front ranks immediately engaged, fighting to close the hole in the line. From the outside Nor troops worked to tear down that portion of the barricades, pulling with pikes, axes, and bare hands at the wood and earth structures. The fighting was close-in, desperate combat, with men on both sides fighting with strength born of desperation.

The 8th was slightly outnumbered, but the troops were fresh. The Nor, despite their numerical advantage, were on the edge of exhaustion and panic, having crossed the field under the hellish fire of Roda Finn's wizardry. Their only hope of survival was to open a hole in the line and keep it open so that their comrades could exploit it.

Parno watched the Battle for the Hole, as it would become known, while Darvo concentrated on the rest of the battlefield. The older man frowned as several Nor regiments noticed the frantic battle for that area of line and headed for it.

"Lad, we need to get more men into that engagement," Darvo told him. "More Nor are on the way."

"Have Captain Moore's company engage the follow on units," Parno ordered a runner. "Have the 12th Tinsee move up to the reserve," he ordered another. "Inform Colonel Chad to move his regiment into the second line, replacing the 12th," Parno ordered a third runner. As the troopers raced off with their orders, Parno turned his attention back to the battle.

"Are we weak anywhere else?" he asked Darvo, having lost track of the overall battle while concentrating on the Hole.

"No, but we're too hard pressed to send troops from along the line to help," Darvo informed him. "It's up to those Militia boys for now, lad."

"I'm going down there," Parno said suddenly, heading for the stairs and donning his helmet.

"Are you daft!?" Darvo nearly roared. "You're needed here, boy!"

"I'm needed there," Parno threw back over his shoulder. "You can handle this better than I can and you know it. Now tend to your knitting and leave me to mine." With that, Parno was gone, racing down the steps, Sprigs and the men of Parno's escort running behind.

-

When Parno arrived at the Hole, the fighting was still desperate and the tide was starting to turn against the Soulan troopers. Parno spotted the 8th Mounted's commander and headed for him.

"Hot day, aye Major?" Parno asked, grinning.

"Are you insane?" Major Dory Leman screeched. "What are you doing down here? Milord," he managed to remember to add.

Parno's grin broadened. "Looked like you could use a hand. Don't worry, there's help on the way."

"I don't know if any help will be enough, milord," Leman admitted. "They're pressing hard and there are more and more Nor troops behind them. If we could get the pressure off long enough, we might could restore the line, but as it is all we can do is try to hold them out."

"I'll see if I can get you some help with that," Parno nodded, turning to Sprigs.

"Tell Lars I want a few special rounds laid into the Nor, about fifty yards of so over the line. I need to break the back of their attack so we can repair the line."

"Milord, that's very close to. . . ." Sprigs started to object, but Parno cut him off.

"I know how close it is! My men are dying to keep this hole from breaching! Now you have your orders!" Sprigs hurried away, objections gone.

Parno turned to his escort. "Follow me," he said simply and turned toward the fighting without waiting to see if they followed. Running to where the fighting looked the hottest, Parno saw two Nor soldiers trying to overwhelm a single Soulan trooper. With sword and shield the Soulan infantryman was holding his own, but he was also tiring. Parno headed straight into the fight, clubbing one of the Nor with his shield and engaging the other with his sword.

The men of his escort fell in behind him, shoring up the weakest area of the 8th Mounted's defense. The escort were all Black Sheep, hard men with little mercy. They fell onto the Nor with a vengeance, striking left, right and front without regard to their own safety. Fighting as a unit, the twenty men formed a phalanx, moving forward together, forcing the Nor to give ground under their assault.

Whenever a trooper went down, the phalanx closed around him, reformed, and continued forward. Several of the 8th Mounted saw them and fell onto their flanks, trying to support the wedge of steel now slicing into the Nor.

Parno, meanwhile, dispatched his opponent with ease, the Nor soldier being no match for the young Prince. Turning, he saw his men moving forward without orders, forcing the Nor line to give ground by simply taking it from them. Parno hurried to join them.

"Well done, Sergeant!" Parno shouted over the din, as Sergeant Berry, the commander of Parno's escort troop, dispatched another Nor warrior.

"Thank you, milord," Berry replied calmly. "All in a day's work."

"So it is," Parno laughed and joined the phalanx, his men making room for him in the center, near Berry's point position.

Together they continued to move forward slowly, but steadily. Seeing them forcing the Nor back in one area gave new life to the 8th Mounted and the men rallied around their Major, striking savagely at the Nor troops still pouring over the barricade.

Suddenly a line of explosions erupted from behind the Nor as Lars landed his first salvo. The artillery Captain had sweated profusely, laying in the catapults himself, worried about the proximity to his own men...and to the Prince.

Sighing in relief as the rounds landed in close as his liege had ordered, Lars ordered another round.

As the rolling explosions boomed across the field, the Nor began to break. The pressure of the follow-on troops eased, as oncoming Nor hesitated in the face of this new threat. Those Nor soldiers already inside fought on, knowing they had to either win or die. Some of those closest to the line joined them, trying to push the Soulan troopers back.

But the 12th Tinsee Cavalry had arrived by then and hurriedly went into the line, swords drawn and shields ready. Another string of explosions rocked the ground, a bit further back from the line this time, and the Nor outside began to break. The rest of the Soulan line was still intact and flight after flight of arrows and crossbow bolts were decimating their ranks.

In the end the ferocity of the Soulan counter-attack was too much. The Nor still outside the line turned and ran for their own lines, leaving their brethren inside to whatever fate found them.

Those inside, unaware that their fellows had deserted them, continued to fight desperately until there were so few left they could not continue. As they threw down their arms, attempting to surrender, Parno stepped forward.

"There's no surrender here," he told them quietly. "Go back to you own lines and tell your comrades. We won't take prisoners. You're lucky, since I need someone to deliver that message for me. Now go, and take your dead with you."

Several of the Nor hesitated, not relishing returning to their own lines. One tried to approach Parno directly, only to be cut down with a crossbow bolt to the throat.

"GO!" Parno yelled, and the Nor went, some grabbing their injured comrades as ordered, others simply hurrying over the lines. Parno eyed the carnage with a jaundiced eye.

"My God," he breathed.

"Milord?" Parno turned to see Major Leman standing next to him.

"Major, we need to get this breach repaired right away. Get some of your men on that at once. Major Strong," Parno addressed the 12th Cavalry's commander, "I want your men to take over this section of line. Have half of them assist with the rebuilding and cleanup, the others to stand watch. I suspect that today isn't over quite yet."

"What do we do with them, milord?" Strong nodded to the Nor bodies, not all of which were dead.

"Toss them over," Parno replied coldly. "We haven't the strength to guard them or the personnel to aide them. Allow the Nor to come and get them if they want. Place them fifty or so yards away from the line."

"Aye, milord," Strong nodded and began bellowing orders.

"Milord?" Sprigs spoke, and Parno turned to look at his Lieutenant.

"Colonel Nidiad requests your presence on the tower, milord."

Parno took one last look at the carnage before him, and nodded.

"Tell him I'm on my way."

-

Parno glanced at the sun overhead as he made his way back to the command post. He sighed, realizing that it was hardly past nine, if that. This would be a long day. He trudged up the stairs to where Darvo and Feng waited. Darvo looked at Sprigs.

"You can wait below, Lieutenant." Sprigs cast a look at Parno, who nodded, then hurried back the way he had come.

"Go ahead and say it," Parno sighed, removing his helmet and laying on the table. "Get it out of the way."

"Of all the headstrong, stupid, idiotic things I have seen in my long and storied career, that had to be the dumbest!" Darvo almost exploded. "You could have been killed! If not by the Nor, then by your own orders to lay those exploding. . .things…of Finn's right in on top of your position!"

"Had to be done," Parno shrugged. "We were going to lose the line."

"You aren't supposed to be on the line!" Darvo shot back. "Your place is here, in command."

"Darvo, I'm not even half as qualified as you are to lead these men," Parno spoke reasonably, "but I am a fair hand with a sword and I can't ask these men to do things I won't do myself."

"That's what command means, lad!" Darvo parried. "You send men into battle. They may live or die, but you remain in command."

"I had to do it," Parno said quietly, his eyes drifting over the battlefield. "You've seen combat, Darvo. You know what it is to ask men to do horrible things. I don't…or at least I didn't." He turned to look at his mentor.

"I can't stand here asking men to do something I can't, won't, or haven't done. Maybe someone else can, but I can't. Understand? These men followed me here and trusted me to make this work. They deserve to know that I'll fight with them or for them."

Darvo's frown softened at that. Intellectually he knew that Parno was right but seeing the man he had come to love as a son risking his life had rattled the older man…rattled him in a way that nothing else ever had. He had been about to reply, but instead held his tongue.

"You did well, my Prince," Cho Feng spoke softly. "Do not mistake the Colonel's words for rebuke. He is proud of you as well. He speaks as a father would. Not as a subordinate."

Parno nodded, understanding. He knew that Darvo thought of him as a son. The old soldier had practically raised him.

"Darvo, you taught me all I know about being a man," Parno's words were soft, but firm. "You raised me when no one else would. I did exactly what you would have done, because that's the man you raised me, taught me, to be…and I'll likely do it again before this battle ends."

"I know, boy," Darvo nodded, his eyes also wandering over the battlefield. "I know." He didn't turn to face the younger man, lest Parno see his eyes water.

"I'm sorry if I worried you," Parno went on, "but we all know this battle can only have one outcome. Today, or tomorrow, or the day after if we're uncommonly fortunate, all of us will be dead. There's no point in my not helping my men when I can."

"Just remember that these men are inspired by you," Darvo replied, voice strained. "If you fall early in the battle, then they may lose heart. Fall earlier than if you were still here, encouraging them. There's more to leading men than leading them into battle."

Parno thought about that for a moment. "I'll remember," he promised. He hadn't considered that. All he had thought of was that the wall was falling and that he could help. He had to start thinking more like a commander and less like a knight errant.

"In any case," Cho Feng smiled, "I think your men are sufficiently aware of your willingness to engage the enemy in combat. Already your men are talking about your actions and word is spreading across the Fort. They have, indeed, taken heart from your stand."

"Good," Parno nodded. "It may be all I have to give them."

"We shall see," Cho replied. "We shall see."

"Any word on our casualties?" Parno asked, hoping to get off the current subject.

"One hundred and seven dead, two hundred eighty-six wounded. One ballista lost." Darvo recited the words tonelessly. Almost four hundred men. Nearly ten percent of their force.

"Who was hit hardest?" Parno asked, dreading the answer.

"11th Cavalry was holding the line where the ballista round exploded," Darvo told him. "Their casualties are the highest, followed by the 8th Mounted. Our men fared better, with eleven dead and sixteen wounded."

"Not bad, I suppose," Parno sighed. "I can't even fathom how bad we've hurt the Nor. Their bodies seem endless out on the field."

"Estimates are between two thousand and twenty-two hundred dead," Darvo informed him. "They're estimates, mind you, but they seem fairly accurate. Conservative, if anything, and those are only the dead left on the field. Throw in the wounded who made it back and the number will be higher."

"Good Lord," Parno breathed. "I had no idea."

"You've stung them hard, lad," Darvo smiled for the first time since Parno had returned to the tower. "Hurt them badly."

"I can't believe we managed to turn them back," Parno shook his head. "They had the numbers to overwhelm us. Why didn't they?"

"Two things," Darvo used his lecture voice. "One—Finn's exploding weapons. The shock value alone was worth another regiment of men, not to mention the actual damage. Two—the ferocity of your counter-attack. The two combined shook their confidence. They lost their edge and broke. Simple as that."

"Let us not forget the value of a strong position," Cho put in. "You have such a position and have planned your defense well. The enemy has to pass you in order to continue. You have placed him in a position where he must either fight or withdraw. He has no other option."

"I'd be glad to see him withdraw," Parno admitted, "but I don't think that's going to happen."

"Not likely," Darvo agreed. "They've bled too much trying to take this place to leave it standing. The only thing saving us so far is the terrain. They simply can't cram enough men into this pass at one time to batter us down."

"They came damn close," Parno objected.

"Only due to the damage caused by the ballista exploding," Darvo corrected him. "If not for that we would have seen some hard fighting, yes, but I don't believe, with all other things being the same, they could have breached the line."

"Then maybe we can hold for a while longer than I thought." Parno's voice was tinged with hope.

"Perhaps," Darvo agreed cautiously. "Were I in his shoes," he pointed across the battlefield to the Nor position, "my next attack would be my last. One wave after another, after another, until my men were either broken in defeat or this place was a smoking ruin…and I wouldn't put it past whoever is in charge over there to do just that, either. So far, their General has shown a decided lack of caring where the lives of his men are concerned."

"He is in an untenable position," Cho remarked. "As I said, he must go through this pass in order to fulfill his objective, whatever that is. You are blocking his way. He must either defeat you or withdraw. I believe, based on what I have seen so far, that failure must carry a very heavy penalty among these Nor."

"I should imagine it does," Parno nodded thoughtfully. "Their regime is known for cruelty. Their people live in great fear of the government, I'm told."

"Their Emperor has gone to great lengths to stage this war," he continued, remembering the events leading up to the war. "He has spent a great deal of time, money, and resources to bring this about. I suspect that he would not be pleased if it were to fail."

"Just so," Darvo agreed, "and that means our opponent will likely become desperate as the battle goes on. Which leads me back to my original statement; expect him to throw his men into this grinder until he breaks us or we break them."

"With their numbers I fear it will be us that breaks," Parno murmured. "If we had more men we could probably hold this place indefinitely. Even one division of infantry, even light infantry, would make this place nearly impregnable."

"Might as well ask for two divisions, so long as you're wishing," Darvo chuckled mirthlessly, "but we'll make do…at least for a while."

"I'm going to walk the line," Parno said abruptly. "I want to see the men, gauge their condition for myself. Let them know I'm not just sitting up here, watching them die."

"They already know that, lad," Darvo patted the younger man's shoulder fondly, "but it will likely do them good to see you among them."

"I'll be back," Parno promised, "and I'll come straight back if another attack comes," he added. Darvo nodded.

"I'd appreciate that very much."

-

When Parno reached the bottom of the stairs Sergeant Berry and the remaining fourteen men of his detail stood, but Parno waved them back.

"Stay here, and rest," he ordered. "I'm going to walk the line, that's all. If fighting breaks out I'll return here at once. Tend to your wounds."

"I'd rather we accompanied you, milord," Berry objected. "It's our duty to see you safe."

"I'll be fine, so long as I don't rush headlong into another fight, Sergeant," Parno smiled, "and I promise I won't without you at my side."

"Very well, milord," Berry reluctantly agreed.

Parno motioned for Sprigs to follow, along with two runners. As he walked, Sprigs risked speaking.

"Are you all right, milord?"

"I'm fine, Sprigs. I just want to see the line and talk to the men."

"Of course, sir," Sprigs nodded. "I. . .milord, I owe you an apology for earlier," he stammered. "I didn't intend to question your orders. I was concerned about your proximity to the salvo you ordered. I allowed that concern to interfere with my duty."

"Don't worry about it," Parno waved the apology aside. "I know you meant well and I appreciate it."

"Sir," Sprigs nodded, clearly relieved. They made the rest of the walk in silence. Parno started on the right flank, where Landers' men were still clearing away debris from the battle.

"Milord," Landers smiled as he saw Parno. "A rather hot morning, yes?"

"A bit warm, certainly," Parno managed to say with a straight face before grinning.

"Your men did very well, Colonel."

"All of the men did well, sir," Landers agreed. "I thought at one point that we would surely be overwhelmed. I cannot say enough about the bravery of these men."

"Nor can I, Colonel," Parno replied. "I am proud to be among them." The troopers near enough to overhear their conversation straightened a bit at that. Parno pretended not to notice.

"Anything you need, Colonel?" he asked. Landers pondered that for a moment before replying.

"Not that I can think of, milord. I did wonder, are you going to leave the 12th in place on the line?"

"I am," Parno nodded. "I think the line needs to be strengthened. I'll leave the 8th in reserve, and Colonel Chad's men are now on the interior line, along with the Provisional Battalion."

"Very good, milord," Landers nodded. "I asked only to see if I needed to reorient my unit."

"I'll leave that to you, Colonel," Parno ordered. "You have command of the 12th in any case. Place them as you see fit."

"Thank you, milord," Landers beamed at the implied confidence. The two men shook hands and Parno started up the line, offering an occasional comment to the men as he went. He liked what he saw, he decided, as he made his tour. Morale was high for the moment. Every soldier on the front knew how close they had come to losing the first line and that they had managed to hold it against staggering odds.

That knowledge gave them renewed confidence, not only in themselves, but each other and in Parno himself. Everyone knew, by now, how the young Prince had led his own escort into the fray, fighting to hold the line until reinforcements could arrive. The soldiers took pride in knowing that they were following a fighting member of the Royal Family and that made them want to fight harder, so as not to disappoint their scion.

Parno paused at the Hole, seeing that the work was progressing nicely. Major Strong noticed him and walked over.

"We're making good time on the repairs, milord," Strong informed him. "I'd estimate we'll be finished in another half hour, if the heathens give us that long."

"Don't count on it, Major," Parno warned. "They may well give us half the day, for all I know, but hurry the work as much as possible. I don't want our men exposed any more than necessary should another attack come."

"We'll get it done, milord," Strong promised, "and if I may? I saw your action earlier, milord. I just wanted to say, that was the finest bit of soldiering I've ever been privileged to see. It's an honor to fight with you, sir."

"Thank you, Major," Parno managed not to murmur. "I appreciate that. Colonel Landers will still be in command of this section of line and he may want to realign everyone once the work is done. Take your cues from him. If I have direct orders for you they'll arrive by runner. Please send two men to the tower for that purpose. I prefer to use men from the units, as they'll be more familiar with the area and the command structure."

"I'll see to it at once, sir," Strong replied.

"Very well, then, Major. I leave you to it." Parno continued on his way, slowly making his way to where his own regiment was entrenched. When he arrived his men cheered, rushing out to meet him. Parno grinned at their enthusiasm, shaking out thrust hands and enduring many claps to the back.

"Here now!" Brenack Wysin waded through the group. "You'll break the man's spine, carryin' on so!" Everyone laughed at that, but ceased the informal contact.

"I'm very proud of you, men!" Parno called out. "You fought well! Kept your discipline and took the fight to the Nor! I couldn't be more proud." Cheers erupted again at that and Parno had to smile. He was proud of them. All of them.

"All right!" Karls Willard boomed. "We've got work still to do, lads. Back at it now, before the bloody Nor come looking for more pain and suffering at the hands of Parno's Black Sheep!" With one last cheer at the regiment's new name, the men drifted back to their posts. A beaming Willard closed with Parno and gripped his hand tightly.

"How are you, milord?" he asked. "I heard you were in the thick of things for a while, earlier."

"I was at that," Parno agreed, clasping Willard's hand equally firm. "Berry and his men did most of the work, mind you, but I was there to cheer them on." Willard cast a glance at Sprigs, who rolled his eyes. Willard grinned and turned back to his liege.

"We've done well so far, milord," he turned serious, "but I expect we'll see a much stronger attack this time."

"Darvo says the same," Parno told him, "and so do I. I think the Nor General over there is between a rock and a hard place, Karls. He has to carry this place. He'll keep throwing men at us until he does."

"And we'll keep throwing them back!" a voice yelled out of the crowd, renewing the cheers from Parno's men.

"You do that!" Parno laughed. "That's what I want to hear!"

"We'll hold them, milord," Karls added. "For a while, at least."

"I know," Parno assured him. "You've done well, Karls. In a better world you'd be a General after this."

"I'm happy where I am, milord," Karls smiled. "I wouldn't be anywhere else, even if the opportunity was available. This will be a fight long remembered by our people and they will sing songs, write poems, and retell this story for so long as memory holds it. I'm proud to be here with you."

Parno looked at the other man for a long time, seeing in Karls eyes the truth of what he said. Parno suddenly embraced him fiercely. An embrace which Karls returned.

"You're more of a brother to me than my own blood, Karls," Parno told him quietly. "I couldn't ask for a better man to stand with me."

"I feel the same way, Parno," Karls replied, using the Prince's first name, something he very rarely did. The two men parted then, with nods of respect for each other. Karls returned to supervising the work of the regiment and Parno started back to the tower. Sprigs followed at a respectful distance, instinctively knowing that his commander would want some time to himself.

When Parno arrived at the tower he climbed slowly to the top, reflecting on what he had seen along the line. All of the men were in good spirits and determined to fight to the finish. He couldn't ask for better. If only. . . .

"Lad, I think the Nor are about ready for another try," Darvo's words broke Parno out of his thoughts. He took up his glass and looked across the field to the woods. Sure enough, there were signs of activity within the trees.

"Send word to all units that the Nor are marshaling for another attack," Parno ordered Sprigs, "and have Captain Lars report all available ammunition, please." Sprigs nodded and hurried down the tower to the waiting runners.

Parno turned to Darvo. "What do you think?"

"The first attack was by a division of infantry supported by a brigade of cavalry," the older man rubbed his chin in thought. "The second was two infantry divisions, at least. I doubt they'll send anymore horsemen at us in this terrain. I'd look for at least three divisions this go round, likely stacked one atop the other."

"I don't know that we can hold them again, lad," he admitted.

"We'll try, at any rate," Parno replied. "I'll have Lars open up with the exploding rounds as soon as the Nor are in range this time. That should disrupt their order, at least."

"Just so," Darvo agreed, "so long as they last."

"We have enough to last the day," Parno assured him, "after that it will depend on what Roda's managed to accomplish and how much we use today, of course."

"Well, as you said, if we don't survive the day it won't matter what's left."

-

Across the field General Brasher was seething. He had already ordered the two generals who had led their divisions in the last attack executed for incompetence. That should, he reasoned, be an incentive to the generals leading this next attack.

This time three divisions would attack in echelon. Wave after wave of soldiers, shoulder to shoulder. Their casualties would be heavy, thanks to the Soulan devil weapons, but they should carry the position and he would still have sufficient strength to threaten the Soulan capital city of Nasil.

He had to break this defense. His orders were very strict on timing and Brasher was already behind schedule. Every minute of delay here was another minute that Soulan would have to react to his presence in their heartland and that meant that the odds against him were growing by the minute.

He cursed his failure to anticipate this suicidal stand in the Gap. Had he been more careful in his strategic thinking, he could have sent his two best mounted divisions ahead at a gallop, with orders to seize and hold this Gap until the rest of his army could arrive.

Lost opportunities, he shook his head, nothing for it now but to press ahead. If he failed the Emperor would have his head and likely those of his family.

"I will not fail!" He mused.

"Sir," his second in command approached carefully. "We're ready for the next attack."

"Have you expressed my displeasure with the former attack to the division commanders?" Brasher asked coldly.

"I have, sir," his second nodded. "They are well aware of the price for failure."

"Good," Brasher nodded in satisfaction. "Sound the advance."

-

Parno frowned as he heard the sound of bugles echoing across the field. The Nor General was through playing around, judging from the number of calls.

"Looks like you were right, Darvo," he said tonelessly. The older man snorted.

"Of course, I was!" Darvo sounded mildly offended, but grinned as he said it. His grin faded soon, however.

Line after line of Nor soldiers emerged from the woods, reforming their lines on the move, headed straight across the field. Parno turned to his artillery runner.

"My compliments to Captain Lars and he may open fire. Special rounds to start, and then every third salvo until further orders." The runner took off.

"Order Captain Moore to engage the third line of mines at his discretion, but not before the third rank approaches, and not until there's a solid line around them," he told another runner who headed for the sharpshooter company.

"How many more of those mines have you out there lad?" Darvo asked.

"After this round, three more," Parno replied. "They're set in groups of fifty."

"They've worked well," Darvo admitted. "I'm glad we had them."

"We should have another round, or maybe two, to leave in the Gap when we finally have to withdraw to the second line."

The two watched as the Nor came, doggedly working their way across the rough terrain, now strewn with the bodies of their fellow soldiers and horses that had fallen in the first attack. The going was rough, but the penalty for stopping was rougher.

"I think they're having to force their soldiers to fight, Darvo," Parno commented, noting how the officers were close behind each rank.

"I'd thought that myself," Darvo agreed. "That could work for or against us, depending on how hard we make it on them."

"I'd opt for it being harder," Parno decided. "They might be killed in the attack, true, but if they withdraw they will be killed by their own. Not much of a choice, really."

"True enough."

Silence reigned then as the two concentrated on the approaching Nor. Parno heard the catapults and trebuchets engage, heard the deep rumbling of the gears working, and heard the now familiar "thunk" of released pressure as the mighty weapons fired. Lars first salvo landed staggered among the first three lines of infantry, wreaking havoc among the enemy, yet the Nor seemed to shrug it off and continued their advance.

Archers on the front line began to loft arrows at the approaching lines, once again seeding them with the exploding Hubbel arrows. Cross bowmen readied their weapons, taking their places on the platforms behind the berm. Suddenly they fired, nearly in unison, and a ripple seemed to work its way through the first rank of Nor.

The leading line of the attack staggered this time and almost halted. Only the pressure of their officers and the following line of troops kept them moving. Parno smiled grimly at that.

Lars' second salvo, this time of stones and boulders, tumbled through the follow on ranks, crushing dozens of soldiers at the time. Parno grimaced at the images the action conjured into his mind, but he shook it off. There was no place in this business for sentiment where the enemy was concerned.

The remaining eleven ballistae were firing, their wickedly hooked large bolts tearing great holes in the first and second ranks. Archers continued to loft their arrows and Nor troops continued to fall. Lars' third salvo sailed overhead, once more tumbling among the leading ranks of the Nor.

"Next salvo will be exploding rounds," Parno said to no one in particular.

"He's cutting it close, lad," Darvo warned. "We can't afford to have one of those things land among the line. It would be worse than the ballista and this time they'll have the numbers to press the attack." Parno considered that for a second, then turned to the second artillery runner.

"Compliments to Captain Lars and he is to raise his fire to no less than one hundred yards distant from the line, unless ordered otherwise." The runner bowed slightly and flew down the stairs. Parno turned to look at his mentor.

"That will let them keep hammering the follow on ranks fairly heavily."

"Good deal, lad," Darvo nodded, never taking his eyes from the field.

The battle waged on. Most of the Nor first rank was gone, now, either lying on the field, or absorbed by the second. The second rank was clearly wavering but were now within fifty yards of the first line of defense. Their own bowmen were now firing and Soulan troopers began falling. Not nearly as quickly as their adversaries, but there were far fewer of them.

"You will be forced to defend the wall, my Prince," Cho said quietly, having observed in silence until now. "Their numbers will allow them to reach you, eventually."

"I know," Parno nodded. "I strengthened the line with another battalion. I think…I hope…that will make the difference." Cho nodded, his eyes also not leaving the field of battle. Parno wondered for a second what Cho was seeing. What he was thinking.

"War is as terrible as it is exciting," Cho almost whispered, as if he could hear Parno's thoughts. The young Prince was inclined to agree.

As the next salvo of exploding artillery rounds fell among the advancing enemy, Captain Moore's sharpshooters engaged the next line of mines, hidden among the third and fourth ranks of the enemy. This time all but four of the clay mines exploded, hurling bits and balls of iron throughout the lines.

For a second the entire Nor advance staggered to a halt, the men dazed by the round of explosions. Then the threats of their officers pressed them forward once again, though the front ranks were noticeably more reluctant. Several shirkers were cut down by their own officers, an example to the rest.

The advance began again, though its momentum was lost at least temporarily. Parno tensed in anticipation, knowing that the line would soon be under direct attack.

For the next several minutes the fighting was close in, and desperate. Nor troops began to reach the line and assault it. Pikes found their way over the barricades and pry poles hooked to the stakes along the berms and trenches of the fortifications. The sheer muscle of the Nor numbers began to tell as several of the wooden obstacles began to fall.

Yet the Soulan troopers were fighting hard as well. Soulan pike-men lunged over the berm, sinking their long spears into enemy flesh. Crossbow bolts shot through men at close range, often continuing out their backs and hitting the man behind.

Meanwhile, Soulan archers continued to loft flight after flight of arrows over the berms, into the following ranks of the Nor attack. Soulan troopers began to mount the wall, swords in hand, to repel those Nor fortunate, or unfortunate, enough to make it to the top. In several spots Nor troops actually managed to cross over the line only to be fell upon by Soulan troopers with swords.

But this time the weight of numbers was on the side of the Nor. For every enemy soldier Parno's men killed or maimed, there were two more to take his place—and Parno's own men were falling now at an alarming rate.

"Lad, we may need to think about falling back to the second line," Darvo said at last, watching the desperate battle unfold.

"I know," the Prince agreed. He was reluctant to abandon the forward line, but could see the strain that holding it was placing on his men. He turned to the rank of runners behind him.

"Order all commanders to prepare to fall back," he told them. "Have Captain Moore hit the fourth rank of mines, then fall back to the second line at once to help cover our withdrawal. Order the ballista teams to fall back now and have Captain Lars lift his fire to within fifty yards of the line and be prepared to loft three solid salvos of exploding rounds, staggered all along our line to help cover our withdrawal. He is to await my command before commencing his fire. Archery Company 'B' is to loft one, and one only, volley of the Hubbel arrows just before withdrawing." Runners departed in a flurry as Parno continued issuing orders.

"Have the 8th Mounted gather all wounded at once and get them behind the lines. I want no one left behind if we can help it. Order Colonel Chad to have his men prepared to leave the line in order to cover the withdrawal if needed." He turned back to Darvo.

"Have I missed anything?" He asked.

"Not that I can see, lad," the old soldier shook his head. "Not that I can see."

"We'll have to abandon this tower once we give the order to fall back," Parno mused. "I hate to lose this observation post."

"Can't be helped," Darvo shrugged. "We can't remain here. We'll be targets for every Nor with a bow at this range."

Parno watched as his orders began to take hold. The ballistae were already pulling out of the line, their men working to get them behind the second line of entrenchments. As he looked on Captain Moore's sharpshooters stood and delivered a volley into the next rank of mines. Despite the press of bodies in the field, they managed to strike thirty-eight of the clay jars, sending another ripple through the Nor lines. Immediately the crossbow men turned to head for the second line of defense, reloading their bows as they moved.

Men from the reserve moved in to gather the wounded, hurrying to clear the field before the line broke. Parno was pleased to see that they weren't in a panic, despite the nearing collapse of the front line. Instead they worked quickly and efficiently. He glanced over to where Colonel Chad's men stood waiting, ready to defend the second line or to move forward to support the others, whichever was needed.

"I think it's near time, Darvo," Parno finally said, hating every word.

"That it is, lad," Darvo nodded. He turned to the waiting runners.

"Gather your things, take all the gear from here and report to the secondary command post. Hurry now." The men needed no urging. Nor arrows were already falling around the tower.

Parno dropped to the ground where Berry and his guard waited. The sergeant looked apprehensive.

"Milord, we should get you back from here," he said calmly.

"Nonsense," Parno scoffed. "We left the tower because it was so exposed. Our men are about to leave the first line, retreating behind this one. I can't be out of touch when that happens. Keep your men down, so much as possible. There is a chance," he added, "that the Nor will be able to pursue quickly and try to carry this line as well. We cannot allow that to happen."

"Yes Sir." Berry acknowledged. He looked unhappy at that, but would not object. Darvo came down the stairs last.

"The tower's empty," he informed Berry. "No one is to go up again." Berry nodded and ordered two of his men into place to guard the tower. Parno scrambled to where he could see over the second berm, eying the withdrawal.

The ballistae were already coming into the line with Moore's men in place to cover the others. He turned to his artillery runner.

"Order Captain Lars to commence firing," he yelled. Without waiting for a response he turned to the front.

"FALL BACK!" he bellowed at the top of his lungs. "ALL UNITS, FALL BACK!"

Landers and Karls Willard both began withdrawing their men by companies, with archers falling back first to cover the others. Parno watched pensively, hoping that everything went according to plan.

Sensing that the Soulan line was weakening, the Nor redoubled their efforts, forcing men over top of one another in an attempt to get inside the line and keep the Soulan troopers from retiring. The battle turned desperate for Soulan for a minute as much of the fighting fell to hand-to-hand combat. Swords clashed and shields beat as one force tried to overwhelm the other. Roland's 'B' company lofted their flight of explosive arrows which cut deep into the Nor front lines, but more enemy soldiers appeared to replace those who had fallen.

Just when Parno was sure all was lost, Lars launched his first salvo. A ripple of explosions fell just outside the first line, literally walking its way down the line. The continuous boom of exploding rounds stunned the Nor long enough to allow most of the troops to disengage. They, in turn, aided their fellows in putting down the most stubborn of the Nor troops, then ran for the second line.

Crossbows twanged all along the second line as the Provisional Battalion and the 12th Kent Militia sent their bolts into the pursuing Nor. Archers behind the line began to rain arrows on the enemy and the front ranks again seemed to stagger, men falling in droves with each volley.

Another string of explosions, these falling just inside the front line, wrought complete havoc with the Nor soldiers who had made it inside the perimeter. Between the artillery and the archery, the advance stopped cold, with men running about in a panic.

The Soulan troopers took full advantage of that, hurrying inside the traps designed to allow passage outside of the second berm. Covered by a final walking salvo of explosions, these once again outside the perimeter, the remainder of Parno's command managed to escape, pouring through the siege gates and into the second line of defense.

But the danger was not passed.

There were still five more full ranks of Nor coming and the Soulan troopers had no time to spare. Hurrying onto the line, the survivors of the first line joined those on the second line, forming a strong position where men stood literally shoulder to shoulder.

"Keep a sharp eye out for their artillery!" Parno called to his lookouts. With the front line fallen, Nor artillery might have a chance to deploy. He wanted to prevent that if he could.

Running up and down the line, Parno surveyed his men and their deployments. Satisfied with what he saw, he made his way to a high point on the third line where he could see marginally better and had a better over-all view of the battlefield.

The Nor were streaming inside the old line now, reforming on the move to hit the second line as hard as they could. A brief tinge of disappointment passed through Parno at the thought of losing that first line. He had desperately wanted to hold that line for the entire day, even if he'd had to abandon it after dark. He shrugged mentally. He'd done what he could with what he had.

Soulan archery was taking a harsh toll now, laying droves of Norland infantry low with every volley. Parno watched closely, wondering how much more the Nor could endure. Surely, they were near their breaking point.

That thought made him re-examine his own command. How many of them were near to breaking? As he studied them, however, Parno realized that his men were not in such straits. True, they were tired, some even near exhaustion, but they were holding firm and showing no signs of panic.

As the Nor closed on the new line, Soulan troopers once more mounted the parapet, swords in hand, to repel them. For a few desperate moments Parno worried that this line would fall as well, but the second line was shorter, more compact, than the first and almost all of his troops were now on the line. With more swords per foot than before, the Soulanies were better suited to holding this line, even against a determined attack, and the Nor they were fighting were no longer so determined.

"Have Captain Lars lay a line of regular shot inside the first line," Parno ordered the artillery runner. "Have the ballistae began firing as soon as they're on line," he ordered another. "Tell Captain Moore to hold his men in readiness for now, behind the main line," he instructed yet another. All three ran to obey. Parno turned his attention back to the line.

The press of Nor bodies was beginning to ease, he noticed. Their casualties had been horrendous so far, their strength sapped in taking the first line of defenses. Just as Parno began to feel confident about their chances, Darvo grabbed his shoulder.

"A new division coming, lad!" he yelled, pointing beyond the current battle. Parno followed his finger, seeing new ranks of Nor emerging from the trees. Files after file of fresh troops. Dismayed, he turned to Darvo.

"Can the men keep fighting like this?" he asked.

"They've no choice, lad," Darvo told him. "They'll keep at it." Parno nodded, and turned to his artillery runner.

"Inform Captain Lars to begin taking the new lines under fire with explosive rounds." The young man nodded and headed to the artillery line.

"If we can beat them up before they get here, then their weight may not hurt us so badly," he told Darvo, who nodded.

"Worth a try," He said.

Parno looked out over the battle now raging much closer to the Fort. His men had performed brilliantly so far, but how long could they face such continuous combat?

How long could they keep the Nor at bay? And would it be long enough to matter?

# CHAPTER TWENTY-SIX

-

Memmnon read Parno's report for a second time, unable to comprehend the magnitude of the impending disaster it warned of.

He tried to warn us, Memmnon thought. We should have listened.

He hurried along the hallway to his father's apartments. 1st Corps had already left Nasil, Therron at its head, on the way to reinforce General Davies. The situation in Western Kent was dire, to say the least. General Raines was holding in Shelby for now, having prevented a river crossing four days earlier, but he had warned that the Wild Folk had assistance from at least two Nor divisions and he didn't have the troops to patrol the length of the Great River in order to prevent a boat crossing such as the one that had overwhelmed Davies in Kent.

As a result, 5th Corps was moving west, to take up a position in Misi province, near Vix, a moderate sized city and river port. Once there, they could take over patrolling the Great River for much of the area south of Shelby. General Herrick, commanding 5th Corps, would need most of a week to get into position, pushing his men and horses beyond all reason to do so that quickly and it would take days longer to establish patrols covering the river.

Memmnon shook his head. Everything was happening too fast. There was no time to try and regroup or to plan a strong counterattack. All Soulan could do was react to what the Nor were doing.

And now this.

He arrived at his father's office and walked in unannounced. Tammon looked up, startled, from his consultation with several of his closest advisers.

"Memmnon?"

"We need to talk, father," Memmnon informed him. "At once. It cannot wait," he added when his father indicated the men seated around his desk. Tammon eyed his son for a moment, then nodded.

"Excuse us for a moment, please gentlemen," he ordered. The various ministers gathered their valises and left the room. Once they were alone, Tammon turned to his oldest son.

"This had better be important," he warned. Memmnon thrust the letter toward his father.

"Oh, it's important, all right," he commented. "This is from Parno." Tammon's face grew taunt.

"Memmnon, I haven't the time to read his litany of complaints about. . . ."

"READ IT!" Memmnon almost screamed. The door to Tammon's office burst open at once as two guards reacted to the outburst.

"GET OUT!" Memmnon did scream at them. "See that no one disturbs us!" The guards looked to the King, who nodded, eyeing his son as if he'd never seen him before. Without another word, he took the letter and began to read.

"Memmnon,

Word has reached me that a large force of Nor troopers approaching fifty thousand strong has been detached from the forces currently battling General Davies and are heading for the Gap of Cumberland. I have moved my regiment to the Gap and am currently preparing to defend it. There are less than four-thousand of us all totaled, but we are erecting barricades and earthworks in preparation for a stand. Units are currently in the field trying to slow the advance of the enemy and I will join one of them shortly to see things for myself. If the reports are correct, and I believe that they are, then we have at most a week and likely less before they are upon us. It is unlikely that we will be able to hold for long, brother. The numbers are simply too great. We will hold as long as possible, however, and bleed this enemy force as badly as we can.

Once they are into the Gap. . . .well, you know as well as I do what that will mean. I feel confident that we can give you at least two days and perhaps even three. After that, every minute we buy you is a gift. Use it wisely.

Good luck, Memmnon, in the days ahead. This war is unlike any of the previous attacks on our land. I think that the Nor are determined to conquer us this time and willing to pay the price to do it.

Parno"

Tammon looked up from the letter, eyes wide in comprehension. His mouth worked to try and speak, but no words would come.

"Parno is going to die," Memmnon said quietly. "He warned us not to ignore this threat and we did. Therron is riding even now to reinforce General Davies and may even be there already while the forces against him are depleted from sending this army into the Gap—an army that no one but Parno and a handful of militia are in a position to stop. We have blundered."

"Send word to Therron immediately," Tammon ordered, his voice trembling. "Tell him to move at once to the Gap and defend it at all costs."

"It will take two days for word to reach him," Memmnon sighed. He'd already done the math. "Even then he will likely argue, which will take further time…and he will move slowly, against his will."

"I'll send the runner," Tammon declared. "He won't argue with me!"

"No?" Memmnon asked, eyebrows raised. "Perhaps not," he nodded. "Let us hope so, at any rate. Because if he does, and Parno fails, then this war is all but over."

Tammon summoned his personal courier and dictated a quick set of orders. Memmnon watched, his mind working. Was there any way to get help to Parno in time? If there was, he couldn't see it.

After the runner had gone, Tammon looked out his window for a time, silence laying heavy between father and son. Finally the older man turned.

"I'm going to the Gap," Tammon said quietly. "I will take whatever forces are still in the city and my personal regiment. If we ride hard we can be there in three days."

"You cannot be serious!" Memmnon was alarmed. "We're at war, Father! Your place is here, like it or not."

"My place is with my son," Tammon said softly. "I have wronged him in so many ways. . . ." He looked at Memmnon with haunted eyes.

"I haven't been a father to him at all," he admitted for the first time in his life. "The least I can do is try to get there before. . . ."

"Before he dies?" Memmnon asked scathingly. "A bit late for sentiment, Milord. He has tried for years to win our love or even just our respect. Despite everything we've done and said to him he is about to give his life for us and for this Kingdom. Whatever your feelings, you cannot simply ride out and join him. There is a war to be fought."

"You can see to those things as well as I," Tammon told him flatly. "Perhaps better, since you tried to tell me not to ignore Parno." Tammon tugged on the rope that would summon his personal servant.

"I leave the Kingdom in your hands, Memmnon," Tammon said formally. "You are the Crown Prince. It will be for you to do someday. Perhaps I can help your brother save something for you to rule. Gather whatever troops you can lay hands to and have them ready to ride in one hour. I'll be down as soon as I can."

-

"Do you understand my orders?" Tammon asked. The man before him was his personal Royal Courier, one of the most trusted men in Tammon's Court.

"I do, My King," the man bowed stiffly. "Your instructions will be followed to the letter."

"I know," Tammon spared the man a rare smile. "I hope I'm wrong, of course, but . . . ."

"There is much at risk, sire," the courier agreed.

"Off with you then," Tammon ordered suddenly, all business again. The Courier spurred his horse, a truly magnificent animal, and shot away, galloping toward 1st Corps. Tammon watched him out of sight then turned to his own horse.

Memmnon had used the time Tammon had taken to dictate his messages to turn out the House Guard and Tammon's personal regiment, along with every other soldier he could lay hands to quickly. When Tammon departed, the only military unit worthy of the name still in Nasil would be Memmnon's personal regiment. They would be responsible for protecting the palace in the absence of the House Guard.

"All is in readiness, Father," Memmnon said quietly, coming up behind his father. Tammon looked down from his saddle and nodded.

"Many of the troops are in wagons," Memmnon warned. "Sufficient horses couldn't be gotten on such short notice."

"They'll be fighting on foot, anyway, I'd imagine," Tammon shrugged. He leaned down, offering Memmnon his hand.

"Good luck, son," he said softly. "In the event I don't return, I'm afraid my troubles will become yours."

"You will return," Memmnon replied with more confidence than he felt. "I'll see you soon enough."

Enri Willard rode up just then.

"The House Guard is ready, milords," he reported. Colonel Strong, commander of Tammon's personal regiment was right behind him.

"We're mounted and ready to ride, sire," he stated.

"Let's be off, then," Tammon ordered. "Time is precious, gentlemen. Waste not a minute of it."

-

Tammon's courier rode all through the night. He stopped briefly, twice, at courier stations to exchange mounts, wolfing down sandwiches at each stop with hot coffee to ward off the cold. Otherwise, he rode steadily, following the road with little trouble.

As a result, he rode into the camps of 1st Corps just short of two days after leaving Nasil. As the King's Courier, he was escorted directly to the Lord Marshall. He placed the King's orders in his hands, then stood back to wait.

Therron McLeod looked at the message in his hands, his face showing both anger and disbelief.

"And this came from the King, himself?" he asked the Royal Courier. Therron wanted to make sure the order came directly from his father and not from Memmnon.

"I waited as the King dictated the message, sire," the courier nodded.

"I want clarification on this before I act on it," Therron said suddenly. "I'm not about to up and move my entire command based on the word of Parno!"

"His Majesty, the King, said that might be your response, milord," the Royal Courier almost smirked. He reached into his bag, pulling another envelope, sealed with wax bearing the Royal Seal. He handed the envelope over without comment.

Therron practically snarled as he ripped open the envelope, tearing the letter within out. Written this time in his father's own hand, this message informed him tersely that, yes, he was going to move his men toward the Gap at once, and without hesitation, or face the consequences. Therron's hands trembled in rage as he read.

"Trouble, milord?" General Davies' asked, walking into the tent which served as headquarters for the entire army. He also held a courier envelope, though it did not bear the royal seal.

"The King has ordered me to abandon you," Therron bit out, "and move east to assist my brother," he made the word sound like a curse, "at the Gap of Cumberland. Immediately."

"I suspected as much," Davies nodded, not surprised. "I just received a message from a detached militia unit. It's Colonel informs me that a large force has broken off from the main army and is, or was, currently headed for the Gap. The message took several days to find us."

"What?" Therron looked stunned.

"Colonel Chad estimates that the force numbers some fifty-plus thousand," Davies continued grimly, "and there is nothing to stand in their way once through the Gap. They can reach Nasil before we can."

"Are you certain of this, Davies?" Therron asked. "Is this Chad reliable? He is militia, after all, and not. . . ."

"He is a decorated soldier and a good one, milord," Davies managed to hold his tongue for the most part. "Well trained, too. If he sent this, he was sure of it."

Therron absorbed this without comment. It seemed that his idiot brother might well have stumbled upon a real battle, despite his being ordered to sit tight in his small fort. Well, he'd see about that once this war was over.

"Very well, then," Therron released a long breath. "I have my orders, whether I agree with them or not. Have you seen the pressure ease on your front at all?"

"It has weakened some," Davies agreed. "Especially in the last two to three days. It's almost as if they're tired. In all honesty it makes sense," he shrugged, "and we haven't gotten a good look at their numbers since the second day. As many of them as there are, it's entirely feasible that a large group could have slipped away and we'd not have noted it."

"I still think this move on the Gap is a feint," Therron insisted stubbornly, "every instinct I have tells me this is the main push, while the other attacks are meant to drain off manpower from your front. I'm going to compromise. I'll send two divisions toward the Gap, keeping the bulk of 1st Corps here."

"Milord," the Royal Courier tried to speak, but the Lord Marshall cut him off.

"I have made my decision," Therron spoke abruptly.

"The King will be displeased," the courier warned. As personal courier to the King, the man was more at liberty to speak than most. He carried the weight of the crown behind him. "His orders to you were quite specific."

"I don't need some delivery man to tell me my duty!" Therron screeched. "I'll prepare a response to the King's order, which I expect you to deliver."

"I will lay it in his hands myself," the courier nodded.

"Prepare the 6th Cavalry and the 5th Mounted Infantry for immediate movement to the Gap," Therron ordered Davies. "I want them on the way in one hour, if at all possible."

"Aye, milord," Davies sighed, full of misgiving. But Therron McLeod was the Lord Marshall. His word on the battlefield was law.

The Courier waited as Therron wrote a hasty reply to his father, and then, without so much as a "by your leave", mounted a fresh horse for his return to Nasil.

The King would not be happy.

-

Tammon McLeod twisted in his saddle, looking back at the column trailing his regiment. The line wasn't nearly as long as he wished…or needed.

Memmnon had stripped guards from every building in the city and turned out every company left in the area to raise the men following the King. Many of the troops were infantry and there had not been enough ready horses to mount them all. As a result several wagons were bumping along the trail behind the horses, pulling both men and equipment.

Tammon sighed as he turned back forward, shaking his head in distress. There was no way that this slow moving outfit would be able to reach the Gap in time to make a difference. Beside him, Enri Willard saw the King's discomfort.

"We'll make it, sire," he said softly, so that only the King could hear.

"I don't see how, Enri," Tammon replied. "We're moving too slow."

"It won't help them if we arrive too worn out to be of use, sire," Willard said reasonably. "We need to be ready to fight as soon as we get to the field."

"I know," Tammon nodded, "but I worry there won't be anyone left to help when we get there. If Parno's numbers are even close to accurate then he and the men with him are outnumbered ten-to-one or more."

"It is good terrain, sire," Willard offered, "and don't sell short your son. I know better than most," he grinned at that, "that Parno McLeod is nothing if not a fighter…and an uncanny one at that."

"Yes, he is," Tammon smiled sadly at that. Whatever Parno was, it had nothing to do with him, the King knew. For the first time in his life, that hurt. Sighing again, he looked down the trail before them.

"Let's try to pick up the speed a bit," he ordered. "An extra mile or two a day may make the difference."

-

Parno McLeod was starting to feel like a small boy, trying to throw water from a sinking boat. No matter what he tried it never seemed like enough.

The Nor had thrown yet another division into the attack, seeing that the first Soulan line had broken. Even as one fresh division neared the line, another emerged from the tree line, forming on the move. That made five divisions against three regiments and two battalions, plus another of literal volunteers.

The remnants of five divisions, he reminded himself, cheering a bit at that thought. His men had cut the heart out of at least three Nor divisions during the day and another the day before. They were hurting the Nor.

Just not enough.

"Lad, we're going to be sorely pressed, soon, I'm afraid," Darvo told him.

"I know," Parno agreed. "Have Captain Lars switch to regular shot for now," he ordered the artillery runner. He turned back to Darvo.

"I need to go and see Roda Finn for a moment, Darvo. I have an idea and he's been working on it. I need to see how far along he is with it. It might buy us a little time. If we can last out the day, I plan to withdraw to the third line after dark."

"Good," Darvo nodded. "I was going to suggest that. We need to shorten our lines and form a reserve. As it is now, we're dangerously thin."

"We'll make do," Parno patted the older man's shoulder. "Don't get killed while I'm gone," he added, grinning.

"I'm trying not to get killed at all," Darvo growled. "Off with you."

Parno hurried along past the third line and into the Fort itself. Going through the rear gate he went directly to the bunker where Finn's work was stored. He found the inventor outside, pacing back and forth, with a scrap of papyrus in his hands.

"Roda, have you figured out what we can do?" he called out before he even got close. Finn looked around him wildly for a second before spotting Parno. He sighed.

"I thought I was hearing things," he admitted, wiping his brow, "and yes, I have, milord, but it's not to your liking, I'm afraid. The best we can do, according to my estimates, is to hurl a half barrel of pitch some three hundred ninety yards. It's possible we'll get more, but that's the most I'm prepared to promise."

"I'll take it," Parno said at once. "Our situation is precarious to say the least. Our first line has fallen and the second in hard pressed."

"If the artillery has fallen back, then my estimate will be short of what. . . ." Finn began.

"The artillery is still in place for the time being," Parno cut him off, "but that won't last longer than today. We'll have to withdraw by evening. If I'm going to use the pitch and get the use I want from it, we have to do it now."

"It will require that the catapults be re-sprung, milord," Finn admitted hesitantly. "That will take at least a half-hour."

Parno cursed under his breath. He couldn't afford for the catapults to be out of action that long. He couldn't afford for them to be out of action half that long. He thought for bare seconds before making his decision.

"We'll use two catapults for the fire," he decided. "Go at once and inform Captain Lars what must be done. Are the barrels ready?"

"Yes, milord," Finn nodded. "Fifteen of them. There should be another ready by now, actually," he added.

"Have your men begin bringing whatever is ready forward. I want to be firing as soon as the catapults are prepared." Finn nodded and screeched for his assistant. Parno ignored them, looking at the sky. There was at least five hours of light left. His men had been fighting all morning, all day in fact—some of them since dawn.

If this idea worked it should at least slacken the efforts the Nor were making to add to their attack.

He turned and hurried back to the line, hoping that there was enough time.

-

Karls Willard walked the line behind his regiment, encouraging, exhorting, and checking on his men. He had never imagined being in command of the regiment like this. He had always assumed that when the time came for them to join in battle, Darvo Nidiad would lead them.

Circumstances had dictated otherwise, though, and now Willard found himself in true command for the first time in his life. He was also in a desperate battle against odds so great that the only possible outcome was defeat. He laughed silently at the irony.

His men had been on the line from the start and he marveled that they were still able to function, let alone do so effectively. He spared a glance at the other units down the line, seeing a real difference in the other troops. Cho Feng's conditioning had done wonders for the Black Sheep.

Black Sheep. Willard played that name over in his mind, smiling. The men themselves had taken that name, after the speech Parno himself had given the day he has informed the regiment of the impending war. They seemed to take great pride in it, and in the fact that they, the cast-offs, were performing even better than the regular troops, let alone the militia.

The men of Parno's Company had become hard and lean. They had taken well to their training once they had seen the seriousness of it, becoming a true fighting unit—one of the best Karls had ever seen. The young Colonel was convinced that without them the battle would have long been over. Numerous times during the day the Black Sheep had helped other units all along the line, their strength being great thanks to their rigid training regimen.

But they had paid a price of their own, Willard acknowledged to himself, sadly. The ranks of his regiment had thinned since this morning. Yet, the men showed a resilience he could only credit to their near fanatical devotion to Parno himself. Many of them were fighting on, even wounded. They had left the line long enough to be treated, then returned of their own free will, unwilling to abandon their brethren.

Sudden movement caught Willard's eye, drawing him from the minute of thought. A young Soulan trooper was battling three Nor troopers who had managed to gain the top of the second line. Willard jumped to help him.

Before he could get there, though, two other Black Sheep had already pounced on the Nor, cutting them down without pause. They covered the younger man, who had been injured, and then remained on the wall, taking his place. The youngster, bleeding from a deep cut on his arm, sank to the ground and began trying to wrap the wound himself, rather than go to the medics. He looked up, startled, as Willard's shadow fell over him.

"See the medic, trooper," Karls ordered. "Have that wound tended to."

"Ain't but a scratch, sir," the man grinned slightly. "I'll be back on the wall in a minute."

"We aren't likely to run out of Nor before you can have that properly bandaged and return, soldier," Willard smiled in spite of himself. "Have it seen to properly, then you can return, if you're able."

"Yes, sir," the man agreed, finally, rising to his feet. He set off to the aid station behind the line, where the slightly wounded could be tended without going to the over worked field hospital in the Fort. Willard shook his head, watching the man go.

"You two need help?" he called to the men who had rescued the other. One looked over his shoulder.

"We can take it, sir," he nodded. "Ain't but a few Nor, after all."

"Well said!" Willard replied, and the man grinned before turning back to the wall.

Willard resumed his inspection, wondering how long his men could keep this up and how long before they were all wounded, to some degree or another.

-

"What is it you're planning, lad?" Darvo asked, seeing Parno looking past the battle to the trees.

"I'm going to try and set the woods on fire," Parno admitted, lowering his glass and looking at Darvo. "They're using the trees as a marshaling point. I'm betting there's another division in there, right now, waiting to attack. If we can start a good-sized fire, maybe even threaten some of their supplies and equipment, it should take some of the pressure off of us, at least for a while."

"And if they ignore it?" Darvo asked calmly.

"Then I've wasted a few shots of pitch," Parno shrugged. "I think it will work. It hasn't rained here in several days. The sun and the wind have dried the effects of the rains. Everything is dry. Dusty, even. If we can loft enough pitch far enough then the woods should burn nicely. With luck, it might even spread to their camps. I'll take whatever I can get at the moment," he added. "Desperate times call for desperate measures."

"It's worth a try," Darvo admitted. "We're getting more pressure on the right," he pointed. Parno looked to where Landers was rallying his men to throw back a troop of Nor who had managed to gain the top of the barricade and berm.

"Landers will take care of it," Parno replied, confidently. "He's a good man."

"With tired troops," Darvo pointed out. "He could use some help."

"There's none to send him, at the moment," Parno shrugged, then paused. "Send Moore's men down there. They can pick off the Nor as they get atop the berm. That will help."

"Good thinking," Darvo nodded, and sent a runner on his way with order to do just that. The artillery runner appeared.

"Captain Lars reports ready on catapults three and five for the pitch, milord," he informed Parno breathlessly.

"Tell him to open fire at once," Parno ordered eagerly, "and to spread the fire several degrees with each shot, left to his discretion. I want the maximum spread possible and tell him that the faster he can fire, the better." The runner snapped a bow and left.

It was three anxious minutes before Parno saw the first smoking half-barrels sail over his head. He kept his eye on the two all the way to the tree line, flinching in disappointment when they fell just a few feet short of the woods.

"Not enough," Parno murmured. "I need them inside the tree line." It required the greatest exercise in patience to wait for the next salvo. Men frantically cranked at the catapults, readying them for another shot, while more men wrestled the next half-barrel into place. As soon as it was on the bowl, a man touched the torch to it, lighting it afire. Seconds later it was airborne and sailing toward the enemy.

Parno again followed them with his own eyes, not even daring to blink as they traveled the distance. One crashed just into the tree line, starting a small fire. But the other traveled past the trees and crashed into the woods themselves. Flames instantly sprang from the pitch and Parno could see several tree tops aflame in addition to the fire on the ground.

"Yes!" he shouted, elated. "Let's have some more like that!"

Over the next few minutes, three more flights of half-barrels sailed over the battlefield. One fell short, causing no damage other than to set fire to trees already on the ground. Another fell inside the line, spreading fire all along the ground. Still another flamed out entirely, spreading raw pitch over a good part of the woods, but without the fire.

The other three carried well over the tree line and into the woods, shattering against old growth trees, and raining fire everywhere. Even as Lars prepared another salvo, Parno watched as the flames literally exploded, quickly growing on the dry fuel of the woods and the leaves beneath.

"Look, lad!" Darvo pointed, one hand still on his glass. "You were right!" Parno adjusted his glass down and saw immediately what had gotten Darvo's attention.

The Nor had been massing a new attack inside the trees. Parno could see man shaped figures, now awash in flames, running through the trees, spreading flames even as they ran. Some of the flaming pitch had landed squarely on troops preparing to enter the battle, setting them ablaze along with the trees and brush.

Parno swallowed at that, imagining how horrible it must be in those woods. He had unleashed that hell himself.

You had no choice, he reminded himself doggedly. They invaded your home, killed your people. They're to blame for this, not you.

"It's war, young Prince," Cho Feng spoke almost in his ear. "If you cannot bear the result, you should not start a war. You are defending your people and are not the aggressor. This is the price they pay for belligerence."

Parno nodded at that, not trusting himself to speak. What Cho said was true but that didn't change the facts. He continued to watch in silence as the flames spread, great columns of smoke rising into the sky. Thankfully, no more human torches were visible and the din of the battle kept the screaming of the burning men from reaching his ears, but it was easy enough to imagine.

As the minutes past, the battle began to ebb. Parno didn't notice it at first, so intent was he on the fires, but Darvo did. He examined the line and noted that the Nor were actually beginning to pull back, heading toward their own lines. Whether to help with the fire or using it as an excuse to escape the battle, he didn't know…or care.

Gradually the other Nor noticed this and they too began to pull back. Slowly at first, as if reluctant to give up their advantage, then faster and faster.

Ten minutes later, the front was quiet again.

There was no cheering this time. No one had the energy.

-

"Let's start moving the men, Darvo," Parno said quietly. The flames across the battlefield had spread, even now burning their way across the ridge to the front and down into the valley beyond. The valley where Parno suspected the Nor had their camps.

Good riddance

"Are you sure, lad?" Darvo asked. "There's still enough light for them to try again."

"They won't try again, not today," Parno sighed. "It'll take them the rest of the night to get straightened out, I'd imagine. We'll leave a force here to watch and give warning, but I want everyone else, and everything else, behind the third line before dark."

"There's a lot of equipment to move and a lot of wounded to carry out. The men need rest and food. Let's see to them while we can so that they can rest tonight. They'll need it tomorrow. The Nor will come calling with blood in their eyes after this."

Darvo took one more look at the fires blazing out of control on the other side of the pass, and nodded.

"I'd say you're right. Very well, lad. I'll get things moving."

Parno watched him go, lacking the will, or the energy to follow.

He had won. For now.

-

It was nearing darkness when Parno stumbled over to his own small camp. His steward had already prepared his meal and Parno sat heavily in his camp chair, eating without really tasting his food. He was hungry, but had no desire to eat.

The tally of dead and wounded had come in and the news was not good. Landers regulars, the 11th Soulan Cavalry, had suffered nearly thirty percent losses. Theirs had been the unit nearly over run when the ballista had exploded, creating a hole for the Nor to exploit. The two militia battalions had suffered nearly as much, both losing nearly twenty-five percent of their number.

Chad's men had fared better, with losses of just under ten percent, as they had not seen any fighting early on. The Provisional Battalion had escaped with only fifteen percent losses, which Parno thought was extraordinary, considering.

His own men had lost roughly eighteen percent of their fighting strength. Unlike the other units, however, Parno's regiment was still in good shape. Thanks to a very rigid training regimen, the Black Sheep, (he still smiled every time he thought of that name), were far tougher than the other troops. But they had also been fighting since before dawn.

After withdrawing from the second line, Parno had decided to place Chad's men, along with the Provisional Battalion and the 12th Tinsee Militia Cavalry, on the line to start the day. He would allow Landers' regulars and the 8th Mounted to form a reserve along with the Black Sheep.

The reserve would be behind the line, out of direct combat, but every archer in those units would be pressed into service, firing over the line into the Nor masses.

The third line was more compact. Located at the start of the narrowest part of the Gap, the line was one hundred yards shorter than the first and second had been and was anchored into the rock walls on either side. Darvo had taken great care with this line's construction, as well, knowing that it would be the best defensive position of all. There was a slight grade for the Nor to climb as they tried to attack, which would help, and the range of Soulan artillery and arrows would be aided by the grade, if only slightly. At this point, Parno would take all the help he could get.

"Evening, milord," Karls Willard called as he walked into the light of the fire.

"Hello, Karls," Parno smiled. "How are you?"

"I'm well, milord, thank you. How are you?" Parno could hear the concern in Karls' voice.

"I'm good," he assured the young Colonel. "How are the men?"

"Ready to go, believe it or not," Karls shook his head. "They take great pride in the fact that they are in better shape than the 'real' soldiers and, honestly, they are. Ready to go, I mean. I've never seen men more able, I think. You did well, milord."

"We did well, my friend," Parno corrected gently. "There's more than me involved in this. You, Darvo, Cho, everyone who helped train and prepare them. They've made me proud. All of you have."

"We don't want to disappoint you, milord," Karls said sincerely. "They were wondering why they were to be in the reserve tomorrow," he added, eying Parno closely.

"I want them rested," Parno said bluntly. "They are in better shape and better prepared than the rest. Tomorrow's fight will be ugly, I fear, after what I did this afternoon. The Nor will be out for blood come morning. If they manage to break the line, I want the Sheep ready to fall on them and hopefully close any holes in the line."

"I'll pass that along," Karls smiled. "It will make them happy to hear it."

"We've managed to do well, today," Parno said suddenly. "If we had only one brigade of troops or even just two more regiments to call upon I would feel confident of outright victory. As it is," he shook his head, "I think we can hold tomorrow and perhaps the day after."

"We might surprise you, milord," Karls ventured, though he felt the same way himself. "And we've definitely bloodied their noses."

"That we have," Parno nodded thoughtfully. "Even if they manage to overrun us and get loose into the valley, we have so weakened them that a single cavalry division, well led, should be able to run them to ground."

"Well, that's what we were fighting for," Karls noted. "Anything beyond that is just icing."

"True enough," Parno chuckled. "I just wish I could see a way for some of us to live through it. That would make it a true victory."

"If it helps us win the war, then it's a true victory, even if none of us live to see it," Karls replied solemnly. "That's the important thing. That Soulan lives."

"Yes," Parno agreed. "That is the important thing."

"You two look like something the cat drug up," Darvo Nidiad said lightly, walking up to the fire with a plate in hand.

"You don't look any better, sir," Karls shot back, grinning.

"I'm not as young as you children," Darvo sniffed. "Man my age has a right to look a bit long after a day like this. You two, though, ought to be fresh as daisies on a spring morn."

"I am," Parno replied with a straight face. "So long as the daisies have been trampled underfoot by a herd of stampeding cattle, that is." All three men laughed at that and it made them all feel better. Cho Feng joined them as the laughter was dying down.

"When one can laugh, then all is not lost," he smiled. "I see that you are all in high spirits."

"Might as well be," Darvo shrugged philosophically. "Not much we can do, otherwise."

"True," Cho nodded. "You all did very well, today. I am very proud to be a part of your company. I have never seen better fighting, nor better leadership."

"It wasn't that great," Parno remarked. "We lost the first two lines on the very first day of battle."

"No," Cho objected. "You lost one and surrendered the second for a better position. You have also made the enemy pay a heavy price for the little ground he did gain today. You have no reason to feel badly, Parno. You and your men have done great things this day. Far better than you had any right to expect."

"I agree," Darvo added, talking around a mouthful of food. "We did do well, lad. We've butchered the Nor today at every hand's turn, and with just a fraction of their strength." He put his now empty plate down.

"I've ordered some scouts out to see if they can find out what damage the fire may have done to the Nor and I've ordered the fires lit again. Captain Moore's men slipped out this evening, early, and moved the last of the mines as well."

"Good," Parno looked shocked at that. He hadn't even thought of those things.

"Well, I get by," Darvo smirked. "I still don't entirely trust those wizard gimmicks of Finn's, but I have to admit they have made the difference. Without them, we couldn't have held out as long as we did."

"We may have to learn to get by without them," Parno said sourly. "We're using them faster than I'd hoped. Over half of what we had ready are gone and Finn has only been able to replace about half of what we've used. We should be okay for tomorrow," he added, seeing Darvo's concern. "After that, we'll have to see."

"After tomorrow I doubt they'll make much difference, lad," the old soldier said softly. "If we suffer as many casualties tomorrow as we did today, we'll not be able to hold this line, nor likely the last, either."

"Then we might as well use up everything tomorrow, right?" Karls asked brightly. "No sense in wasting them."

"Ah, the enthusiasm of youth," Darvo's sarcasm was thick. He looked to Cho. "Have you ever seen the like?"

"Age brings wisdom, it is true," Cho smiled, "but without the strength of youth, the wisdom is less usable, I'm afraid." Darvo guffawed at that.

"I think that's the best way I've ever heard that put!"

-

Most of the fires were out.

General Brasher looked at what remained of his camp, anger coursing through his very bones. Just when he'd been sure of victory the enemy had launched the pitch, catching his next division in the process of marshaling for a follow-up attack.

Sure victory snatched from him in the blink of an eye. The fires had spread wildly and many of his men now lay in the woods, little more than ash. Most of the division he had been about to commit to battle had died in the blaze as had many others.

"Sir." Brasher turned at the sound of his second in command.

"Report," he said dully.

"We've managed to put out the majority of the fires," came the hesitant reply. "But… sir… we've... we lost more than half our train, sir. Most of our supplies are gone as well as a goodly supply of arrows. Horse fodder and tack, farrowing equipment, almost all is a total loss."

"Have the wagon train commander executed for incompetence," Brasher ordered.

"He. . .sir… he died fighting the fire."

"Execute his deputy, then!" Brasher demanded.

"Yes, sir." The man knew better than to object. Brasher looked at him.

"I want every man still able to draw a sword or a bow ready to attack one hour before dawn." Brasher's voice betrayed his rage. "Every man. Any wounded who are able to walk will join the attack as well. I want every possible man on that field by sun-up, beating down those damn defenses, and I want that entire rabble slaughtered to a man. Am I clear?"

"Yes, sir," his second nodded. "I'll see to it at once."

"Go."

Brasher watched the man run away, snorting in disgust. He was surrounded by incompetents. The Emperor would be furious at this loss and likely take it out upon Brasher himself.

Only a victory now could save him…and that was uncertain.

But he would have victory if it cost him the lives of every man under his command. Soulan would fall, and he, Brasher, would do his part in seeing it happen.

# CHAPTER TWENTY-SEVEN

-

Parno was up long before sunup, walking the line, inspecting his defenses. Most of his troopers were still asleep. Cooks were working already, preparing a hot meal for the men. It would be the last meal for many of them, Parno knew. Maybe for all of them.

It would be today, Parno knew. He hadn't bothered sharing that with anyone. There was no point. His men and his commanders had great confidence that they would hold, but Parno knew better. The Commander across the field would be furious after the fire, with blood in his eye and on his mind.

In his place, Parno would muster every last man capable of carrying a sword or drawing a bow and carry the fort by sheer weight of numbers.

He expected no less from his opponent.

"Good morning, my Prince," Cho Feng's soft voice carried to him. Parno turned to see Cho wearing his own armor this morning, two slim swords strapped across his back. He frowned at that.

"Good morning, Master Feng," he tried to smile. "You're looking rather military this morning."

"Today will be different, I think," Cho shrugged casually. "I thought it best to be prepared for that."

"You know, then?" Parno said, eying his teacher closely.

"One last day, Parno," Cho smiled. "One last day of glory. Yes, I know."

"You don't seem worried about it," Parno smiled crookedly and Cho returned it.

"There is no need of worry. One's fate is not always in his hands."

"You could leave, you know," Parno said softly. "No one would blame you. This isn't really your. . . ."

"Don't finish that, Parno," Cho warned, his voice hard. "I have trained you and your men. I have worked with you, ate and slept with you, and rode with you. This is now my land as well as your own. If I were to leave then I would blame me, no matter what anyone else said."

"I know," Parno sighed. "I just didn't want this to be how you were repaid after all you've done for me."

"My payment has been my freedom and the opportunity to see my hard work come to fruition."

"Fair enough," the young prince smiled. "Will you walk with me? I need to have a look at the lines while there is time. I don't expect to get the chance, later on."

"I will." Cho replied.

The two walked together then, master and novice, teacher and pupil, in silence.

-

Darvo and Karls were seated at Parno's campfire eating when Parno and Cho returned from the inspection. Both looked up as the other two came walking in.

"Mornin' lad," Darvo spoke around a mouthful of bread. "Cho."

"Morning," Parno replied, while Cho nodded in greeting. "The line looks good. I think we'll do okay for at least a while." Parno and Cho accepted a tray of food each from a steward and settled in to eat.

"This line's some shorter," Karls agreed, "and it's anchored good. We put a bit of extra effort into this one, as the Colonel thought this would be our best place to make a strong stand."

"I concur," Cho nodded. "This is very good ground. Ideal for a force so small as ours."

"You look some different than usual, Master Feng," Karls noted. "Nice armor."

"I thought that it might come in handy," Cho explained. "No sense in missing out on everything." Karls chuckled quietly at that. Parno looked at his youngest subordinate.

"How are the men?" he asked.

"Ready," Karls nodded. "They're quiet, but confident. I think they know that this is probably it today. They're concerned, of course, but unafraid. Or at least," he added, "they aren't letting their fear rule them. They know what's at stake and they don't want to let you down, either."

"They've already made sure of that," Parno smiled wanly. "I couldn't be more proud of them. I fear they'll bear the brunt of the fighting today before all is said and done."

"They'll like that," Karls smiled. "So will I. When you need us, milord, we'll be there."

"I know." Parno fell quiet for a moment and all of them ate in silence for a time. When he finished, Parno looked at his three friends.

These men were his family. They had believed in him when no one else did or would. They had helped him build his regiment, something that was meant to be a joke, into a force of fighting men that literally had no equal in the Kingdom. Each, in his own way, had contributed to that work something that Parno could not have.

Cho had taught them sword work that was far beyond what most Soulan soldiers were capable of and had taught them lessons of war learned through experiences that even Darvo couldn't match. He had also trained them physically, giving them all the conditioning that made them tough, rugged soldiers, capable of fighting on any terrain.

Karls had brought them enthusiasm and instilled a sense of pride among the men by his own conduct. Through him and his men the Black Sheep had learned what it was to be a professional soldier and to take pride in it. They had also learned the importance of camaraderie and team work, to place the unit above themselves.

And then there was Darvo Nidiad.

Parno sighed as he contemplated the man who had been more like a father to him than a mentor. It was Darvo who had taught him how to be a man. Who had helped him survive in a hostile environment, surrounded by a father who despised him and by siblings who, more often than not, had wished him dead.

It was Darvo who kept him from worse trouble than he'd managed to get himself into and who had picked up the pieces when Parno had failed to live up to what he'd been taught. It was Darvo that he had gone to when afraid or alone. Darvo had always been there when Parno needed him.

"I want you all to know," he spoke quietly, "that I have never had better friends, better family, than the three of you. You have all helped me to become a better man and a fair leader of men. I wish. . . ." Parno trailed off then, unsure how to say what he felt. These men, so dear to him, would probably die today. Try as he might, Parno simply could not see a way to prevent that.

"Parno," Cho spoke just as quietly. "We know what you feel. You wear it plainly upon you, for those of us who know you well." Darvo and Karls nodded in silent agreement.

"You grieve for what's comin' lad," Darvo spoke then. "Want some way to make this unnecessary, but there is none. This had to be done. We all knew coming here that it could only end one way. We came anyway. You aren't to blame for this."

"I've been soldier since I was old enough to join the army," Karls told him. "It's all I know, all I've ever done, but until I was assigned to you, milord, I didn't know what it meant to be a true soldier. A man willing to sacrifice everything for the cause of his people and his land. That, I learned from you."

Parno looked at each man in turn, wondering as he had countless times, how he deserved their loyalty.

"I'm indebted to you all," he told them. "If this is the way it has to be then I couldn't ask for better company. Thank you." The four of them sat in silence for a moment. The spell was broken only when Landers and the other commanders approached the fire for their morning meeting.

"I won't mince words, gentlemen," Parno said a few moments later as everyone gathered around him. "We aren't likely to live out the day. You know that as well as I do." The assembled men nodded grimly.

"What we have done, these past few days, has bought precious time for our land. Time for the army to shift in order to meet this threat. More than that, we have bloodied the enemy well, weakened them with our stand here. When the army is able to meet them they won't be near the threat they were just five days or even two days ago. We have done what we set out to do."

"I'm proud to be here with you. I'm honored to be among you…and this Kingdom is blessed to have you." He paused as the men took in what he had said.

"Everyone has their assignments," he said at last. "We've managed to shorten our lines and create a reserve. Our men are packed tight, behind a strong position. Captain Lars," he looked at the artillery officer, "we'll depend on you a great deal today, especially to prevent their artillery from becoming a factor." The man nodded gravely, accepting that responsibility with a calm air.

"All archers will be engaged from the start," Parno informed them. "The reserve will fire over the barricades from blind ambush so it will fall to the front line commanders to spot for them, shifting their fire as needed. If the enemy pack in tight, and I expect he will, then all archers will fall back off the line as soon as the enemy begins to reach our barricades. All swordsmen will go to the line and repel the Nor while the archers continue to thin their follow-on ranks. Captain Moore, your men will hit the first rank of mines when the Nor's third line reaches it. Hit the last as soon as the fifth rank files in or before the enemy can obscure them, whichever comes first." Moore likewise nodded his understanding.

"If Soulan survives this war, it will be in large part because of what we've done here today. Don't forget that, and don't let your men forget it, either. Are there any questions?" There were none. Today didn't require much in the way of instruction.

"Then take your posts, gentlemen, and Godspeed." The men hesitated for a moment and Parno frowned. What was wrong?

"Sir," Landers spoke then. "The men asked me to speak for everyone, milord," he explained. "We. . .we wanted you to know, Parno McLeod, of the House McLeod, that we are honored to have fought by your side. We will proudly carry your banner today and give for it the last full measure of ourselves in its service. We have never served a finer officer, sir." As one man, the group of commanders slowly saluted. Parno looked at them for a long moment, then drew himself erect and returned their honor.

"Thank you, gentlemen," he said softly.

"Everyone to your posts," Landers ordered, and the men filed away, heading into the darkness to prepare their commands.

"Good bye, Parno," Karls waited until the others had gone. "Die well." Parno took his hand, then embraced him as well.

"And you, Karls. And you." The younger man then followed the others into the dark, leaving only Cho and Darvo with him.

"Well, I don't aim to hug you," Darvo sniffed airily. Parno laughed.

"Nor do I," Cho smiled, a soft and knowing smile. "It is unseemly."

"C'mon, you two," Parno started for the smaller tower that had been erected during the night. It was almost time.

-

Across the field, Norland's General Brasher looked at his men, even now forming in line of battle out of sight of the small fort in the Gap. He frowned as he recalled his second's review of their line of battle.

After the first two days battle and the fire the night before the Norland 3rd Field Army could field slightly less than twenty-five thousand men, roughly half of his original force.

Brasher swore violently at that realization. A pitiful handful of southern soldiers had decimated his once proud fighting force, using the terrain and their sorcery to kill and maim his men as they tried to carry the enemy position.

His men had suffered greatly, though Brasher was less concerned with their suffering than with the loss to his strength. Many of his men still lived but were so horribly maimed that they would never again be useful to Norland. Men missing limbs, blinded by fragments of those barbarous weapons, and burned beyond recognition. All of them lay even now in crowded tent hospitals or on the ground outside the overflowing tents.

"We're almost into line, sir," his second appeared out of the dark, carrying a shielded battle lantern. "Ten more minutes and we'll be ready to advance."

"Fine," Brasher nodded curtly. "I want the men to maintain complete silence. Have their officers strip the men of anything that might rattle or might trip them up. I want us to advance under cover of darkness. Get as close as we can to their wall before sun-up. In fact, if we can hit their wall before sun-up, that would be even better."

"Very good, sir," the other man replied. "I'll see to it at once."

Brasher watched him depart, then turned his gaze south toward the Gap. He would throw everything he had at the Southrons today. Every man who was able to move under his own power.

Today, the line would break under the weight of his troops.

Once that was done, he would mount every able-bodied man on horseback and head straight for the Soulan capital of Nasil, capturing it. With their capital gone, the southerners would break and he, Brasher, would be hailed as a hero of Norland. His failure to break the Gap yesterday would lie forgotten under the lapel of victory in Nasil. In fact, the hard-fought battle might even add to his stature, proving him as a man who would not fail even under the most adverse of conditions.

Yes. Today would be a day of glory.

He smiled at that thought, even as his troops began moving forward. He watched carefully, satisfied that, for once, his orders were being followed. Men moved quietly, seeming to glide over the ground rather than make contact with it. Anyone who made noise during the advance would be executed on the spot by his order. He wanted nothing to warn the southerners that he was coming.

Coming to destroy them all.

-

Soulan scouts were spread all over the battlefield, watching and listening for anything that might indicate that the Nor were coming in the dark. Prince Parno had instructed them himself, warning them that the duty was as important as it was hazardous. They had taken his warnings to heart and were lying quiet and still.

Once scout was far afield, having crawled carefully out on his belly some one hundred yards to the front of the original battle line. Anthony Felds had been raised in the mountains of Eastern Tinsee and had been taught the value of stillness and patience from the time he was able to walk.

As he lay in the dark, eyes long accustomed to hunting in the dark scanned the field before him. He knew that he was the farthest out of all the scouts, having heard the others as they fell out of line to take up positions. His senses were strained now as he controlled his breathing, working to keep his own heartbeat from hammering in his ears. Suddenly he stiffened slightly and raised his head.

Until this instant, he had been hearing the chirping of crickets and night fowl as they prowled the battlefield. Burned over ground and fallen soldiers had left easy pickings for them and they had returned during the night after the battle had ended.

Now they had gone silent. Felds knew that only one thing would cause that.

Suddenly he heard a flock of birds take flight to his front, catching a fleeting glimpse of their outlines against the sky. A muffled exclamation carried to him, followed by a groan and the sound of a body hitting the ground.

The Nor were coming.

Felds turned at once and began to make his way back to the lines. He worked his way carefully through the obstacles of fallen timber and fallen bodies until he was within fifty yards of the lines, then stood in a crouch, running silently over the ground. As he went he gave a warbling cry, mimicking a night bird's call. Replies came from all around as the other scouts acknowledged his call and likewise began making their way back.

The Nor would find Soulan ready and waiting when they came to call.

-

"You're certain, lad?" Darvo Nidiad asked Felds. The young man nodded quickly.

"Aye, Colonel. They're coming. No idea of the number, but it's a flock of 'em, sure enough."

"Well done, boy," Darvo clapped the young man on the shoulder. "Get to your unit, then." Felds beamed at the compliment and hurried to rejoin his outfit. Darvo turned to Parno.

"What about it, lad?" Parno turned to the artillery runner.

"Order Captain Lars to launch the pitch with the first volley, then open up with special rounds until further notice." The young man bowed quickly in acknowledgment and ran to obey. Parno turned to the other runners.

"Pass the word, Nor are advancing. Quickly now!" The others scattered to their respective areas carrying the Prince's orders.

Parno, Darvo, and Cho remained on the small tower, waiting for the battle to join. The wait wasn't long. Sounds of artillery pieces being fired echoed across the line and half-barrels of flaming pitch sailed overhead on their way to the Nor lines.

The flaming pitch fell deep inside the lines of the advancing enemy, illuminating the entire area. Parno looked on in shock at the sheer number of troops arrayed against him.

"They aren't playing today, lad," Darvo said grimly. "He's hitting us with everything at once." Parno nodded. The three watched in silence as once again Nor troops scattered, many aflame with the pitch that had covered them. Orders were bellowed down the line as Soulan archers were ordered to prepare to fire.

The artillery cycled quickly and another salvo sailed over the line toward the enemy. This time instead of fire a line of explosions walked its way across the Nor troops, falling farther along the battlefield into the follow-on ranks. Parno had ordered Lars to concentrate his fire not on the front ranks, but on those coming up in support. It would fall to his soldiers to halt those Nor who reached the line.

As the first exploding rounds fell behind them, the front ranks of the Nor advance, still recovering from the effect of the pitch, were hit by thousands of arrows as the first volley of archery fire swept their ranks. Though the darkness and the distance prevented accurate aimed fire, the Nor were packed in so tight that it was hard to miss. Several of the enemy were struck by more than one arrow, but the front ranks were cut up badly by the volley. Another was on the way before the first had finished its flight.

"We're in it now," Darvo's comment was almost lost as another, more ragged volley of artillery took flight. Faster crews were getting their shots off quicker than some of their counter parts, but all the rounds were aimed at a particular point along the battlefield so the effect was not diminished greatly.

"So we are," Parno replied. He felt almost sick looking across the fire illuminated ground before him, seeing tens of thousands of enemy soldiers coming toward his thin lines.

We'll never last the day, he thought gloomily. We'll be lucky to last the morning.

But his troopers were fighting hard. Flight after flight of arrows sailed into the oncoming horde of enemy and the artillery continued to loft Roda Finn's 'bombs' into the following ranks.

No one had thought to tell the Soulan troops that they couldn't do the impossible.

-

Across the way General Brasher cursed as his plan fell apart. He didn't know what had happened but the southern line had known his men were coming. His men had been attacked before getting even half way across the distance between themselves and the Soulan lines.

He watched through his glass as him men fought to continue against the southern wizardry and archery. His men fell in windrows, lying in heaps like wheat to be harvested, but they were still pushing. Still moving forward. The butcher's bill for this would be higher than he'd hoped and while he didn't care about the lives of his individual soldiers, he needed enough of them to continue his campaign.

If they were quick enough, broke through fast enough, then he would have his ultimate victory. Either way, this outpost would fall.

-

The sun was beginning to light the eastern sky into dawn as Parno watched the battle unfold before him. Even as he watched Moore's men rose up, launching their bolts at the first line of mines. The newly reorganized Nor lines were ripped again as forty-one of the clay jars exploded in their midst, showering the troops near them with iron shards. Other crossbow armed archers were on the wall now, firing directly into the front ranks of the oncoming horde whilst their longbow armed companions continued to shower those behind with arrows. Moore's men quickly reloaded and awaited their next command to fire. Once the last mines were detonated they would join the others shooting individual Nor soldiers.

Even as the Nor tried to reform Moore's men rose again and hit the last group. The effect was instantaneous. Those Nor in the front ranks who had survived to this point were routed and turned to flee. Many, if not most, were cut down by their own men. Parno shrugged mentally at that. He didn't care what stopped them, so long as they were stopped.

"We're getting our licks in, anyway," Darvo noted, his eyes scanning the battlefield. "They're already routing up front and they've not even reached the lines yet."

"That won't last," Parno predicted. "They'll keep coming."

"Aye," Darvo nodded grimly, "but they'll pay for it."

And pay they did.

Flight after flight of arrows soared across the Soulan line, landing among the struggling Nor. Soulan artillery lofted round after round against those out of bow-shot, tearing into follow on ranks. Parno felt a brief surge of hope as the battle raged and still the Nor were largely kept off the line. A few hardy Nor managed to reach the barricades at times, only to be put down by crossbow or sword.

"I think we've. . . ." Darvo's comment was cut off as several large boulders hit the Soulan lines. Landing behind the barricades, the stones wreaked havoc on the bowline, crushing dozens of men as they went.

The Nor artillery had taken the field. Parno's glass flew to his eye as he strained to see the enemy position in the dim light.

"Order Lars to engage that artillery!" Darvo screamed over the cries of pain and confusion around them. A runner took off in the direction of the artillery, but Lars had already made provisions for this.

Four catapults had remained silent during the battle, unengaged. Now Lars went to those crews and issued swift orders. Within seconds, two half-barrels of pitch and two exploding rounds were on their way across the battlefield. Arcing high above the enemy troops, these rounds landed on or near the Nor artillery, peppering them with the blazing pitch and iron shards from the bombs. Two Nor artillery pieces were destroyed outright, with another one heavily damaged. Still another was awash in flames.

"That was fast," Darvo murmured, but another Nor salvo was on its way and once again oversize boulders and a shower of smaller rocks rained down on the Soulan troopers. Parno could only watch in fury as his men were now on the receiving end of the same hell he himself had unleashed on his opponent's men.

Medics and hospital bearers hurried among the fallen, looking for those who still lived. There were far too few of them as the heavy boulders left little life in their path.

Lars launched another return salvo, but the shots were not nearly so effective as the first, having been laid in haste. One Nor catapult took the brunt of two exploding rounds, while another caught one half-barrel. The other fell harmlessly between the enemy artillery crews.

"Damn it!" Parno swore. "Have Lars direct more fire at the enemy artillery," he ordered a runner. "If we don't knock them off line soon, they're going to tear us apart."

But Lars had his own troubles. A new volley of Nor artillery walked through the rear of the Soulan position, striking the artillery area. In under a minute Lars had lost three catapults and two trebuchets, effectively cutting his firepower by one third.

Yet the artillery men were not deterred by the loss of their fellows. With scarcely a missed beat, their pieces let fly, again lofting rounds high over the Soulan lines and far down field. Half the rounds were exploding, the other half flaming pitch. As soon as the rounds were launched, Lars ordered everything reloaded with boulders. Even as the new volley of fire reached out for the enemy, hands frantically cranked pieces back into firing position.

This time, their aim was better.

The Nor still had over twenty pieces of artillery in operation against the Soulan lines, despite their earlier losses and those of this morning. The Soulan rounds fell among them with a vengeance.

Half of the Nor artillery was destroyed outright as machines broke and buckled. Several were set ablaze as pitch barrels landed squarely atop catapults or trebuchets. Even where the piece itself failed to ignite, the ropes used to fire the heavy artillery pieces were burned through and the tar-soaked ropes burned hot enough to ignite the wood.

The remainder of the Nor artillery was damaged to one degree or another, as iron shards cut ropes and killed crews. Flaming pitch set fires all around the positions and splashed across artillery men. Worse, the Nor had been about to launch a round of pitch themselves.

As General Brasher watched in silent fury, a Nor artillery man, burning like a beacon on the coast, stumbled into the barrels of pitch setting ready to fire. One was knocked over, spreading pitch everywhere among the barrels. In seconds the entire supply was ablaze, the heat enough to sear nearby crews and melt or damage the iron parts on the Nor catapults and trebuchets.

"That's givin' it to 'em!" Darvo yelled in delight. Parno looked over at his mentor grinning only to see Darvo Nidiad looking down at a Nor arrow protruding from his chest, as if wondering how it had gotten there.

"Lad?"

"Darvo!" Parno screamed, grabbing the older man as he collapsed. He lowered Darvo carefully to the floor.

"Get a stretcher!" he screamed at the runners. Half of them ran off in a bunch to retrieve a stretcher.

"Can't. . .leave the battle, boy," Darvo gasped. "Men n. . .need direction."

"They can do fine until I see you cared for," Parno said sternly.

"Get back to your post, boy!" Darvo ordered harshly. "You'll see more than me fall before this day is gone. Your job is to lead. Now lead!"

Parno blinked at Darvo's harsh tone.

"He tells you what is true," Cho said softly, kneeling by Darvo's other side. "You cannot help him. You can help your men, young Prince. You must do your duty. I will watch over him until the doctor arrives."

"Have me carried down," Darvo objected. "Get me out of here and make him run this battle."

"I. . .I can't, Darvo," Parno almost whispered. "I'm not you. I don't. . . ."

"Shut that talk!" Darvo cut him off. "You've been doin' it! You just won't have me to fall back on now so make sure you do things right the first time. Now you get ba. . .back on that line, before I kick your pompous little ass!" Darvo was struggling to breath now and blood flecked around his mouth.

"You must get back," Cho ordered, more sternly than before. "He is killing himself talking to you. Return to your post, Prince of Soulan."

Parno hesitated for another second or two, looking from one man to the other. He realized that Darvo was right. He couldn't leave the battle with no direction and

Cho was right that there was nothing that he, Parno, could do for Darvo's wound.

"All right," he sighed. "I. . .you take care, Darvo. You have to have permission to die."

"Think th. . .that might be bey. . .yond what you ca. . .can make happen, son," Darvo almost smiled. "You watch yourself." With that Parno nodded and motioned for the runners to get the Colonel off the tower.

"Be easy and carry him to the Fort. Have Doctor Corsin see to him as soon as she's found." With that, Parno turned his attention back to the battle before him.

He had work to do.

-

Tammon McLeod resisted the mighty urge to bellow in anger as he once more turned to see the slow-moving column behind him. They were near the Gap, now. Perhaps twenty miles distant at most. He seethed with the slowness of the movement, though he knew that the wagons were doing their best in the rough terrain. Enri Willard watched his King for a moment.

"Milord, we're moving fairly well. . . ." he started.

"I know," Tammon cut him off, "and I have not said anything, Enri. I am just anxious."

"I know, sire," Willard nodded in sympathy. "I. . . ." he trailed off as he heard a distant rumble. Instinctively, he looked toward the sky.

"Was that thunder?" Tammon asked, also looking skyward.

"I. . .I don't know, sire," Enri admitted, his voice puzzled as he scanned the sky. "I can't see a cloud anywhere in the sky but it did sound like. . . ." Once more Willard trailed off as the rumble was heard again and this time a slight tremble was felt for just a second.

"An earthquake?" Tammon's voice revealed his puzzlement.

"I don't think so, sire," Willard shrugged helplessly. "Surely a shaker would not be so intermittent and would last longer." Tammon nodded in thoughtful agreement.

"Then what in blazes are we hearing?"

Willard had no answer for that. McLeod turned suddenly, beckoning to the Lieutenant commanding the first troop in the line. The young man raced to his King.

"Milord?"

"Take your men and patrol ahead," Tammon ordered. "See if you can determine the source of that. . .whatever that was." The young man nodded his head slightly in respect, then raced away. In less than a minute his men were following him down the trail, heading out away from the column at a good gait.

"Enri, ride back along the column," Tammon said suddenly. "We're picking up the pace. Everyone is to keep up as best they can, but we're moving. I want us into the Gap no later than nightfall. Before if possible."

"Yes, Milord," Willard inclined his head and hurried to inform the column.

Restless and angry, Tammon McLeod resumed his march to relieve his son.

-

"Milord, Captain Lars' compliments and we are down to three salvos of the special rounds. He wished to know if you want him to save them or use them now."

Parno sighed at the news, looking to the sky. It was only about noon and that meant several hours of light remained. He had known that he was using too many of Roda's bombs, but they had been the only thing keeping the Nor from crashing over the Soulan lines.

"Order him to hold them in reserve," Parno ordered reluctantly, "and to lower his fire, switching to stones." The runner nodded and hurried to relay the orders.

"We're running out of time, Cho," Parno grimaced. "I don't think we can hold till dark. Even if we do," he continued after a pause, "the Nor will likely continue their attack, even in the dark."

"I believe you are correct," Cho nodded. "Yet, there is no alternative but to continue."

"I know," Parno sighed. "I've tried to think of something that would help our chances, but I've played all my cards to hold this long."

"You might withdraw to the next lines," Cho offered. "Those position are undamaged and would be stronger than these," he nodded to the present line of defense. During the day the line had been breached more than once. Each time the reserve had managed to plug the holes, but the cost had been murderous. Parno doubted that he could hold another breach.

"I don't know if we can withdraw under this pressure," Parno replied. "We could be caught moving and the Nor would destroy us."

"Might I make a suggestion?" Cho said softly.

"I'm open to anything that gives us a chance," Parno nodded. Cho spoke quietly for two minutes. Parno listened, wide-eyed at first, but with realization dawning as Cho went on. When he finished, Parno was nodding.

"Get me Colonel Landers," he ordered.

-

"Are you out of your mind?" Landers almost screeched after Parno had outlined his plan. Parno shook his head.

"No Colonel, I'm not. This is the only way to try and keep the fight going a bit longer. We can't hold this line and you know that as well as I do—the damage to the defenses is too great. We have a line less than fifty yards behind us that is strong and undamaged."

"In order for us to withdraw in good order we have to relieve the pressure against us and this is the only way we can do that."

"It's suicide," Landers spat. "I won't allow it! I can't allow it!"

"It's not for you to allow or not," Parno replied grimly. "I'm in command here, Colonel, and you have your orders."

"I won't do it," Landers said quietly. "I refuse."

Refusal of an officer to follow a Royal order was punishable by death and Landers knew it. He had also come to know Parno McLeod. The young Prince merely smiled.

"You have to, Brian," he spoke firmly but gently. "I need you to do this. You're the only man for the job and it has to be done. It will be done. Am I clear?"

Landers face reddened slightly at the mild rebuke. Finally, reluctantly, he nodded.

"Fine," he snapped. "For the record, I do this under protest. It's wasteful, and wrong."

"I'll see to it that your protest is logged," Parno told him. Landers snorted at that and stomped away, fury boiling over at the orders he'd just received.

"He will do fine," Cho assured Parno, watching the Colonel go.

"I know," Parno nodded, his voice sad and weary. He was tired of telling me to die. Soon, he wouldn't have to worry over it anymore.

"Let's get ready to go," he said suddenly.

-

Parno looked at what remained of his regiment. Many of the men still fighting were wounded to some degree or another. They were tired, dirty, covered in blood. By rights they should be near collapse.

But they weren't. Not only were they ready to go, they were eager.

"I won't make it an order," Parno said, his voice carrying over the din of battle. "Anyone who does this will do it on their own decision. I wanted you to know how things lie."

"When do we go?" one man asked.

"We're ready," another spoke up.

"My boys are ready," still another spoke up.

"All right, then," Parno nodded. "Form up and be ready. Colonel Landers will be the one to start things up."

-

Colonel Brian Landers looked over the line one last time, making sure that all was in readiness. This would be touch and go as it was. Satisfied that things were as good as he could make them, he nodded to his runners.

"Prepare to disengage!" he bellowed and heard the call echoed up and down the line. The artillery as already gone, even now setting up behind the fourth and final line of defense. It was time to withdraw what was left of their men.

Most of them. Landers' anger threatened to surface again at Parno's plan, but he shook it off. If he and his men were to survive he needed his wits about him.

"Fall BACK!" he yelled above the din of battle. "FALL BACK!"

All along the line units began withdrawing, archers falling back to the front of the next line, then the swordsmen falling back, shields up. The withdrawal was orderly, for now, but any minute the Nor would notice. . . .

It happened at a span of barricade that had already failed once. Nor troopers tore and pulled at the structure until it gave way entirely and a gap of nearly twenty feet across appeared in the wall. Enemy troops poured in, pursuing the retreating Soulan warriors.

Crossbows twanged and the front lines of Nor fell in heaps, bolts at this range penetrating so deep in many cases that the same bolt would strike a second man after exiting the first. Swordsmen braced for the weight of the rush, knowing they would not be able to contain it.

"DOUBLE TIME!" Landers yelled. "INTO THE TRAPS!"

Startled, the Soulan troopers wavered in confusion for several seconds, then turned and headed for the traps along the line that would allow them inside the barricades.

The Nor troops, sensing victory at long last, streamed after them, hoping to catch the fleeing Soulan troopers before they could get behind their new line. Just as it seemed they would, a solid wall of swords and shields appeared within the flow of retreating southerners. Hesitating at the sight, the Nor looked on.

Standing in front of the fleeing Soulan troops, the Black Sheep had formed a three deep wall of men, shields gleaming and swords threatening. In front of them stood three men.

Parno McLeod smiled slightly at his enemy's consternation, then raised his sword.

"BLACK SHEEP! AT THEM!"

With a wild yell of fury, fear, and raw power, the Black Sheep of Soulan surged forward into the wall of oncoming Nor troops.

-

From his vantage point, General Brasher had seen the line breaking and watched as his troops poured into the Soulan interior lines.

"Yes!" he had exclaimed quietly, watching. They had done it! The line was broken and the enemy retreating in disorder. He turned to one of his runners, intending to send instructions that the Soulan troops were to be hammered as hard as possible. One of his aides grabbed the General's arm, however.

"Sir!" the man exclaimed. "The Southrons are. . .sir, they're counterattacking!"

"What?" Brasher whirled back to look at the battle line. "Impossible!"

But they were counter attacking, at least some of them anyway. Incredibly, even as Brasher watched what looked like the remains of a single regiment stood before his teeming masses, blunting his attack.

Brasher looked on as his troops hurled themselves at the phalanx of enemy soldiers over and over again, each time being repulsed. True, the enemy were falling as well, but their disciplined way of battle made it difficult to break them and protected them from harm to a great extent.

"Damn them!" Brasher swore. He turned to a runner.

"Order the rear ranks to surge forward again!" he demanded. "Have them carry that position at all costs!" The runner hurried to obey. Brasher turned back to the battle.

"Sir, they're. . ." the aide stopped, unable to continue.

"They're what?" Brasher snarled. He lifted his own glass, seeing for himself.

"They're advancing!"

-

"Forward!"

Parno was at the front of his men, Cho by his side, as he screamed the order. Karls Willard was to his other side, sword hacking and slashing as well. Behind him, his men let out a mighty cry.

"PARNO!" The Sheep surged forward, swords hacking and cutting in near desperation. Fear and anger added to their strength, though they remembered their training. Cho Feng, with a sword in each hand, spun and slashed alongside them, killing Nor troopers faster than any two Soulan soldiers. His swords seemed to be alive as they wove in and out of the mass of enemy soldiers, a deadly dance of blood and death.

"Drive them back!" Parno yelled, his own sword striking nearly as rapidly as Cho's. Parno might not be the most gifted commander on the battlefield, but he had few equals with the sword and now he proved it. To himself, his men, and to his enemies.

The Black Sheep of Soulan slowly began advancing, paying for that advance in blood, but moving forward none-the-less. Nor troops continued to stream into the gap in the line, while still more Nor worked to widen the breach or open others. Try as they might, the Nor could not withstand the advance of Parno's Regiment.

But that wouldn't last, Parno knew. He glanced over his shoulder, seeing that most of the others were now safely behind the new line. Some were lingering, assisting wounded Black Sheep to get inside. Parno waited perhaps one minute longer, then lifted his head.

"FALL BACK!" he yelled over the battle. "FALL BACK!"

As he gave that command, every archer that Landers still had appeared over the top of the fourth line, arrows flying into the Nor and staggering their attack. Taking advantage of that, the Sheep ran for their own lines, the hale and hearty assisting the wounded, in some cases carrying the dead. Karls Willard watched to see that the regiment kept its form. To break now would mean death to them all.

Parno was the last man to move and the last to enter the lines, with Karls just ahead of him. He leaned against the line for a brief time, regaining his strength. Amazed that any of them had survived, he pushed himself off the wall wearily and made his way to where Landers stood, directing the battle.

"Keep your command, Colonel," Parno told him. "I need to see to my men and get them reformed."

"Aye, milord," Landers nodded. "That was the damnedest thing I ever saw, milord. Well done."

"Does this mean you withdraw your protest?" Parno grinned tiredly.

"Absolutely not!" Landers replied at once. "That was the stupidest thing I've ever seen in all my years as a soldier!" Parno laughed and staggered tiredly over to where his men were reforming under the watchful eye of Karls Willard.

"How badly were we hurt?" Parno asked the young colonel. Willard looked haggard.

"We have just over three hundred men either missing, confirmed dead, or known to be wounded, milord," he said sorrowfully. Parno felt dismayed. The attack had gutted his men. He looked at the soldiers still present. They were haggard and tired, their strength gone.

"I'm sorry," Parno said to no one in particular. Several heads came up at that.

"What's that, milord?" one asked. "Sorry? For what?"

"For asking this of you," Parno admitted. "I'm sorry for so many losses, so much pain."

"Think it's all your fault, is that it?" one of his men asked. "Don't be sorry for things you got no control over, milord." His men agreed, heads nodding all around him.

"This here," another man commented, "this ain't no doin' o' yers, milord. Them stinkin' Nor heathens is to blame fer this and we'll kill 'em all 'fore it's all said, you wait and see if we don't!" The entire regiment cheered at that and Parno smiled. His men were tired, but not broken.

"Rest here for a bit," he ordered Karls. "I'll have need of you one last time, I suspect. After that, we'll all be resting." Karls nodded, knowing what Parno meant.

"We'll be ready, milord." Parno walked back to where Landers was directing the battle.

"How are we doing, Colonel?" Parno asked. Landers spared him a glance, then turned his attention back to the battle.

"We're holding, for now, milord," Landers assured him. "Our losses have been heavy, I'm afraid. Most of our units are mustering well below half strength. There is no reserve, other than your personal regiment and they have been sorely used."

"They'll be ready, if you have need," Parno said with quiet pride. He had never thought of them as his personal regiment. Indeed, all male members of the Royal Family had one, except for Parno himself. Until now, anyway.

"I'm sure they will," Landers nodded, "but we are near the end, sir. You have to know that." Parno nodded.

"Yes, I do," he agreed. "But we'll continue to hold as long as we can, Colonel. Once this lot is into the open we may never run them to ground. We have to bleed them here, while we can."

"We will, milord," Landers promised. "They seem to be drawing their rearward units together for another push," he added, looking out over the battlefield. Parno followed his gaze and was shocked to see so many bodies piled high.

"We've hurt them, Colonel. Hurt them badly. I had no idea."

"We have that, milord," Landers nodded in satisfaction. "They may gain possession of the field in the end, but we've scored a victory here. Never doubt that."

"You've been a large part of that, Colonel," Parno told him sincerely. "I can never thank you enough for that. I need to draft a message for my brother and have it dispatched. I will make sure that the Crown is aware of your service here. It's little enough to offer after all of this, but it's all I have."

"I'm flattered, milord," Landers replied honestly. "I never imagined that I would have this kind of opportunity to serve in a battle so important to Soulan. It's been an honor."

"The honor belongs to Soulan, Colonel. In having sired a man of your quality and in being fortunate enough to have your loyalty and your service." Landers flushed slightly at the praise.

"Thank you, milord."

"I'll be nearby, if you need me."

-

"I want you to deliver this personally, Lieutenant," Parno told Sprigs, after reading and signing what he was sure was his last bit of correspondence. Sprigs stiffened at that.

"Sir, my place is with you," the young man objected quietly. "I should. . . ."

"Your delivering this message is far more important than anything you can accomplish by dying here, Harry."

"Sir, don't do this to me!" Sprigs begged. "Everyone knows how this is to end. I'll be shamed for the rest of my life!" Parno looked at the young man, understanding how he felt.

"Harrel," he said softly. "Someone has to live. I need to get this report to my brother so that the heroism shown here over the last few days is known…and to let the Crown know that the force here has been hurt badly. I can't entrust just anyone to do that. I need someone I can trust. Someone I can rely on, and that person is you."

"Milord, please," Sprigs was almost in tears. "Don't make me leave all of you like this."

"I am truly sorry," Parno told him, meaning every word, "but I have no choice. Select a good horse and a remount. I want you on the trail within the hour. Godspeed, Lieutenant, and thank you for your service."

Parno turned away as the younger man slumped in defeat, sobbing quietly. In his letter to Memmnon, Parno had requested that his brother look after the young lieutenant, knowing that some would likely accuse him of cowardice. Such was the world.

But Parno had meant what he said. Sprigs' delivery of that report was more important than anything he might accomplish on the battlefield.

He was also confident that, someday, the young Lieutenant would forgive him.

-

Seeing Sprigs depart, Parno walked to the small building behind the Fort proper, where Darvo Nidiad lay after Stephanie had seen to him. Parno found her, dirty, disheveled, and covered in blood. She saw him coming and left the orderlies she was instructing to come to him.

"How is he?" Parno asked without preamble.

"The wound is grievous, Parno, and the damage great. He hangs on because of his great strength, I believe, and little else. I am sorry." She lowered her head for a moment, then looked back up. "He hasn't got long, Parno."

Numbly, Parno eased into the room, walking to the bed that held his old teacher and mentor. Darvo was sleeping fitfully, mumbling. Parno sat down beside him, wanting to spend just a few more minutes in his company. As he settled into the chair, he found Darvo looking at him.

"What are you doing here, boy?" the old man demanded gruffly.

"I see you're recovering," Parno replied sarcastically, "and yes, I'm fine, thanks for asking."

"How goes the battle?" the old colonel demanded.

"Fair, for now," Parno admitted. "Just a matter of time, I'm afraid. We managed to withdraw behind the last line a little while ago. Our losses are high, I fear. I doubt that we'll hold out the day."

"All the more reason for you to be out there and not in here!" Darvo pointed out.

"Darvo, I can spare a few minutes to say good-bye to my dearest friend," Parno sighed, and Darvo nodded, after a bit.

"'Spect that's so, lad," he smiled slightly. "It is good to see you, I'll admit."

"Well, good God, don't hold back," Parno laughed and Darvo chuckled, only to have it cut off by a round of coughing. Blood flecked around his lips and Parno took a cloth from the bedside and wiped his mouth.

"Damn Nor archer," Darvo grumped. "'Fraid he got me good, lad," he looked up. "I'm sorry to leave you like this, boy."

"It's okay, Darvo," Parno assured him, returning the cloth.

"I always thought on you as my own son, boy," Darvo said suddenly and Parno nodded. "I always did. You're a good lad and a fine man. You remember the things I taught you growing up, son. You stick to that and you'll do fine. Hear me?"

"I hear you," Parno nodded. His eyes were misting over for some reason.

"You look after my daughter, Parno," Darvo ordered. "See her married well or not at all. There's no one else to see after her now."

"I swear I'll look after as if she were my own," Parno promised. "If you like, I'll ask Edema to look after her. She can strain her suitors and find a suitable one, I promise." In truth, the dispatch he'd just sent off contained a request to Edema to do just that…and for Memmnon to make sure that no problems arose for the girl.

"Long as you make sure," Darvo nodded. "Parno, boy, I'm going to miss you. . ." Parno looked up as Darvo trailed off. Darvo's eyes were still open, but they were sightless now, and Darvo's labored breathing had stilled. Parno reached over and closed the eyes gently. He then took Darvo's hand for a moment, gripping it tightly.

"I'll miss you too, my old friend." He carefully folded Darvo's hands across his chest, trying not to sob. Then he leaned over and kissed the old man on his forehead.

Standing, Parno left the building without looking back. Darvo had seen his last battle.

Now it was his turn.

-

Corsin-Freeman was waiting for him as he exited the room.

"I want you and your staff ready to leave in fifteen minutes," he ordered brusquely. "I'll have a small escort ready. All civilians attached to the hospital are to leave when you do."

"We'll stay," she shook her head. "Some of the wounded won't make it if we..."

"They aren't going to make it anyway," Parno told her flatly. "We won't last much longer and none of you, most especially including you, are staying. Don't argue with me," he added when she seemed about to protest. "I'm too tired for it. You can load the wounded that can be safely moved and carry them in the wagons. I know there's not enough for all of them," he raised his hand again to forestall her complaint. "Carry those with the best chance of survival."

"So, you'll just let the rest die?" she asked in anger.

"What the hell did you expect?" Parno suddenly demanded. "I told you what was going to happen, remember? You wanted to come anyway. I only agreed on the promise, your promise, that when I said it was time for you to go, you would. Are you going back on your word, Doctor?" Parno's stiff and formal speech caught Stephanie by surprise.

"No, My Lord, I am not," she replied formally. "I'll assemble the staff at once."

"Thank you. For. . .for everything," Parno said suddenly, his voice softer. "Your escort will carry all of you to Nasil. Nowhere closer will be safe, I fear. At least there you'll have a chance."

"What will you do, Parno?" she asked, then mentally berated herself. She knew what was coming.

"I'll do what I set out to do," he actually smiled a little. "I'll make sure that this force is so bloodied and battered that they aren't a threat to Soulan. That's. . .that's all I can do." He took her hand, holding it softly in his own.

"Good bye, Stephanie. I'm glad to have known you." With a gentle kiss to her cheek, Parno turned without another word, and left her.

She watched for a moment, her eyes misty. Then she turned and started snapping out orders.

-

Harrel Sprigs ran his mount as fast as he thought safe over the rough terrain.

Partly he pushed the animal because of the urgency of his mission. Part of it, though, was the anger he felt coursing through him at the thought of the men he had left behind.

Dying.

So consumed was he in that cloud of anger and despair that he was almost run through by a lance held in the arms of Soulan Cavalry Trooper.

"Halt!" the man ordered, "in the name of the King!" Sprigs fought to slow his mount, looking at the squad of men before him.

"The King?" Sprigs asked, unwilling to believe his good fortune.

"Who are you?" the officer in charge asked.

"Lieutenant Harrel Sprigs, of Prince Parno's regiment!" Sprigs informed him, "and who are you?"

"Lieutenant Marion Manness, of His Majesty's Personal Regiment!" the officer replied. "Did you say you were part of Prince Parno's regiment?"

"I am milord Parno's aide," Sprigs nodded. "I bear important correspondence for Prince Memmnon, in Nasil."

"The King is closer," Manness informed him. "Come, we'll take you to His Majesty."

With that, the squad reformed and headed toward the King as fast as their horses would fly.

-

"You've just come from the Gap?" Tammon asked, looking at Sprigs. The young man nodded.

"Prince Parno dispatched me to deliver his report to Prince Memmnon, sire. I have been in the saddle less than two hours."

"What is the situation at the Gap, lad?" the King asked.

"The line was holding when I left, sire," Sprigs informed the King, "but the Nor are pressing hard against it. Milord Parno believes that it is only a matter of time before the line fails completely. It... it may well have fallen already, sire."

"How strong is the force facing my son?"

"They did number near fifty thousand, sire," Sprigs replied, "but we have hurt them badly, thanks to Prince Parno. Estimates are that the Nor have lost nearly half their number in the last three days."

"What?" Tammon was shocked at that.

"Milord Parno's new weapons and his tactics have enabled us to inflict massive casualties upon the heathen, sire," Sprigs said proudly. "And the men have all fought above and beyond what even they themselves thought possible, inspired by the Prince. He is a gifted leader," he finished.

"I see," Tammon said, more to cover his shock than anything. What had Parno done to be able to hurt the Nor so badly? He shook his head. None of that mattered now. He turned to Enri Willard and Colonel Strong, the commander of his personal regiment.

"How many men can we mount?" he demanded tersely. The two men considered that for less than a minute.

"With our regiment," Strong answered, "the House Regiment, and the men we mounted from the City Guard, we can muster around twenty-five hundred mounted troopers, sire."

"I want them ready to ride in five minutes," Tammon ordered. "The wagons are to follow at best speed, horses and wagons are not to be spared. Move!" he bellowed. Both men scurried to obey. Tammon turned back to Sprigs.

"You will ride with me," he ordered, "and tell me of my son."

Scant minutes later, the countryside around them thundered with the sound of over two thousand horses racing across the land as fast as their riders could coax them.

At their head, Tammon McLeod rode in silence, digesting what Sprigs had told him of Parno's efforts over the past week. His face was grim and gaunt.

Parno had been alive, and his force holding, two hours ago. He hoped, he prayed, that would still be the case when he and his men arrived.

There was much he needed to say to his youngest son.

-

Stephanie Freeman-Corsin watched as the last of the wounded were loaded on the wagons.

The last that can be moved without killing them, she reminded herself. So many men lost. She shook her head. No time for that now.

"Ma'am."

She turned, seeing Lieutenant Parsons holding the reins of her own horse. Her personal ambulance she had turned over to the wounded. Taking the reins, she climbed aboard.

"We'll see you, and them, safely home, ma'am," Parsons promised.

"I know," she smiled weakly. "I'm just sorry to be leaving so many in need."

"I understand, ma'am," Parson's nodded. He wasn't happy himself, but orders were orders, and these had come directly from the Prince.

"Head'em out!" Parsons called. He nodded to one of his subordinates, Stephanie couldn't recall his name, and that man and three others set out at a gallop ahead of the small wagon train.

She made sure that everyone was loaded and moving, then kneed her horse alongside Parsons'. As the wagon train started rolling she didn't look back.

It required more effort than she'd imagined.

# CHAPTER TWENTY-EIGHT

-

Parno watched through his glass as the Nor reformed across the battlefield. He could only imagine what shape the enemy troops were in, but fervently hoped it was bad.

"They look tired," he commented quietly to Cho Feng, who stood by his side. The oriental nodded.

"They are near the end of their usefulness," he observed. "They have lost faith in themselves and their commander. Only fear of reprisal keeps them going."

"I wish they feared us more than they feared him," Parno muttered. "If they hit us again with everything they have left we'll likely be finished."

"I must agree," Cho replied calmly. He looked at the sky, gauging the time until dark. "There is sufficient light remaining to mount a coordinated attack and follow it through. Time is very much on their side, my young Prince."

"I know," Parno sighed. "I'd love to be able to hold them one more day," he added forlornly, "but I just don't see that happening."

"Nor do I," Cho agreed. "We will see."

"Sooner rather than later, it appears," Parno told him, lowering his glass. "Seems they've gotten their infusion of courage. Here they come." He turned to his runners.

"Order Captain Lars to use the remaining explosive rounds as soon as the enemy is in range, then continuous fire for as long as possible. Notify your respective commands that the enemy is about to make a major push against our position." The runners all saluted and hurried off to find their commanders.

Parno watched them go then turned his attention to the line below. His men were dirty, exhausted, and just plain worn out. They had fought bravely but they, too, were near the end of their rope. Casualties had been horrendous during this day's fighting already with well less than half of their number still able to make muster. The dead were being stacked like cord wood behind the lines and the wounded were spread upon the ground inside the small fort itself, there being no more room for them in the makeshift hospitals and tents.

Over two thousand men lost in the last three days. It was small comfort that the Nor had lost many times that, if their count was anything like accurate. Nor dead littered the battlefield so heavily that Parno could have walked across the field without placing his feet upon the ground. The awful effect of Roda Finn's gadgetry. Had it not been for Finn's weaponry, the Nor would simply have rolled over them and kept going.

But not now.

The once strong enemy army had been bled mightily by the small force of Soulan soldiers. Estimates were that the Soulan defense had cost the Nor commander fully half of his command. Scouts reported that the fire had also destroyed a great deal of their train. Those who were left when the battle finally ended would be short of everything.

Maybe they'll starve, he thought bleakly. It wasn't harvest season so foraging would be difficult. This area was sparsely populated to begin with and the raging battle had warned most of the country side to flee. The small farmsteads in this area would yield little in the way of sustenance for the Nor troops. In that weakened condition his father should be able to run the remainder to ground, at least he fervently hoped so.

"Don't let this be for nothing", he prayed silently. "Don't let all these brave men die for nothing."

"They are coming, my prince," Cho said softly, bringing Parno back to the present. He nodded.

"Now we'll see, I suppose."

-

Tammon McLeod drew reign as one of his scouts appeared in front of his column. The King halted his horse, irritated by the pause.

"What?" he demanded gruffly.

"Sire," the scout swallowed nervously. "We have encountered the leading elements of two Soulan divisions, the 6th Cavalry, and the 5th Mounted. They are on their way to the Gap as well, by order of the Lord Marshall."

"Excellent," Tammon smiled for the first time in days. "When will the rest of 1st Corps be up?"

"Sire, they are alone," the scout reported. "Those two divisions are all that are coming." Tammon looked at the scout for a moment, his eyes ablaze.

"Are you sure about that?" he asked, his voice deadly calm.

"Yes, Sire," the scout nodded nervously. "They claim they were sent to investigate a rumor of Nor activity in the area."

"Take me to them. At once," Tammon ordered. A rumor? He had ordered Therron to send the entire Corps to the Gap at once. His son had disobeyed him.

And now the Kingdom lay in peril because of it.

As he followed the scout toward the newly arriving troops, Tammon made a decision. His second son had defied him. Openly. He couldn't allow that to stand. Once this trouble was seen to, he would have to reign Therron in. His face was hard as he rode.

At least he would no longer be leaving the problem for Memmnon to deal with.

Less than twenty minutes later, Tammon McLeod, followed by his own men, emerged into a small clearing where the bulk of two divisions of Soulan's finest soldiers sat waiting. Everyone snapped up straight at the sight of the King, but Tammon ignored that. He rode directly to the head of their column, stopping his horse in front of the Generals commanding the two divisions.

"I understand that you are the only part of 1st Corps ordered to the Gap. Is that correct?"

"Yes, Sire," General Thomas, senior of the two division commanders replied. "That is so."

"Who issued that order?" Tammon asked, eyes narrowing. Thomas looked nervously to his counterpart, then back to his King.

"L. . .Lord Marshall Therron, sire," was the shaky reply. Tammon's eyes hardened at that. So it was true.

"Very well," he nodded. "We have no time to waste, General. We are but a short ride from. . ." He broke off as that strange rumbling came to him once more and the ground trembled slightly.

"We must hurry," Tammon instructed. "Have your men follow, General, and be prepared to fight as soon as we reach the field."

"Yes, sire!" the two generals replied in unison and turned to their aides and runners.

"Move out!" Tammon called loudly and spurred his horse savagely. The great beast leaped forward, unaccustomed to such treatment. But it knew who its master was and went willingly.

Now with over twelve thousand troops at his back, Tammon McLeod raced once more for the Gap. With luck, they could get there in the next hour. He only hoped that was soon enough for his son…and his Kingdom.

-

"Milord, they're pressing the left very hard," a runner informed Parno. "Colonel Chad says he may not be able to hold the line." Parno nodded and turned to one of his own runners.

"Order Colonel Willard to detach Captain Seymour to support Colonel Chad."

The two runners departed, leaving Parno behind with Cho Feng.

"We won't be able to hold much longer, Cho," Parno said softly. "The Nor aren't going to stop this time and I'm fresh out of tricks."

"It has been a great battle, my prince," Cho replied. "One worthy of pen and ink. You should be proud." Parno looked at Cho.

"Proud? Proud?" Parno's voice rose slightly. "I've killed or ordered killed thousands of men in the last three days, Cho. Ordered good me to die rather than give ground! What in hell is there to be proud about?"

"Your humanity has survived, I see," Cho surprised him by smiling. "That is good, Parno. It is often the first casualty of war. But yes, you should be proud. You have served your people well here. Your men have served you well. That is the mark of a great leader, Parno McLeod. Don't forget that."

"No more time than I have left, I'll probably be able to keep it in mind," Parno remarked dryly. "There's no. . . ." He was cut off as a breathless runner hurried to him.

"Colonel Landers reports that the right is in danger, milord!" he gasped out. "We have lost too many men to hold the Nor at bay." Parno turned to order reinforcements for the right, but before he could speak, he heard the cracking of timber. Turning, he saw a portion of the line crumble before his eyes and Nor began to pour through the opening.

"Black Sheep! FORWARD!" he heard Karls Willard cry, and then the regiment was among the Nor, fighting desperately. Parno sighed and drew his sword. Beside him, Cho Feng drew his own blades.

"It's time, my prince," he said solemnly.

Parno nodded. "So, it is."

Without another word, the two men leapt from the small observation point and headed for the battle.

-

Across the field now out in the open since the hellish witch weapons had fallen silent, General Brasher smiled in triumph.

"We've done it!" he cried to no one on particular. "Order all commands to head for that breach, widen it, and press the attack to the hilt!" His runners rushed to obey.

He would beat this ragged bunch of Southrons and then nothing would stand between him and the Soulan capital. He would win this war for his Emperor and reap the benefits.

Smiling, he urged his own horse forward, wanting to see the final defeat of this cursed position for himself. His guard followed nervously.

-

"We're losing the position, milord!" Karls called to Parno over the din of battle. "There are too many of them to hold!"

The barricade had failed in another position now, near the center. Landers' men had lost over half of their remaining strength trying to stem the initial breach and now staggered back under the weight of this new push.

Parno considered his options for a few seconds, then started snapping orders.

"Order all commands to fall back and form a box!" he ordered his runners. "Militia and provisional battalions to form second ranks, except for Chad's men, who will form on the first rank! Move!" The runners all took off as fast as their feet would carry them.

Parno looked at Karls. "Form a box!" he shouted, and the younger man nodded. Parno looked to where Landers was still leading his men in an attempt to hold the Nor at bay.

"Landers! Fall back and form a box!" he called. The colonel nodded in reply, then stiffened, a puzzled look upon his face. Parno noticed a pike point protruding from his chest.

"Brian!" Parno called, forcing his way forward. He arrived just as the grinning Nor soldier jerked the pike from Landers' body. The colonel fell to his knees, blood streaming from his mouth and nose. Enraged, Parno flung himself at the Nor soldier, who tried to bring the long pike to bear on his new target.

Parno's sword bit deep into the pike shaft, slicing it cleanly off. Before the Nor could react, Parno's blade flashed again and the Nor's head went sailing. Kneeling by Landers, Parno tried to help the man to his feet.

"No...no time, mi... milord," Landers gasped, blood frothing around his mouth. "I'm done. . .done for."

"You'll be fine!" Parno shouted. "Just hold on until I can...."

"Leave me, Parno," Brian Landers smiled up at him. "It has been my greatest honor to serve you, milord...." Landers eyes glazed and with one final cough of blood, he went still. Parno let him go, rising.

"Fall back!" he shouted through tears of rage. "Fall back and form a box, men!" The soldiers around him began to retreat, their numbers dwindling steadily. As Parno watched two Nor approached him, swords swinging. Parno almost smiled.

He stepped forward, feinting suddenly at the man on the left, then striking at the man on the right. His sword bit deep into the man's side, and Parno twisted the blade in his hand, widening the wound. The other Nor took advantage of that to strike, but Parno was far too fast. His blade slid from his first target and blocked the incoming slash, then snaked out toward the Nor's throat. The man managed to deflect the blow enough to save his throat, the blade sinking instead into his shoulder at the seam of his armor. He grimaced, but managed to pull himself free of Parno's blade. The prince followed him, however, and this time sank his blade nearly hilt deep into the man's belly. He fell as if boned.

"Milord!" Parno turned at the cry, just in time to see two more Nor bearing down on him, with three more behind. Parno set himself but before he could attack, Cho Feng's swords flashed in from the side, slicing one man to his backbone and tearing a chunk of flesh from the neck of another. A Soulan trooper, seeing his liege in peril, attacked from the side, felling another of the attackers, but then falling himself as one of the remaining Nor ran him through from behind.

Parno leaped forward, catching the back stabber with his sword still caught and taking his head off with a broad sweep. He turned in time to see Cho take the last one, slicing the man's arm nearly off.

"Let's go!" Parno ordered, and the slight oriental man nodded, following. The two of them raced toward what remained of the small force that had fought so hard for so long. Now in a box, backs to one another, with a second rank inside it, the balance of Parno's forces prepared for one final stand.

Without a word, the front rank made room for Parno and Cho Feng. He smiled at the men around him, nodding. Then the Nor were upon them and there was no time for anything other than the battle.

-

This time Tammon didn't halt the column when the scout appeared. The man galloped toward the column, slowing and turning his horse to fall in beside his King.

"Sire! The men at the Fort are still fighting! They are sorely pressed, and have lost their line, but are still fighting!"

"Forward at a gallop, Colonel," the King ordered, spurring his horse again.

"Column, gallop!" Strong yelled. If either General took offense to the Colonel being the one giving the orders, they remained silent about it.

Artificial thunder shook the ground as the hooves of over ten thousand warhorses pounded the landscape, riding hard in hopes of arriving before the battle was over.

At their head rode their King, his face set in a mask of determination.

-

Parno had lost sight of the battle, fighting in the front line along with soldiers from private to sergeant. He would not retreat any further.

"Milord, you should be to the middle ground!" one shouted.

"I can see better from here!" Parno threw back, smiling. His blood and grime covered face looked more like a demon than a Prince of the Realm. He no longer cared.

"Lad, you do not need to be here!" the rumbling voice of Brenack Wysin sounded in his ear. "It's among them you're most needed!"

"There's nothing left for me to do there, my friend," Parno replied, deftly parrying a Nor sword at the same time. Before he could slash back, Wysin's mighty hammer fell on the Nor soldier's head, crushing it. Parno looked at the smith, stunned.

"I said I had no skill with a blade," Wysin smirked. "I used a hammah all my life, milord."

"Thanks," Parno grinned back and turned his attention back to the front. Only he wasn't in the front anymore. Taking advantage of his brief distraction, three of the Black Sheep had moved to place themselves between Parno and the Nor. He frowned at that, but a hand fell on his shoulder before he could object.

"Milord!" Karls Willard shouted. "Walk the line! Let the men see you and know you're safe!" Parno nodded dumbly, not having thought about that. He immediately began moving inside the box, up one line and down the other.

"That's the spirit, boys!" he shouted and the soldiers cheered in spite of their predicament.

"Hold 'em as long as we can, milord!" one shouted back without turning. Giving deed to his words, he used his shield to slice the throat of a Nor who had gotten too close.

Parno nodded in satisfaction.

They had lost, true. But they were not yet beaten.

Not quite yet.

-

"Why is it taking so long?" Brasher demanded of no one in particular. One of his aides galloped ahead to see what the problem was. He passed another aide, returning.

"General, sir," the man reported. "The enemy have formed a box and refused their flanks. Brigadier Semmes reports that casualties are high, higher than expected that is, but he is confident that the position will be in our hands in minutes."

"Tell him it damn well better be!" Brasher replied harshly. With that the aide whirled away, on his way back to the line. Brasher watched him go, seething. How could it take his tens of thousands of men so long to roll over a few thousand backwoods troops? He would have someone's. . . .

"General," his personal aide said in his ear. "We may have a problem."

"What?" he yelled, looking wild-eyed at the man by his side. The aide wasn't looking at him, however. As Brasher watched, the man lifted a hand, index finger extended.

Following the pointed finger, Brasher looked to see what the idiot was babbling. . . .

-

Tammon McLeod took one look at the battle below and turned to the Generals behind him.

"Deploy your men at once, and hit their flank. Ride them down and pursue until the field is ours. Move!" Both men turned and started yelling. Tammon looked at Strong and Willard.

"Take your men and move to support and relieve the survivors," he ordered more calmly. "They have to be near the end of their rope."

"Aye, Milord." Both men likewise began barking orders.

Two minutes later, the air once more filling with the sound of thundering hooves, a battle cry rose from more than ten thousand throats.

"SOULAN! McLEOD!"

Tammon watched them go, surrounded by his personal guard.

He prayed they were in time to save the few who remained.

-

Parno was exhausted. His voice was almost gone and he was once again on the line, having stepped up to take the place of a fallen militia man when there was no one else to do the job. His sword arm was growing weary and he could only imagine how the men who had been fighting all day were feeling. There had to be a limit to. . . .

"Milord!" Karls Willard was grasping his shoulder. "Look!" Parno followed Karls outstretched finger, looking back to the west. There, in all their glory, came thousands of Soulan horsemen.

"My God!" Parno breathed. He hadn't expected any help. To see them now, when all was lost, was almost too much. As he watched, however, the troopers kept coming.

And coming.

"It's 1st Corps!" Karls shouted. "And look there! The King's Own!"

Sure enough, his father's personal regiment was thundering down upon his own position, along with what looked like the House Guard.

A Nor swordsman who hadn't seen the approaching reinforcements, took advantage of Parno's distraction and slashed across at the young prince. Parno's reflexes reacted on their own, but he knew he was too slow. He watched as the sword fell, almost in slow motion.

Only to be stopped cold by a hammer. A very large hammer. As the Nor soldier stood there, stunned, a slim sword blade flicked out from Parno's other side, and disemboweled the man. He fell with the look of shock locked permanently upon his face. Parno turned to see Brenack Wysin and Cho Feng both standing there, smiling.

"You can't keep outta trouble, can ya lad?" Wysin smiled gently, then proceeded to hammer a Nor soldier into the ground effortlessly. Cho met two more who were coming and both fell in seconds, one beheaded, the other sliced almost in half.

"We cannot have you make it this far, then lose you, my prince," Cho threw over his shoulder.

"Thanks," Parno mumbled. He didn't know what else to say.

"Welcome, milord," Wysin nodded, not taking his eyes from the battlefield.

Suddenly the Nor were moving away. No, Parno decided, not so much moving as being pushed. Pushed away from the ragged band of men who had fought an entire Nor army to a standstill in the wild back lands of Soulan.

The King's Own and the House Guard ran amok among the dismounted Nor, hacking and thrusting with strength and determination. In less than a minute the two commands had interposed themselves between what remained of Parno's men and the Nor. Enri Willard loomed over him out of the dust, grinning wildly.

"I see you're still in trouble, milord!" he called, then saw his brother.

Enri reached down to grasp his younger brother's arm. "I'm glad to see you well, Karls," he said quietly.

Karls grinned up at him, tiredly. "I'm glad to see you at all!" he replied, and the elder Willard laughed.

"I have work to do, but I'll see you in a bit," he promised, then turned his horse to return to his own men. In the distance, Parno could see what could only be the divisions of 1st Corps hitting the Nor in the flank and driving them back.

The Nor, afoot due to the terrain between their camp and the battlefield, and caught in the open, were being slaughtered by the highly skilled Soulan troopers.

For the first time in days, Parno began to wonder what the rest of his life might be like.

And to think on how much this battle had cost him.

-

"Sir, we can't hold them," Brasher's aide said softly. "Wouldn't it be better to try and save what we can?"

"We can't be beaten!" Brasher screamed, his eyes wild and bloodshot. "We're the superior people! The greater force! There is no way we can lose."

"Sir, we've already lost," his second in command entered the argument. "Our men are exhausted and theirs are fresh. Ours are on foot, theirs are mounted. We have lost."

"We have not lost!" Brasher screamed, turning to face the two. . .traitors. He drew his sword.

"I'll kill the next man who mutters such drivel!"

But General Brasher, in his need to see the crushing defeat of his enemy, had ventured too close to the battle. He saw his aide's eyes widen in terror and had time to realize what must have happened.

Then his head flew from his shoulders, cleaved by the sharp sword of an inferior Soulan trooper, whose mates charged hard after the General's party.

The Nor 3rd Field Army had been routed. Now it was headless.

General Brasher would not be called upon to answer to the Emperor for his failure. He would not be called upon at all.

Ever again.

-

"Let's get the wounded seen to," Parno ordered his men. He looked over the carnage that had once been his force, and tried not to let his dismay show. So many good men.

"It is the way of war, Parno," Cho said softly, and Parno chuckled bitterly.

"One day, you're going to have to tell me how you do that."

"What?" Cho asked.

"Know what I'm thinking."

"You are not the first man I have watched lead men in war for the first time, Parno," Cho told him. "I have seen it before. It is not so hard to know what is in your mind."

"Good thing that Nor General didn't know," he laughed outright at that.

"Son?" a voice called.

Parno froze at that, and turned slowly. He saw his father, astride his great horse, looking down at him.

"Hello, Sire," Parno replied respectfully. "You shouldn't be here, Father."

"I'm still King," Tammon replied gruffly, dismounting. "I go where I please." He walked over to his son, looking him over from head to toe.

"You've done well, Parno," he said softly. "I'm proud of you."

"Proud of me," Parno repeated the words tiredly. "Believe it or not, that's not why I did this, father. I had a better reason than that to lead all these men to their deaths." He rested his hand on the hilt of his sword. "I did it for my people. For my land…and so did they." He waved at the men littering the battlefield behind him.

"I know," Tammon nodded respectfully. "I'm still proud of you. I'm sure Darvo is as well. Where is he?"

Parno's stiffness left him at that. He fought to keep his face neutral and managed to do it, barely.

"Colonel Darvo Nidiad has fallen in battle," he reported evenly. "Killed in action just this morning, late." Tammon's face fell.

"I'm so very sorry, my son," he murmured, and went to embrace his youngest son.

Parno rebuffed that embrace, however. "If you will excuse me, Sire, I need to see to my men. I didn't spend enough time training them and I fear they have suffered for that. My complete report will be finished as soon as possible, but I commend to you Colonel Brian Landers, commander of this garrison, who fell in the line of duty, protecting his post. He should be recognized for his bravery."

Without another word, Parno turned away. Tammon, pain etched on his face, watched him go. He turned to Cho Feng.

"Give him time, King McLeod," the oriental war master told him. "He is hurting and not just from the loss of Colonel Nidiad. He feels every death among the men who followed him as if he had, himself, took their life. It weighs upon him heavily." He smiled. "But he will bear it well. He has the mark of a great man. A very great man."

"I hope so," Tammon replied without thinking. "Because I'm going to need him."

# CHAPTER TWENTY-NINE

-

Parno McLeod stood on the porch of his home inside Cove Canton. He was wearing his dress uniform along with his ceremonial sword. There were no decorations on his uniform although both the King and the Crown Prince had tried to convince him to accept medals for his work at the Gap, but Parno had flatly refused. He couldn't bring himself to accept awards for something that had left so many of his men dead. He didn't deserve them anyway, he figured.

Which brought him to the final piece of business where the Gap was concerned.

Sighing, he placed his cap on his head and began the slow walk out of the abandoned encampment.

-

What remained of the Black Sheep, and it wasn't much Parno noted sadly, were assembled in two lines outside the gate of the Canton. The line was extended by the survivors of the other units involved in the defense of the Gap. A new unit, the Tinsee 3rd Infantry, was already on post at the gap, rebuilding the defenses and garrisoning the post.

Parno stopped at the gate next to Karls Willard. He nodded to the young bugler across from him and the nervous young man lifted his horn to his lips. The notes of the call were clear and sweet in the cool mountain air.

Slowly a caisson drawn by six horses emerged from the Canton, a single coffin in back. The driver was resplendent in dress uniform. Behind the caisson walked Dahlia Nidiad, along with Edema Willows, both dressed in black, with veils.

"Render Honors! FRONT!" Willard commanded. The entire line snapped to a salute and held it as the caisson slowly made its way down the line. Parno and Karls fell in with Dahlia and Edema as the caisson eased past them. Soldiers down the line dropped their salutes as the wagon passed by, falling into trail in column of four.

Following Colonel Darvo Nidiad one last time.

-

The ceremony at the grave site was short. Tammon McLeod himself was in attendance, as was Crown Prince Memmnon. Neither had been asked to speak. Neither had protested.

Parno stood silently by Dahlia's side as the Regimental Chaplain read from the bible over the casket that carried his oldest friend and faithful mentor.

"What will I do now, Darvo?" Parno asked thoughtfully. "Where will I go when I need advice? Turn to when I'm in trouble? Who will bail me out when I screw up?"

There was no answer to these questions, of course. There was no one to answer them anymore.

Parno gave his attention back to the ceremony as the honor guard came forward. Slowly, with the reverence usually reserved for heads of state, they lowered their commander's body into the grave. Finally, mercifully, it was over. Willard dismissed the men and turned to Dahlia. The two of them had become close over the time spent in Cove Canton and Parno suspected that Karls would like nothing more than to marry the young woman. If so, Parno doubted that Darvo would have protested.

Parno caught Edema's eye and nodded to Karls. She smiled briefly, returning his nod, and invited Karls to accompany them back to the house. Dahlia would soon be moving to Cumberland House, under Edema's care. It wasn't too far from here, Parno thought, and Karls could easily make the. . . .

He broke off that train of thought, remembering that there was still a great war being waged. One that Soulan wasn't winning. Dahlia might lose Karls, as well, before it was over, and they might lose the war.

Parno sighed in despair, turning his gaze to the valley beneath them. It really was beautiful country, he decided. A man with a future could take a small farm here, raise cows or horses, marry and have fat babies. Live a wonderful, peaceful life. Except for the Nor, of course. Without any conscious thought, he began walking toward the edge of the hillside, a sharp drop off. There was a small trail there which took him up onto the higher ridge, just a hundred yards or so walk.

Once there he took a seat on the ground, knees drawn up, hands gathered together in front of his boots. He'd come a long way Parno decided, sitting there on that mountain top. From the 'playboy prince' to a soldier. A leader of soldiers. He, with the help of others, had recruited and trained a regiment of fighting men that had no equal in modern times.

Then he had all but destroyed it in just a few days, fighting over a piece of ground too small for much more than a garden, perhaps a house and barn, and a few horses. Suddenly, the grief was too much for a prince not yet twenty-one years old and tears leaked from his eyes. Before he knew it he was sobbing uncontrollably, his face held in his hands.

"Oh God, Darvo, I am so sorry!" he almost wailed. It came out as little more than a harsh whisper, his throat constricted by the sobs of grief that wracked his body and closed his throat. He had not allowed himself to cry since he was seven years old. Refusing to allow his family to see the sadness that enveloped him as a result of the hostility that he had grown up surrounded by.

Now, a lifetime of grief poured out of him as he sat alone.

For he was now truly alone. The only person who had ever loved him, ever taken care of him, was gone, and it was as much his fault as it had been the Nor. Darvo hadn't wanted to be a part of the regiment but Parno had insisted, badgered him into it. He'd had no idea at the time that a great war loomed on the horizon.

And, if he was honest, he had never imagined that Darvo Nidiad was anything but indestructible. He had always been there. Always.

But not anymore, Parno thought to himself. One more thing I can take credit for.

"My Prince?" he heard Cho Feng call. Quickly drying his tears, Parno took a second to try and compose himself.

"Over here, Cho," he called softly, trying to keep his voice firm. The smaller man appeared a few seconds later. He stood there, looking down at Parno for a moment, then folded his legs underneath him, taking a seat beside his young Lord.

"There is no shame in grief, Parno," Feng said softly. "It is not a weakness to grieve for a friend."

"No, it isn't," Parno agreed. "But I can't. . .I have to. . ." Parno broke off, unable to put into words what he was thinking.

"You seek to shield your men from your grief," Feng nodded. "You are a good man, my Prince, and a gifted leader. It is no wonder that your men love you." Parno looked up at him, snorting.

"They might have, once," he said scornfully. "But now? Don't try to kid a kidder, Cho. They can't have any love for a man who led so many of them to their deaths." He returned his gaze to the valley floor below.

"You think not?" Cho asked him mildly. "Did you note, Parno, that none of your men fled you in the heat of battle. Even at the end they were loyal to you, knowing they were doomed to die. Loyal to the end, Prince. Not to Soulan, not to a flag, or a banner, or a King…but to a man who shared their hardships, who gave them a chance to be men. Someone who treated them as men. Never doubt that those who remain love you still. Follow you still, and will follow no other, I think."

"I'm not a leader," Parno said gruffly. "Never was. Just a fool who thought he could change things."

"You have changed things for many," Cho told him, "and will for many more. Your destiny awaits you, Prince, and you cannot escape it." Feng stood.

"You were born into gilded misery, Parno McLeod. You are accustomed to pain and suffering. You are alone against all that stands before you and that has made you strong. Very strong indeed. All things in your life have led you to this great crossroads that now lies before you. You can accept it or you can step aside. There are consequences for each action. Think carefully before you choose. There are things in motion that cannot be stopped, by you or any other man."

"The King and the Crown Prince are asking to speak with you," he said formally. "They wait for you in your office." Parno looked up at him.

"What do they want?" he demanded.

"They hold the key to your future, Parno McLeod. It is for you to decide if you will accept it or not."

-

At that same moment Tammon and Memmnon McLeod were discussing that future.

Heatedly.

"You're practically signing his death warrant!" Memmnon raged at his father. "Is that how you repay him for saving your Kingdom?"

"I don't have a choice," his father raged back, equally frustrated. "If I did, I would take it! But I don't…you don't!… we don't, Memmnon! Not if we are to defend this kingdom and its people."

"It's wrong," Memmnon maintained stubbornly.

"It is," Tammon surprised him by agreeing. "and I'd give anything not to have to do it, but there is no choice. None. It's this or nothing and we can't afford nothing. Not anymore."

Their argument broke off abruptly as they heard Parno entering the outer office. The younger prince walked into his small office, looking at his father and brother with wariness.

"I was told you wanted to see me," he said neutrally. "I'm sorry it took so long. After the funeral, I took a walk."

"There is no need to explain, my son," Tammon said quietly. "We understand." Parno looked at his father carefully and saw that he really did understand. He shrugged.

"I'm here, now," he said, taking a seat behind his small desk. "What did you need from me?" The two men across from him looked at each other. Memmon's face was set, thin lines at his eyes and mouth betraying his anger. He nodded in capitulation, reluctantly. Tammon studied his heir closely for another few seconds, then turned to his youngest son.

"I have a problem, Parno," he said without preamble. "A serious problem. One that could threaten the course of the war and bring about the downfall of the dynasty, taking this kingdom with it." Parno's eyes opened a bit wider at that.

"I know the solution to this problem," Tammon continued. "The only solution, in fact, if we are to survive…but that solution will create still more problems, both now and in the foreseeable future."

"That must be some problem," was all Parno could say. Tammon snorted, and Memmnon's face set even tighter, if that was possible. "What has happened?" He didn't bother to hide his confusion. His father had never talked to him about anything of any importance.

"Therron disobeyed a direct order from me, written in my hand, and delivered by my personal courier," the King told him flatly. Parno blinked at that, stunned. Had his brother taken leave of his senses?

"I… what?" Parno said.

"He deliberately flaunted my orders in front of General Davies," Tammon went on. "I have to relieve him. It saddens me that it has come to this, but I have no choice. I cannot let him disobey me. He is the Lord Marshall, but I am King. He has often argued with me, but never directly disobeyed me. Never. I cannot let this lie."

"I… I understand, Sire," Parno nodded. "What has this to do with me?"

"You and your men, all of the men at the Gap, are heroes, Parno," Tammon spoke quietly. "I can't send Memmnon, because of his position as Crown Prince. I can't have any of my Generals relieve him. Some of them won't react well to Therron being relieved as it is. There is only one person I can appoint in Therron's place with any hope that it will not divide the army."

"That person is you, Parno." Tammon lowered the boom quickly and calmly. Parno blinked slowly at that. What? Finally, the import of the words sank in.

"Me?" he demanded, his voice rising. "Are you insane?"

"You," Tammon nodded, ignoring his son's outburst. In truth he didn't blame him.

"You are insane," Parno murmured. "Father, there is no way that I can be Lord Marshall. Therron already hates me. This would drive him into a homicidal rage! I would never be safe from him!"

"I know," Tammon's voice was sad. Almost weak. "Was there another way, I swear I would take it, my son, and not put you in this difficult place…but there is none. This Kingdom stands on the verge of ruin if we cannot turn this war around. I need a fighting soldier commanding the armies of Soulan. Your brother will need it, when he assumes the Crown." Parno looked at Memmnon. The Crown Prince's face was carefully neutral.

"What the hell are you talking about?" Parno demanded. Tammon sighed.

"I'm not a young man, Parno," he said quietly, "and I'm not always well. I've known that for some time but the strain of this war and the strain of Therron's actions have made it even more apparent. I am able to rule, for now," he assured his youngest son, "but for how long, I cannot know. This is a problem I have to deal with. Now," he added, with heavy emphasis. "While I am still able."

"This really is the only way, Parno," Memmnon told him, helping his father out. "You have done a great thing in defending the Gap. As the architect of that victory, the only victory to date in fact, you will be acceptable to the army, as well as the people…and you have the ability. You proved that at the Gap." Memmnon's voice held a note of pride.

"I… I argued against it, because of the trouble it will cause you with Therron, but in truth, I have to agree with Father. This really is the only solution. I am forbidden, by law, from leading our armies in the field. Otherwise, I would do so, and take Therron's wrath upon myself." Memmnon concluded.

Parno studied his brother closely for a moment, deciding that Memmnon spoke truthfully. He nodded ever so slightly.

"The Inspector General of the Army will bring Therron up on charges of insubordination and failure to follow a binding order of his sovereign," Memmnon said coldly. "His actions could have cost us everything, had you not held your ground. He did as he did because of personal reasons. He must pay the price for it."

"He could. . .the penalty for those crimes is. . ." Parno trailed off.

"He won't be executed," Tammon's voice was hard, "but he will be stripped of his position, duties, and rank. He will no longer have any authority in the army. Nor," the King added, his voice quieter, "will he occupy the second seat of succession."

"What?" Parno's shock could only grow at that.

"That will also fall to you, my son," Tammon told him carefully. "Sherron cannot hold the throne, save in the absence of a male heir. Once Memmnon has fathered an heir, then you will be released from that duty, save for the need of a regent. Which we all hope won't be needed," he added, smiling thinly at Memmnon.

"Father, I don't. . .I don't think I can do it," Parno managed to sputter. "I haven't the training that Therron has, nor the know-how, and I no longer have Darvo to keep me from making mistakes," he added, his voice cloudy at the mention, or even thought, of his late mentor.

"I have thought of that," Tammon nodded. "But you do have the ability to inspire men, Parno, and to get more from them than even they know they are capable of. You're a leader, boy, and right now I need a leader."

"I will assign Enri Willard to you as a military adviser. He has almost as much training and know how as Therron, and more sense. He'll also be loyal to you, rather than to Therron. He will serve as your Chief-of-Staff for all intents and purposes. With the rank of Brigadier."

Parno looked for some way to convince his father that this was a bad idea. If this happened, sooner or later he'd be forced to kill Therron. Kill his own brother. In all honesty, the idea didn't disturb him as much as he thought it should, but something else did. He looked at his father, eyes narrowing with suspicion.

"You know that one day I'll have to kill Therron, don't you," Parno said flatly, his voice hard. Tammon hesitated a minute, then nodded.

"That is likely," he agreed. "As I said, if there was another way, I would take it. I would not put this on you, were the stakes not so high." Parno shot a look at his brother, whose face was once again blank.

"Are you doing this so I'll be the one who has to deal with him? So that neither of you will have to do this deed?" His voice was harsh now and his eyes flinty. Parno had killed many men in the last week. He was beyond fear of anyone or anything. Both his father, and his brother, looked uncomfortable.

"You are, aren't you?" Parno chuckled scornfully. "Using me to fight your battles for you. Do your dirty work."

"No," Tammon's voice took on a hard edge now. "I'm using you to defend this kingdom! Just like I've used everyone else. I must have a Lord Marshall who can and will follow my orders. One that can and will fight! That can turn this army around and lead us to victory. The trouble you may or may not have with Therron will be because of that and nothing else." Parno's snort told both men what he thought of that.

"There is no one else, Parno," Memmnon told him. "It has to be this way. Please," he added quietly. "I'm asking you to do this for Soulan, if not for us." Parno's eyes narrowed even further at that.

"Well, if I were to do it, it would be for Soulan. That much you at least have right," he almost growled. "I owe the two of you nothing." The last word was almost a hiss. Both his father and his brother recoiled as if struck physically.

"I warned you not to ignore the heartland," Parno seethed. "I warned you that the Gap left us vulnerable. But when I point out problems, you snort at them. When I ask where my men are to go, Therron claims they're worthless—and you, both of you—" this directed at Memmnon, "agreed with him which left me in the position of having to defend the Gap against your own orders!" He sighed, trying to let go of his anger. The other two McLeod's said nothing. There was nothing they could say. Every word Parno had spoken was true.

"This war is far from over," Memmnon finally spoke. "Your victory aside, we are losing, Parno. Everywhere. Times are desperate. Please, don't allow personal feelings to cloud your judgment or keep you from your duty."

"My duty?" Parno was incredulous. "I've done my duty, Memmnon. Time and again, and it cost me dearly. Every time. Don't dare speak to me again of my duty. What have you done?" The challenge was quiet. All the more wounding because of it.

"Enough," Tammon declared, rising. "I had thought. . .well, it matters not. I cannot make you accept this, Parno. You know that. The decision is yours to make." He paused for a moment, considering his words carefully.

"I've been no kind of father to you," he said finally. "I can't change what I've done to you. I would, if it were possible, but I can't. I've been a fool for your entire life. You have no reason to be loyal to me or to do as I ask…and I am asking. This isn't about you, or me, or Memmnon. Its not even about Therron when it comes down to it. It's about whether or not our people live under Norland domination in the future. About whether we live free, or as slaves."

"I will take my leave, now," he continued. "I have said what had to be said. I don't blame you for your feelings and I won't blame you if you refuse. I ask that you at least consider it, but don't consider for too long. We haven't the time to spare." With that Tammon walked from the office with as much dignity as a man who knew he was a fool could muster. Memmnon stayed behind for a moment.

"I know it's asking a great deal of you," Memmnon said softly, "and I wish there was no need of it. By rights you, and your men, should be through with war. But the war is only just beginning, brother, and I tell you, truthfully, that we are not doing well." He sighed softly.

"Please do this if you can." Memmnon said. With that, Memmnon, too, departed. Leaving Parno alone.

Alone to contemplate the greatest decision he had ever had to make.

"Darvo, what should I do?"

-

Parno walked slowly through the camp later that afternoon. Those soldiers who were fit for duty were working, repairing gear and equipment damaged at the Gap. Judging whether gear could be repaired or if it must be replaced. Many of the wounded were involved with bandages covering their wounds.

All paused as they became aware of their Prince among them, watching. Not only the Black Sheep, but the remnants of the other units that had fought at the Gap. Even so, there were far fewer than had once walked these grounds.

"Evenin', milord," man after man nodded respectively. Parno returned their greetings almost automatically. He sensed no hostility among them. Not toward him, at least.

"Evening, men," Parno finally said, loud enough that all could hear. Gradually work stopped as the men on the field gave Parno their attention.

"I wanted to thank you," Parno told them earnestly. "What you managed to do at the Gap may have saved our land. I know the cost was high," he fought to keep his composure. "Many of our mess mates will not sit at table with us again in this lifetime."

"And I'm sorry," he continued. "I'm sorry it was necessary and that you suffered like you did."

"You're sorry?" one man spoke, standing straighter. Parno recognized him as one of Chad's men, but couldn't think of his name. "Beggin' yer pardon, sir, but I can't see as how this is your fault. With respect, milord," he added.

"He's right, milord," another nodded, this one from what remained of Brian Landers' regulars. "This wasn't any of your fault. It's just war, sir. The Nor attack, we defend. Would o' happened was you there or not. Only difference you bein' there made was that some of us are still alive and the Nor lost. Can't see where as you got need o' bein' sorry for that." Others growled their agreement, heads nodding.

"As to that," another spoke, "we'd like. . .that is, with your blessin', sir, we'd like to be a part o' your Regiment. I think I speak fer all of us, when I say we'd follow you anywhere you wanted to lead us, milord. Into the Nor country, or straight to hell itself, come to that." Again, growls of agreement flowed from the assembled men.

"I appreciate that," Parno smiled…and he meant it.

"Then we can?" the man pressed. "I don't mean to be insolent, milord, it's just that, well, if'n we can't stay with you, then we'll have to go somewhere for reassignment soon, and we'd really like to follow you wherever it is you're aimin' ta go."

Parno looked at him for a moment, then nodded dumbly. "I'd be proud to have any of you as part of the Black Sheep. I don't think any of them will mind, either."

"We don't," Brenack Wysin spoke. Parno looked to see the giant blacksmith standing to the side with perhaps thirty of the Sheep. They all nodded.

"Be right glad to have you boys," one said, smiling, "and more than glad to share the work details with ya," he added with a snicker. That drew laughter from all over the grounds.

"Very well, then," Parno nodded again. "I'll see to it. Is there anything else you need?"

"Some of us have family 'hind the lines," one spoke softly. "Mayhap we can get to 'em, maybe? Bring 'em here?"

"We can try," Parno agreed, "and we will," he promised. "I swear it."

"Thank you, milord," several of the men said quietly.

"Well, carry on with your work, gentlemen," Parno said finally. "Can't have your officers angry with me for keeping you from your assigned tasks," he smiled. That drew more laughter.

Parno watched them go back to work then continued on his way. Several more times he was stopped and several more times men asked to be included in his Regiment. As he went on, Parno began to realize that perhaps Cho had been correct. Maybe these men did still believe in him.

"They have faith in you," Feng's voice drifted from the shadows. Parno didn't bother to look around.

"You know what they want from me?" he asked softly.

"I do," Feng replied calmly. "As I said, your destiny awaits you, Parno McLeod. The choice is still yours. You needn't take it."

"Do I really have a choice?" Parno wondered aloud.

"No," Feng answered him simply. "Not and remain the man you are. Without you, your people may well be conquered, enslaved or slaughtered. You may or may not be able to prevent it but no one else can, young Prince. There is no one else." Parno sighed deeply. He didn't want to do it.

"It is a heavy burden," Cho nodded, walking forward to stand beside him, "and it will cause you great grief and misery. Such as you have never known, possibly," he added. "You must ask yourself, is it worth it should that save your people?"

Parno looked away into the distant setting of the sun. Low clouds were hanging on the horizon, their colors blending with the reds and oranges of the sunset. Blood colored, he noted idly.

"No, I don't have a choice", he realized finally. "I've never really had one, though, have I? Some people are destined to be unhappy and alone. I'm one of them, I think, and, if it means that my people live free then I can, I believe, live with that."

He turned suddenly to face Cho Feng.

"I already know great misery and grief, my friend," he said softly. "What difference can a little more possibly make?" With that he started off to find his father and brother.

Cho Feng watched him go, a shade of sadness passing across his face. "Your mother's prophesy will come true, Parno," he whispered. "May God have mercy on you for it."

-

Tammon looked up sharply as his door opened. He and Memmnon were in a small house within Cove Canton. Surrounded by guards. Only...

"Hello, father," Parno said softly, walking into the room. "Memmnon," he added, nodding to his brother.

"I take it you have reached a decision," Tammon said at once, noting the calm about his youngest son.

"I have," Parno nodded. "I will accept," he said simply. Tammon released a breath he hadn't known he was holding.

"I have some conditions," Parno continued, and Tammon's short lived relief almost turned to anger.

"Conditions?"

"Yes," Parno replied evenly. "They are not painful, Father," he almost smiled, "but they are non-negotiable and none of them are for me." Tammon lost his look of ire, it having been replaced with a look of confusion.

"Name them, then."

-

Tammon McLeod faced the assembly of soldiers with a solemn look. The Black Sheep, those who remained of the original group, stood before him. The men from the other battalions stood in formation as well, but it was the men before him that he addressed at the moment.

"Men," the King's voice carried over the ground. "You have served this Kingdom well in the past few days, fighting against great odds and with little hope of success. You stood your ground and held it, giving this Kingdom time to shift its forces to meet an invasion force that, if left unchecked, could well have changed the course of this war in favor of the enemy."

"You were taken from prisons as dregs of society and given a chance to serve your land and your people in order to satisfy your debt. It is the opinion of the Crown that said debt has been faithfully discharged. Your service to the Crown will never be forgotten, so long as there is a Soulan to retell your tales."

"It is with great pleasure that I stand before you today and offer you all the official thanks of the Crown and myself, personally. I have ordered prepared, and have signed, full pardons for every man in this regiment. You are all, as of now, free men."

A cheer erupted from the ranks of the Sheep and the officers, many of them among the pardoned, made only a halfhearted attempt to quell them. Tammon endured the interruption with a smile. These men had earned his forbearance. He continued once the cheering had subsided.

"Now that you are free you may leave the service of the Crown if you so desire. That choice is yours to make, though Lord knows Soulan needs men such as you." He looked at them for a moment, his eyes meeting the eyes of those men in the front ranks. It had been at Parno's urging that he had offered them the chance to leave the army, in repayment for what they had accomplished. It had been one of his 'conditions'. Tammon hadn't liked the idea, but he knew he owed them much more than that.

The men stirred slightly as the King's words sunk home. In the front rank, Doak Parsons walked up and down the line, speaking quietly to the rest of the men. Tammon waited patiently, wondering what he was saying.

Finally, Parsons spun on his heels and walked to the front of the formation. Doing a crisp right-face, he approached the podium where the King stood.

"Permission to speak, Sire!" Parsons called out, his bearing military to the core.

"Granted, Captain," Tammon replied.

"With your permission, Sire, we'd prefer to remain in the Prince's service, at least until the war is decided." Behind him, the remnants of Parno's Company cheered loudly.

"Parno! Parno! Parno!" Parsons raised a hand after the third cheer and the men fell instantly quiet. Tammon McLeod had to fight to suppress both a smile and his surprise. He glanced at his son, whose face was a mask of shock.

"Is this your decision as a unit, Captain?" Tammon asked, an idea suddenly springing forth in his mind.

"It is, Sire," Parsons nodded. "To a man." Tammon looked to the other battalions.

"And it is your desire to join the Prince's Black Sheep?" he asked, using the name they had themselves chosen without thought.

"Yes, sire!" Colonel Bret Chad answered for them as the highest-ranking officer still alive among the other survivors.

The King paused for effect, seeming to ponder the request. Suddenly, he nodded.

"Done!" he exclaimed, and cheering broke out again. The King held his hands up and once more there was instant silence.

"By Royal Decree, you are henceforth the Fourth Royal Regiment of House McLeod, commanded by the Prince, Parno McLeod. May your banner never falter—and never fail!"

This time the cheering wouldn't be stopped. The men were still a bit wild, despite the savage discipline in their ranks, and Tammon was glad to see it. He wished the entire army was made of such men. His Kingdom would have need of all of them he could get before the war ended.

THE END

To be continued in the forthcoming book,
**<u>PARNO'S DESTINY</u>**

A Note from the Author:

I hope you have enjoyed Parno's Company. This has been a year's long labor of a project that began with an idea and went through many creative changes over the years. The final adaptation, which you have just read, was the culmination of months of notes, research, ideas formed and then discarded, and a lot of frustration. I hope the final project has been worth it. It has taken a long time for me to be completely happy with it. Sometimes I'm still not sure that I am.

This is the first of a multi-part story centering on Parno McLeod. I hope you've been entertained by this book since that's why I write—to entertain, to give you, me, and anyone who reads a time away from the worries of life. A place of refuge, if you will, if for only a short while, where our own problems are at rest while we live vicariously through imaginary characters with all too familiar problems.

I hope you will do me the favor of leaving a review since that's the bulk of my advertising, so to speak. Word of mouth and reviews and recommendations are the life blood of books like mine. Please also check out my WordPress blog when you get a chance at "Writings and Ramblings of Bad Karma00." There are snippets of other stories there, some fan fiction that I wrote a good while ago, and links to other books as well. While you're there, be sure and follow me on Facebook and Twitter. I announce all new releases through those two mediums and my website. Please also check out my publisher's website at www.creativetexts.com where you can find my other books and news releases on upcoming promotions.

Thank you again for your patronage. I appreciate it, and hope I've made it worth your time.

N.C. Reed

# THANK YOU FOR READING!

If you enjoyed this book, we would appreciate your customer review on your book seller's website or on Goodreads.

Also, we would like for you to know that you can find more great books like this one at www.CreativeTexts.com